Praise for *Esfir Is Alive*

"Once again Andrea Simon has given us a work of power and poignancy as she narrates the story of a young girl caught up in turmoil of pre-war Poland and then in the dual occupations of the Soviet Union and of Nazi Germany. Her writing is crisp and moving. Her grasp of history is assured and her sensitivity to the historical turmoil as experienced by a young girl is pronounced. Enter this world of darkness, grief and loss with young Esfir and you will experience the depth of evil and the travails of human endurance. The power with which Andrea Simon brings Esfir and her era back to life will only magnify your sense of loss for the world that was and the people who were murdered in the Shoah."

> — Michael Berenbaum, director, Sigi Ziering Institute: Exploring the Ethical and Religious Implications of the Holocaust and Professor of Jewish Studies, American Jewish University, Los Angeles, California; former president of the Survivors of the Shoah Visual History Foundation

Praise for Andrea Simon's *Bashert: A Granddaughter's Holocaust Quest*

"Makes a significant contribution to our understanding and perception of the Holocaust in eastern Poland (Belarus) . . . . Balances impressions of life before and during the Holocaust in eastern Poland with other fragments of family life in the U.S. and other parts of the world from roughly 1915 to the present day. This has the welcome effect of demonstrating the quality, beauty and despair of those lives that were destroyed . . . The very personal approach and the attempt to reconstruct fragments of the quality of life . . . give it a special and enduring quality."

> —Dr. Martin Dean, author of *C ''    tion in the Holocaust*

D1213437

"Simon's writing makes us care, care about her, her grandmother, her town and her self-discovery. Pilgrimage is the most ancient of religious rituals, a journey forth that is also a journey into self and Bashert is an admirable account of Simon's pilgrimage. We learn as she learns, we engage, we remember, we cry out and we even at times laugh. Perhaps the first—or at least one of the first—of a new genre of Holocaust writing that will become more familiar and more urgent as the survivors are no longer with us and their descendants are forced to uncover from history what they once could encounter directly from memory."

> — Michael Berenbaum, director, Sigi Ziering Institute: Exploring the Ethical and Religious Implications of the Holocaust and Professor of Jewish Studies, American Jewish University, Los Angeles, California; former president of the Survivors of the Shoah Visual History Foundation

"Bashert is essential reading . . . . Bashert opens our eyes to the personal story of a strong and determined young woman, who lost her home and family . . . and found a new life in America. Masha will take a place in your heart as she did in her granddaughter's and mine and create a pocket of warmth and pride that will forever remind you of how the strength of one person can change the destiny of an entire family. I urge you to read Bashert, but please be sure to have a hanky at hand."

> —Michael D. Fein, editor, *The Gantseh Megillah*

"*Bashert: A Granddaughter's Holocaust Quest* delivers something much more than a story about the author's kin. It carries a message that transcends all cultures, races and generations . . . . Ms. Simon's memoir whispers a warning to all who read it: do not let the past become the future."

> —Melanie McMillan, *The Litchfield County Times*

Other books by Andrea Simon

*Bashert: A Granddaughter's Holocaust Quest*
(University Press of Mississippi, 2002)

# ESFIR IS ALIVE

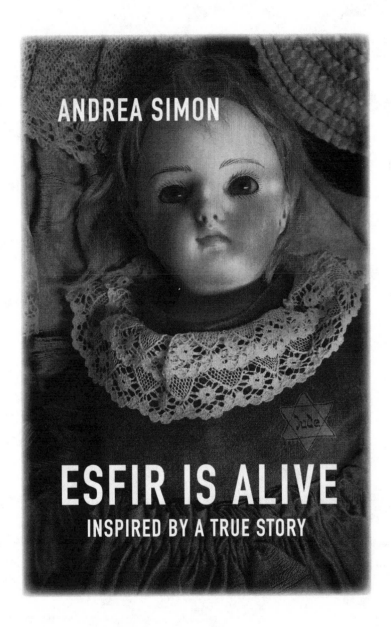

ANDREA SIMON

# ESFIR IS ALIVE
## INSPIRED BY A TRUE STORY

*Bink Books*
Bedazzled Ink Publishing Company • Fairfield, California

978-1-943837-60-1 paperback
978-1-943837-61-8 epub
978-1-943837-90-8 mobi

Includes Glossary of Yiddish Words and Phrases and Reading Guide.

Cover Design
by

DESIGNS

Some of the English translations that appear here have been previously published in the following:

*Paper Bridges: Selected Poems of Kadya Molodowsky.* Translated, introduced, and edited by Kathryn Hellerstein. Detroit: Wayne State University Press, 1999. ("Otwock" and "Merciful God")

*Kartuz-Bereza Yizkor, Our Town Memorial Book.* JewishGen, Inc., 1993. (Elizabeta Zilbershtein [Leah Berkovitz], "By the Common Grave" and Reizel Navi Tuchman, "Brona Gora")

Bink Books
a division of
Bedazzled Ink Publishing, LLC
Fairfield, California
http://www.bedazzledink.com

*To the real Esfir Manevich, wherever she may be.*

In the midst of this streaming rain the little half-naked boy jumped onto a boulder, and throwing back his head, all windblown, he put the flat of his hands against his mouth and whistled for all he was worth. His whistling cut the darkness, the rain, and the thunder like a knife, and it kept growing bolder and clearer:

"I'll make you listen to me! You will have to hear me!"

—I.L.Peretz, "My Memoirs"

# PART I
## Polish Rule

*In 1921, a treaty was signed by Poland and Russia that shifted Poland's borders to include parts of western Belorussia [White Russia] and portions of Ukraine. The formerly named city of Brest-Litovsk or Brisk D'Lita [Brest of Lithuania in Yiddish] was now known in Polish as Brześć nad Bugiem, literally meaning Brest on the River Bug.*

# Prologue

WHEN I WAS five years old, my father, normally a man of precision, drew a crude map of Kobrin and made an "x" to represent our house on Pinsker Street. Though in reality, Pinsker Street (officially called Third of May Street) had its twists and turns, on my father's map, it was a fairly straight line, parallel to the train station and the Mukhavets River; and, while he fashioned other longer, thicker-ruled streets and double-lined avenues, it was clear to me then that everything important took place on Pinsker Street. I could walk from my house to the market to the synagogue to the Jewish hospital and, when I was older, to my school— even to the old cemetery—in one direction or another, depending on my coming or going. Easy as it was for me to get around, and for my mother Sheyne, a woman of worry, to calmly send me on my way, I was not always happy to follow a prescribed route. Sometimes, I longed to make a sharp right or left turn, and see where that would take me. On occasion, my best friend Gittel and I snuck off for our adventures, dipping our feet in the river or tracking mud on the steps of City Hall. Later, there came a time when Pinsker Street not only changed its name again, but the faces of its inhabitants belonged to strangers and I was lost for the first—and last—time.

# One

THE PUBLIC PRIMARY school that I attended was a two-story complex of white stone buildings, partially offset by a picket fence and flanked by large oak trees, and named after the famous Polish leader Józef Pilsudski. There were about forty students in my class, including ten Jews. We sat at long wooden desks, about eight students packed in a row, plus there were a few two-student desks in the front. The buildings were cold and draughty, though shafts of rectangular window light warmed our arms if we sat in their direct path. Even on a day like this, a Saturday in early November 1936, most children, including me, wore sweaters.

Although the Jewish students were required to go to school on *Shabbes*, they didn't have to write. Remaining with their hands folded was enough to show the others that they were different, but the Jewish kids knew they had to be quiet, too. They tried to blend in with the other dark-headed students, forming a kind of Semitic humming chorus, attending the Catholic morning prayers and religious classes.

All, that is, except for me. At seven, I was next to the youngest of the Jewish students. I was thin and pale, with blond hair and blue eyes, and the priest sometimes confused me with being Polish, as if it were a compliment. But I always fingered my silver Star of David necklace that my father buffed every Sunday night when he polished everything else in the house that was worthy of a shine. It wasn't only my looks that made me stand out from the other Jewish students; it was the fact that I never quite learned to keep my mouth shut. And that included singing the Catholic hymns, which I only understood this morning not to do when the priest walked down the aisle, stopped in front of me, and, with his bible, slapped me on the head.

If they were lucky, students brought lunch, including dark break with butter, cheese, or a hard-boiled egg. And if it wasn't too cold, they sometimes ate in the fenced-in yard, under the mammoth oak trees. The boys often threw acorns at each other.

On this day, one of the Jewish boys, Berl, had fallen asleep sitting on a bench in the yard after eating his lunch. He woke up when a group of Polish and Belorussian boys pinned down his arms. One of them, from a higher grade, took out a bottle of ink and a brush and painted a cross on Berl's shirt, while another boy, whom I recognized as the bus driver's son, Feliks, stuffed crumpled paper in Berl's large bat-shaped ears. Berl coughed and sputtered, finally spitting on Feliks who punched him in the nose. Blood spurted down Berl's face onto his white shirt, and the boys disappeared as quickly as cabbage-stuffed rabbits chased by a nap-awoken gardener.

I was standing on the other end of the yard and ran over to Berl. Taking my sweater that had been draped around my shoulders, I offered him a sleeve to wipe the blood from his face. Berl started to cry and snot leaked from his nose. I cringed when he rubbed it onto my brown woolen sweater sleeve. When Berl seemed able to stand, I returned to my original spot where I had left my notebook. All over the cover, there was ink, the same blue-black color that was on Berl's shirt. Instead of the boys, though, a half-dozen Polish girls stood in a small circle, pointing at me, singsonging, "the Jew girl," and cackling like witches.

Determined not to show them I cared, I took the sweater I had lent Berl and, with the clean sleeve, swiped my notebook cover. Now I had one sleeve red with blood and the other stained with ink. I managed to last the rest of the day, but as soon as school was over, I ran home, looking over my shoulder every few minutes, not sure if I expected the bullying boys or the girls to follow me. I knew one thing: I never wanted to set foot in that school again.

When I got home, I walked into the parlor and my mother let out a scream, "Esfir Manevich, what happened to you?" She rushed to my side and rubbed her hand over my reddened sleeve. "What is this? Is it blood?"

"Yes, but it's not mine."

"Not yours? Did you hurt someone?"

"No!" I screamed, and scampered up the stairs to the attic room I shared with my two sisters, Rivke and Drora. Out of breath, my mother came up behind me and peeled the sweater from my body and ran her fingers along the sweater's grooves. "This sleeve doesn't look like blood," she said, holding her thumb to her nose. "Is this ink?"

"Don't you want to know who I spilled ink on?" I said, swearing to myself that I wasn't going to tell my mother the truth.

"When your father comes home, he will get to the bottom of this, even if he has to go to your school."

My mother knew the right words, and I began to cry, not in a snotty, sobbing way like Berl, but in a quiet, soft manner as if my tear ducts were leaking on their own accord. My mother gave a half-smile and I told her the whole story of Berl and the boys and the witch-like girls, and even the behavior of the priest.

"I am sorry, Esfir, that you had to endure this. I am proud that you helped Berl, but the next time, you have to ignore these children. You can't draw attention to yourself. You can't even sing in church. You could get expelled from school, and worse can happen to our family."

Worse? What could happen to them? Could my family go to prison if I sang glory to God, a god that wasn't Jewish?

I decided that I wouldn't admit to my mother that these same girls had taunted me before. I had tried to sit away from them, but last week they caught me near the trash can, and one girl reached inside and grabbed a rotten apple and smushed it into my face. The next day, the girls called me, "Apple Sauce," and that became their regular name for me. And what I would never confess even to my sisters is that the third day they called me Apple Sauce, I hid in the woods after school and threw an apple at their feet as they walked down the road. They didn't see me and squealed. I heard one of them say, "That must have been little Casmir." It disturbed me that they thought they were being pursued by a boy, but I controlled myself and ran home, remembering how my uncle was badly beaten in his bakery because he spoke out against a man comparing him to "Jewish lice."

On Monday morning, my father, Avrum, held my hand and took me to school, the first time for both actions. Although terrified of an adult fight, I was thrilled to have this private time with a man who usually said only a few words to me. He had planned on talking to my teacher or the headmaster. Later he described that while he waited for over an hour in a small room, a woman entered whom he thought was my teacher. Instead, it was Berl's mother coming to complain about what had happened to her son.

"Mr. Manevich," Berl's mother had said, "while my husband and I are very upset over the violence toward our Berl, we are angrier at what the teacher told their class."

"And what was that?" my father asked.

"That the gentiles should not give work to Jewish craftsmen. They should boycott Jewish stores. This teacher even called us Communists."

"She may have well called us dirty Jews," my father said.

After this remark, my father had excused himself, wished Berl's mother luck, and walked to my classroom. He opened the door and there was a united murmur.

"Can I help you?" my teacher asked.

"I am Esfir's father and I came to take her home."

"Is there something I should know about?" she asked.

"We are late for a Communist meeting," he said, giving me a hand-rolling motion, and nodding. I gathered my books and scurried out of the room.

On our way home, I tried to hold my father's hand, but he shook it off. His face was red and crinkled, and I knew it wasn't a good time to ask him anything. When we got in the door, I announced to my mother, "My father came to take me to a Communist meeting."

"What?" she said.

"Papa came to school and announced to the teacher that he came to take me to the meeting."

"Are you crazy, Avrum?"

"She is *not* going back to that school, now or ever."

"Maybe she needs a change," my mother said.

"Maybe we all need a change."


ONLY TWO DAYS later, after I said good-bye to my sisters and my brother, Velvel, I watched my mother pack a valise, carefully layering my cotton nightgown over two freshly ironed white blouses: my fancy one with a bow and little glass buttons, and my everyday one with embroidered flowers, dots, and vines. Even at seven years old, this was not the first time I had left my home but it was the first time I needed to bring a valise.

"Now, Esfir," my mother said in that lecturing voice, "remember Kobrin is not that far away, and you can come home whenever you want."

"I know," I said, afraid to say more because I might cry.

"And I don't have to tell you to behave. Your aunt Perl has much to do, and you must help her."

I nodded. Aunt Perl owned a boardinghouse in the big city of Brest, or *Brisk* as we called it in Yiddish. Perl was my mother's older sister, and about five years ago, she had inherited a large three-story house with an attic when her husband was murdered by a crazy boarder over the weekly rent. Perl had been married by then only seven years. She never remarried and took extra care on my brother, sisters, and me because she had no children.

Since I was the youngest, and maybe the neediest, Perl liked me best and tried to get me to stay by her, even if she had to come and take me back to Brest herself. This time, one of her former boarders, a cigarette factory owner who went to Kobrin for business, drove Perl to my house in a classy black car, of all things.

Perl opened our front door, and I flew into her arms. Although she was heavier than my mother, with stout legs and meaty arms, she looked glamorous in a tan pinstriped suit with her sandy hair in curls hanging from a brown wide-brimmed felt hat. Unlike my mother who, according to my sister Drora, the fashion queen, wore *shmates*, Perl pranced around the room, showing herself off like a magazine model. But Perl didn't take herself seriously; she was laughing the whole time, saying, "Esfele, shake your feathers. We have a man outside ready to step on the gas."

Perl pecked my mother on the cheek and shoved me out the door before I could give my mother a big hug. Instead, I waved. My mother scuttled to the backseat, where I was sitting, and kissed the window in the same spot where my face was pressed inside. Maybe it's good that I didn't get a chance to hug my mother, because this way I didn't have to spend the car ride crying like a baby.

As the car pulled away and I turned to look at my mother's tall, slim frame and soft pink cheeks, I almost yelled, "Stop!" What was I doing leaving her? But my mother waved once, her hand jerking into a fist as if she was tightening a faucet. She quickly turned around. Walking back toward the house, she lifted a stray linden branch from her path and tossed it to the side field. I watched her shrink to a speck and sat back, pulling at the chapped skin on my lips. I almost expected my mother to yell at me, but a heaviness in the air pushed down on my chest as the car made a right off Pinkser Street.

EVEN THOUGH HIS business was cigarettes, this man—I never got his name—smoked cigars nonstop. He would puff even when he spoke and insisted we keep the windows closed because he didn't want to get dust in his brand-new car. The air was cloudy, and it stank like a pile of old burning leaves. I didn't know if I was going to choke or throw up, and when I told this to Perl, the man screamed through an extra plume of smoke, "Open the window this instant!" He must have realized vomit would look worse than soot on his shiny black leather seats.

I loved going to Perl's. Her house was a wonderland. There was a big pantry off the kitchen with shelves and shelves lined with jars of pickles and homemade preserves; ceramic canisters of flour, salt, and sugar; a barrel of potatoes; and burlap bags of garden cabbages, beets, turnips, carrots—all for her boarders, but enough for my family to eat in a year.

Part of Perl's pantry was closed off to make a private space for a bathtub, made of tin instead of the usual wood. In her kitchen, there was a sink. It had a plug leading outside the house. Standing nearby was a barrel with a faucet that held four or five pails of water. No one I knew but Perl had a sink in their house! And in some of the rooms, you could pull a string or chain and the lights went on. This was miraculous.

Best of all, Perl would put me in whatever room had a free bed. At home, I shared one bed with Rivke who was two years older; and sometimes the eldest, Drora, about to become a teenager with the bleeding and all, would plop part of her body on us as our beds were squished close to each other.

Since Perl's house was close to the Tarbut Hebrew Gymnasium, like a high school, Perl usually boarded Jewish students during the school year. Not to make the parents worry, she took only female students; and if she had a male boarder, it was usually an older businessman whom she kept on the first floor, away from the girls. I hadn't been to Perl's since the summer, when the students went home, so I didn't know what to expect, who would be there, or where I would sleep.

So for most of the ride, I stuck my head out the window. As the air whipped my hair into a blinding thicket, I thought of what I was leaving and going to, feeling as exhilarated and burdened as a fluttering butterfly weighed down by a rainstorm. Mostly, though, I was relieved that I saved my family from going to prison for pretending to be Communists.

# Two

WHEN WE ARRIVED at the boardinghouse, Perl took me upstairs and opened the door to one of the three small bedrooms on the second floor. Lounging in one bed was a girl with burnt-orange-brown hair in ropey braids pinned up in the back. Her name was Rachel, and she hadn't gone to school because of a bad cold. The other bed was unoccupied.

"Rachel, this is my niece Esfir," Aunt Perl said.

Rachel blew her nose into a lace handkerchief and continued flipping through the pages of a magazine.

"Rachel, I'm speaking to you, if you don't mind."

Rachel looked up and forced a half-crooked smile. "I heard you, Mrs. Epstein."

"Then give me the courtesy of a response." Perl said in a rush, "My niece will be staying with us for a while. She will take this bed and share your room."

"You expect me to share a room with a child? My father didn't pay for me to babysit!"

"I can sleep on the sofa," I said, feeling embarrassed more for my aunt, that this girl could talk to her in such a voice.

"No you will not," Perl said. "Rachel, Esfir is capable of taking care of herself. She needs no special treatment from you, and you won't even know she is here."

"In that case," Rachel said, "if she isn't really here, I don't have to acknowledge her presence."

I had never heard a girl with such *chutzpah*. As I watched Aunt Perl unpack, laying my underwear in the two drawers of the night table, I marveled at my aunt's patience. In my family, Perl was known for her quick and loud temper. Maybe since Rachel was a paying customer, Perl didn't want to risk losing her. But still . . .

I didn't know what to do. Should I say something nice to Rachel? I just couldn't, but I kept thinking of ways to make my little space more my own.

After Perl left and closed the door, I placed a small cardboard box with my hair barrettes on the night table next to my favorite picture book, *120 Adventures of Silly Billy Goat*. I lay a sock puppet, Zusa, sown by my sister Rivke, on my pillow and pushed my shoes under the bed. Afraid to make noise, I sat on the bed, my back erect, and clasped my hands.

"Are you going to sit there like a stone?" Rachel asked. Then she added some words in Hebrew that I didn't understand. I knew they taught Hebrew at Rachel's school, but at mine, the language was Polish.

"I will read my book," I said, even though I wasn't such a good reader and needed help. I would never admit this to Rachel.

"You're making noise, Esther," she said, sniffing in her phlegm, which was like a bus motor compared to my feathery sounds. She mumbled something else in Hebrew.

"I don't understand you, Rachel. And my name is Esfir, not Esther."

"Esther, Esfir, what's the difference. You're still a baby."

I got up and tiptoed out the door, closed it softly, and tumbled down the stairs, then darted directly into the kitchen where I assumed Perl would be making dinner. I was right about her being there, but she was sitting at the small white enamel, red-rimmed foldout table, massaging her temples.

"Esfele, what is it? You sounded like my uncle Hymie's pair of horses."

"Aunt Perl, I want to go home."

"I thought you like it here," she said, licking her fingers and smoothing my bangs to the side.

I didn't answer because, as in the car, I was afraid of crying.

"Esfir, why are you so quiet? It's not like you."

"Rachel doesn't like me."

"Rachel doesn't like anyone—even herself, if you must know the truth."

One look at my crossed eyes and Perl must have guessed that I would rather go back home and squeeze in bed between my two sisters than sleep in the same room as this snooty girl.

In her forties, Aunt Perl was always cooking, cleaning, going to the market—never sitting still—so that my mother called her *vants*, the Yiddish word for bedbug. Usually the word is given to a little person, but in Perl's case, she got it because she twittered about like she had these critters in her pants. This was a rare moment that my aunt was still.

"Come here, Esfele." Perl wrapped her arm tightly around me and gave me a wet, slobbering kiss.

"You're squeezing me to death, Aunt Perl," I said in a pretend-annoyed tone. My mother would never have been so sloppy.

By the time I went and came back from the outhouse, Aunt Perl had rearranged my belongings in another room; she put a different girl with Rachel. I felt terrible for that poor girl, Fanny.

I was sitting on a bed in the room next to Rachel's. Like the others, this room had two single beds and two night tables. On each wall there were four large hooks. I noticed a white blouse, gray sweater, blue skirt, and a bulging knapsack hanging from them, and a small clock and a stack of books on the night table near the other bed.

Suddenly, about five o'clock, when it was already as dark as nighttime, a towering female vision burst into the room and threw schoolbooks on her bed. With a pencil, I was making a picture to send to Rivke and got so involved I almost didn't look up except for the whoosh of air from the opened door and the slap of books.

She was tall, maybe the tallest girl I had ever seen, definitely the tallest fourteen year old, even taller than my twelve-year-old sister Drora, who was two heads taller than me. Her tallness went with her. She was big boned too, healthy looking. My mother would have said "substantial," but this girl wasn't heavy or fat. She fit into her skin like a stuffed derma.

"Hello, Esfir, I'm Ida," she said, barely looking at me. She continued to unload her schoolwork.

I knew a Polish girl—funnily, her name was Polina—and she was tall almost like Ida. But Ida was different. She didn't have Polina's fair skin or blue eyes. I could have been Polina's little sister, having the same coloring and all. Of course, more than the priest in my school mistook me for a Pole. Just last month, a Polish policeman in my neighborhood asked my mother, "Is the girl Polish?" When my mother had answered that I was Jewish, he was puzzled, as if to accuse her of lying. Then he said, shaking his head, "She could pass for a Pole." He didn't say what was on his face: "What a waste!"

Everything about Ida was dark: from her deep olive skin tone, black-coffee eyes, long and thick ripply Oriental-black hair, and ruby lips, to the maroon circles around her tan nipples, which I got to see later when she undressed in front of me, thinking I was napping.

Though Ida wore the school-required white blouse, she had folded her mud-brown sweater over her arm—it was a warm fall day—and with her top buttons undone, I could see the outlines of her front. Its *V* shape pointed to her full breasts, revealing the tip of a cleavage just like my mother's.

Maybe she was coming from some place outdoors where she needed to contain her hair from the wind, because she was wearing a black head kerchief, unlike the other schoolgirls I had seen on the streets. Only a slight shade darker than her hair and decorated with a magenta bird pattern almost the color of her lips, it halved her forehead and was tied in the back of her neck. At first, I didn't notice it and thought she had small birds nested in her hair.

She didn't look like a common peasant girl. No, she was grand, a gypsy princess, and she had come, I knew immediately, to save me from Rachel.

Unlike Rachel, who spoke to me partly in Hebrew, Ida said in Yiddish, "*Nu,* Esfir, *vos makhstu?*"

I said, "*Gants gut,*" pretty good. Her asking how I was in a familiar way made me feel immediately at ease, and, before long, she was sitting on my bed, questioning *me* as if I were some sort of movie queen.

"Why did you come to Perl's now?" she asked, surprising me with her directness.

"One of my teachers said that the gentiles should not give work to Jewish craftsmen. They should boycott Jewish stores."

"Yes," Ida said, "that happened in my village, too."

"This teacher even called us Communists."

I didn't admit to Ida my real fear: that my mother was happy to get rid of me. I didn't mean forever, because I thought my mother missed me when I was gone, though she never said so. But there would be fewer mouths to feed, and I was always asking for something more to eat.

Ida said, "Oh, Esfir, you remind me so much of my darling Ester, who follows me around like a shadow. She's only a year older than you and you have a similar name. But you look more like my twelve-year-old sister, Sala, who has blond hair like you. So, Esfir, we may as well be sisters, too."

She must have noticed my beaming. When I realized it, I put my hand over my mouth and mumbled something like "thanks." From that moment on, I tried my best to keep up with Ida's remarks and to be like a sister she could call her own.

In minutes, Ida had me spellbound. "In my village, Volchin," Ida said, "we have a nice house in the middle of the town, the Jewish part that is. My father, Iser is his name, is very handsome, and everyone in the village looks up to him."

"Is he so tall?" I asked.

Ida laughed. "He's tall but not too tall. He's respected, I meant. He's captain of the fire brigade."

"That's nice," I said. "Is that his job?"

"No, he has a shop attached to our house where he sells and repairs Singer sewing machines and bicycles."

"Oh. My father repairs watches," I said.

Ida didn't respond. It was as if she was in a trance. She continued to speak about her father. Being the first born, Ida got special privileges. He taught her how to fix bikes; and they often tried them out together, taking long rides into the countryside. And, Ida boasted, he was aware of the latest news and politics, which he talked about all the time.

I knew what it was like to have a busy father, with his hands in the entire town's business, but I didn't want to say "I know" or "mine too" and take away from Ida's pride. I never spoke about my father in that way. Ida's talking did make me see my father more kindly; I wasn't so mad at him for never being home. The part about not paying attention to me was a different story.

Ida suddenly stopped talking about her father and said, "Esfir, I'm sorry, I'm going on and on and I do want to hear about your family. You said your father repairs watches."

"Yes," I said. "I like to help him, too. Maybe some day he will take me to visit you in Volchin."

"But, Esfir, we won't be living in Volchin forever."

"What do you mean?" I asked, suddenly worried that I would be losing my roommate before I got to know her.

"My father's entire birth family—parents, sisters, brothers, and even grandparents—have gone to America. You know where that is?"

Without waiting for my answer, she said, "They write to him regularly. My father is saving money for us to join them, and we will someday soon because life is becoming worse for Jews. I can't wait to be in Brooklyn, New York City."

I hardly knew Ida, but this news that she could be leaving in the near future crushed me like one of Aunt Perl's embraces. Was it possible to feel so abandoned by someone you just met?

And then she said the most surprising thing. "Where my relatives are, there are many Jews like we have in the biggest cities like Brest. And they are allowed to do a lot of things, like the Poles do."

On our way to the dining room, Ida said, "Esfir, if you want, I'd be happy to tutor you in Hebrew."

Ida must have figured out that Rachel had made me feel stupid by spewing all her Hebrew words, and that must have been the reason I wanted to change rooms. Ida was good at reading people.

Tutor me? I couldn't believe my ears. With all the things she had to do, Ida wanted to spend her precious time with me! I couldn't have been more thrilled, but I tried to control my voice. I didn't want Ida to see how strong my feelings were; I didn't want to scare her away. So I said, "Ida, are you sure it isn't too much trouble?"

Ida looked at me as if I had insulted her. "Esfir, I don't say what I don't mean."

And that was that. I had my very own tutor, only steps from my bed.

With such information swimming in my head, Ida slipped her arm under mine, and like that we walked down the stairs ready for supper.

# Three

PERL'S DINING ROOM was a long narrow space, right off the kitchen and separated by a swinging door. At one time in the house's history, it had been part of the kitchen, making it one large room. When Perl's husband, Natan, was alive he was a flour mill owner who fell on hard times like many other Jews. So he leased out his mill, which was on the edge of town near the river, and cut the kitchen in two so that there would be a proper dining area. Then he put up a sign in the window, "Room and Board." Perl came along at the right time in his life, so she could cook and clean for the boarders. Not that Perl came along at the right time in *her* life, because she was pretty much a servant and not the wife she had imagined; and later, as a widow, she was stuck with that label. At least she had some income and had inherited fine jewelry and dishes from Natan's family.

By the time Ida and I got to the dining room, there were three girls and a man seated at the long pine table, which took up practically the whole room, except for a mahogany hutch that displayed Perl's cherished Dresden china, adorned with elegant floral patterns, which came all the way from Germany. Perl was standing behind the seat at the head of the table and motioned for me to sit by her right side and for Ida to sit on her left.

The gentleman, a Pole named Jozef Kozak who ran the mill, sat at the opposite end of the table as if he were Perl's husband. I couldn't tell his height then, and I learned later that he was just about an inch or two taller than Perl, who was average height. By sitting, though, he appeared very large, maybe because his shoulders were broad, his hands were large and hairy, and his gray-streaked hair was thick and greasy, matching a considerable wiry mustache that covered his pinkish lips. He winked at me and there was something knowing and affectionate in his large hazel eyes; I liked him immediately.

Ida sat next to Rachel, who was already picking pieces from her roll; she wouldn't wait for anyone, though she didn't have the guts to begin eating her soup. Rachel's long, thin nostrils twitched from side to side. I almost laughed because Rachel looked like she was trying hard not to sneeze. Then she blinked repeatedly as if she were showing off her sweeping eyelashes and translucent pale-blue eyes. Speaking of those eyes, Rachel was talking to a freckled girl sitting next to her about something and she said, "Oh my eyes, they come from the Kohen side of my family, you know male descendents of the first priest Aaron, brother of Moses."

The girl, who looked bored, said, "Well, so sorry, Miss Priestess."

"No need to be so nasty."

I was beginning to understand why the bed in Rachel's room was empty.

"Well, Esfir," Rachel said, "I see that you found your way to the dining room. I guess you could always follow the odors."

"Some odors come from your room as well," Ida said, and the other two girls, Liba and Fanny, giggled. That alone made me like them. When I sat down and looked at them more carefully, I realized they were twins, but wearing different blouses. I was fascinated by this discovery. I had never met girl twins, especially ones that could have been exact copies, though there were twin boys at school in Kobrin.

I later learned that Liba was the older, by three minutes, and the more dominating twin—a perfect match for Ida's adventurous spirit, and a real threat to my longed-for friendship with Ida. The twins had one thing that saved me from total jealousy. They were noncompetitive and shared a mystical bodily bond—each guessing the other's aches and pains—and felt incomplete without the other.

Sometimes Perl had household help from a Polish woman named Sonia who lived in the countryside. By suppertime, Sonia got a wagon ride from a neighbor and went home to her family. So on this night, Perl did most of the work, cooking and serving.

"Can I help you, Perl?" I asked.

"No, Esfele, sit. This is your first night here and you are probably tired. Now everyone, eat. Before it gets cold." She then disappeared into the kitchen.

In front of each person was a large white china soup bowl filled with a clear broth and one big *matzoh* ball. I took a few spoonfuls and hacked off a bit of the *matzoh* ball by the time Perl returned with a tray of small dishes containing *gefilte* fish. I was ecstatic since I loved this dish, especially the way Perl made it kind of sweet and not jellylike as my mother's. I hadn't had *gefilte* fish for a long time, especially not on a weekday. At home on school days, my family had black bread, sometimes with butter, Swiss cheese, and milk in the morning, the same for lunch at eleven, watery porridge and bread in the late afternoon, and milk in the evening.

To have more than one or two courses was a big treat for me. I tried hard not to eat too fast, to savor each delicious bite and to rest and look around, not to seem as if I was desperate to eat everything on my plate. Perl finally sat down and the door to the kitchen swung open, and another girl came out with a tray holding two bowls of boiled potatoes, a large serving dish of boiled flanken, and cups of mixed carrots and celery. I couldn't believe my eyes; it was like a *Pesach Seder*, all this bounty.

Though getting food was becoming harder and harder for Jews, especially for men like my father—with a big Jewish clientele—there was nothing more important to Perl than providing a decent meal and she was, my mother said, "a magician in plucking potatoes from thin air." As she cooked, Perl tasted everything over and over, sometimes taking a break with samples, her favorite being stuffed cabbage or onion rolls straight from the oven. She wasn't chunky for no reason.

The girl with the tray, it turned out, was the last boarder from the Tarbut high school. Her name was Freyde and she shared a room with Liba. A short girl with enormous glass-green eyes, Freyde was too skinny to be pretty; her high cheekbones, wide forehead, and pointy chin stuck out against her tight skin.

Freyde's family was from Smolensk in western Russia and relocated to Bereza Kartuska, northeast of my town of Kobrin. When she sat down, the girls had been talking about books, and Freyde said, "Everyone knows that the Russians are better than the Germans, just look at Pushkin and Tolstoy."

Liba said, "I don't agree."

Fanny said, "Neither do I."

Rachel piped in, "Of course you don't, Fanny. You copy whatever Liba says."

"Okay, enough, Rachel," Liba said. "Freyde you know that our parents were born and raised in Germany. But not only because of that, I think the Germans are very refined, and most of the famous composers were either German or Austrian."

"Isn't this why your parents decided to put you girls into separate rooms this year?" Rachel said. "Because the Germans have the latest thinking about education and psychology, twins should have independence and all that."

"That's true," Liba said. I was waiting for a sarcastic comment to follow, but Liba seemed to actually agree with Rachel. I guess everything Rachel said and did wasn't terrible all the time.

They were speaking in Yiddish, and Mr. Kozak didn't understand. I felt uncomfortable as if they had been leaving him out. I didn't know where I got so bold, but I said, "Well, I don't know too much, but I think the Poles and our Belorussians are very smart."

Well, you could have dropped all the platters at once from the sudden silence. All eyes were on me. I was a little *pisher*, a nobody, and what did I know? I should have kept quiet. Ida gave me a wink, my second for the evening. I couldn't really call this discussion a fight; it was more like a showing off, because in our hearts we knew what every Jewish person knew: it didn't matter what country or region we were from or which one we liked the best; to the world, we were Jews beyond all else.

Even with Rachel's snobby ways, and Fanny's shy personality, they were a close-knit group maybe because they were among the small number of students who didn't live in Brest and boarded out. While they weren't the most popular girls—not that Rachel would ever admit this—they were certainly known as the most spirited. It didn't take long for me to find out that if there ever was any trouble in school, and the suspect was a girl, the other students assumed one of my housemates had something to do with it.

After my remark about the local people, I didn't say too much. I ate and took in all these new people. I noticed that Rachel wiped her lips constantly with the linen napkin, and that she stirred her food around her plate and left over the meat. Ida ate everything quickly and efficiently, talking the whole time. The twins tasted each other's food, even though they had the same things on their plates, and Freyde was up and clearing the dishes before she finished her meal. Ida explained later that Freyde got a discount on her rooming fee for helping with the chores.

When I was cutting a potato, there were several loud knocks on the door.

"Who can it be at this hour?" Perl said.

"Do you want me to see who it is?" Mr. Kozak asked.

"No, no, I'll go." Perl muttered curse words in Yiddish on her way to the door. Then there were muffled voices, and the door slammed. Perl returned to the table, sat down, and resumed eating.

"Was it someone for me?" Mr. Kozak finally said.

"It was nobody," Perl said. "But Rachel, certain nobodys came to speak to you, and I chased them away. If you want to conduct business with such people, don't invite them to this house." Her lips pouted shut and she breathed heavily.

I looked around. Everyone seemed suddenly very involved in their food. I continued to check my potato but swallowed a piece that was too big and began to wheeze and cough. Ida handed me a glass of water and hit me on the back.

Rachel pushed back her chair, got up, and rushed to the door. I could hear it open and close, and she didn't return until Freyde brought in a tray with baked apples. Rachel sat down and twirled the apple's stem with her thumb and forefinger until it fell onto her plate.

"I'm sorry, Mrs. Epstein, for the disruption. It couldn't be helped."

"You have business with a bunch of troublemaker boys?"

"It's nothing, really," Rachel said, in a cottony voice. I didn't know Rachel well, but I could swear that somebody was very happy about nobody and nothing.

Perl didn't respond. She tried to keep the meal moving, nodding every now and then to Freyde, who popped up to bring a pitcher of water and then a tray carrying a small plate for each person with a damp towel that had been heated on the stove. I had a friend who was orthodox and her family washed their hands or fingers with a cup of water before or after certain portions of the meal. But this towel had nothing to do with religion. Somewhere Perl read that this custom meant you were high class.

She couldn't have been doing this too long, because Mr. Kozak held the towel and didn't seem to know what to do with it. He grunted and Perl said to no one in particular, but spoke in Polish, "Well, everyone, our little Freyde heated the damp towels to save us the trouble of washing our faces with the pitcher and bowls in our rooms. So we should all thank Freyde for her thoughtfulness."

We all muttered, "thanks," and I took an extra swipe around my face and hands, sure that all this food must have stuck to every crevice of my body that was so desperate for its nourishment. I kept a sliver of flanken stuck in my teeth, planning to pluck it out once I was alone in my bed so I could relish it properly.

After glasses of tea, we all helped carry the dishes to the kitchen. There was a loud knock on the front door and Mr. Kozak said, "I will get it," now without a question. My heart started pounding because I suspected that my aunt would not let Rachel get away with her interlopers a second time.

Perl said, "No, this is still my house and I will go."

We scurried into the kitchen, busying ourselves with washing and drying the dishes. Perl came into the kitchen without fanfare. Her cheeks were flushed and she was breathing hard.

"What is it?" Mr. Kozak asked, following Perl.

"I want to speak to Esfir," she said, almost panting. Everyone scattered out of the kitchen like the parting of the Red Sea. They were leaning against the other side of the kitchen door. I could hear them and see it moving; Perl and I were alone.

"Esfele, I want you should sit down," she said softly, reverting to Yiddish.

I knew this was going to be bad and felt an immediate kick in my stomach. Acid traveled up my throat and I creaked, "What? What? Did those boys say bad things about me?"

"No, it wasn't them. That was a messenger by the door. He had a telegram from your mother."

A telegram? I had never heard of my mother sending a telegram. I didn't even know how she did it. I was going to ask Perl if my mother had to go to the post office to send it, when I realized this was not the time to ask such a question, but I wanted to do anything to prolong whatever it was that Perl had to tell me.

"Esfele, now I need you to be a good little girl."

I had trouble focusing on Perl's words. I saw her mouth open and her lips stretching into a long oval, revealing enormous pointy teeth.

"Your papa had a heart attack," she said. "They took him to the

Jewish hospital. Your mother wrote that he must rest for a while but should make a full recovery."

"But I should go home," I said, breathing as fast as my aunt. Everything happened so quickly that I somehow believed that Rachel had made this up and Perl was going to tell me this was a very bad joke.

"I have to go home," I said, practically screaming. "You can put me on the bus, and my sisters or brother can meet me at the station."

"No, your mother expressly wrote, 'Tell Esfir to stay with you. It will be easier. Tell her not to worry and give her a big kiss from her mother who loves her very much.'"

A heart attack. I didn't know what that meant. It sounded so horrible. Your heart was attacked—attacked by what? I excused myself, grabbed a lit kerosene lantern hanging from a nail on the kitchen wall, and plowed through the back door to the outhouse. I almost didn't make it in time. After setting the lamp on the dirt floor, I held my head over the hole and threw up. It went on and on as each new spasm spewed out yellow-brown-green liquidy, chunky masses. When I thought I had nothing else left in my system, I squeaked open the wooden door. Ida was there with one of Freyde's wet towels.

Like when we had gone down to supper, Ida supported her arm under mine, and we walked in the house and upstairs to our room. We didn't say much after that, changing quickly into nightgowns and slipping into our beds. Ida asked if I wanted to talk, and I whispered "no." I lay awhile in the darkness, thinking of my father and all the things we never did together. My tongue felt the sliver of flanken, the one I had been saving. I pulled it from between my front teeth and flicked it across the room. Nothing would ever taste that good again.

# Four

PERL TOOK ME to the post office, and we phoned the branch in Kobrin to leave a message for my mother to call us the next day at one p.m. She didn't call back. Then we sent her a telegram begging for word on my father's health. At Perl's, I stood by the door and watched out the nearby window for the telegram delivery man; and when I didn't see him, I paced up and down the block, searching, thinking maybe he got the address wrong. I began to count male heads, telling myself that by the twenty-fifth, he would surely come, and then upping the number to fifty and a hundred. One by one, the girls came home from school and greeted me. Fanny even walked with me up and down the street for a half hour and we counted to two hundred and fifty, adding our names after each number to prolong the counting.

Rachel saw us pacing and asked who we were waiting for.

I said, "A telegram man."

Rachel said, "Aren't you someone special, getting a telegram."

"It's about her father," Fanny said.

"So, I've gotten a telegram many times." Rachel didn't say anything about my father, but kept looking over her shoulder. Then she asked, "Has anyone else stopped you to talk?"

"Just a few neighbors," Fanny said. "Why?"

"Oh, no reason," Rachel said, and went into the house.

Perl had come out a few times, trying to entice me back inside, offering tea and even a slice of *challah*. For the first time I could recall, I wasn't interested in food.

When Ida got home, I pleaded with Perl again. "Please, let me go home. I can go myself. I'm not afraid."

"I'll go with her," Ida said.

"Just wait a little longer," Perl said. "We will hear from your mother soon. I know so."

I pulled a chair near the window and continued my vigil for the telegram man. I kept picturing my father and how much pain he must have experienced. I was terrified that the reason my mother didn't contact me was because my father was dead. Or maybe worse, maybe *my mother* died from a heart attack from the news of his death.

I had heard that in August, the Polish government ordered all shops to put the name of the owners on their business signs. Perl had explained that this was announcing to the people that they were Jewish and this was very bad for business, scaring away the non-Jews who may have been customers. Between them and the Jews who didn't have enough money to buy or fix watches, maybe no one came to the shop anymore and my family couldn't afford food. Maybe my sisters and brother were alone and they were starving to death. Death was my theme, and there was no getting away from it. It was hard to believe that only a day before, I had been so happy to be Ida's new roommate and sometime pupil.

Ida tried to distract me. She insisted that we have a Hebrew lesson. This was the last thing I wanted to do. I couldn't concentrate on memorizing words, not when I was soon going to be an orphan. Besides, I was convinced that if I stopped counting heads, the telegram man would never come.

Ida said, "It's bad luck to be watching for something to happen. You have a better chance of it happening if you don't pay attention."

I agreed to go with her to the nearby park despite the overcast weather. We sat on the first bench. Ida opened the Hebrew book, pointed to a few words, and directed me to write the Polish equivalent in my lesson notebook. I stared at the blank page. Then I turned and began to watch two boys my age chasing each other around a linden tree. One had a bloody and scraped face, and the other was laughing in that mean way that tries to hide a guilty conscience.

"Esfir, are you with me?"

I jerked my head around and wrote the date on the page. I wanted to show Ida that I wasn't dumb, but I didn't remember what I was supposed to do.

On another bench in my line of view, a young woman sat with her legs crossed and her head down, her dark brown hair sweeping her thighs. I thought she was reading and twisted to see her closer. The woman's lap was empty except for her arms folded tightly as if she was hugging herself.

Ida motioned for me to stand, and then I realized that the woman was crying. I couldn't help staring; Ida grabbed my arm and pulled me away and we headed back to the boardinghouse.

Suddenly, I felt something hard smack me in the back. Ida yelled, "Ouch," and blood was dripping from a gash on her cheek. Objects were hitting us and I realized they were rocks of all sizes.

"Duck," Ida yelled, pulling me back to the bench, away from the direction of the onslaught. Ida had carried a blanket to protect our laps from the cold weather and draped it over our heads. We huddled on the bench and I peeked out from under the blanket. I saw four teen boys aiming at us. A younger one was waving his hands as if he was at a parade. Ida told me to get under, and she also peeled the blanket aside and saw the band of boys and yelled, "Stop it! You're going to hurt us. There is a child here."

"Go to Africa where you belong," one of the boys shouted.

"Go away," Ida screamed. Then she whispered to me that we should stand and place the books over our heads and the blanket over the books. "Follow me," she ordered, and we took baby steps sideways away from the line of fire.

"Jew girls, Jew girls, go to Africa. Monkeys to monkeys."

"I am going for the police," Ida screeched. I didn't know why that got them to stop because everyone knew that the police wouldn't help. But, we continued to walk with increasing speed toward the boardinghouse and didn't feel any more pelts.

When we opened the door, we almost fell inside because the door was partially opened and Rachel was standing there.

"Quick, close the door," Ida said. As I got from under our "tents," I glanced out the window and saw the boys running and yelling. Perl appeared by the door when she heard us screaming.

"What happened?" she asked. "Oh my God, you have blood on your face, Ida."

"These boys threw rocks at us in the park," I said, the hysteria building up. Before long, I was crying for real.

Perl opened the door and screamed, "Do not come here again, do you hear?"

"Did you see them?" Rachel asked Perl.

"Yes, I caught sight of them rushing down the street. I think they are the same boys that came to the house, to see you."

"And why would they do that, Rachel? How do you know them?" Ida asked.

"Oh, it's nothing," Rachel said. "I once met them with my father at the train station and saw them hanging around the neighborhood. They wanted to speak to my father about a job."

Meanwhile, Perl brought a wet rag and was dabbing at Ida's cheek. Ida winced and held the rag tightly against her face.

"Rachel," Perl asked, "I will ask you this once and one time only. What do you have to do with these boys?"

"Nothing, I swear. I had no idea they could be so brutal."

"So you had something to do with them?"

"No, no, as I said, I only met them one time. I am so sorry about what happened."

"Rachel," Perl said, her voice even and strong, "if I hear that you were involved with these boys and what they did, you will leave this house. Is this clear?"

"Yes, Mrs. Epstein."

Rachel gave Perl a head bow and backed away in little steps, inching toward the stairs, which she climbed on tiptoes. I heard her door slam, and it sounded like she was throwing something around her room. Ida later described Rachel as acting like a Japanese Geisha, whatever that was.

"That girl is trouble," Perl said. "Keep your eyes open around her."

I didn't know if Perl was talking to me or to Ida, but it didn't matter. She wasn't telling us anything we didn't know. But one thing was clear: Rachel's jealously was now making its way out of Perl's house.

"What did they mean about us going to the monkeys?" I asked, determined to change the subject.

"Oh, don't worry about that," Ida said.

But Perl didn't let it go and wanted an explanation, too.

Finally, Ida said, "You know that the Polish government is looking into using an African place to send the Jews."

"You mean Madagascar?" Perl asked.

"Yes," Ida said.

"Where is that?" I asked.

"It's an island off the southeastern coast of Africa, a French colony."

"Is Africa where they have the monkeys?"

"Yes, only in Madagascar they have funny animals called lemurs. There is one kind with a long black-and-white ringed tail. We saw pictures of them in school," Ida explained. "They dance and jump very high, from tree to tree."

"Do they look like monkeys?" I asked.

"Well they have fox-like faces and are like huge rodents."

"Why should Jews go to this lemur place?"

"So we should be very, very far away."

Silently, we took off our coats and went into the dining room. I was shivering. As Perl attended to Ida's wound with brown medicine, I kept envisioning all the Jews I knew, locked in cages, surrounded by giant screaming, leaping rats. Even if I had to creep out of the house in darkness and walk, I was more determined to go to Kobrin that night and warn my family not to go to this terrible place in Africa no matter what the government ordered.


AFTER DINNER, THERE was another knock on the door. Luckily, this time, we heard a familiar voice outside and it was a woman Perl knew. She said that Perl's aunt in Kobrin sent word to her big-mouthed half-cousin in Brest, who told this woman at the marketplace, that "Avrum was well enough to make Sheyne crazy from being under her feet."

This was just an expression but I had a laugh thinking of my mother digging her calloused big toes into my father's lumpy back. This half-cousin was a source of much family criticism so I didn't know if I should believe her version. I still couldn't understand why we hadn't received a telegram, but Perl seemed satisfied with this news and told me that I was worse than an old lady with my worrying, and that she knew things were okay. I began to breathe a little more easily about my father. Bad gossip made me feel like maybe things were back to normal.

The next day after school, Ida decided that I was ready to return to my Hebrew studies. But nothing and nobody—even Ida—could get me to that park again.

"I know what," Ida said. "Sit by me and we will have a little fun." She pulled a chair next to hers and wrapped a wool shawl around my shoulders. "Why don't we call this Story Time, and I will begin with one.

It could be a true story or a made-up one, or a combination. I'll sprinkle a few Hebrew words now and then so you can learn them within the story. When it's over, we can take a little break, have tea, and then it will be your turn. I'll interrupt you occasionally and point out a Hebrew translation. What do you say?"

Only two days before, I would have said, "Yes, yes, yes. Ida, I'd love to hear your stories." But how could I tell her now that despite Perl's reassurances, all I could think about was my father? I should be by his side. Maybe *he* was the one who needed a glass of tea. Maybe my mother had to help in his watch-making business. Maybe my sisters and brother were too busy with school and other activities. And maybe, my father had no one there and was angry at me for deserting him.

I could get his book. I could bring him his eyeglasses. I could even read a story or two from my own books even if they were baby stories to him. I could sing Yiddish songs; I knew the ones he liked. Recently he had heard at a Yiddish Theater concert, "*Belz, Mayn Shtetele Belz,*" about missing a childhood town. He shed tears when they sang it, my mother had said. But I didn't tell Ida any of this because something inside me knew that if I was near my father now, I'd be the last person he'd want with him.

It got worse for me because Ida began Story Time by relating about when she and her father had to go to the town of Visoke, about seven miles from Volchin, to deliver two bikes to a factory. "As we got into the wagon," she said, "our horse started to neigh and jump. The sky was getting dark as it is turning now, and you could see storm clouds." Ida stopped the story to tell me that the Hebrew word for storm was *seara* and rain was *geshem*.

"Then," Ida continued, "my father put a tarp over the bikes and my mother Bashke handed me an umbrella. After going a few feet, the sky burst open and huge hail balls came flying down." This was the first time I learned the Hebrew word for hail, *barad*.

"I was about your age then, Esfir," she said. "My mother wanted us to wait out the storm. But my father didn't want to disappoint his customer. Suddenly he jumped off the wagon and went into the shed while I ran inside the house—the *bayit*."

It was hard for me to focus on Ida's words. I tried to picture the last time I was on *my* father's wagon; my sister Rivke and I had been helping him unload sacks of scrap metal and old tools. "Take the smaller ones," he had said, "and make sure you don't drop anything." As soon as my father said that, the sack slipped from my hands, and I dove into the dirt and picked up a few pieces of bent metal. "I'm so sorry," I had said, but my father pushed me aside, mumbling, "clumsy girl."

"Esfir, are you listening?"

"Yes, Ida, please continue."

"After a while," she said, "my father knocked on the door and presented his creation: it was a carton, maybe half the size of my body. He had made two holes and screwed a small glass jar into each hole. This was for my eyes. He gouged a large hole for my nose and mouth, and sliced slits for my ears. To top it off, he nailed a rubber hose to the back, pinning each end so that it formed an arc. For effect, he hung the umbrella from the hose."

"That sounds nice," I said.

"And so, we went to Visoke," Ida continued, her voice rushing now, "me with my helmet, hearing the hail pounding my cardboard-covered head. I must have been some sight, like out of a Jules Verne underwater story, but Esfir, I didn't care what I looked like."

I pretended to know who Jules Verne was, and I forced out laughs not to insult Ida. It was a funny story, but to me, it was an arrow through my heart. Finally, when I didn't say anything more, Ida said, "Esfir, is there something about my story you didn't like?"

I couldn't hold it in anymore and blurted, "Ida, you are so lucky."

"Why, Esfir?"

"Because your father loves you so."

"I'm sure your father loves you, too, Esfir. Just because he sent you to Perl doesn't mean he doesn't want you home."

This was not what I had meant, but I was too embarrassed to confess to Ida that being at Perl's wasn't the problem. In all my life, I couldn't think of one good experience with my father that I could tell Ida when it was my turn for Story Time. And now with this heart-attack business, maybe I'd never get the chance

# Five

AT THE TARBUT Gymnasium, Ida discovered that there was another man who could inspire her. All the girls had a crush on Mendel Feigen, a soft-spoken man in his twenties, who taught natural science. Ida was very specific about his distinguished facial marks: "Matching fingerprint-size cheek dimples, a triangular chin cleft so deep it was more of a gouge, and two temple-to-temple forehead lines, sweeping chevrons activated by raised eyebrows."

Surely, the girls were taken by these unique indentations, but they basically liked him, she explained, "because he was the only male teacher who talked to us in the school halls, not in a flirtatious way, but in a way that said, 'Hello, you are interesting and I wish I could get to know you.'"

The night of my first Story Time, Freyde came into our room.

"Can I borrow your history book?" she asked Ida.

"Sure, but I need it later."

"Oh, Ida, I forgot to tell you something about my brother Yossel." Freyde's voice lowered and even I suspected that the only thing she had forgotten was that her cheek was smeared with jam.

"What about Yossel?"

"I saw him after school. He mentioned that he had spent a recent evening with Mr. Feigen at a political rally."

Freyde must have also "mentioned" this news to the other girls because soon they crammed into our room, squeezing onto our beds.

Fanny, one of the twins, asked, "Do you know where Mr. Feigen lives?" After Fredye shook her head, Fanny said, "Maybe near the Fortress? Remember when he took our class there, he seemed to know the neighborhood well?"

Her sister Liba seemed more interested in Yossel's activities, questioning Freyde about the location of her older brother's rooming house. Then she asked what was on everyone's mind: "Ask Yossel if Mr. Feigen is married. He doesn't wear a ring. But that doesn't always mean something."

"I'd like to know if he attends a synagogue," Rachel said in an accusing tone.

"Of course he must," Fanny said, her head darting from girl to girl, trying to make peace.

"Why? Many of the teachers are against religion." Rachel, of course, knew everything about everyone.

Strangely, Ida was silent.

Freyde was overwhelmed by all the questions and wrote them down in a notebook, promising she would ask her brother. "But," she said, "I want to do it in a natural-like conversation, otherwise Yossel will become protective—like boys can get—and not reveal anything."

After the girls left our room, Ida said, "Esfir, this is the best lesson for you."

"Are we having another Story Time?" I asked.

"No, Esfir. I just want you should know that there's a time to ask questions and a time to keep your mouth shut."

Sometimes Ida talked in riddles. I didn't want her to think me stupid again, so I smiled.

"When you show others how much you are interested in something or someone," she said, "suddenly that thing or person becomes more interesting to everyone. People want to know all kinds of things, even too personal. They don't care if that person may be offended by such interest."

"But how can I know the difference between good questions and bad ones?" At this point I was so confused. The other day, Ida was asking Freyde about Mr. Feigen's talk at some important meeting. And now, she acted like she didn't want to learn anything about him.

"You don't have to know this now," she said. "You'll understand the difference when you get older."

Everybody always said that to me. Would the knowledge of what to say and do come to me in a flash? Would I gather a little each day until it formed a set of rules I could follow? Or would I go through the rest of my life listening to others, scrutinizing them to see how I should be acting?

The next day, Freyde came home from school and announced her findings in the dining room where the other girls were doing homework at the table: "Yossel says Mr. Feigen lives with his elderly parents on Bialostocka Street near the Jewish Hospital. He is *not*, I repeat, *not* married; and he is a Zionist big shot. He plans to actually go to Palestine—to join his older brother who lives in a kibbutz. And get *this*: he is *very* interested in girls. I mean in what women think. Many girls come to these meetings, too."

"They do?" Fanny asked.

"I heard someone in school say he was a Bundist," Ida said.

"What's that?" I asked, risking laughter. It sounded like a terrible disease.

"It's a group that represents the Jewish workers' union. Bundists believe that Jews should make conditions better where they live now."

"Maybe he's changed his mind," Rachel said. "You know you can believe in the rights of workers here *and* a better life for them somewhere else."

Rachel was always happy to point out that Ida didn't get it right. Besides, Rachel's father belonged to another group called the Right Poale Zion, which she said was "a moderate Socialist-Democratic party that supported the modern Hebrew movement." There were so many words, I wrote them down to ask Ida to explain them later.

Meanwhile, I was lost. Should Jews make a life in another place altogether? Did they have those crazy lemurs in Palestine? Shouldn't we stay where we knew how to find everything? Should we speak Yiddish or Hebrew? There seemed to be so many views, so many groups, so many possible ways of life. Maybe for a Jewish person, this was not unusual. My aunt Perl said, in her own version of a popular saying, that in a roomful of a hundred Jews at a bar mitzvah, you'd get a hundred-and-one different toasts to the boy's family.

"Yes," Freyde said, "there's so much political fighting. But these meetings that Mr. Feigen attends are about serious changes in society."

"You mean like Karl Marx, revolutionary?" Ida's voice was breathless and she quickly turned her head as if she was expecting a policeman to arrest her.

"Well, that would be part of the Bundist ideals, but Mr. Feigen doesn't follow Russian doctrine. He's part of the Revisionist Zionist movement, which prepares people for life in Palestine."

"How?"

"I think they organize kibbutzim—you know collective settlements—in Poland."

I didn't know what Freyde was talking about but I was impressed anyhow. She knew a lot of big words that got instant attention.

"And you know," Freyde continued, "he believes in Hebrew as our national language. He has certainly corrected enough of our Hebrew at school."

Ida nodded, probably unable to admit to such a total immersion. Even though most of the students who attended the Tarbut came from secular Socialist families, we didn't know anyone who actually did anything more than talk, not like Mr. Feigen's brother, Freyde said, who gave up a doctor's career to toil on arid land in Palestine.

"Can we go to a meeting?" Ida pleaded. "I mean can you ask Yossel?"

"I already did." Freyde waved a piece of paper. "I have the date and time."

Ida jumped off her chair and hugged Freyde. "You're wonderful," she cried. "When are we going?"

For the first time in what seemed like forever, I stopped thinking about my father. Catching Ida's enthusiasm, I begged Aunt Perl to let me go to the meeting with the girls. She said "absolutely not" more than once. When I showed her the flyer and she read that the topic of discussion was the founding of the Revisionist Zionist movement started by Vladimir Jabotinsky, Perl's soft brown eyes lit up like a lantern wick.

"Oh, Esfir, Jabotinsky," she said, crooning. "Years ago I went to one of his lectures. What a voice, like velvet! And what passion! We were all transported. He gave us what we hadn't had before—pride in our own people and hope for the future."

I had never heard my aunt talk like this. To me, she was a plump, good-natured, graying woman—a *balaboste,* the number-one homemaker in my family, even if she no longer had a husband.

Perl could spend hours talking about material for curtains or argue about the ingredients of borscht. I loved to snuggle against her as she exaggerated funny family stories or read from the big color picture book of bible tales. But I couldn't imagine that she had such worldly ideas.

Although she had read many articles and speeches about Zionism, Perl said Jabotinsky had kindled a fire under her to do more than talk.

"If it wasn't for my husband and his obligations to his aging parents, I would have gathered my gardening tools and made the pilgrimage to Palestine, right then and there."

Perl was dying to go to the meeting, too. But if she went it would mean no one would be in the house except me and Mr. Kozak. Not that Perl didn't trust him, but it didn't look nice to leave a young girl with a man alone.

So Perl compromised. "Esfir, you'll come with me and the girls. I will only stay for a little while, maybe thirty minutes. Then I will grab your hand and you won't say a thing. Do you understand?"

Do I understand? To be able to go, I would have agreed to silence for a year.

# Six

THE MEETING WAS held at the Zionist Center, a three-story building on Topolowa Street. It was a castle-like complex with an expansive courtyard where many events took place. At this time of the year, the guests gathered inside the main hall. A small lump of men stood by the entrance smoking cigars, but they may as well have been a hundred of them standing in the center of the room, because the dense fumes wafted inside and clung to the air like unlidded kettles of boiling cabbage.

Dressed in a sweater and wool coat for the long walk to the Center, I was sweating since it was an unusually warm evening. Even though I was with Perl and the girls, I kept looking around for those rock-throwing boys.

Once inside, I was in no mood to push through bodies to get a peek at the speakers. I was holding Perl's hand, who was holding Ida's hand, who was holding Freyde's, followed by Rachel and the twins. Like a wired Chinese paper dragon that I saw in a magazine, we wound our way through the crowd until we condensed, accordion-style, to form a tight unit facing the stage. We were still in the back of the auditorium; at least we were close to the last row of seats.

Some air must have come through the windows and leaked out under the closed curtains as they occasionally billowed out, but all I felt was the overwhelming oppression of stale breath, dank underarms, and coat residues of sulfuric stick matches and cigar ash. As we fidgeted, we all complained, except for Ida, whose olive skin was as smooth and cool and dry as the silk lining of my velvet muffler.

I heard a woman address the audience in Hebrew. She was hesitant and hushed, and my Hebrew was not good enough to catch all the words without being able to see her lips so I missed most of what she said. I did get that she pledged her dedication to Palestinian settlement, calling for the participation of more women, and gave a schedule of future meetings. Then she introduced, "her good friend and comrade Menachem."

Suddenly, I got a jab at my side and Ida said, "That's him. That's Mendel!"

"But the man's name is Menachem."

"That woman, Shoshana, must have used the Hebraic name for Mendel. Shoshana is a Hebrew name, too."

Ida lifted me by the waist so I could see him, and I have to say I was surprised. The way the girls had spoken about him, I was expecting a movie star. He was nothing special. He had thick brown hair, tight to his scalp with a slight puffiness on top and a widow's peak, and large ears that stuck out. His eyebrows formed a continuous line passing over the brim of his long and straight nose. Though he did appear neat, I had to admit, wearing a pressed white shirt, striped tie, and light-brown jacket. That's it. He looked like any good Jewish boy, I mean "man."

We noticed empty seats as some people—maybe they had been with Shoshana—got up and walked toward the door. We snaked down the aisle and found seats midway to the stage. We couldn't all be together, but I got to sit between Perl and Ida; the other girls were a few rows behind us.

If I sat on my knees, I could see Mendel better. I was struck by his eyes: dark brown, set wide apart, and penetrating like darts that got you to stare him down. Mendel started out in similar soft tones as Shoshana, but in Polish, and I began to doubt his ability as a speaker. He discussed his brother's life on a kibbutz in the Galilee region, when his eyes landed on Ida. Then he changed focus, his voice taking on a thoughtful, almost dreamy, tone.

"My mother's father was an orthodox rabbi," he said, "who was deeply upset by the religious disillusionment of his daughter's husband, my father. Later on, my mother, who tried to maintain a kosher home, lapsed into more secular ways. When I also abandoned my Talmudic studies and began to quote Karl Marx, my grandmother said she was glad her parents didn't live to hear such a thing. It's not easy being a disappointment to one's close relatives—to those you love and respect. It still gives me great emotional pain. But I console myself with the realization that my parents were my first real teachers. They had the courage to thwart *their* tradition for what they believed in." Mendel's words were mostly right because Ida took careful notes and later copied and expanded them into the *Journal of Important Words* that she would give me.

"As a young man," Mendel explained, "I joined the Betar movement. I wore a uniform. I was drilled; I learned to shoot. I was ready for action in a way that was anathema to many of my relatives. I wanted to be a new kind of Jew, an independent and courageous person who could defend his people. Most of the youngsters in my neighborhood also joined, and we began to see the hopelessness of Jews living in the Diaspora, essentially nationless, who have been persecuted for generations.

"And I am ready to go and fight for our people's rightful land. My brother, who made his *aliyah,* his immigration to the Land of Israel, with the third major wave in 1924, has urged me to come. But first, he said, I must spread the word. I must gather more of us—our strong and able young people—to leave this land of oppression, which was never our true home."

He stopped to take a sip of water from a glass at the lectern. Nobody fidgeted, coughed, or whispered. Ida's eyes were moist and transfixed. I could feel her breathing intensify, and I was afraid she would collapse in her chair and slide to the floor. This must have been how Perl felt when she heard Jabotinsky speak that night seven years ago.

Then Mendel read a passage from Jabotinsky, whom he called, "the great Zionist visionary and warrior." Mendel cleared his throat and his voice was strong yet soothing. "Jabotinksy wrote, 'We are a people as all other peoples; we do not have any intentions to be better than the rest. As one of the first conditions for equality we demand the right to have our own villains, exactly as other people have them . . . . We are what we are, we are good for ourselves, we will not change, nor do we want to.'"

Mendel ended with an excerpt from the great Yiddish writer, I.L. Peretz's play *A Night in the Old Marketplace,* recited by the Jester:

> Life must be taken by force,
> And if you don't have the strength,
> Pluck it from the cedar and the oak –
> Suck it from the juices of the grass –
> Steal it from the fire of the sun!
> Take from the lilies their white,
> From the roses—their red . . .

Without waiting for the dying of the applause or for questions, Mendel did the strangest thing. He stepped off the stage and came to our row. Ida was in the aisle seat.

"Come," he said, now practically singing. He reached out his hand, spread his fingers, directing the pointer toward Ida like the picture of Michelangelo's God that I saw in one of Ida's art books. "Come," he implored, "take my hand."

I felt Ida rise. She edged closer to him and stretched out her arm.

"Yes," he said fervidly, "yes, *you,* take my hand. Take my hand and lend your other hand to someone behind you. And that person lend a hand to another. Look at that person and without words, make a pledge: 'We have work to do.'"

A chorus echoed the words. Then the audience broke out in wild applause. I knew that Zionists were basically secular, but this exchange was the closest I had seen to a religious spell since I had attended a Hasidic *shul* with my devout cousin a year ago.

Ida let her hand go from the human chain and fell into Mendel's embracing arms. Perl reached out to Ida, tugging at her blouse. But Mendel led Ida down the aisle, passing the other girls.

"Ida Midler!" Rachel screamed. "Come back here!"

I didn't know why Ida decided to listen to Rachel, a girl she distrusted. But she whispered something to Mendel and disengaged from him.

We walked home after the meeting, each girl alone with her thoughts. After a while, Fanny complained that her feet hurt, and Rachel said the heat in that room was suffocating and she wouldn't be caught dead stuffing herself in with all those smelly, poorly dressed people again. And Ida, oh Ida, Ida, Ida. She wouldn't tell us how she felt for anything. She talked a little about having to improve her Hebrew, and that could mean only one thing to me.

Later at Perl's, Rachel claimed that she prevented Ida from making a public spectacle of herself and from getting kicked out of school.

"Don't pretend that you care about me," Ida said, touching her cheek where her rock wound was healing to a large scratch.

"What do you mean *pretend*?"

"I still can't understand your friendship with those boys who hit us."

"They are not my friends. I don't associate with people like that."

But Rachel didn't fool us. We knew she had been up to something bad. We knew she was jealous, jealous so badly that she thrashed in her bed that night, making all kinds of sounds. I knew because Fanny grumbled that Rachel woke her up several times.

From then on, there was a lot of talk about Mendel at the dining room table.

Perl said, "I was very impressed with him and he almost lived up to Jabotinsky's speech from my memory."

Liba, I think, suspecting that Ida was crazy about Mendel, wanted to help out her friend. She pried Freyde with more questions. "Come on, can you ask Yossel what he knows about the love life of our science teacher?"

"Why are you so interested?" Rachel asked Liba. "You must have a crush on Mendel." When I caught Liba winking at Ida, I was sure of her true intentions.

But Freyde took her responsibilities seriously. She enlisted the least troubling girl, Fanny, and then went on a fact-finding mission; they would be the first ones to report to Ida. They would tell her as if they came across the information naturally, like maybe from Yossel, because they knew Ida would kill them if she knew their methods.

Coming early to class, they began snooping around Mendel's desk. They opened drawers and searched the laboratory area. When they heard someone opening the door, they got so scared somehow they knocked over chemical vials and there was a long bang with puffs of smoke. Thank God the person at the door was only Liba. The girls tried to clean up the spill, though the chemicals stayed on their hands. When Mendel came into the room, he wriggled his nose. "What is that smell?" he asked, narrowing his eyes and scanning the room.

Fanny swallowed and raised her hand. Fredye glared at her and mouthed, "No, don't."

Fanny said, "Mr. Feigen, I was thinking about crop rotation use in the Jewish community."

Freyde beamed. Just because Fanny was the docile twin, it didn't mean that she couldn't fling an arrow straight to the bullseye. And Mr. Feigen was like a noodle taking shape in boiling water, expanding and wriggling as the temperature got hotter. Before long, he was lecturing excitedly about "the necessity of water utilization schemes in the semiarid land of Palestine."

The girls were lucky then, but they scrubbed their hands repeatedly when they got home. I overheard one interesting tidbit of information. Fanny told Freyde that she did see some papers in his desk drawer, and there was a note with the name of Ida Midler and it was circled. I didn't know how they were going to pass this information to Ida, but I had no doubt they would think of something.

# Seven

THE DAY AFTER the Zionist meeting, Perl invited me to have a glass of tea with her in the living room. It was early afternoon. As an extra treat, she brought two plates, each with a *rugelach*. I just adored that little crescent-shaped pastry. This version was stuffed with apricot preserves, raisins, and almonds. She had been practicing for Chanukah, when she would present a basket, covered with a red-and-white checkered dish towel. Underneath, there would be the "cookies" with different experimental fillings.

"Esfele, sit," Perl said, patting the couch pillow next to her. "*Nu, es!*" She ordered me to eat, not that I needed a push. I felt so grown-up sitting with her as if we were about to discuss world affairs. After I had a bite of the *rugelach*, careful not to gulp down the whole thing, she asked me if I was happy with her.

I couldn't tell her that I was terrified of going to the park and those rock-throwing boys. I didn't confess my fear about my father's health and the well-being of my family. So I said, "Yes."

"Childhood should be happy," Perl said, her eyelids fluttering as if she were drifting to sleep, "and I loved growing up in Brest."

"How was it?" I asked.

I didn't know much about those years; my mother didn't speak about Brest. She had tried to make Kobrin, my father's birthplace, her home and pointed out its virtues to us children, especially to me, at every opportunity. Seeing how I was drawn to Brest, she tried to brainwash me against it, which is funny because she's the one who sent me to stay with Perl in the first place.

Perl began her story. "When I was your age—yes even I was once young—at the beginning of the century, a million years ago, rich Jewish merchants would sit on the balconies of their newly built homes on warm summer days, drinking tea from samovars. Before the Great War, there were silent movies at the beautiful theatre, elegant shops displaying fruits and cakes, teahouses with cool cellars and gypsy violinists playing Russian songs."

With this memory, Perl closed her eyes and hummed a melody. I didn't question her; it seemed private.

"The old marketplace used to be busy during the week with Jewish shops on all four sides, overflowing with the best. I loved this tiny, old woman's potato cakes—hot, hefty, and steamy."

"It sounds delicious," I said.

"I never could replicate them with my *latkes*."

I suddenly longed for a *latke*. We were a few weeks from Chanukah; I couldn't wait.

"As a family," Perl said, "we had *bopkes*, nothing, compared to these rich people. We didn't know we were any different."

"And now?"

"Nowadays, everyone has *bopkes*. As you know, the Jews close their stores on Saturdays. With the new laws, they are not allowed to operate on Sundays, too. So they have less business, and their shops may as well be branded with the Jewish star. And the markets today, you're lucky to find a ripe tomato and everyone is suspicious of everyone."

"Not everything is different," I said, feeling the need to justify our current life like Fanny often did.

"Before the Russian Revolution of 1917, during the tsarist regime, there were political rallies and speakers and singing of revolutionary songs. Jews, from the wealthy to the poor, gathered in plazas and parks. Girls even recited the poetry of Pushkin and Lermontov. It was a world, then," Perl said in a sad voice. "Like always, there was Jewish suffering. But we were gay and full of life. Now, you know this already, is not a good time for Jews."

I knew we were poor, too, I mean this is why I went to live with Perl. Unlike how Perl was in her youth, my family felt it. Perl's memories were making me even more worried about them. I wished I had been born when Perl was a girl.

"Enough with the stories," Perl said with a sigh. "Esfir, you do this to me all the time, with your questions. I have things to do."

I didn't contradict Perl. I had only asked her two questions. She was like the samovar—all you had to do was turn the spigot and she poured out her heart.

PERL DID ERRANDS and when she returned, I helped her change the sheets and towels. Before we knew it, the girls arrived. Rachel zoomed past us, announcing that she had to pee badly; Freyde sifted through the mail, piled on the parlor table, always anxious to hear from her parents; Fanny grabbed Perl's untouched *rugelach* on the table; and Ida ran upstairs, motioning Liba to follow. I was as invisible as a bat in the evening.

I went upstairs, planning to open my *Journal of Important Words* and write down some of the ones that Perl mentioned like *Lermontov* and *tsar*. Ida would surely admire my new vocabulary. I didn't get the chance then because the door to my room was closed and I heard Liba and Ida talking. I didn't catch everything but I understood enough. It seemed that Yossel met Liba outdoors during lunch break and invited her for a short walk. Behind an oak tree, he kissed her.

The girls' voices got softer. I could hear Ida ask, "How was it?" followed by murmurs. Finally, Ida screamed, "Esfir, if you're out there, I am counting to three, and you'd better be gone."

I probably made some noise, but then I tiptoed down the hall, slipped inside Fanny and Rachel's room, and closed the door. Thank God Fanny was alone. "What is it?" she asked, sitting on her bed reading a geography schoolbook.

"Oh, nothing," I said. "I just wanted to know if you need me to do anything."

"That's nice of you, Esfir," Fanny said. "I don't need anything now." Then seeing my scrunched face, she said, "But I could use a little company. Come sit with me and I'll show you the map I'm studying."

I didn't report that right now her twin was scheming with my "big sister" about boys.

After dinner that night, Perl asked me to help her with the dishes. She dismissed the other girls, making it clear she wanted to have a special word with me.

"Esfir, I spoke to your mother on the phone at the post office."

"When?"

"After our tea."

"What did she say? How is my father?"

"He is getting back to normal. Everyone is fine. But we discussed something about you."

"What? What did I do?"

"Nothing, Esfir. Why must you always think the worst? When you came to stay with me, we thought it would be for a short while. Now, since your father is still a little weak and your mother helps him more, we thought you cannot stay with me this long and do nothing."

"But I don't do nothing. I help you. And Ida teaches me. I'm learning more than I would in school."

"Yes, Ida has been wonderful. She has gone way beyond my wishes."

"Your wishes?"

"When Ida became your roommate, I asked her to take an interest in you."

"An interest?"

"Why are you repeating what I'm saying? An interest isn't a bad thing. You are very young and here without your family, children your age. It's good to have an older person watch out for you."

"Did you pay her to be nice to me? Did you pay her to be my tutor?" The insides of my heart and head battered around like raw eggs whipped in a ceramic bowl.

"Of course not! Ida was only too happy to befriend you. She, too, missed her sisters, especially the younger one. They are very close. You may think she is above human emotions, but she needs warmth and acceptance also."

"But, still, you didn't have to ask her."

"Trust me, Esfele, she was very glad to be with you. You don't give yourself credit for being the lovable person you are. All I had to do was give her a little prod. The rest—all the affection she has for you—came naturally. It had nothing to do with me."

When I didn't answer, Perl said, "And Ida has a gift for teaching. Surely, you can see that, Esfir."

My internal movements stopped, returning me to my former self, maybe a little older. "So why can't we find more books for her to teach me from?" I asked.

"It isn't enough, Esfir. You need an education, a real one. This is why you will be going to school after the weekend, this Monday."

"No!" I yelled. "I don't want to go to school."

"I know you had a bad experience with school in Kobrin. Unfortunately we can't afford to send you to a Jewish school, but last week I went to the Polish elementary school a few blocks away and spoke to the headmaster. He was very encouraging and called in a teacher, too. I was impressed with them and I think you will find this a better atmosphere."

"I'm not going!" With that, I stormed out of the kitchen.

"Yes you are, Esfir Manevich, yes you are!"

At that moment, I didn't just feel invisible like that nighttime bat. I felt like the bat's baby left alone in a dark, treeless field of spiky leaves.

# Eight

HER NAME WAS Ania. I hadn't noticed her on that first morning in school. I had been so miserable, I kept my head down, staring at my notebook. The teacher, Miss Petra, had introduced me as the "new girl," and directed me to an empty seat in the back of the classroom.

A shapely redhead, Miss Petra was giving a lesson in Polish history. I had been taught that information at my school in Kobrin, but I didn't raise my hand when the teacher asked a question. It was bad enough that I was the "new girl." I didn't want the others to think I was conceited. I'd never tell this to Ida because she would yell at me. She said to me recently, "Esfir, never hide your knowledge. It is something to be proud of."

So this girl with licorice-black, straight hair came up to me in the lunchroom while I was eating my dark bread with butter, cheese, and a hard-boiled egg that Perl had packed for me. She was small and petite like me, with a smooth white-pink complexion and tiny freckles around her nose, and her ears protruded through her hair. "Can I sit next to you," she asked, but sat before I answered. I nodded slightly and looked at her carefully, expecting some major imperfection that would cause her to abandon her friends. I found nothing but the clearest baby blue eyes and the widest smile.

I had a lingering fear that this was a setup, that behind the coat closet, a group of giggling girls whispered, silently directing this girl to her prey. I continued eating and tried to ignore her.

Finally, she said, "I'm Ania. I know you are Esther."

"Esfir," I corrected. She looked wounded and I said, "Everyone gets my name wrong, don't worry. My aunt says that Esther is called Esfir in Russian, so it gets even more complicated."

I found out that Ania lived two blocks from Perl's house, that she had five older brothers. "And my uncle is the priest who teaches at school," she announced loudly with her back straight. I got the feeling that this uncle was a star in her family. A few minutes later, while she was munching on an apple, two girls—one very short and the other very tall—appeared and asked Ania to come with them. She followed without a word to me. I couldn't tell then whether I was in love with Ania or if I hated her.

When I related this to Ida, she had a definite reaction. She said, "Ania was probably really friendly and had the courage to risk approaching a new girl, but not enough to resist the pressure of her friends."

By Monday, a week later, I still hated school. The teacher asked me to read aloud and complimented me; I was happy though I could feel my cheeks redden. Those two mismatched girls sneered at me then, but I could swear that Ania gave me the squished lips of approval. I hated to feel so different. Another girl, Sara, was also friendly to me at our lunch break; she was Jewish, too.

When I was picking up a book from the shelf in the library, I saw Ania huddled with these same two Polish girls, whom I now recognized to be Ania's constant bodyguards. Ania broke free and stepped back. "But Esfir is Jewish," the taller one, said, raising her voice on *Jewish* as if she had just seen a boy pulling down his pants. I felt the hair on my arms prickle and a burning behind my neck. This happened to me in the first grade when I had three nosebleeds in three days, and a boy named Hershel threatened to tell everyone not to sit next to me. And Hershel was Jewish.

"So what, Janina?" Ania said to the taller one.

I didn't hear what followed but I saw Janina putting her arm around Ania, drawing her close. Ania shrugged and they continued in their secrets. That was it; I had been right. I couldn't trust Ania.

When school was over, I lingered by the coatracks so that most of the others would leave before me. I put on my coat and went outside. I heard running feet behind me and soon Ania was by my side.

"Do you mind if I walk with you?" she asked.

I turned around to make sure Janina wasn't nearby. "If you like," I said, keeping my voice steady.

We walked a few blocks and then Ania asked if I had to go home right away.

I said "no" with a mix of dread, waiting for the footsteps of Ania's friends, and the thrill of thinking that maybe Ania really wanted to be with me.

Farther along, at the side of a beautiful square with fountains, there was a majestic Roman Catholic Church.

Ania said, "I have to go inside. My uncle is waiting for me. It will only take a few minutes. Will you come with me?"

My heart started to gallop. Go into a church? My grandmother would have had a fit. I could hear her say, "*Nisht far dir gedakht!*" I didn't know what to do. I couldn't let Ania think I was unfriendly or unaccepting. I closed my eyes and walked up the steps behind her. She dipped her fingers into a small liquid-filled, half-bowl topped with a praying angel, nailed to the wall near the entrance. Then she faced the front, knelt on one knee, and placed the fingers of her right hand to her forehead and down and then to her left and right shoulders, and murmured a prayer. I didn't understand what was happening, but I had seen this motion before from the priest in my Kobrin school and knew that she made the sign of the cross.

I stood in front of the liquid vessel. An elderly woman with a head scarf was behind me and whispered for me to go ahead. I put my pinky in the liquid, which surprised me to be water, moved inside the church, and quickly copied Ania's movements. Then I felt so guilty that I circled my palm over my face and chest in a symbolic gesture to erase whatever sin I had just committed. I tried to trace a Star of David with my finger. If God was watching me, he would have sent for a doctor because I looked like I had that disease with the fits.

Ania excused herself and slipped into a side room. Soon she emerged with a slender priest with gray hair. "Esfir, this is my uncle, I mean, Father Janusz." He gave me a slight bow and said, "Charmed." I bowed back, not knowing what to say in return.

"Now Ania, please give this to your mother for me." Father Janusz handed Ania a package wrapped in white paper.

We thanked the Father and left, Ania clutching the package.

"What is it?" I asked.

"Just some food," she said. "My uncle spoils us."

The way she said it, I was sure that this package was not filled with treats but with necessities. We began to skip and sing a Polish song we learned in school about a happy bird. By the time I got home, it started to snow. Luckily, Perl didn't ask me what took so long.

I didn't take any chances. I went immediately to the kitchen sink,

put a cloth in the basin of icy water, and rubbed my forehead. Then I
ran up the stairs to change my blouse in case there had been any sign of
the cross.

# Nine

IT HAD BEEN snowing on and off for a week, and Perl and I worried that we wouldn't be able to go to Kobrin for Chanukah. Two days before we were planning to leave, the sun came out and workers began to clear the roads and train tracks.

On the morning of our departure, I said good-bye to Ida who was going home to Volchin that afternoon. She would be taking the train the twenty-five miles to Visoke where her father would meet her with his horse and wagon. The night before, she had borrowed my *Journal of Important Words* and included entries for me to read, or have Perl read to me, on the train or when I got home. I kept asking her if she really wanted to write in my journal. She looked at me as if I was crazy and continued writing. "It is up to you what you share with your sisters or your brother," she said, "but I hope you will at least show Drora." The oldest of my two sisters, Drora was the closest to Ida's age being two years younger than her.

The twins had left the day before. Yossel picked up Freyde with two pairs of skis. They had planned to go to Brest's outskirts, where they'd hitch a ride from an army truck that was going their way.

Rachel, who had bragged about the expensive clothes she would get for Chanukah, sat on a bench in the vestibule wearing her wool coat, her small hard suitcase between her legs. She didn't live that far away, in Chernavchich, about eight miles from Brest. Ida had been there once visiting a relative. I was surprised when Ida told me that Chernavchich was probably smaller than Volchin with maybe 430 Jews to about 500 in Volchin, which seemed almost the same to me. With all of Rachel's airs, you would think she was from a large city like Minsk and had dined at the finest restaurants and lived in the fanciest house.

"How long have you been sitting here?" Perl asked.

"Not long," Rachel said.

Although it was cold in the house away from the kitchen stove, it wasn't so cold that Rachel had to wear her coat, and I noticed she had sweat beads above her upper lip. She must have been there for at least two hours. It was still dark outside when I had gone downstairs for a glass of water, and her shadowy form on the bench almost scared me to death.

I didn't contradict Rachel and said that I hope she has a good holiday.

Perl seemed agitated though and sat next to Rachel. "Who are you expecting?" she asked, conspiratorially, as if twenty people were straining to listen.

"My father and uncle are driving in my uncle's new car. My uncle is coming from Bialystok so I'm not sure how long it will take to get here."

"Did you get a postcard from your father?"

"Yes," Rachel said and bit her lip as if she were trying not to cry.

"When did he say he was coming?"

Rachel said she couldn't remember, but Perl pressed her. My aunt insisted that we wouldn't leave until we were sure Rachel was safe with her father; and if it meant missing our train, so be it. I was getting real mad because I knew how hard it was to get our tickets during the holidays. Mr. Kozak had to pull strings; he seemed to know the right people. We didn't have money to buy new tickets in case they couldn't be exchanged, so Perl was taking a big chance. If I didn't get to see my mother and sisters soon, I was going to scream, especially if the reason had to do with Rachel. Anyone could see at this point that Rachel was hiding something.

Finally, after she realized Perl was serious and wouldn't budge, she admitted that no one was going to pick her up; she had been lying. She hadn't gotten any postcard, letter, or message from her father, uncle, or aunt. Rachel was an only child as her mother died in childbirth.

"Maybe they forgot me," she said, a tear slipping down her cheek.

Perl said, "Nonsense. There has to be a logical explanation. You will come with us, and we will contact your father from Kobrin. In the meantime, you'll spend the holiday with our family." I guess she assumed Rachel would have money for a ticket, maybe paying a little extra to get any available seat or as a lure for a passenger to give up an existing seat.

I could have killed Perl. The last thing I wanted was for Rachel to spoil my homecoming. It would be just like Rachel to cozy up to Drora or say bad things about me to Rivke or even flirt with Velvel. Since Ida and I suspected her of plotting with the rock-throwing boys, God knows what she was capable of. And I just knew my father would fall for her tricks. I remember how silly he always acted near Drora's friend, Tauba, who, as my mother said, "was too pretty for her own good."

Just as we were getting up to go, with Rachel at our side, someone pushed and pulled the door knocker a few times.

I drew back the heavy curtain, looked out the window, and saw a droshky carriage with a beautiful black-maned, liver-spotted horse.

Perl opened the door and a short, portly man in an opened wool overcoat, revealing a tight, button-popping vest, stood with his hand raised as if he were about to knock again.

"Daddy," Rachel screamed.

"We didn't know when to expect you," Perl said in a sarcastic tone.

"Yes, I had some business to take care of and wondered if Rachel wants to go to my brother's with me."

"Of course she does," Perl said. "Where else would she go except to her family?"

With this remark, Rachel ducked under her father's raised hand and snuck out the door without even saying good-bye. I peeked out the window and saw her getting into the droshky and her father taking the reins. I didn't see a driver.

Minutes later, another drosky came to take Perl and me to the train station. I was hoping we could catch up with Rachel so I could see where she was heading. With her, I didn't know what to believe.

"I wonder what happened to her uncle and his new car," I said.

Perl shook her head.

At that moment, I realized something big and took out my *Journal of Important Words*. In the back, there was a section I reserved for random thoughts. I raised my pencil that was attached by a string and wrote, "I don't hate Rachel anymore."

I LOVED THE train. I loved everything about it. I loved the whistles, clanging, bells, and the rhythmic wheel churning. I loved the elegant railroad station. I loved the vendors selling ice cream and balloons, and those shoving bread through the opened windows. I loved walking down the train's aisles, teetering, and trying to hold onto a bar for support. I loved the conductors inspecting the tickets and punching them with a gadget that made little holes.

On previous trips, we had sat in open crowded cars, and I would study the other passengers and get up often to look out the window. This time, Mr. Kozak bribed someone, and we got to sit in an expensive compartment with sliding doors. Our seats were on a couchette that could fold into a bed. There was this rich wood surrounding the windows. And I couldn't believe there was a wooden tray that popped out if you wanted to put something on it like a book or hunk of bread.

I can't remember whether there were other passengers or not in our compartment. In my mind, Perl and I were alone and I had the seat near the window, which was framed like a personal cinema screen.

I do remember pressing my face against the glass, observing my breath fog part of the view. I ran my fingers in the cloudiness and wrote my name. I wiped off a large oval and saw an entirely new scene, self-contained like a drawing in a book, rolling through its boundary so that just when I got a good look, it was in my rear view.

Away from the station, there wasn't much to see because most everything was covered with snow. I made it a game to find as many objects as I could that popped out from the whiteness and wrote them in my journal: red barns, horse fences, hazy distant homes beyond brown thick trees, faint footsteps along an empty road, fir trees heavy with the burden of new snow, a stone wishing well, snowflakes like polka dots of white against my glass viewfinder, thin branches whitewashed along their sides, a slick and smooth pond with small skating figures, rivers bisected as ice meets snow-covered water.

Then it began to snow heavily and my view became more and more blurred. Snow smashed against the window until all I could see were dark branches and gray waterways obscured by white splotches. It was as if I were a painter and flicked a white-dipped brush onto a gray/brown-washed canvas, surprised where the blotches appeared.

"I hope the train doesn't get stuck," Perl said. "It looks like a bad storm."

That was the last I heard because the gray and white and brown blobs mesmerized me, and the next thing I knew, my head was in Perl's lap and she was shaking me awake, saying, "Esfir, wake up, we're here."

# Ten

VELVEL MET US at the station. Even though it was snowing so hard, I would have recognized him anywhere in his fur-brimmed Russian hat with the side flaps, slumped on the seat of the wagon, wrapped in a blanket. He was almost a ghost; his ashen face and dirty blond hair paled into the snow fog and all I could see were shades of gray.

We waved to him and I shouted his name. He shook the snow from the blanket and cleared a space for us in the wagon. Not bothering to get down and hug us, he said, "Hurry, get in. The snow is piling up and I'm not sure old Ben will make it."

Believe it or not, Ben was really gray. He looked like a gigantic monster, whinnying in protest. I scrunched next to Velvel and he gave me a peck on the cheek. There were icicles dripping from his long white-blond eyelashes.

Soon, we were off and the poor horse trod and stopped and jerked his head, smacking flying snow in our faces. Velvel concentrated on the road ahead, which was barely visible. I had never heard my seventeen-year-old brother curse so much, and I cringed as he kept slapping Ben in the rear with the whip. Once I told him to stop, and Perl squeezed my hand and put a finger vertical to her lips warning me to shut my mouth. I was shivering so, even wrapped in the scratchy green wool blanket, which was like being cuddled inside a sheet gathering ice on a winter's clothesline. When we got to Pinsker Street, I recognized the sign lit by a gas lamp, and my house was aglow in the grayness due to burning candles in the windows.

My father was shoveling a path leading behind the house to a shed that stored firewood, and farther back to a small stable where Ben was protected from the elements. The way the horse was breathing was scary. My mother, Sheyne, stood in front of the house, screaming at my father, "Avrum, you'll get another heart attack. Let Velvel do it."

Velvel, a walking snowman, grabbed the shovel from my father and took over without a word. My father, already hunched, looked like he was shrinking before my eyes.

"Come in, come in," my mother said, sweeping her arm as if to include all the neighbors. "You'll catch your death from this weather."

We huddled in the hallway. My father put his wet coat and hat on hooks and took off his boots. He was panting and my mother yelled, "Rivke, bring your father a glass of water. And Drora, why are you standing there like a dummy? Can't you see that your aunt and sister are wet also? Help them with their clothing."

Drora scrunched her thin lips, stood straight, and was even taller than she was when I left only a month and a half ago. Her saddle-brown hair was pulled back in a neck scarf, and I noticed that she had red pimples on her chin. When Rivke returned, I was so happy to see her round dimple-cheeked face and long rusty braids that I almost ran up to her, but I was stopped by her serious expression. She didn't even look at me.

Perl ignored all and said, "Who's bringing us glasses of tea to warm our bones?"

I gripped her hand, still afraid that my family was no longer my family. After Rivke gave the glass of water to my father, she ran to me and twirled me in a circle.

"Oh Esfir, you look so grown up. I've missed you so."

In the train, I had decided I wouldn't cry when I saw my mother. I wanted my family to think I was mature now that I spent time in the big city. It was no use. Another squeeze from Rivke and I was a blubbering fool, going around and hugging Drora, my mother, and, when I was about to approach my father, Velvel came through the door. He shook off the snow, hung up his coat and hat, and, without even taking off his boots, yelled, "Come here, *feygele,* give your old brother an official hug." Little bird was his pet name for me. I looked at my father, who should have been next, but he went to the parlor.

My mother screamed, "Avrum, aren't you going to welcome Esfir home and say something to Perl?" I couldn't believe my mother had such *chutzpah.* Usually, she deferred to my father and never said such brave things to him, especially in front of the family.

There was no answer from my father. He looked very sad.

When he was at his peak, my father was a master of all timepieces. He had a collection of antique parts and made new ones. He could not only fix old wristwatches and pocket watches and just about make them from scratch, but could repair a variety of clocks, the bigger the better for him. He had studied old drawings of clocks' insides and memorized the intricate pieces and mechanisms.

Nothing could give him more pleasure than to work on an old grandfather clock. One time he showed us a color drawing of an eight-foot cherry beauty he'd seen at a rich mansion in Pinsk. He had been intrigued with everything, from the massive shiny brass circle pendulum behind the beveled-glass panel in its coffin-like case, to the split swan-neck pediment crown adorned with elaborate carvings, to the golden clock face with black Roman numerals. I saved a magazine drawing of a similar clock that I found in one of Ida's magazines and glued it into my journal. I liked to smoothe my fingers over the polished wood as if the real object was in front of me.

I had been taken by this clock, more by its name and size than anything else. We had such a small house, I couldn't imagine fitting one anywhere. Once I asked my father if there was a grandmother clock, too. You can imagine the laughter from my sisters and brother.

"Don't laugh at your sister," he had said, chuckling with superiority. "There *is* a grandmother clock—anything over five feet. And believe it or not, there is a granddaughter clock that is smaller than five feet. The big daddy, over six feet tall, is the grandfather—as it should be called."

This was the one—and maybe only—time my father came to my defense.

I had been curious about other members of the tall clock family, like about the grandson, but I didn't press my luck. I sensed my father's patience with explanations fading and I basked in my righteous rightness.

From that moment on, I tried to learn as much as I could about the strange objects that made up my father's trade. In his shop, there were lathes, tiny wheels, pinions, hairsprings. These miniature circles and gears fascinated me. When he'd bring such treasures home, my father studied these internal workings with intense concentration. His was a tiny world of ticking motion and he had the power to literally stop time.

That afternoon, when I was in the kitchen with Drora, I learned more. She said that my father rarely went to his watch-repair shop. Occasionally, he attended one of his meetings in the big building with all the groups on Tragota Street. He had been a prominent secretary in one of them; I didn't remember his organization's name, but it had to do with going to Palestine.

Before his heart attack, my father was the busiest person, not only as a respected watchmaker and secretary to the settlement group, but as secretary to a Jewish trade union and a local Jewish sports club. My mother had called him the "Number-One Secretary." He had a different brown ledger for each group.

If he still held those titles, they were dwindling to name only. The ledgers were gathering dust under a stack of magazines. Nowadays, my father sat in his big brown chair in the parlor, reading the Yiddish weekly newspaper, his favorite the *Kobriner Wochenblatt*.

I didn't see my father leave the house that first night we were home. But I was reading in the parlor when he came in the door. Hurriedly, I went to get him a blanket while he sat on his chair, returning to hear my mother yelling at him for giving money to the Jewish National Fund, which developed and bought land in Palestine for Jewish settlements.

"Settlement, schmettlement," she said, "people are hungry here, in *this* settlement, in *this* street, in *this* house!"

My father didn't respond; he reeked from *shnaps*.

PERL USUALLY STAYED at my mother's parents' (Yankel and Elke) house a few streets away. They lived with my mother's middle sister, Khane, and her three children. Feeling that my mother could use her help, Perl now slept on the couch in our parlor, which made my father even more grouchy since he couldn't sit in his favorite chair whenever he wanted.

Perl was her cheerful self and wouldn't let anything or anyone spoil her holiday spirit. Before she went to bed, she came into our attic area carrying her thick cloth satchel. "I'm putting this in the corner," she said, "and if anyone opens it, they're going to get a knock in the head."

"Your things are safe with us," Rivke said, giggling. "Though my little sister here has been known for her nosiness."

I hit Rivke with a pillow.

"So Aunt Perl, how do you find our father?" Drora asked. Rivke took an intake of air and her face suddenly hardened.

"I find him in your house?"

"No, seriously Aunt Perl, he isn't himself."

"Maybe Papa is just saving his strength," I said.

"That's true," Perl said. "After all, it's only been six weeks since his heart attack."

"You don't understand, it's not only because of his health, but because people aren't using him as much," Drora said. "Mama says that repairing or buying watches and clocks are some of the first luxury things people give up. And the gentiles won't come into a Jewish shop." Drora's voice was high-pitched, like she was going to say more but suddenly looked at me and stopped talking.

But Perl wouldn't let it go. "What else does your mother say, Drora? You can tell me. I promise I won't say anything. And you, Esfir, you can get my shawl from the parlor. And see if your brother is home yet."

I started down the stairs, but stopped to hear the rest of the conversation. Drora was saying, "That's why she goes to the shop nearly every day, mostly selling and making minor replacements like a new watchband since she can't do repairs."

"Doesn't he help her?" Perl asked.

"He never asks her about the business, at least not that I know. He no longer wears his beloved watch, you know the one that he had got from his parents for his bar mitzvah."

I didn't make out Perl's response but I got the main part. It seems that anything to do with that part of my father's life suddenly shut down like one of his unfixable clocks.

"And that's not all," Rivke said, finally getting in her two cents. "Lately, Mama spends the evenings with dressmaking jobs."

"From who?"

"Peasant girls from nearby villages. You know how word spreads."

I returned upstairs as soon as I could with Perl's shawl. My brother had just come home and remained in the kitchen.

"I have one thing to tell you girls," Perl said. Her voice was stern.

Drora and Rivke both said, "What?" in a way that meant they were expecting criticism.

Perl said, "Happy Chanukah."

One by one, we wished each other a happy holiday and Perl gave me a big wink when she left. I loved her to death.

# Eleven

EARLY THE NEXT morning, I was awakened by the moldy smell of grated potatoes. It could only mean one thing: *latkes*. We were expecting my grandparents (my father's parents), Morris and Ruth, their daughter-in-law and son Sam and their three children, and my mother needed to prepare at least two dozen *latkes*. She hadn't started to fry them yet; she waited for the last moment so they would be hot. While I helped form the patties, she fried one for me and topped it with sour cream, just the way I liked it. Now, I was in heaven—just me and my beautiful mother in the kitchen, like old times. It was hard to believe that only the night before, I had felt so alone in my own house.

It had finally stopped snowing and the sun was coming up. I put on my coat and opened the front door, ignoring my mother's protestations. I had to take a look at the house. Through the snow, I saw patches of corrugated metal from our low slanting roof; the brown-framed window of the attic where we children slept; and the big linden tree that hid the front entrance when in full bloom, fanning out like a large spread hand and casting spiked shadows on the walls of the pale-yellow wood exterior. I thought I was the only one up besides my mother, but there was Velvel on the street side of our house, his gloved hands wrapped in a big towel, wiping off snow from our light blue-gray, fancy fence—the pride of our family.

My grandfather Morris had worked in a cement factory. After hours, he had fashioned a mold with twelve decorative spokes bisected by a horizontal band of embossed bumps. A curved bottom barely brushed the grass. The top of the mold had a graceful wavy scroll design like a cake's frosting pattern. Morris made six molds, enough to form a unique and elegant fence that set our otherwise plain house apart from our neighbors.

In their later years, Morris and Grandma Ruth moved from this house to a large room at my uncle Sam's, saying they didn't want the bother of taking care of such a big place. We all knew the real reason for the move—to give us our own house, my father being the oldest son. Before that, we were packed in a small apartment shared by another family, separated by a sheet for privacy. As my mother had often reminded my father, "This is no way to live."

My father, at first, didn't want to take the house. He couldn't replace his parents, he said. But my brother, who told us girls the story one night last summer, thought my father was afraid he couldn't afford the upkeep and would lose face with his family. My mother, who had been pregnant with me, gave him an ultimatum. This was another time my mother had showed her *chutzpah*.

That night, we lit the *shamash* on the menorah to begin the eight-day Festival of Lights. My father's tea-colored eyes came alive at the table when he explained to my ten-year-old cousin Leah that the menorah symbolizes the miracle of a day's worth of oil that lasted eight days. He bent his head to look down at the candles on the table. His sparse, gray-streaked, reddish-brown hair drooped to his forehead and he combed it back with his fingers. He sat down, cleared his throat, which rasped from smoking, and went on and on about the victory of the Jews called the Maccabees, who had recaptured their temple in Jerusalem from the ruling Greek-Syrians.

We had a nice, but crowded, first night of Chanukah. My cousins, including Leah's older brothers, Mottel and Alter, and my sisters and brother sang songs and played *dreydl*, spinning the top for the prize of nuts. We all longed for a little Chanukah *gelt*, but those times of extra money were gone. We did get to eat vegetable soup, *kasha kreplach*, and my all-time favorite dessert, *mandelbrot*.

Before we went to sleep, I showed Rivke and Drora my *Journal of Important Words*, which had been entitled by Ida in black ink on the first page with my name on the bottom. I had left a few pages empty in the beginning, saving them for something extra important. On the first empty page, Ida had copied a sentence from the last will of Sholem Aleichem:

"Wherever I may die, let me be buried not among the rich and famous, but among plain Jewish people, the workers, the common folk, so that my tombstone may honor the simple graves around me, and the simple graves honor mine, even as the plain people honored their folk writer in his lifetime."

Drora was very intrigued by this quotation. She had read Sholem Aleichem's stories of simple village life, but this philosophy was underlined and starred by Ida. My oldest sister asked about Ida's political and social views. I didn't think I could explain them properly. So I showed her the chart in my journal that Ida made after I had driven her crazy with questions. Ida had explained that there are many subgroups and these are general categories. Here is her chart:

### Political, Social, Educational Movements in Poland and Russia
(and elsewhere in Eastern Europe)

| Name of Movement | Belief System |
| --- | --- |
| Bund | Non-Zionist, Socialist, Yiddish |
| Halutz | First Pioneer Zionist youth movement |
| Hashomer Hatzair | Left-Wing Socialist-Zionist youth movement (pioneering settlements, scouting) |
| Betar | Revisionist Zionism (Jabotinsky), military education, pioneer settlements |
| Left Poale Zion | Zionist workers, Marxist, Communist, Yiddishist |
| Right Poale Zion | Zionist workers, modern Hebrew, non-Marxist, moderate Socialist |
| Mizrachi | Religious, mainstream, Zionist |
| Agudath Israel | Religious, ultraorthodox (including Hasidim), anti-Zionist |

"Brilliant," Drora exclaimed. "But where does Ida stand, since she likes the quotation about being buried among the plain people?"

"She is her own person," I said. "She goes to the Tarbut, which favors Hebrew, but she loves Yiddish. She's a Zionist, yet loves her country and village and thinks Jews should be able to live happily there, and she wants to go to America someday."

"I can understand that," Drora said, squeezing a ripe pimple. "I guess we're all mixed up."

Before I heard where Drora stood and I'm sure chatterbox Rivke had her own views—or thought she should have them—I fell asleep.

I WOKE UP early and found my handsome brother in the kitchen. Velvel had my coloring, light hair and blue eyes, from my mother's side of the family, whereas my sisters were a cross between my mother and father, who had darker skin and brown eyes. Velvel was also tall like Drora, but he was muscular and lean. His hair was wavy on top and his features were perfectly sculpted—Perl said like a Greek God. I figured the girls all had a crush on him, but he was also very bookish and shy.

Like Ida's teacher, Mendel, Velvel was fired up politically. He went to meetings of Hashomer Hatzair, which was Hebrew for The Young Guard, and often wore the group's shirt and neck scarf, borrowed from a cousin who was much smaller.

Velvel was sitting in a chair by the stove, warming his enormous feet. "So how is life in Brest?" he asked nonchalantly.

"Good," I said. "Perl has been wonderful to me and I have a roommate and teacher, Ida, and I made a friend in school named Ania."

"Is she Polish?"

"Yes, why?"

"Just asking."

Perl must have heard us talking from her bed on the couch in the next room and joined us wrapped in her woolen shawl.

"It's freezing in here," she whined.

"Come by the stove, *tante*," Velvel said.

In the midst of a warm and friendly conversation, with a lot of kidding and jokes, I began to see a new side of Velvel, one that wasn't so serious. The line that stuck in my memory is when Perl said, "I've heard from my cousin in Brooklyn, New York City."

Dutifully, Velvel and I asked about this cousin's news from America.

"He wished us a Happy Chanukah, of course. And guess what? He says the Americans Jews copy the *goyim* about Christmas."

"Do they have a Santa Claus?" I asked excitedly.

"Maybe some do. Bernard said that it is a custom there to exchange gifts for Chanukah like Christmas presents. Usually, a small gift is presented on each day of the holiday."

"Eight presents?" I was aghast, not only by the shock of the practice, but by the obvious wealth of American Jews.

"We can be American here, too," Perl said. "And I'll show you all later."

Velvel guessed that Perl would give us Chanukah *gelt*—a zloty or two, or maybe a fake coin made of chocolate, wrapped in gold foil. I couldn't wait.

But we had to wait, at least until that evening, because my grandmother Elke and Aunt Khane came over. My mother was angry because they just dropped by at lunchtime and she hardly had enough food for us. She managed to scrape together some leftovers, careful not to mix meat and dairy as my grandmother followed kosher rules, and added boiled potatoes and more carrots to the soup.

While we were eating, Aunt Khane bragged that my grandmother had given her money to buy a new coat.

"Oh?" Perl said. She waited for a word from her mother, but my grandmother was silent, smiling, proud that she could buy something for her daughter.

Perl exploded, without warning. I must say I was a little scared to see her this way. "Just because I have a boardinghouse doesn't mean I have all the money in the world."

"Do you have to begrudge your poor sister a simple coat?" my grandmother asked.

"Yeah, it's always about poor Khane this and poor Khane that." Perl's chubby cheeks expanded.

"Perl Cohen Epstein! Your sister is all alone in this world with three children."

"You forget that my husband is dead, too."

"Oh Perl, Perl. There is nothing I can ever do to please you. You have things that Khane doesn't."

Perl was too proud to tell her mother that she, too, had bills she couldn't pay. The big difference was that Perl lived larger than she was and Khane was just the opposite.

"It's not just that," Perl said, sounding like a teenager. "Other people can use things too, like your other daughter, Mother. Sheyne wears this worn-out coat from twenty years ago, and as I recall Khane already had a fairly new coat."

"I don't need anything," my mother said, in a way that showed she was pretending. She smoothed down the sides of her wool skirt, too big for her slim figure.

"Don't be such a martyr," Perl said to my mother.

"What's a martyr?" I asked.

"This is not *your* business," Perl said.

My face felt hot and I was holding in my crying. I didn't remember Perl ever talking to me this way.

"I'm sorry, *bubele*. I didn't mean that." She beckoned to me.

I must have forgiven her because Perl was the one person besides Ida who could get me to her side in an instant. The nasty remarks went on, and I realized this was how my mother and her sisters always talked to each other. It was hard to believe that they were still vying for their mother's attention at their ages.

If she couldn't cajole her mother and sisters, Perl had no trouble with her nephew and nieces. At bedtime, she walked upstairs to the attic with us girls in two beds and Velvel, who usually slept on the couch, on a *perene*, a featherbed, in the nearby storage area.

"Children, I have something for all of you," she called.

Velvel lumbered to our side of the attic. We watched her with our mouths agape, like baby robins in a nest waiting for a worm.

Perl carried over her large satchel, which she had brought up earlier. She opened the clasp. I thought it had been filled with her clothes even though she had also taken a small valise that she was using in the parlor.

"Now, these are for Chanukah, like they do in America. It's not a lot, but I want you should be modern, too." With this announcement, she pulled out a skull-size box wrapped in red tissue paper and handed it to Drora.

Drora looked stunned and kept the box in her lap.

"Open it," Perl ordered.

Drora still didn't move and when she realized that we were staring at her, she slid her fingers under the tape and lifted the paper gently so she wouldn't rip it.

Velvel said, "Just open it already."

Drora said, "But the paper is so beautiful. Maybe I can use it for something."

At that, we all sighed, realizing that Drora had to do things slowly and methodically. This was her way. Finally, she opened the box. It was a small globe on a stand. The continents were raised like brown and tan bumpy animals, and Drora ran her fingers over them as if she were tracing the route for an upcoming voyage.

"It's wonderful!" she crooned.

I was happy for Drora but a little jealous. I couldn't imagine that my gift could be half as good.

Next, Perl handed a soft, bulky object to Rivke. It was also wrapped in tissue paper, only this time it was green. With these Christmas colors, I knew my parents—and certainly my grandparents—would have a fit. Unlike Drora, Rivke tore the paper open to reveal a brown-and-gold striped cardigan. Perl had knitted it, she said, just for Rivke.

"Oh," Rivke said, holding it up against her chest. I knew Rivke was disappointed. She wanted a store-bought present like Drora's. With our prodding, Rivke tried it on. When she put her arms in the sleeves, it was obvious the sweater was much too small, so she didn't try to button it. But Perl insisted, and Rivke yanked the middle button to its hole and it just about made it, straining the wool across her chest. Rivke wouldn't button any more, clearly humiliated by her pudgy stomach. It was more than that, though. She hadn't grown so much since Perl had seen her last. Perl was an expert knitter; she should have known Rivke's size.

"I'll wear it," Rivke said, without conviction.

"Don't be silly, Rivele. Give it to Esfir. I'll make you another."

Rivke handed me her sweater; it was useless to protest.

"And for you my little Esfir, I have something special." This remark only made me feel more embarrassed for Rivke, so I couldn't show my excitement. The rectangular box was the length of one and a half rulers. This one was wrapped in yellow paper. Being more like my sister Drora in some ways, I carefully unwrapped the paper. When I opened the box, I inhaled so deeply and held it in for so long that I almost fainted.

It was a beautiful doll with a full-length, ruby taffeta dress trimmed in fancy lace. Her hair was blond like mine and she had a round, rouge-cheeked porcelain face with large blue eyes also like mine. Embedded in sockets, her glass eyes stared intently and were fringed in lush lashes that looked like real hair. She had a tiny upturned nose and red-painted cherubic lips. She wore dainty black velvet slippers. If there was ever a doll that looked like me, this was it.

What my sisters didn't know was that a few weeks before, Perl and I had gone to the market. On the way, we'd passed a small shop that sold women's hats and accessories. In the window, there was a doll with a sign propped up against it, announcing a sale. At the time, I said to Perl, "Oh I would give anything to have that doll. If I had it, I'd never ask for anything again."

I hadn't been hinting to Perl. There was no reason for her to buy me anything; I hadn't yet known about her new Chanukah gift policy. And the doll cost more than two week's groceries. It was a fortune.

And wonder of wonders, this was the very same doll. To this day, I don't know how Perl afforded it; then, I didn't think about it. All I could do was stroke the doll's dress and hold her tightly to my chest.

"Oh, Esfir, she's beautiful," Drora said.

"Can I hold her?" Rivke asked. Reluctantly, I gave her my doll, but for only a few minutes.

Even though my sisters were too old for a doll, I can say this now, I don't think they were really happy for me. It was bad enough I lived with Perl. But now, I got the best present by far.

Perl sat on the bed, smirking. She didn't make a motion and we were staring at her. There were no more gifts in her satchel, and Velvel glared at Drora's globe as if he hadn't noticed.

Perl stood and reached into her sweater's wide pockets. "Don't think I have forgotten you, Velvel." She handed him a tiny netted bag filled with gold-foil chocolate *gelt*. "I know how much you like sweets," she added.

"Thank you Aunt Perl," he said, shoving the bag into *his* sweater pocket and not offering us a bite.

I was enamored with my doll, grabbing it back from Rivke. I couldn't wait to show it to Ania. She had a doll too but, compared to mine, it was nothing special. I decided to call my doll, Mary, after Jesus's mother and because it was one of Ania's favorite names. Perl almost had a stroke. "Mary is not really a Jewish name," she said, angrily.

"But wasn't Jesus Jewish?" I asked.

Rivke said my name loudly in such a way that I knew I shouldn't argue. So I renamed her Miriam and Perl was happy. I went to bed thinking that this was the only time I had such a wonderful gift, my first real doll. It was the best Chanukah in my life.

THE DAY BEFORE Perl and I were leaving for Brest, at the beginning of the new year, 1937, I woke up early and surprised Rivke in the kitchen. She was sitting at the table massaging a soapy mixture into Miriam's hair.

Horrified, I snatched Miriam from Rivke and frantically dried the doll's hair with a towel. "What are you doing?" I screamed. "You've ruined Miriam's beautiful hair."

"I was only washing it," she said, adding, "to surprise you," as if those last words could convince me of her sincerity.

"Why?" I asked, still bewildered that my beloved sister could do this behind my back.

"So that Miriam has clean hair for your trip back to Brest."

I didn't say anything more, but the rest of that day, I walked around with Miriam tied to my waist. I thought and thought about Rivke's actions and was so hurt, I could barely look at her the rest of our time there. It wasn't until I got back to Brest that Fanny and Liba used some of their hair products to get Miriam's hair in an acceptable style. My Miriam was never the same, though I loved her even more.

On the train back to Brest, I realized that it hadn't been such a wonderful holiday. Yes, it was so cold and we had little to keep us warm except for our clothes and the kitchen stove. But there had been other kinds of hot and cold.

When my grandmother and Aunt Khane came unexpectedly, my mother had been furious at them, and probably at Perl too for assuming she'd entertain in her stride. My mother's normally pale complexion had reddened and her blue-green eyes—then more green—glowered. Perl had been enraged at her mother and jealous of Khane about the new coat. My sisters and brother were jealous of me. Jealousy was passed on like an outdated dress with patchwork hemlines.

During that vacation, my brother became glum and had disappeared on mysterious missions causing loud arguments with my father. My father was away even more and didn't appear to have missed me at all. My sisters, too, were busy, with what I can't remember. I spent a lot of time with my next-door neighbor, Gittel, and my doll, Miriam.

Yes, much happened during our time home that winter. However, there was a far more significant reason that holiday is seared into my brain. It was the last Chanukah my whole family spent together.

# Twelve

I HAD BORROWED Perl's satchel that first day of school after the vacation so that I could bring Miriam to show Ania. After my experience with Rivke and the hair washing, I didn't want to leave Miriam out of my sight. I soon found out that bringing the doll was a mistake because I couldn't fit the satchel under my desk, and the teacher made me hang it with my coat. Whenever I had a chance, I ran to the coatrack and checked on Miriam.

Ania was very impressed with the doll and I could see that my status rose in her eyes. Before, she must have thought I was poor since I didn't have many changes of clothes; now she looked at me in wonder as if I must be a wealthy person. She was careful with Miriam and admired her from a distance. It was worth my worrying, though I decided I would leave Miriam in my room from then on.

That morning, I forgot my lunch bag, which happened routinely, so I went to get it from Perl's (of course, taking Miriam) during recess. When I walked in her door, I was in a good mood. Usually, Perl was in the kitchen or the parlor. I couldn't locate her so I assumed she was out doing errands. I went upstairs to find a safe place for Miriam. I laid her in a box without the lid so she wouldn't suffocate, and slid it under my bed.

When Perl appeared at my door, I screamed. "I thought no one was home," I said. "You scared me."

"I'm sorry," she said, leaning against the door. She was wearing a wrinkled housecoat and an old, holey sweater and her upswept bun expanded like a flattened bird's nest as if she had been sleeping on it.

"I came back for my lunch. Did I wake you?" I asked.

"No, Esfir."

I was beginning to get scared. She looked sick. I was praying it wasn't *her* heart, too.

"Sit down, Esfir," she said softly.

Dread struck me like an arrow. That was what she had said when my father suffered a heart attack. "Did Papa have another heart attack?" I asked.

She nodded.

Okay, I thought. This had happened before and everything turned out okay, or at least mostly okay.

"Is he in the hospital?"

Perl nodded again. Tears slid down her cheeks and she wiped them with her sweater sleeve. It wasn't like Perl to be so slovenly. She usually wore a freshly starched and ironed blouse and she even ironed her apron. She was picky about anyone seeing her before her hair and makeup were perfectly done. Even when she slept at my house on the couch, she fussed in front of her hand mirror before greeting an early riser.

I didn't want to know any more. I didn't feel like I was going to vomit like I had last time. I no longer felt my heart racing. I was as calm as Kobrin's Mukhavets River on a stagnant summer day. My hands, on their own, palms outward, crisscrossed my face; it seemed easier than shaking my head. For the first time since I came to Perl's, I wasn't cold or hungry. I could have sat there the whole day with all my bodily systems still.

Perl started crying for real. "Esfir," she said under strangulated breaths, "your papa is dead."

"Okay," I said. She sat next to me on the couch and put her arm around my shoulders, squeezing me toward her. I stiffened and pulled away.

"Esfir, did you understand what I said?"

"I'm not stupid," I said, sarcastically. "How do you know? You could be wrong."

"No, *bubele*. I got a telegram when you were in school. It was from Velvel. There is no mistaking the news."

I must have risen because somehow I was in my room, bending under my bed. I took Miriam out of the box and sat on the floor, curving my arm around her shoulders just the way Perl had done to me. I sat there with Miriam for I don't know how long. I have a slight recollection of Perl kneeling in front of me, her hand on my knee and me jerking Miriam away from her potential clasp. Out of all my memories until now, this day is the cloudiest.

What I do remember is that I became crazy with time, like I was one of my father's timepieces needing constant oiling and checking. I figured that he had died some time between the morning that Mr. Kozak picked us up in his company's car and made two stops for his business, and early evening when we had arrived in Brest. This second day of the new year was the first day in my life that my father was not alive.

DURING HIS LUNCH break, Mr. Kozak was kind enough to drive us back to Kobrin. There were cursory kisses and hugs all around, then hysteria from Rivke and muted tears from Velvel. My father's parents, Morris and Ruth, appeared to have shrunken overnight. Drora and my mother were getting ready for the funeral, selecting clothes for us and sending a messenger to relatives' homes.

The day before, shortly after my father died, Grandpa Morris and Velvel, still in shock, went to the synagogue for funeral arrangements. In Jewish law, we had to bury him quickly and my mother was so worried that Perl and I wouldn't arrive in time.

Before we left for the funeral, my brother had produced a knife and made a slice into the collar of my blouse. He did the same for my sisters, my mother, and himself. I was horrified. Perl explained that it had something to do with my father's soul lasting forever but I couldn't understand the connection. And I couldn't comprehend all these religious rites for a man who never went to *shul* except for bar mitzvahs.

Befitting my father, everything was simple. His coffin was plain pine; the rabbi spoke about my father's accomplishments and read a short prayer glorifying God, not my father. My mother sat in the women's section with Drora, Rivke, me, and my grandmother Ruth. Behind us were Perl, Grandma Elke, Aunt Khane, my father's brothers' wives, my cousin Leah, and other female relatives. The men went to their section and included, of course, Velvel, Grandpa Morris, my father's two brothers, and my other grandfather, Yankel. The rest of the *shul* was full; at least as far as I could see turning around. There were neighbors, customers, members of my father's political and social groups, and even peasants from the countryside who remembered my father delivering a repaired clock to them, carried in his old wagon led by Ben.

I couldn't believe my father knew all these people and that they could find out about his funeral in less than a day. As Ida once said to me, "Bad news travels like the wind."

When the cantor began to chant "El Male Rachamim," I could feel my mother's shoulders shaking. I pressed into her as if I could stop her movements. I didn't understand most of the words, but I knew that the cantor was saying my father should rest in peace. Maybe it was those words or his whispering and wailing voice that got the women going. Suddenly I recognized Perl's voice, sobbing so loudly that I turned around to make sure this was really my happy-go-lucky aunt. My grandmother Ruth kept murmuring, "*Mayn zun, mayn zun.*"

My mother was still trembling but her face was dry. Her eyes were closed and she nodded silently. I squeezed her hand, which was resting on my thigh. "No," I willed my mother. "Don't cry, don't cry."

My father was buried in the nearby Jewish cemetery in his family's plot. We stood in the below-freezing weather while the rabbi said *Kaddish,* the mourners' prayer, and then we officially began *shivah.* Miraculously, at home, platters of food appeared on our table. The house smelled of hard-boiled eggs. Someone I didn't know ordered me to remove my shoes and sit on a low bench that wasn't from my house. That person instructed me not to leave the house or take a bath, not that I would do either in such freezing weather. When I went to check on my collar tear, the mirror was covered. I guessed that this had something to do with not looking at ourselves since we weren't allowed to bathe.

A lot of other strange things happened that week. Everyone who came said the same thing: "May the Almighty comfort you among the mourners of Zion and Jerusalem." I recalled Ida's chart and all the Zionist groups. Were people in Palestine already crying for my father? It wasn't just this phrase, but all the talk of God and things we could and couldn't do scared me. If I forgot to do one thing, my father wouldn't get to visit God. I tried to study everybody and act right. It wasn't so much of an effort because during that week, I hardly moved. People kept coming up to me on my bench and tried to stuff food into my mouth. I took a bite here and there to make them happy; anything I swallowed felt like a rock.

People were supposed to say nice things about my father. After a while, it seemed that everyone was competing for my father's attention even though he was dead. My uncle Sam said he was the first to help my father rebuild the shed after a fire; his old business partner said he was the first one to go with my father to Warsaw; Perl said she introduced my father to Mozart—even I knew that one was not true. My brother said he was the first to go with my father on the new bus; Rivke was the first to show my father the latest baby chicks; and Drora had the first of her blinding headaches in my father's lap. My mother topped them all: she was the first to find my father dead. There was not one thing I did that involved a first with my father, except that being the youngest, I'd be the first child to forget him. Even at the young age that I was then, I had the sense that I would be looking for something I never had for the rest of my life. Something big closed inside me.

My mother shut her door at night and we could hear her sobbing.

My brother snuck out late one evening, I'm sure for one of his secret meetings, and my mother, who had gotten up for a drink, discovered him coming home. I had never heard my mother scream so loudly. Usually she was quiet in her anger, sort of sticking it in your face when you didn't expect it. Now it was: "Velvel I am so disappointed in you. You couldn't even honor the *shivah* week; your father hasn't been dead for five days even. What is wrong with you? Do you have no feelings for him or at least for us?"

"I'm sorry, Mama," he whined. "I had to go; it couldn't be helped."

"What is more important than the death of your father?"

"I didn't say that Papa's death isn't important. It's not a question of what's more important. It was something I was committed to. People expected me and I couldn't let them down. Besides, Papa didn't believe in all these religious customs."

My mother didn't answer him. She ran into her room, slammed the door, and I heard things shatter and bang all night. She must have disobeyed the custom of *shivah* because the mirror had to unveil as it crashed.

The next morning, the mother I knew was gone. In her place was a wild woman: My mother's once-iridescent eyes popped out of darkened crescents; her fine tawny hair stuck out as if she had removed a sweater over her head and created static electricity. Only she also had bald patches. I once heard the expression, "tearing one's hair out." This is what described my mother.

# Thirteeen

WE RESUMED OUR life in Brest. Ania, Ida, and all the boardinghouse girls treated me like I was a princess. Children at school gestured and whispered in small clusters, but generally they were nicer to me than usual.

On my first day back, my teacher, Miss Petra, called on me to read, lately becoming one of my most enjoyable activities to do in school. I had to admit I was a good reader and I liked to show it off. I read two paragraphs of a Polish book about a boy and his dog. I had no expression in my voice, and Miss Petra told me to sit down and called on Ania to continue, something that would have humiliated me in the past. Then I was relieved.

January and February passed and I was lonely all the time. It didn't matter if I was surrounded by the girls at Perl's or a yard of schoolchildren. Like when my father was sick, I had this awful feeling of guilt and misplacement.

I should have been helping Drora buy food at the market. I should have helped her store it in the cold cellar, ducking spiderwebs and sidestepping scattering mice. At the first good thaw, I should be helping her dig up the potatoes, packed with straw last autumn, buried deep in holes by the edge of our backyard garden.

I should have been helping Rivke on laundry day, soaking the piled-up clothes in a hot soapy tub, squeezing and rubbing them on the metal ridged washboard. I should have helped her lift the clothes to the huge copper boiler on our stove, where they "cooked," and then rinse them in a clear-water tub, adding bleach when necessary. I should have helped her wring out the heavy clothes and hang them in the attic if it was snowing or outdoors on the clothesline to dry in the sun. I should have helped her lift the still-frozen shapes as if locked in a waltz position, to thaw inside, or fold them outside during the first warm days.

I should have been sitting in the cart with Velvel as he lugged pails of icy water from the well or from the river to supplement the barrels delivered from the horse-drawn water carriers. I should have been comforting my grandparents, who had lost their firstborn. And with my mother, the list was endless. I should have been there for all.

Days, weeks, went by without me. Spring came and I wasn't there to notice the first daffodils by our front door. Worst of all, nobody wrote or left a message for me to come home.

Not surprising, it was Ida who eventually got me to feel almost normal again.

*Pesach* came early this year. It was the last Friday in March and everyone was scrambling to get home before sundown. The twins left the night before, Rachel before lunch, and Freyde went to an aunt's house in Brest. Perl and I were leaving on the two p.m. train, and I came home from school at lunchtime to get ready.

There was a strange man in the vestibule, sitting on the bench. He got up the second I opened the door. He didn't do anything to alarm me, but I screamed anyhow. I always hated the unexpected. He was very tall and handsome, older than Mendel but younger than my father. My first reaction was that he must be someone with bad news, maybe an official from the government or post office. Then I thought he must be a theater actor since he was so good-looking and wore a stylish double-breasted jacket and silk blue tie. His hair was light brown and it was parted to the side, the top high with ridges. With his classy clothes and aristocratic air, the thought occurred to me that maybe he was related to Rachel, but I was shocked to see Ida run down the stairs right into his waiting arms; and he lifted her twice and spun her around as if she were a child and not a young woman almost his height.

A closer look to compare Ida with this man, her father, Iser Midler, and I noticed similar hair coloring and texture—and bearing, but that was it. Iser's features were fine and sensitive; his long narrow nose ended in a dimpled tip, his eyes were powder blue. Physically, father and daughter didn't go together, but their bond was as clear as his eyes. After they embraced and giggled like lovers, Ida introduced me and, surprise of surprises, he knew who I was. I couldn't believe it. My father, or even my mother, hadn't known the names of my schoolmates at home unless they lived nearby and they encountered their family at a social or political group. In my mother's case, she could have recognized someone from our synagogue.

Mr. Midler remembered everyone's names and asked about each girl. He had met Perl a few times during other visits to Brest and when he first brought Ida to school at the beginning of the school year.

"Are you going home for *Pesach*?" he asked me.

I whispered, "Yes."

He took off his jacket and hung it on the hall coatrack. He wasn't so fit on closer inspection. He was high-waisted and had a paunch. His tie was tucked into his belt, from which hung a pocket watch chain. I was about to ask him about his "fob" to show him I knew the name for this chain, when he said, "I'm very sorry to hear about your father, Esfir. I heard he was only forty-two, two years older than me. A shame so young."

A glob of grief jammed into my vocal cords.

"I wish I could have met him. I have a great interest in watches myself."

"Thank you, sir," I eeked out.

"No need to be so formal," he said, crinkling his soft blue eyes.

"Esfir, do you mind if I show my father our room?" Ida asked.

She had to be kidding. Did I mind? I was so honored that this man was going to see where I slept that I felt as if someone reached into my gullet and siphoned out my salty tears, replacing them with a well of seltzer. I scampered up the stairs to make sure my bed was made well, and cleared the clothes that I had been packing from the bed so Mr. Midler could sit down if he wanted to talk to Ida across from him.

Ida and Iser were soon in the doorway. Ida directed her father to her books and showed him the view from the window, looking out on the large oak tree.

"Very beautiful," he said.

"Esfir, do you have your journal?" Ida asked.

"Yes, it's in my valise. Why?"

"I want you should show it to my father."

"But Ida?" I was dumbfounded. Show my private thoughts to Ida's father! I hadn't shared my journal with anyone except Ida and my sisters. With my sisters, they just read some quotations, not my own words.

"Yes, Esfir. Just the parts from the authors and some of the pictures you drew."

Mr. Midler joined me on my bed, and I flipped through the middle section where most of the drawings were. There were pencil sketches of Ida's face, my horse Ben, the oak tree outside the window, Perl's stubby hands, which she couldn't keep still. Then I turned to the beginning with the quotations.

"This is one of my favorites, by the eloquent Yiddish master himself," Mr. Midler said, reading a saying by I.L. Peretz: "You, as an artist, don't react to things that are actually happening now. You deal in memories."

I smiled.

"Do you understand that?"

"Not really."

"Well, I can see from your drawings that you are very talented and display much promise for such a young person. You didn't show me the section on your thoughts, but this means that you are a creative person, expressing yourself in different ways. There are those who need to do this, either because they are lonely or because they have something inside that compels them. For you, my little friend, maybe both reasons are true."

All this fancy talk. I didn't want Mr. Midler to think I was just an ignorant child, but I couldn't think of a clever remark, so I just said, "Thank you very much."

He patted me on the head and said to Ida, "So are you ready?"

That was something I knew the answer to. Ida had hung clothes on the line, and from the window I could see them flapping. There were books and underwear on her bed and her little suitcase was empty.

"Just give me a few minutes," Ida said, throwing things into her valise.

Then Mr. Midler showed a different side. In a flash, he screamed, "Ida Midler, *what* is wrong with you? You knew I was coming. We don't have much time or we will miss the train."

"I'm sorry, Iser," she said.

I did a double take, thinking I misheard when she called her father by his first name.

"You always do this, Ida," Mr. Midler reprimanded. "Not everyone can conform to your time schedule."

Ida rushed out the room and I heard her tumbling down the stairs. From my bed, I could see, beyond the oak tree, a hand yanking something from the clothesline.

Ida was ready in record time and she was gasping for breath when she hugged me and wished me a good *Pesach*.

"Yes, have a good holiday, Esfir," Mr. Midler said, shaking my hand as if we hadn't just looked at my journal together.

So now I knew more things about Ida. She was special to her father; she was often late; and her father was kind but had a quick temper. Surprisingly, the temper part made me feel better, like maybe this man whom I desperately had wished was *my* father, wasn't so perfect after all.


THERE'S NOT MUCH to say about our *Pesach* holiday. It was a good time for me to be away from Brest because that Sunday was Easter and Ania would be busy with her family.

I expected that when I arrived home, we wouldn't have a regular *Pesach* because of my father's death. I was so right.

Last *Pesach*, Velvel had gotten a grown-up suit and Drora a new dress. Rivke and I had received hand-me-downs, but fixed to our sizes. For days, my mother had cleaned the house, from top to bottom. The day before *Pesach*, my mother bought meat and eggs and at night she went to the *mikve*, the ritual bathhouse. Last year, she had taken Drora who had gotten her first period that winter. Rivke and I washed in the wooden tub my father brought into the kitchen. The next morning, my father and Velvel went to the *mikve*.

Drora had described the *mikve* to me. The place was divided into two sections. The walls were tiled and you reached the water from steps. A large furnace heated the water. There were tubs that connected to hot and cold water and rows of overhead showers. The second section was a *shvitsbod*, steambath, where you lay on wooden benches and got enveloped by steam so thick you could hardly see anyone. On the bench, you rubbed or massaged each other's backs with a short broom made from birch twigs. Afterward, you took a shower.

It was bad enough that blood came out of a woman down there, but this nakedness in front of others was beyond imagining. I swore that I'd never go.

I remembered we had eaten our last *chometz* meal at around ten on Saturday morning. It was *challah* and milk. Then my mother, my grandmothers, and my aunts prepared the *Seder* meal for the first night of *Pesach*. Prepare, prepare. There was so much to do, for the women, that is, but everyone was happy about being together and looking forward to the food and the reading and the singing.

This year, everything changed. There was no cleaning of the house, no *mikve*, no food preparation. We went to my uncle Sam's house for the first *Seder*. Being the youngest, without a boy close to my age, I asked my uncle, my father's middle brother, the Four Questions, with a little help in the reading department from Drora, starting with the main question, "Why is this night different from all other nights?" and following with the four subquestions. The questions should have been directed to my father, and the answers involved unleavened bread and herbs and *matzoh*, and slavery and freedom.

I didn't pay much attention to the answers or the rest of the *Pesach* stories, songs, or rituals until I realized that Velvel's voice was raised.

"The questions should be, 'why are we different from all other people?'"

"Please, not now," my mother said.

"No, let's hear what the boy has to say," Uncle Sam said.

"Jews are different, that's all," Velvel said.

"Yes, we are the chosen people."

"Chosen to be defined by others. Like those German laws. What is a Jew? You must have three or four Jewish grandparents. And if you are a Jew, you can't be a German citizen or marry one."

"Why?" I asked.

"Because the German race must remain pure."

I didn't understand what Velvel was saying. He went on and on about different categories of German Jews, but not measured by their religion but by their racial mixture. I thought of Miss Petra in school, who once confided in me that her cousin had just married a Jewish man and they wanted to have many children.

I snapped off little pieces of *matzoh*, smashed them under my glass, spit on my thumb, pressed on the bumpy bits, and lay them on my tongue. When I layered my entire tongue, I swallowed. The mixture got stuck in my throat and I started to cough until the coughs turned into chokes. My uncle Sam slapped my back and handed me his wine glass, ordering me to "drink."

I took a few sips before I realized its sweet burning taste. My uncle was bald and had a graying mustache. Otherwise, he looked just like my father.

That night was different from all other nights.

# Fourteen

THE *PESACH* AND Easter holiday break was over and I resumed my life in Brest. Just as it had been in Kobrin, being in a Polish public school spelled trouble for Jewish children. Before Christmas, for example, the class memorized carols. Jewish kids were exempt from singing, but they had to attend rehearsals. I loved the songs and had a good voice. It killed me not to use it. I got up my nerve to ask Miss Petra if I could sing like the others. She was sorry, she said, but she couldn't go against policy. To make up for the loss, Ania and I sang the songs loudly on our way home.

In the mornings, I joined the class for prayers, again banned from oral expression. I also went to religion class, though the priest never called on me and I spent most of the time drawing pictures in my journal. One that I worked on for a few days depicted a cartoon of a little girl sitting on a bench with a black-inked bubble over her head. Inside the bubble, it had the lyrics of "God Is Being Born," a Polish Christmas carol. My latest was a copy of a drawing that was pasted on the wall of a lamb surrounded by large Easter eggs. I left out the huge crucifix painted in the center. When the priest passed me, he grabbed my journal and took my hand as I was holding a pencil and guided it to form a large cross in the middle of the page. He then nodded and walked away.

Ania had an eleven-year-old brother named Piotr. He was in the sixth grade and got great pleasure in torturing me. One day, after school, in early April, I went home with Ania. We planned to play jacks in her backyard. As I was throwing the little ball upward, Piotr reached and caught it. He kept tossing the ball way high and catching it, running in circles, yelling, "Come and get it." At first, I was happy that he would spend time playing with us and held my wrists up chasing him. Ania didn't join. She stood with her folded hands pressed into her waist, her legs splayed, as if she were going to dare somebody. And she did.

"Give Esfir that ball, Piotr right now!" That was one reason I adored Ania. She wasn't afraid of anything, even her stocky brother, whose wide nose flattened like a pig, which she let him know, calling him "Pig Face" when he didn't give me the ball. Piotr went wild. He threw the ball far over the house, into the neighbor's wheat field. It was gone for good, this we knew.

There was something about Piotr that seemed familiar. Probably, I had seen him around the neighborhood and hanging around the school. But there was another thing needling me, the way he tossed the ball, in a waving motion, that caught in my mind. Then it dawned on me. He was with that band of older boys throwing rocks at Ida and me in the park.

I didn't know what to do. Should I confront him? Should I say something to Ania about her brother? I didn't have proof. The whole incident had happened so quickly. I couldn't be sure that he was responsible for directing anything at us; I was certain, though, that he was following the other boys.

Later on, we were in Ania's kitchen drinking milk, and Piotr sat down and began reading a schoolbook and eating sunflower seeds, making loud crunching noises, spitting the residue on the floor. We tried to ignore him.

"Got a new Polish language textbook," he said in a showing-off tone. "You want to see?"

Again I fell for it. I peered over his shoulder to an open spread. There was a picture of Jesus Christ. He read what was written underneath. I can't recall it all, but it was something like, "This statue stands in the village of . . . on this spot where the last Jew of the village had lived." Piotr was smirking and chortling, but I didn't understand what was bad. So if the statue stands where a Jew lived, what was wrong with that?

I should have known that Piotr wouldn't stop until he got to me. "Look at this," he said, turning a page. There was nothing but words so I didn't look hard. "You can't read this anyway; you're just a baby."

"What does it say?" I asked.

Ania looked like she was going to kill me. I was just trying to be nice to her brother.

"There are stories here, good stories, all about Jewish people—how they swindle us poor Christians."

"Enough!" Ania ordered. She grabbed the book, slapped it shut, threw it to the floor, and stood on top of it.

"You want to read it, then you have to get it from under my feet. And if you lay a hand on me, I'm going to tell Father Janusz."

That stopped Piotr. He sat and sulked. It was now a waiting game. Finally, I said I had to go home, and Ania walked me to the door, picked up the book, and slammed it on the table. She said, "Take your stupid book. A stupid book for a stupid boy." I then decided not to say anything to Ania. She already knew who her brother was.


A FEW DAYS later at religion class, I sat in the back with the ten other Jewish kids as I usually did. I got out my journal, intending to draw a picture of the priest when I heard him tell the class that the Jews killed Jesus. I didn't listen to his explanation, if he had any, because the other children turned behind to stare at us Jews, most of the boys snickering and some of the girls whispering.

At lunchtime in the schoolyard, a group of boys surrounded a shy, short, and pudgy Jewish girl named Sadie. She was the type that got picked on even by other Jews. They started to chant, "Dirty *Zyd,*" Jew in Polish. "Beat the *Zyd!*" "Christ killer!" Then there was a lot of scuffling and screaming. Since I was short, I couldn't see what the boys were doing to Sadie. I noticed Ania rush toward a male teacher. She was clearly agitated, pointing to the group. The teacher shook his head.

Timidly, I approached the group, sure that I would be the next victim. I cleared my throat and croaked, "Please stop what you are doing to Sadie." I don't think anyone heard me. I began to shout, "Stop," but it was useless. One boy shoved me and said that I'd better go away or else . . . He didn't have to finish the sentence.

The teacher blew a whistle, signaling the end of the lunch period, and the boys reluctantly broke up. There, on the ground lay Sadie, her face bloodied and her right eye closed. Her skirt was pushed up and her legs were scratched. Sobbing, Sadie wobbled up and held onto me. I straightened her clothes the best I could and spit on a handkerchief and tried to wipe her face, but it looked more like smeared muddy blood.

Miss Petra appeared and took Sadie by the hand. When they returned to class, Sadie's face and legs were cleaned, but her right eye was puffy and still didn't open.

WHAT HAPPENED IN school was the topic of conversation around Perl's dinner table. Luckily Mr. Kozak was out of town so we could talk freely. I related the events and Freyde said her cousin, who went to public school, joined Jewish friends and called the Polish students who had taunted them, "dogs." So, as far as she was concerned, the bad remarks went both ways.

"That's true, everyone can say mean things," Fanny said, always trying to find the good in a situation. She, more than her twin Liba, suffered terribly from people unsure of who was who. I learned later that they were really mirror twins; everything about them was opposite. Liba was right-handed, Fanny was left; Liba had a beauty mark on her right cheek, Fanny's on her left. Though many thought they looked alike, with the same bushy black eyebrows, oval chestnut-brown eyes, and chubby freckled cheeks, I could tell them apart a mile away. From her sashaying walk, tweezed eyebrows, and coiffed hair, Liba was as different from Fanny, with her raggedy-doll floppiness, as a slice of pumpernickel from a *matzoh*.

And to prove my point about their differences, Liba said, "I heard about a bunch of Belorussian boys in another town who surrounded a Jewish classmate and called him a 'Christ killer' and threw stones at him as he ran home."

This was the second time in a day that I heard the expression, "Christ killer." To no one in particular, I asked softly, "What *is* a Christ killer?"

"Speak up, Esfir," Perl said, tugging her earlobe.

"Oh no!" Rachel said with exasperation. "Here we go again, the same old accusations. Just forget it, Esfir, we are above answering to *them*."

"You're not helping," Ida said, throwing Rachel a dirty look. "Esfir, it is a person or people who helped kill Jesus Christ, who died in a terrible way."

"I saw him nailed to the cross at Ania's church."

"You went to her *church*!" Perl said, adding, "Without my permission?"

"It's okay," I said. "Ania's uncle is a priest there."

"That's comforting," Rachel said sarcastically.

This time it was Liba who yelled, "Rachel!" as if she would stuff a sock in her mouth.

"I need to learn more," I said. "If someone calls me this, I have to know what to say."

"Okay, Esfir," Ida said, despite Perl's lip pursing and her expression that said, "Must you?" Ida continued, "First you have to know that Jesus Christ was a Jew."

"I knew that."

Perl got up and mumbled that she would not be a part of this conversation and went into the kitchen. She was talking to herself.

Ida said, "Christ was a young man who spoke great messages to masses of people about love and helping each other. There were those who were threatened by his words, thinking their own power over the people would be gone. Some were Romans, who were very big rulers then."

"Like from the Bible?"

"Yes, like the stories Perl reads to you. Jesus was betrayed and tortured before he was crucified."

"So the Jews didn't kill Christ?"

"Not really. It was the Roman soldiers, but other people, like some Jews, didn't or couldn't intervene. So maybe there was guilt by knowing about it."

"Like people who don't speak out about bad things others say about the Jews?"

"Yes, Esfir, there are people who do bad things. And there are also people who watch others do bad things and remain silent."

"You said it!" Rachel roared, leaving the table. Obviously, she had enough of the conversation. Perl returned with a plate of cookies. I couldn't make out Perl's position. First her mouth was all screwed up and she was talking to herself and the next minute she was stuffing us with sweets.

"Should I say I'm sorry if anyone says my people killed Christ?" I asked.

"Never, never!" Liba and Ida shouted simultaneously.

"First," Ida said, "it is not really true. Second, *you* did not kill Christ. No one should condemn an entire people for the actions of others. Even the Poles, the Russians, the Belorussians, the Germans, whatever they do to us, the Jews, we have to step back and ask, 'Why are they doing this?' 'Did *I* do anything wrong?'"

"That's a lot to remember to ask," I said.

"It doesn't help," Freyde said, "that some in the clergy encourage Jewish hatred." As usual, Freyde was the one with the facts. "Cardinal Hlond was the one to say, 'There will be a Jewish problem as long as the Jews remain . . .'"

"That reminds me," Liba said. "Last August, our family stayed at a guesthouse near the Bug River, south of Brest, not far from the pine forest."

"Yeah," Fanny said, dreamily, "there were girls from the Polish gymnasium in Brest. They thought they were so wonderful."

"That's not the point Fanny," Liba said, losing her patience. "We went for long walks in the forest and picnicked on a small sandy embankment by the river. We swam in the river."

"It sounds lovely," Freyde said.

"So did something happen there?" Ida asked in her direct way.

"Local boys threw sticks at Fanny and me when we were waiting for our parents who were swimming in the deep water."

"That's terrible," Freyde said.

"It's not the worst. A monk appeared on his daily walk and witnessed the boys taunting us. Instead of shooing them away, he said to us, 'You people are in great danger and should leave.' I told my parents and this was the first time they agreed so quickly with a Christian religious leader. We left the next day. Fanny and I were crushed."

"But Ania's uncle, Father Janusz, is not like that," I said. "He is very sympathetic to Jews. Ania says he does things for the Jews that could be very dangerous for him."

Freyde said, "Yes, Esfir, as in every religion, there are the good and the bad."

Once in my room, I opened my journal to a fresh page and asked Ida to write down some of the explanations. She scribbled and soon filled the page. When she was finished, she closed the journal and said, "Esfir, remember we don't know how much was true or were just stories. You will understand as you get older."

That was the same thing she had said when she tried to explain the difference between good and bad questions, regarding Mendel Feigen. I waited for that day of comprehension—or I should say I yearned for that day.

WHEN I AWOKE and saw that Ida was missing, I rushed downstairs. No one was at the table. Perl heard me barreling down the stairs and met me in the dining room.

"What?" I asked. "Where is everyone?" "Is it a holiday or something?"

"No," Perl said. "The girls went off to school. We didn't want to wake you."

"Why? I'm not sick."

"I know, Esfir. But from what you told us yesterday, I made a decision. You are *not* going back to that school for a while. I asked Ida to stop at the post office and send a message to the Kobrin branch. Sheyne usually goes there in the early afternoon. I asked your mother to call me at four. I will go to our post office then and if she calls, I will tell her my decision."

"But, I don't mind what they say. I promise I won't answer them if they call me a 'Christ killer.' "

"I know you're a good girl, Esfir. Let's leave it like this and see what your mother has to say. In the meantime, you can stay home with me today. What do you say? Maybe we can bake some *rugelach*."

Normally, I'd be so happy to stay home and bake with Perl, but I was scared what my mother would say. Would she agree with Perl or be angry at her? Would she make me come home? What would happen to me, leaving not just one public school but now two? Would I go to prison?

The question I dreaded the answer to the most was, "If I have to leave school, will Ania still be my friend?"

# Fifteen

THERE WERE MORE and more frightening stories, perhaps because I was now home with Perl and I heard her speak with neighbors, people at the market, her friends and relatives. I was a silent bug on the wall of a multistory house of cards; one tip and the sides would cave in, leaving a pile of mismatched suits.

Perl, my dear, dear aunt couldn't keep her mouth shut. I thought I had a vomit mouth, but she expressed her every thought and action. She had never been so bad before. Now she talked to herself, forgetting I was in the room, and ran a running commentary like, "I am going into the kitchen. I am washing down the table. I am sifting flour over rolled dough." It was as if she feared a moment of silence would create a vacuum and allow the wind to blow down *her* walls, as shaky as that house of cards.

At first I thought I was to blame, that she had to worry about providing some kind of education for me. Since my mother called on the day that Perl ordered me to stay away from school, there was more tension in the family, not that we needed more. My mother, Perl had reported, agreed that I should remain home. Enough was enough with these public schools. My mother would think of something for me, Perl said, and not to fret. I did overhear Perl talking to Mr. Kozak outside her bedroom door on my way to the kitchen one night, fast becoming my usual pursuit to cure sleeplessness.

"I don't know what to do with her," Perl had said.

"Let her be for now," he said. "Wait awhile. Things always get better."

"Spoken like a true *goy*," she said.

Then I heard laughing and shushing and I tiptoed up the stairs. Whatever they were saying next, I had the good sense to realize it wasn't for my ears.

In the long days I spent with Perl, when she wasn't talking to herself, she related more stories about her life as a girl and as a young woman.

During lunch one day, Perl reported that before the Big War, Brest had a large Jewish community of over thirty thousand, or sixty-five percent of the population. But it might as well have been a hundred percent. The commercial row at the market, with four hundred stores, had only one Christian shop. "Even my mother had a stall. She sold bread, eggs, and vegetables. In the winter, she kept warm by putting a pot of hot charcoal by her feet."

Perl's father, my grandfather Yankel, drank tea early in the morning from a shiny copper samovar and attended synagogue. Then he went to his fabric shop near the river in the tradesmen district. Bolts of colorful material lay on a long table in tight, tubed rows like organ pipes. There were all kinds of fabrics: cotton, wool, and more delicate ones like silk and satin. There were florals and plain colors. Quilted bolts were also popular.

By now, Perl's face was softening and I could swear she looked ten years younger. "Customers would point to one," she explained, "and my father would pick up the tube and unravel just enough material for the person to examine."

When we finished our lunch, Perl insisted we go for a walk and that I take my journal. "You can't stay cooped up here in the house," she said. Before long, we were in the park. Perl directed me to a bench and patted the seat.

"I don't want to sit there," I said.

"What is wrong with this bench?" she asked.

I shrugged and stood immobile, pulling Perl's hand backward. Finally, I said, "That is the bench Ida and I sat on when the boys threw rocks at us."

"I see," Perl said. "Then we should definitely sit there."

I didn't protest; there was no use in arguing with Perl when she decided on something, but I was already thinking of what I would say to get Perl to leave.

"Now, Esfir," Perl said, "let's continue our lesson. Where was I? Is there anything you want to know about?"

"Yes," I said, noticing that a woman with a baby carriage stopped to sneeze and cough and she aimed her face right near the baby's. "Did Sheyne ever get sick?" I asked. I was always desperate to know about my mother.

PERL CLOSED HER eyes then. "Of course, we all got sick. But with the bad diseases, not your mother." Perl was quiet as if the subject was finished, but I was beginning to read the rising and falling of her voice.

"Then who?"

"Maybe it's time for you to know."

"Know what?" I asked, thinking that maybe my mother had some horrible illness that was inherited.

"I am not the firstborn child. I had an older brother, Isaac. He was a spunky, adorable child, the kind everyone idolizes. When he was six, I was three—your mother wasn't born yet for a year—he got diphtheria and died. I don't remember the details, except that he stayed for a few weeks in the house with my mother. They were quarantined. We couldn't go home. My father, me, and Khane, who was only a year old, had to stay with my grandparents. I missed my mother so much, and Khane was hysterical all the time."

"And then?" I asked, suspecting the rest.

"Isaac died in his sleep. It wasn't until years later that my mother told me that there had also been a baby girl between Isaac and me who died when she was a month old."

I didn't realize it until Perl stopped that I had been crying.

"Don't cry," Perl said, which made me cry more. "I'm sorry I told you."

"Maybe now that I'm not in school, I should go home," I said, suddenly missing my family terribly, even if they didn't miss me.

"Not yet, Esfele. Soon, I promise."

"I have to use the bathroom," I said, figuring this would get Perl moving. She turned my head toward her and stared into my eyes. Then, she stood, extended her arm—a signal that she was ready to go, though I don't think she believed me. As we walked toward the park's entrance, I felt a smack on the back of my shoulder.

"What?" I yelled and scrunched my neck, waiting for a blow. I turned and saw Ida and gave a loud, "whew."

"Sorry, I scared you, Esfir, but I saw you two walking."

"Where are the other girls?" Perl asked.

"I don't know. I didn't wait for them. It's such a beautiful day, the first warm one in April so far, that I wanted to walk home through the park. Can you sit awhile?"

I immediately went back to the bench, my fears lessening with Ida's bubbly spirit.

"I was giving Esfir a little history lesson," Perl said, caving with relief onto the seat, "though I am surely not the teacher you are."

"About what?"

"Oh, I was rambling, but mostly about family history. Sad, though many suffered worse."

"Worse than illnesses and death?" I asked.

Perl mopped her damp forehead with a handkerchief from her purse. She licked her lips. "I wish I had some water. I don't know why I'm so thirsty," she said.

I knew why. She hadn't stopped talking for twenty minutes. But Perl was not finished.

"When I was not much younger than you, Ida, in 1905," Perl said, "there were pogroms all over."

"What's a pogrom?" I asked. I had heard that word before from adults, and always, it was followed by shaking of heads.

"A pogrom," she said slowly, taking on her professorial voice, "is organized mass violence toward a minority group, usually spurred on by a local government. What that means is looting, assaults, arson, and I don't want to say."

"Like what?" I asked.

"You don't have to know everything."

"Killing?" I said.

"Okay 'Miss Know-it-All.'"

"How can I be a 'Miss-Know-it-All' when no one tells me everything?"

"She has a point," Ida said, smiling.

"Okay, but promise you won't snitch to your mother."

Informing my mother of anything was becoming a rarity. You couldn't confide in someone you didn't see.

"Actually," Perl said, quickening her voice, "the first wave of pogroms started around 1903. You heard of the Bund?"

"Yes, it's in the chart that Ida made."

"Good. The Bund organized networks among Jewish workers and community members to defend themselves against the bad people. Some of the bad people were in Russia. A group called the Black Hundreds claimed that Jews were enemies of the tsar, and extermination of the

Jews was a patriotic act. They spread these words throughout Russia. And when people are poor, they need someone to blame."

Instinctively, I said, "So then what happened?"

"What happened next is not a pretty story," she said. "It happened on Easter in 1903 in Kishinev, south of Ukraine. In three days of rioting, about fifty Jews were killed. Even worse pogroms occurred later on. Rioters often included the local population who used sticks and knives, often chanting, 'Let's kill the Jews.' "

"That's terrible," I said, beginning to dread the rest.

Perl said, "Write this down in your journal, Esfir."

I opened a clean page and wrote down "Easter, 1903" in case Perl tested me. When someone took on the role of a teacher or gave a lesson, you never knew what they'd expect from you.

My head was pounding. How could I tell my aunt that I didn't want to hear anymore, that I was only almost a third grader? A simple story book was enough for me.

"I won't go over the gory details, but there was also general rioting against the Jews in the summer and fall of 1905. The October Rechitsa Pogrom—Rechitsa is east of Pinsk—was so bad that your beloved Sholom Aleichem wrote to the Russian writer Leo Tolstoy. Now, Esfir, this is something good to copy."

Perl said, "Aleichem wrote: 'Shame and misfortune befell our common homeland, but we poor Jews suffered the most.' " I interrupted Perl so many times for the spelling that she eventually took my journal and wrote it down herself.

"Esfir, I'd like to copy that too," Ida said. "Can you lend me your journal when we get back?"

"Yes."

"You know a lot, Perl," Ida said.

"Just because I run this house doesn't mean I came from the treetops."

Ida, looking embarrassed, said, "I know, Perl."

Perl took a large intake of air. She had more to say. "Then the pogroms came to Mogilev, Vitebsk, Minsk, and the Vilna regions."

"But not here?" I asked, my voice rising.

"Yes, I'm afraid so. There was one here in Brest in May 1905. Many Jews were wounded and killed."

"Oh no," I said.

"Between 1903 and 1906, pogroms had spread to hundreds of cities and towns. Thousands were killed and wounded."

"At least it hasn't happened in a long time," I said.

"Well, you'll probably hear this anyway. But there have been *incidents*. Last March, in a Polish village called Przytyk, a group of Poles attacked local Jews, breaking into their homes and beating the people. They also broke into Jewish stores and stole merchandise. Three Jews died and there were many wounded. The police didn't do a thing to help the Jews. Some of the local adults, yelled, 'Wait until Hitler comes.'"

For me, an unusual thing happened. I was totally speechless. The rocks that the boys had thrown at Ida and me now seemed like particles of dust.

Perl said her last words on the subject, "After these pogroms, I learned what it meant to be a Jew, not in the religious sense, but in the sense of our place in the world. And after last year, with more and more pogroms, I'm afraid we may have no safe place in this world."

# Sixteen

DESPITE THE WARMING weather of spring, I didn't want to go outside. When I wasn't helping Perl around the house, I was in my room having pretend conversations with Miriam. I couldn't tell anyone, even Miriam, what I feared the most: being caught in a pogrom.

On the last Wednesday of April, Ida woke me early and said that I should get dressed for an outing and that she wasn't taking "no" for an answer. I had to go and that was that. I was too tired to argue. I went to the bathroom, washed my face, and brushed my teeth. When I returned to my room to dress, Ida had laid out my clothes—a short-sleeved blouse, blue cotton skirt, and white socks.

We would have time for a quick breakfast, she said. There at the dining table were the girls dressed in school clothes, Perl wearing a floral dress, and my Ania clutching her school books against her chest.

"Ania," I said, "what are you doing here?"

"I'm going with you and the girls to the forest for your holiday. My family doesn't know. They think I went to school like always. Ida met me near school. She told me about it yesterday, and I wouldn't miss it for the world."

"What if your parents find out or your uncle?"

"Yesterday I told Miss Petra that I wasn't feeling well, so she won't be surprised that I don't show up today. I don't think she'd be suspicious 'cause I'm never absent."

"But, does Perl know?"

"Don't worry about your aunt," Ida said. "She thinks we got approval from Ania's family."

"You mean you lied?"

"A white lie, maybe. I'm sure Ania's family would have approved. Last year, her uncle came. They know what fun we're going to have."

Ania nodded with a big grin.

"Sit down," Ida ordered. "Eat your breakfast, and be ready to leave in ten minutes." Ida was like a general and I didn't dare protest.

The holiday was Lag b'Omer, which comes between *Pesach* and Shevuoth, and has something to do with a famous rabbi and the plague. Nobody seems to know why we celebrate it, and, unlike most Jewish holidays, nobody wants to know. The agreement is that whatever the origin, it's a day of celebration and God knows the Jews sorely needed it.

Ida's plan was that Ania, Perl, and I would accompany the Tarbut students on a bus to the forest. From what I overheard from Fanny, the arrangement had a connection to Mendel Feigen, Ida's not-so-secret crush, who was instrumental in organizing the events. Although Ania and I sat in the back of the bus, we heard Mendel who stood up front and spoke loudly. All his speechifying had come in handy.

From the window, we saw parades of young people marching in military fashion toward the Gardens. Bands played patriotic Hebrew songs, with a lot of drum beating. Mendel stopped the bus and ordered us out to get a better viewing spot. Then he yelled out the identities of each group. There were members of Hashomer Hatzair in their shirts and neck scarves, the men wearing shorts and long socks; there were lines of students from Betar units, in their military uniforms. They were led by an older soldier riding a white horse. Less coordinated, another marching group of young Halutzim, the Hebrew word for pioneers, from a nearby village, wore dark shirts and light ties. The crowd cheered when a large contingent from what Mendel explained as "the independent, humanistic, self-labor group," Gordonia, appeared in their scouts uniforms, accompanied by drums, trumpets, and cymbals. Yiddish schoolchildren marched with their teachers. Those in front of each group held the Polish flag and the blue-and-white Zionist flag.

A man appeared and whispered in Mendel's ear, as if anyone could hear him over the din of the parade. Mendel nodded and waved us to follow him. He was screaming, "Come." Apparently, the bus driver was blocking traffic where he was parked and we had to move.

Back on the bus, we were glued to the window, straining to see splashes of color and billowing flags, as we made our way toward the road outside Brest and headed forty-three miles north to the Puszcza Bialowieska National Park, to me known simply as "the forest."

Mendel proved to be a great forest guide. On our walk from the parking lot to a picnic area, he pointed out the names of the old trees,

including the Great Mamamuszi, the thickest oak in the forest. He told
us about the famous rare bison, which scared Ania and me; luckily,
we didn't see one. Mendel identified a fox, squirrel, raccoon, and a
woodpecker, so far not such scary or unusual animals, but there were
also wild boars and wolves and we were relieved to miss them. But being
in a forest, you never knew what was lurking behind the trees. There was
one bird he talked about, the black stork, which we were dying to see,
but I guess being black made it hard to spot.

Before long, we found the picnic area where other Tarbut students
had come with their parents from another bus. They had already
unpacked food baskets. Perl set immediately to work, adding her own
basket filled with hard-boiled eggs, rice pudding, boiled chicken, apples,
dark bread, cookies, and a thermos of tea.

Groups of students had spread out blankets; many were sprawled on
them, laughing and munching on food. It was a day filled with activity.
We sang Hebrew songs, led by a female teacher with a beautiful voice.
Occasionally, a young person stood on one of the tables and recited a
poem, written for the occasion. Parents clapped wildly.

When our stomachs were full, there was a series of speeches. I fell
asleep for a while and woke from a poke in my side from Ania. Mendel
was speaking and the girls on my blanket sat up like trained seals. He
welcomed everyone as if it was his private party. Introducing each Zionist
group, he encouraged members to stand and the crowd applauded.

With everyone riled up, he took out a paper from his pants pocket
and read. I was trying hard to keep my eyes open. Ida copied his words
in her journal so I was able to transfer them later to mine.

Mendel asked if anyone in the crowd attended a meeting of the
Zionist youth organization, Masada, Hebrew for fortress, earlier in the
year. A few held up their hands.

"For the benefit of those who didn't come, I will summarize. It was
electrifying." His eyes engorged with fervor. "The speaker was a Brisker,
now a lawyer in Warsaw, who came home to visit his parents. He now
calls himself Menachem, Menachem Begin. A short man, his stature
rose as he described, with deep feeling, the Jewish situation. I would say
he is second only to Jabotinsky as an orator. This man was one of us. He
went to our schools. Actually, we went to the same Polish gymnasium.
Mr. Begin spoke in Polish, using Yiddish and German phrases. And

what did he say? You have heard it before: the hopelessness of our future in Poland."

Mendel said more; I have in my notes the words, *evacuation plan*, calling for all Eastern European Jewry to move to Palestine. He criticized political infighting and governmental failure, warning of "impending catastrophe" if Jews stayed in Europe.

Ida, still writing, said, "pompous ass," and when she remembered me, she apologized for her language. I smiled because the way she giggled out those words showed that she liked him better than ever.

Mendel was screeching, repeating the word, *Palestine, Palestine, Palestine*, getting people in a frenzy. They raised their fists and shouted, "Jerusalem, Jerusalem." Carefully, he sipped water from a jar and held up his palms for quiet like he was the Pope.

"So, my friends," he said in a very low voice, "think about what *I* said, not only me but what your leaders have pleaded for. I don't want to spoil the day with all this serious talk." With those words, he sat on a chair, more like he collapsed in it, his entire body sagging. Then he rose, self-satisfaction ooozing from his pursed lips, closed eyes, and *davening* torso.

Finally, the fun started. Children ran around chasing each other with bows and arrows. I was longing to use one and asked a boy if I could take a turn. The arrows were rubber-tipped so I aimed one at Ania's feet. She jumped and grabbed the bow from me, and aimed her arrow at a target in a tree. Although it didn't stick, a boy close to it yelled, "Bulls-eye!"

There were more games with bats and balls. Girls joined boys. It wasn't like it usually was, with the boys having all the amusement.

The rest of the day included more eating, speeches, and songs. The most wonderful event was yet to come. As soon as it got dark, I saw orange flames rising in the distance. Perl told us to stay put, but we followed masses of people hypnotically veering toward the light. It was a giant bonfire. We got close enough to see sparks darting in all directions. I was surprised to hear such loud sounds coming from the fire—crackling, pops, bangs, roars. Ania and I circled it from a safe distance and saw the fire take on different shapes, depending on where we stood. Sometimes it looked like black silhouetted figures headed toward the flames, then there were piles of crisscrossing sticks like a funeral pyre I saw in a book on India. I was drawn toward it and found myself getting closer. I heard Ania calling me back, but I was no longer in control of my movements. If others could show their shadows, so could I.

A loud burst followed when someone threw a long, sausage-like object into the orange heap. I went forward, transfixed despite its potential harm, and then inched backward, running as far away as I could.

The story of Jesus came to me. Maybe I thought of it then because of the sticks, which sometimes looked like burning crucifixes. I think also, it was the stories of his miracles and how he mesmerized crowds with mystical powers. This was not Easter, but Jesus was rising from the dead.

Behind a row of tall bushes, I heard yelps and saw a flash of arms. I moved closer and peeked around the side. On a pile of twigs Mendel and Ida were laying down, and Ida rolled over. Mendel crawled next to her and smoothed the dirt from her skirt. His hands ran down her legs and up again, and she seemed to pounce on him. Before long, they were kissing and feeling each other around. At first, I was going to yell her name and then thought of finding Perl. But I saw that Mendel pulled Ida's long black hair back and licked her face. Instead of pushing him away, she moved her head back and closed her eyes, seemingly in a trance. I scooted away and ran back and bumped into Ania.

"Where have you been?" she said. "Perl is looking for you."

"Looking for you," I repeated, my cheeks pulsating with heat, not just from the fire but from the shame of my Ida.

Back on the bus, I slept all the way to Brest. I awoke a few times for a second or two and have a vague memory of humming tunes. Once Ania whispered, "Look, Esfir, Ida and Mendel are sitting together." I didn't want to see and pretended to sleep. By the time we got to the Tarbut to unload, Mendel was standing again, checking a list of students as they disembarked.

I was surprised that the next morning, there was nothing mentioned about Lag b'Omer at breakfast. Freyde was in a rush, as usual, grabbing a roll and running out the door. Fanny and Ida sat drinking tea as they waited for Liba. Leave it to Rachel to bring up the unmentionable.

"So, Ida," she said, her voice rising on the second word, which she dragged out.

"So, Ra-chel," Ida parodied.

"Did you have fun yesterday?"

"Yes. Didn't you?"

"It was okay if you don't mind almost getting burned to death and children practically killing you with bows and arrows."

"Must everything be about you and how you narrowly escaped death?"

"Not everyone gets to nuzzle with their teacher."

Rachel had gone too far this time. I was angry at Ida but more scared for her, hoping that I was the only one who saw them. Everyone knew that Mendel would get in serious trouble if anyone suspected him of showing improper overtures to a student, especially a girl who just turned fifteen.

Ida's face reddened, which surprised me since her complexion was so dark. She once told me that she didn't get sunburned but turned tan or she should have said, "tanner."

At that moment, Liba entered the room. She must have been listening or Rachel was speaking so loudly, Liba could have heard her upstairs.

"I'm ready," she announced, scooping an apple from a bowl on the table and rocking it from one palm to another. "Oh Rachel," she said, on her way toward the vestibule. "Keep your goddamn mouth shut. Jews are in enough trouble in this city. We don't need to make trouble for each other."

Perl didn't like that kind of language, but let it go. Rachel actually looked chastised. She lagged behind as the girls gathered their books from the hall table. I think I was the only one who heard her say "sorry" as she passed me by.

After the girls slammed the door, I raced upstairs. I took Miriam out from under my bed and propped her up against my pillow. "Now Miriam," I said, stroking her not-so-perfect hair. "I must tell you about yesterday. It was the most wonderful day of my life, except for one thing."

# Seventeen

I REMEMBERED THE date, Thursday, May 13. It was a rare day in that I was looking forward to going outdoors. Ania invited me to pick her up after school. We were meeting her oldest brother Erek at his gymnasium and then going to the park to watch him play soccer. On the way to the game, we walked through the New Market and were besieged by rioters. Since Erek wore his Polish school uniform, the rioters let us alone. The swell of the mob blocked our way. They surrounded the market. We watched, horrified, from a safe distance, but close enough to see gangs break into Jewish shops and overturn market stalls. They bashed barrels of herring and tossed torn sacks of food into a heap. A knot of thugs approached a blacksmith's stall and crushed his instruments. His crying wife and young children stood by the entrance and were shoved inside. I waited but didn't see them emerge.

We managed to move a little and halted because of yelling and screaming. Instinctively, we hid in a nearby alleyway with a view of another scene. It was the most horrible thing; I couldn't erase this memory. I was too terrified to move. Men hurled rocks at several Jews as they ran out of their shops. Three men were enclosed in the mob's circle. Rioters hit them with rocks and sticks, and stomped on their bodies. A young man rushed in to help, crying, "Papa, no." A mobster smashed a wooden beam over the son's head. I shouted to stop but my voice was buried in the racket.

Village peasants harnessed their horses and hitched their wagons to get away as fast as possible.

Trying to escape from the violence, we crept in and out of alleys and slunk around corners as if *we* were the thieves. This mob had no such subterfuge; they attacked like feral animals. They ripped off locks and smashed shutters, windows, and doors to get into any Jewish shop or building. They walked out with merchandise and threw what they couldn't carry into the streets. Locals pushed their way and picked through the goods, flinging wrecked items in the air and stuffing what they wanted into makeshift bags. The debris formed into miniature mountains, growing bigger by the seconds. There was glass all over.

Enraged looters drenched piles of useless items with kerosene and set them on fire. Others shook flour over heaps of merchandise, whitening faces and hair—crazed ghosts at a ritual slaughtering.

Finally, I saw Jewish men trying to ward off the mob. Most were workers—the carriers, wagon drivers, meat industry employees. I felt some relief that they would stop the violence. But the police stood observing, many of them laughing. Officers hauled off the Jewish defenders. The hooligans continued looting. They swaggered as they barraged. Some wore swastikas on the right side of their chests. I knew that symbol was very bad. Then they shouted slogans like, "Jewish property belongs to us," "Nobody will stop us," "The police are on our side."

We found a break in the action, and I asked Erek and Ania to walk with me on the side streets toward Perl's. The marauding continued, only now it was happening to people's homes. There were broken doors and windows. Shattered furniture, slashed mattresses, pillows, and bedding were piled in the street. Feathers flew like a blizzard. We didn't know where to turn. Erek tried to lead us to a safe corner. I began to shake violently, certain now that Perl's house would be missing.

When we got to Perl's, the house seemed unscathed. We pounded on the door until Perl eventually opened it. I fell into her arms and was sobbing. But there was no time for comfort. The looters were now entering our neighborhood. Perl insisted that Ania and Erek join us in the shallow cellar. There, the girls were already squeezed tightly; and we pressed into them, lying sideways so we could fit. I heard and felt nothing but the gurgling and rumbling and thumping of my insides. Sure that everyone could hear, I held my breath hoping to quiet myself, but I couldn't hold it in. As the air burst from my mouth, pee released. I started to cry again, more like whimpering. I couldn't see who was on my sides, but each scrunched closer to me and someone whispered, "Shh."

By nightfall, we crept out of hiding and crawled inside the house. Ania and Erek's father came looking for them. "Where have you been all this time?" he asked. "Your mother is screaming to God."

Perl said, "Your children have been heroes. They probably saved Esfir's life."

A religious and quiet man, Ania's father beamed for a second and then turned serious. He was a civil servant and heard about the rest of the city. "I saw several beatings and stabbings. They were a bunch of animals."

Disbelief was written in giant letters on his lined forehead. He reported that synagogues, prayer houses, and Jewish cultural centers had been destroyed. Life as we knew it had ended.

We turned off the lights and moved the sofa against the front door and the dining-room hutch against the back door, leaving a slight opening in case we needed to use the outhouse. We clung to each other in darkness and silence, terrified that any second, a frenzied mob would burst into the house. I safeguarded my two precious possessions, camouflaging my journal and Miriam in the farthest reaches of the attic. Sometimes our bladders and bowels defeated us and we snuck out in groups of three to the outhouse. The two outside scoured the periphery for signs of life.

Night passed somehow. Peeking out from the curtains at dawn, we saw others do the same. One neighbor swept fallen branches from his stoop. An elderly, bent woman shuffled down the block, carrying a basket. Cautiously, we moved the sofa and cupboard back. People began to walk openly down the streets, hungry to get a newspaper, speak to a knowing source. Ania gave me a long hug and silently, she and her family left from the back kitchen door.

By early evening, we learned that we were safe for the moment. Only after a call to central headquarters in Warsaw had auxiliary police been sent. That afternoon, they had ended the pogrom. Two Jews had been killed and many injured. The twenty-four-hour rampage was over.

Though I lived through it, I heard how it happened from the radio, supplemented by word of mouth, and later from those who read the Jewish press. It had begun with one incident. In this case, the last straw had really been the last straw, on the floor of a butcher shop. Previously, the government had issued anti-Semitic laws that restricted the number of cattle that Jews could kill. This lower number was not enough to meet the needs of the Jewish community. The result was illegal killing of animals by local butchers.

A governmental official, assisted by a policeman, would inspect meat at the butcher shops. If they found meat above the allotted quota, they would confiscate it. Often, the police accepted bribes.

A butcher in the New Market stalls couldn't tolerate these practices and protested. The policeman said, "You lying, bloody Jew" and pushed the butcher, who fell. Witnessing this, the butcher's son stabbed and killed the policeman. Governmental leaders used this incident to stir up the public. All of Brest's Jews had to pay for the butcher's son's crime with their "fortunes and blood."

Agitators had waited for such an incident. They had collected an army of peasants and hoodlums while the police stood by with their guns drawn. Police arrested the Jews who tried to resist.

The instigators wanted to empty Jewish shops. They intended to prevent the Jews from carrying on their businesses, hoping that the locals would take over. But the plan failed.

Jewish communities around the world responded immediately through local relief societies. They sent large sums of money, clothing, and goods. Anyhow, the Jews eventually replenished their shops.

Our pogrom was not the beginning or the end. There were pogroms in neighboring cities and towns. Ida said we shouldn't have been surprised. Everything for the Jews changed after Marshal Pilsudski's death in May 1935. He had been kind to the Jews, "a benevolent dictator," Ida wrote in my journal. After his death, right-wing parties, including the *Endecja*, had taken over the Polish government and anti-Semitism had increased.

Perl was beside herself with fury. "Jealousy, jealousy. It's all about jealousy," she said. "The Jews of Brest managed to restore themselves to a full life. They had their trades, their newspapers, theater, schools, sports clubs. They all thought, 'This would never happen here.'"

You can imagine the talk that went on at the Tarbut and at the political organizations. *Exile* was the word of the day. Still, most people around us couldn't believe such violence would last. Not me. One of the few times I had gone outside happily and the world had erupted. My worst fear realized. Oh My God. It was a POGROM. A pogrom! Only it wasn't just a word in a history lesson, an event that happened in another city. A pogrom found us! I was never going out of the house again.

# Eighteen

I GAVE UP my chores around the house and spent most of the day in my room, except for eating and going to the bathroom. If I could have performed those functions without leaving my space, I would have. Even Ida couldn't persuade me to go outdoors. She had asked me to come with her shopping, to go for a hike, to join her friends at a picnic. I had refused all offers.

Then she thought she had something to entice me out of the house. She begged me to attend an upcoming soccer match between the Jewish Maccabi team and a Polish team; she had a special invitation from Freyde's brother, Yossel. But all I imagined were evil people hiding in the stadium's aisles, waiting, waiting to pounce.

Ania also tried. She came and sat on my bed, telling me the news from school. Her big ploy was to bring one of her dolls, asking if we could enact a story with Miriam. Our two "girls" could have an adventure in the park. I was no fool. I wouldn't endanger Miriam for a minute; she was safe in her hiding place.

One late afternoon, about ten days after the pogrom, there was a knock on my door. I whispered, "Come in," expecting one of the girls. I was in shock to see my mother. I had forgotten how her long honey hair wound into a graceful chignon lying softly at her nape, a few wisps falling from the sides. I had forgotted her extended elegant neck and high, rounded cheekbones. I had forgotten my mother's dainty mushroom-shaped ears and aqua eyes that penetrated mine, daring the truth. I had forgotten my mother's girlish appearance, looking years younger, embarrassing Perl when a neighbor once mistook her for Perl's daughter. I had forgotten that my mother was so beautiful.

All my life I longed for someone to say that I looked like her. Mostly, they said, "Mmm, who does Esfir take after?"

It was fitting that my mother's name was Sheyne, translated as *beautiful* in Yiddish. Esfir, a Russian version of Esther, meant, my mother once explained, "*star* in some foreign language."

"Esfele," she said softly.

I gasped.

It was then that I noticed my mother's hair showed gray strands, as fine as thread. It was then that I saw pronounced crow's-feet fanning from her bloodshot eyes.

"*Tsatskele,*" she whispered.

I slid off the bed and stood fixed to the spot. She had not forgotten me. I was her "little treasure."

My mother inched toward me. She held out her arms and I ran into them. She kissed me on my head and crooned, "*Mayn sheyne maideleh,*" my little girl.

I finally got to be *sheyne*, just like my mother.

I buried my head into my mother's chest and let her stroke my hair as I began to shudder and tremble until my pent-up crying came out in heaves. Then I thought of my father, and sobbed in another prolonged spasm. This was the first time I had cried for him.

To be in my mother's arms was everything. As soon as the trains resumed regular runs, she said, she had come to bring me home. I would have followed her anywhere.

Perl came with us to the train station. She was carrying a pouch bag with fruit and cheese, and one of her shawls. "For you, Esfir. God forbid you should starve or catch a cold."

"Aunt Perl, we're not going to Siberia."

"With these trains, you never know. Now give your aunt a big hug."

Perl enveloped me with her round arms and I pressed myself against her large breasts. "I wish you could come with us," I said.

"Me too, darling. But another time. I have the other girls to take care of."

"I know," I said.

"Come, Esfir. We have to get on the train," my mother said.

Minutes later, I was looking out the train window and waving to Perl, my tears blurring my image of her scurrying form. She seemed to go forward in a backward motion. My mother patted the seat next to her and I snuggled, wrapped in Perl's shawl

IT WAS A strange homecoming. Rivke, Dvora, and Velvel acted as if I were a doll; actually, I was more honest with my doll, Miriam. They were polite, asking me if I wanted this or that. On the very first day, I heard my mother tell them when I was out of sight, "Be nice to her. She's been through a lot, especially for someone so young. She is very frightened. Going outside is hard for her. So I don't want to hear any fighting or bossing her around. Do you understand me?"

I didn't hear a response from my siblings so I assumed they had agreed with a nod or closed eyes or something respectful but shy. They were also young and frightened.

At first, I was happy to have my family jump up and attend to my needs. Then, it got on my nerves. I was itching for a good argument; I wanted them back to the way they had been. Luckily, my siblings could be nice for just so long. Within a week, Rivke was bribing me to do her chores; Drora was chasing me away when her friends came over; and Velvel, well, he was rarely home. I was beginning to think that he was becoming like most males I knew, totally absorbed in activities outside the home.

One day in June, he walked inside wearing his Hashomer Hatzair outfit: shorts and a neck scarf. His face was flushed and sweaty, his curly hair stuck to his forehead. There were wet ovals underneath his shirt's armpits. He was out of breath as if he had been in a long-distance running event.

My mother was sitting at the sewing machine in the living room. I was her "assistant," feeding her the proper thread and fabric. Velvel stood in the middle of the room, panting.

"What?" she asked, taking her foot off the pedal.

"I have the most exciting news," he said between gulps of air.

"What is it?" my mother asked insistently. "You're giving me a heart attack."

How could my mother say those words? I snorted and wheezed, holding in my breath. The noise must have got my mother's attention. "I'm sorry," she said. "I didn't mean a *real* heart attack."

Velvel flopped on the couch, gulping water until he emptied the glass. "I'm going," he said. "I'm finally going."

"Going where?" my mother asked, swiveling her stool around to face her son, barely eighteen years old.

"I'm finished with school; it's time for me to get on with my life." Velvel had attended the ORT trade school to become a carpenter.

"Okay, I agree," she said. "Your father and I wanted you to have skills for real work."

"I have experience already. You know I did some building for Kibbutz Shacharia and now I'm helping in the farming. They all come to me to fix the machinery." He hunched toward his knees.

"This is not what your father and I had in mind."

"Why? This is good, honest work, and for a real cause. Not to build a cabinet or chair for some rich person."

"There is nothing wrong with building furniture. People get satisfaction from this."

"Mama, you don't understand. I'm not interested in personal satisfaction or frivolous pursuits. I want to make a difference, for you to be proud of me."

My mother's voice softened. She moved toward the couch and sat next to her son. She rubbed the back of his head. "Velvel, I *am* very proud of you. It isn't easy to be the only male in a family. You have been my rock. I don't want to see you waste your life on dreams. We Jews need practical skills to make us necessary."

"This is just my point, Mama. I want to teach these practical skills to make *more* of us Jews necessary. Necessary to ourselves and not to a country that makes us prove ourselves over and over, changing the rules arbitrarily and dangling false hope like a sadistic monster."

My brother was sounding familiar. Then I remembered listening to Mendel speak at the meeting and during Lag b'Omer. He had that same fiery, overblown manner.

"You are young, Velvel. You don't know the world. You think what you read, what you hear others say, is right. It's good to be idealistic, to believe in the value of human life and nationalistic pride. I don't want to squash your enthusiasm. But we live in hard times. We don't have the luxury to get lost in ideas. We have to feed our children. We have to live."

My mother's voice was congested and the whites of her eyes reddened. She stopped herself as she didn't like us to see her upset, especially to cry.

"I am not speaking in the abstract here," Velvel said, taking the sarcasm out of his tone. "I want you to understand how much I love my country, my home, and my family. But love is not enough. Love doesn't allow us to be. We cannot remain like sheep. We have to act. And that is why we have to make our home elsewhere, and this is why I'm making *aliyah*."

"No!" My mother held her hand over her heart. She didn't say "heart attack" again, but when she pressed her fingers deeply into her chest, she made it clear that Velvel's words were having a lethal effect. "You can't go to Palestine. We need you here."

"You'll be all right. Drora is old enough now to help you in the shop. Grandpa Yankel and Grandma will also help out. I've spoken to them. Rivke can take care of herself. And Perl is only too happy to care for Esfir."

"I see you have it all figured out."

"I've been thinking about this for a long time. This is not an impulsive decision."

Suddenly, my brother sounded old. He was sure of himself, of his plans. He didn't ask our opinions; he delivered his future to us, served on a platter with reheated leftovers.

It was a time of screaming hysterics and unabashed pleas. My mother was beyond desperate, pressing relatives, friends, and business associates to persuade Velvel to change his mind. It was no use.

He had just been wearing shorts and a scarf. Only a few days later, dressed in khaki slacks and a long-sleeved shirt, carrying a small suitcase, Velvel was on his way toward a long, treacherous, and convoluted journey to the Promised Land.

Rivke remembered that almost three years before, a large group of youngsters had gone to Brest on their voyage to Palestine. At the train station, there had been a crowd waving hands and singing *Hatikva*, "The Hope" in Hebrew, and labor movement songs. People brought flowers. The relatives were crying, but they were filled with pride and hope.

When we went to see Velvel off at the station, there was little fanfare. He located his small group of fellow pioneers. I stood on tiptoe and clutched my arms around my brother's skinny waist. He bent and kissed me near my lips and I smothered him with kisses, wetted by tears. His parting words to us were, "I will write to you when I arrive there and am settled. Don't worry, I will work hard and before you know it, I will send for all of you. We will be together again in our own country."

On the way home, I repeated his last words, how we'd be together in Palestine. I knew he meant it, but I couldn't imagine how he could make this happen. Looking at my mother's wan face and stooped posture, she was just as skeptical. He was still a boy to her; he was still her child, lost to the world.

# Nineteen

THAT SUMMER, NOT much was happening, which was all right with me. I discovered that even Drora was becoming involved in Zionist activities, something she kept secret because my mother was so upset over Velvel's parting. Rivke must have found out. I had gotten a little suspicious when they were whispering a lot and not fighting. Then, they started leaving together. When I asked where they were going, they never answered specifically. They were stepping "out," to "visit friends," to the "library," etc.

One day in mid-July, however, I got an opportunity to join them for the day, basically after my mother insisted that they take me someplace so I would get out of the house. They even told me I could invite Gittel, my neighbor friend. I hadn't spent much time with Gittel, not the way I used to in the summers when we'd go to the river and the pick blueberries. Gittel was not as experienced as Ania, but she was a good person and let me boss her around in a way that I could never imagine with Ania.

It was a steamy day and we packed lunches in a basket and headed for the Mukhavets River. We marched on the promenade and crossed the bridge, which divides the city in two. There were barges and boats in the river and we walked toward a large neatly trimmed space where there were crowds of youngsters laying on the grass. Drora took Rivke aside and they looked at Gittel and me with conspiratorial nods.

Rivke led us to another area with poplar trees, and we leaned against a large one and ate our lunch. She promised to take us swimming by the riverbank later.

Although it was obvious that Drora wanted us to be away from the action, I could hear loud chanting. I stood and turned toward the noise. Rivke ordered me to sit down and mind my business, but she couldn't contain me. Forgetting my fears, like at the Lag b'Omer event, I grabbed Gitttel's hand and we scampered in the direction of the activity, caught in the momentum of others with the same idea. If

Drora and her friends wanted their meeting to be a secret, it was no use. That's how it was in my city: the more you tried to hide, the more everyone knew your business.

In the middle of that lawn, Drora and the others had moved their blankets to form a semicircle. In the center, a boy—or I should say, a young man—about Velvel's age was warning the group that they had to be more careful in the future if they wanted to continue their activities. "Meetings should be held in smaller groups, in someone's house or a synagogue," he urged. "Nothing should be discussed away from those quarters. Don't trust outsiders. You could be arrested or worse." He stopped talking when he noticed all of us coming toward him and held up his hands as if to push us away.

"No," he yelled, "please!"

This wasn't enough and the people, mainly youngsters in their teens, swelled forward. Finally, he shouted, "In the name of Palestine, you must go away. It is not good to make such a commotion. From now on, we need to carry on in more discreet ways. Please, I beg you, for your own sakes."

That last plea got to us and independently, singly and in pairs, we dispersed in different directions, many with our heads down as if this posture would not draw attention. Near our spot by the poplar trees, Rivke beckoned us with large curving arm gestures. Drora joined us minutes later.

On our way home, Gittel and I skipped ahead of my sisters, not frightened by the young man's dire predictions. How could we take him seriously when he was drawing a crowd and then telling them to be secret?

I will never be sure of what happened that day because Rivke wouldn't divulge anything. Even though I loved my sister madly, she was ordered by Drora to keep us in the dark as much as possible. Rivke, the middle girl, usually obeyed her older sister's commands, especially, as in this case, when Drora made her feel important. Jealous or not, I wouldn't try to entice Rivke my way. Even at my age, I sensed that she needed to feel special more than I needed to know what was going on. When I got home, I had written in my journal, "Something to do with teenagers, 1937."

A few days later, I went with Rivke to meet Drora outside of her youth group. It was held at the big building on Tragota Street that had been sectioned off to include the main offices of the Jewish cultural youth movements (where my father had performed secretarial duties), four Jewish schools of different orientations, relief organizations, an orphanage (where Gittel and I had volunteered), reading rooms, and libraries.

For the students, the days were for studying. At night, hundreds of young people gathered at the Tragota complex for recreation. While Polish schoolchildren could become members of *Mloda Polska*, Young Poland, an artistic and cultural movement, Tragota was the creative soul of Kobrin's Jewish youth.

Drora was an hour late and Rivke was pacing around the periphery of the complex.

"Should we go inside to the meeting room?" I asked.

"No, Drora said to meet her here. She wasn't sure where her meeting would be held. Finally, we saw Drora running in the street toward us. Her hair was disloged from its pins and it looked pasty with sweat. Her blouse was pulled out of her skirt and her left eyeglass was cracked.

"We have to get out of here," she said in a semi-hysterical tone. "They came and took the house. The police are all over. Let's run, follow me."

I heard a commotion and behind me I could see local police chasing Rivke's friends and other members of Zionist groups. They carried sticks and hit anyone in their way. One young man resisted by holding up his arms and a policeman beat him to the ground. Carriages arrived and mobs—we don't know who they were—loaded what they could take from inside the building. Again, we heard the curse, "Wait. Hitler will come upon you!"

We were lucky and made it home. Drora found out that some Zionist groups found shelter in large homes and rented space elsewhere. Maybe this is why that young man in the park had been urging his followers to be careful because he expected trouble, or maybe the purge had already begun. Anyway, in 1937, the year that Kobrin's fire brigade got a motor pump, the singing stopped on Tragota Street and the Jewish youth's dreams crumbled. And for me, there seemed no safe place. In Brest, I had been in a pogrom and now saw something even sadder: my sister Drora became a frightened and angry young woman.

AT THE END of July, early in the morning, my mother and I went to visit her parents. Though they shared a house with Aunt Khane and her children, it was really my grandparents' house. Khane had moved in when her husband, who was older, had died from a stroke. Slowly, Aunt Khane had taken over a lot of the cleaning and cooking—of course keeping kosher—as my grandmother Elke had a bad back.

My grandparents had moved to a small room on the first floor, so that my grandmother wouldn't have to climb stairs. This gave Khane the main bedroom. So with all these changes, the family soon began to call it Khane's house. My grandparents were probably hurt by that.

We sat in the living room where Grandpa Yankel was praying, standing in the corner. Grandpa was a small man, maybe five feet two inches tall, though he slumped and appeared shorter. He was very thin and always hoisting up his baggy black slacks, or rolling up his sweaters and jacket sleeves, even though Grandma Elke was an excellent seamstress and was only too happy to alter his clothes. He didn't want to bother with changes to his wardrobe, unaware that the cuffs of his slacks dragged on the ground, fraying and attracting mud. Elke had given up nagging him, not only about his clothes.

I wouldn't have been surprised to hear he had tripped over his overlong pant bottoms. My grandma said he looked like a starving peasant. My sisters had been embarrassed by his disheveled appearance.

My grandparents were religious, meaning that they were orthodox. Elke didn't look any different from other women, except that she always wore a dress with long sleeves, wool stockings, and a babushka head scarf covering her long gray hair. My grandpa didn't wear a fur hat and he didn't have *peyes*, or the uniform of the Hasidim. He had his own uniform, his own look that never changed.

My mother and grandmother left to go into the kitchen and I stayed on the couch, supposedly reading a book. Instead, my eyes went toward my grandfather, by now swaying fervently, totally unaware of my presence. He sported a white uneven, triangular-shaped beard, with a reddish brown and gray mustache, a white shirt, black silk vest, a black rumpled jacket, and a black *yarmulke*. During morning prayers, he wrapped his long white *talis* over his shoulders. Outdoors, he wore a black fedora with a black grosgrain band; and in the winter, he added a double-breasted gray overcoat, also wrinkled and too big.

When my grandfather finished his prayers, he turned and walked slowly in my direction, adjusting his eyeglasses as if he wasn't sure he was seeing me or a phantom. They were perched at the end rise of his lumpy nose, broken twice from falls. I was transfixed by his cloudy blue eyes, and I loved his long bony fingers, especially when they traced the lines in a book. I giggled at his constant throat-clearing noises, and was fascinated by his false teeth that were too big for his mouth and made a sucking sound when he ate.

Basically, I was of two minds about my grandpa. Sometimes I thought he was the most distinguished and learned man I knew; and others, I was terrified of his outbursts. Mostly, I felt ignorant around him; I didn't understand his Hebrew, despite his attempts to teach me. The thing that confused me more than anything was the way he spoke in normal conversation. It was usually mixed with proverbs that sounded like curses or the words of Moses. This is how I felt when someone told a joke—that I should laugh because I couldn't admit that I didn't understand the punch line, and was terrified of being asked to explain it.

One of his choice expressions was, "*Afn ganef brent dos hitl.*" I never understood what it meant. My mother explained that, "On the head of a thief, burns his hat," implied that someone always feels guilty for something or a guilty person is always sensitive. This I understood.

As he came to sit by me on the couch, I felt my nerves intensify. I wished my mother and aunt would return. What would I say to him? What if he asked me about something religious, something in his prayers? What if he wanted me to explain the book on my lap, a collection of silly folktales.

Luckily, he lay against the back of the couch and sighed. "Esfele," he said, "I will rest my eyes a little, no?"

"Sure, Grandpa," I said, too quickly. To show my support, I also closed my eyes. I thought about how my parents used to fight about religion. My mother had tried to keep kosher, but abandoned it when my father mixed meat and dairy products and the appropriate plates and utensils. He could never remember what animal or animal parts were permitted and often complained that sticking to the "number of rules regarding the slaughtering and blessings of what we eat could make a man starve to death."

My grandparents had rarely come to our house for a formal meal because, to them, my father was practically a heathen, and they didn't trust my mother to follow the kosher rules. This had hurt my mother very much because she went to great pains to do everything to the letter.

There was one custom she had clung to. Every Friday, just before sunset, whatever my father did, my mother lit the *Shabbes* candles, closed her eyes, motioned her palms over the flame, wafting their fumes toward herself, and recited the prayers. Then the family would sit down to dinner, complete with *challah*s. That was as far as she would go; my father sat respectfully even though he was nonobservant in the extreme.

It's strange, after my father died, when my mother could have reinstituted her orthodox customs, she didn't. She left my father's chair empty and nodded toward it just as she always did to signal the beginning of the *Shabbes* meal. It was more like a reflex. By that time, I figured that my mother herself no longer believed in religious customs.

It was difficult for me to keep up with religious rules. When I went to a relative's house, I was never sure how I should act, what I should say. Perl said that family bickering over religion was common in this day and age. Many from the older generation clung to their ways while their children wanted to assimilate to the culture around them.

"What are you two dreaming about?" my grandmother Elke asked, carrying a tray with glasses of water and cheesecake.

"Nothing," I said, startled from my daydreaming.

My mother joined us and I smushed a piece of cake with my fork and licked off the silky sweet residue. Grandma Elke began to tell us about Grandpa Yankel's brother, Hymie, who lived in Visoke, the Visoke where Ida and her father traveled in the hailstorm. This great-uncle Hymie was very sick with something so terrible that nobody would mention what it was, but it was clear he was dying.

"Since your father found this out," she said to my mother, as if my grandfather was not in the room, "he's been paralyzed. He hasn't gone to his bookkeeping job. He prays. He stares out the window."

My grandfather suddenly jumped up as if he had been bitten by a snake, and said to my grandma, "That does it, Elkele, I'm going to Visoke, to see Hymie."

My grandma nodded, but Grandpa continued as if his wife was forbidding him to go. "After the death of my father, of blessed memory, Hymie took over the bakery even though he wanted to continue his studies. He was the first to teach me how to read the *Talmud*."

"Yes, you should go," my grandmother said. She didn't offer to go along as she had to help with her grandchildren while Khane worked in my uncle Sam's grocery.

With this pronouncement, I went beserk. My grandfather would be going to Visoke, so close to Ida! I had always treated my grandfather with the utmost respect; I rarely said much to him. But now, I was obsessed or I should say possessed.

"Can I go with you?" I asked timidly.

My grandfather didn't answer.

I then badgered my mother and my grandmother to let me go with Grandpa. To my surprise, my grandmother said, "Take the girl, Yankel. She could use a little fresh air."

"So why doesn't she go outdoors?" he said.

"This would be another place."

"I'll be lucky if I get there in time, God willing, without having to wait for a child."

"Esfir will not slow you down." My grandmother had a quiet way of getting what she wanted.

"And what if Esfir cries for her mother?"

"Now, Yankel, Esfir is an experienced traveler. She will be good company for you on the train. She will be able to look after your briefcase when you need to pray, and I'm sure she can be helpful in other ways, too. And Hymie will be very happy to see her."

He thought for a while and said, "*A make unter yenems orem iz nit shver tsu trogen*," which means, "Another person's problems are not difficult for *you* to endure." With that, he made up his mind. "Okay, Esfir can come on one condition."

I yelped.

"Why must there always be a price to pay?" my grandmother asked. Now that she saw him weakening, she got bolder. "*Yeder mentsh hot zayn eygene mishegas.*" In her peculiar way, by saying, "Every person has his own craziness," she was thanking him.

I can't repeat all the epigrams and retorts that ensued. It was a game my grandparents played, and I just sat and listened, reveling in my good luck. Whatever the condition my grandfather was going to impose got lost in their repartee.

My grandmother and my mother made it clear why I was so eager to go with him, explaining that Ida lived close by in Volchin.

"I know where that is," he said, gruffly. "There's no time to wait for her friend to contact us. I may not be able to take her to Volchin, and we don't even know if this Ida is going to be there."

With that, my grandmother answered with another Yiddish expression, which I can't exactly recall, but it is something like, "Things will work out as they are supposed to."

My mother and I went home so I could change my clothes and get ready. Not being a fatalist, my mother gave me money to pay a driver to take me to Volchin and back to Visoke, in case my grandfather wouldn't. She pinned a note to my blouse with Ida's full name, her father's name, and the name of my uncle in Visoke, as if I needed help. I could have spelled Ida's whole name backward if someone asked.

Then we returned to my grandparents. I went in the kitchen to get a bag of fruit my grandmother had prepared for our trip. When she thought I was out of earshot, my mother said, "Father, I have never asked you for anything. Now I am asking you to take care of Esfir. Try your best to take her to Volchin. It would be a *mitzvah*."

Grandpa Yankel didn't come back with a Yiddish saying. This was his way of conceding. But with him, you could never be sure.

I didn't care how I got anywhere. One way or another, I was going to Volchin!

# Twenty

MY GRANDFATHER AND I set out to visit my great-uncle Hymie in Visoke. I don't remember the train ride there or the droshky to his house.

Great-aunt Malka welcomed us. She was frail and small, shuffling around to bring us tea and orange preserves on toast.

Hymie was sitting up in bed and when he saw me, he said, *"A meydl mit a kleydl."* Then he recognized his brother, blurting, *"A pish on a forts iz vi a khasene on a klezmer!"* I knew this meant, "A pee without a fart is like a wedding without a band!" My grandfather laughed and answered, *"Az di bobe volt gehat beytsim volt zigeven mayn zeyde!"* meaning, "If my grandmother had testicles, she'd be my grandfather!"

I was totally flabbergasted. Why were these two brothers speaking to each other in such "dirty" epigrams? But no one seemed to be insulted. Malka clapped her hands and shouted, "So I see you two are at it again."

I almost got it when my grandparents exchanged Yiddishisms, but these were of a different nature. When I was alone with Malka in the kitchen, she explained that this was the brothers' way of hugging; and as long as it continued, she was happy.

Hymie's lips had a bluish tinge and his brown eyes sank into dark-gray semicircles. But he continued to joke and needle my grandfather, so I figured he wasn't as sick as he looked or as I had expected. When we left his bedroom, Hymie yelled that we should live and be well, which made my grandfather suddenly stop. Malka said that Hymie didn't really mean it, and my grandfather blew his nose in his handkerchief and rushed me out the door while Malka was still squashing me with her hugs. I was totally confused. When Hymie finally said something nice, my grandfather acted like he couldn't take it.

It took me a while to realize what was going on. They were saying good-bye.

Hymie's son arrived by wagon to take us to Volchin, about seven miles south of Visoke. I don't remember much of what we saw getting out of Visoke, except that it was a lovely town with lots of grass and trees. On the dirt road to Volchin, we passed houses, fields, cows, and many trees—birches, pines, cypresses. This landscape could just as well have been the outskirts of Kobrin. I had expected it to be more exotic; I had expected that we would enter the village through a commanding arch surrounded by remarkable monuments. Instead, we barely saw the signpost saying "Volchin."

HYMIE'S SON EXPLAINED that Volchin contained three distinct neighborhoods. From Visoke at the northern entrance, there was New Volchin, where most of the Catholics lived. The first site Hymie's son identified was a large field that had been a sand quarry. We could also see the Catholic church and the public school. There was a beautiful palace and a park.

I remember passing a stone bridge over the Pulva River (tributary to the Bug River) and then we were on the main street—a narrow road flanked by wood fences protecting wooden houses with corrugated roofs. It was very pretty and romantic, not like I imagined the poor *shtetls* described in the Sholem Aleichem stories that Perl read to me. This was where the Jews lived.

The southern area was Old Volchin, home of the Russian orthodox, but we didn't make it that far because we were hardly into the Jewish section when Hymie's son announced, "Here is the Midler house." He located it easily, he said, because Iser Midler was a notable village man, and "Everyone knew who he was and where he lived."

My grandfather and I got out of the wagon, and I was surprised that he instructed Hymie's son to go back to Visoke and not wait for us. Usually, my grandfather wouldn't make such a rash decision; he would ensure everything was satisfactory before he acted. We were uncertain what we would find here, whether Ida would even be home. And we only had two hours before we had to return to Visoke to take the train back to Kobrin. This brave risk on his part only made me more excited. Why would I care if we extended our stay in Volchin and had to miss our train to Visoke?

It was a well-kept, wooden house, large by the village standards, but not so compared to Kobrin's or Brest's. It had a low-slanted roof with attic triple windows. The house's side windows swung out vertically, exposing a patterned curtain with fringe lacing billowing in the breezy summer day.

Clearly, this house had the village's most spectacular landscaping. Rose and peony bushes flanked the front door. Plum-purple irises and burnt-orange lilies hugged the sides.

My grandfather squeezed my hand and knocked on the door. There was no noise coming from inside. We walked to the side window and he tapped on the glass. A woman's head popped out, her face scowling like she was going to yell at one of her kids. When she saw strangers, she changed her expression to puzzlement. From Ida's description, I knew this was her mother, Bashke.

"Forgive us for startling you, Mrs. Midler," my grandfather said, introducing himself and explaining that I was a young friend of Ida's who shared a room with her at Perl's in Brest.

Bashke, I mean Mrs. Midler, immediately raised her head; I thought she would bang it on the window frame. "Oh, oh," she said, "please go around to the front. Please come in."

While Mrs. Midler welcomed us inside, wiping her hands on her apron, she appeared nervous and shy. She paced around the hallway, saying "Oh my," several times until she invited us to sit in the large dining/living room, motioning to the couch and overstuffed chairs. She apologized for the unapparent disarray and said that she was the only one home, that she was expecting the girls soon. Sala, which I knew was Sara's nickname, and Ester were swimming at the lake. Ida was at some large building in the center of the village. Across from the Russian orthodox church, it had a stage for theatrical productions. Every week the youngsters attended dances there, too.

Why Mrs. Midler was reporting this, I couldn't understand. I wasn't going to a dance or the theater, and we had informed her that we were only staying a short while. Finally, she explained, "Ida is there rehearsing for *King Lear*," adding and nodding to my grandfather, "you know by Shakespeare." My grandfather nodded back and waved his hand as if to say, "go on."

"My Ida is going to be the treacherous older daughter, Goneril. I wish she would have gotten a nicer role."

It was clear to me that if anyone would relish playing a villainess, it would be Ida.

This building, Bashke said, was also where her husband met for the volunteer fire brigade. He was a captain, she couldn't wait to slip in.

"Oh, the fire brigade," my grandfather said. "When I lived in Brest, a long time ago, in 1895 and 1901, there were great fires. More than half of Brest burned down."

"I didn't know this," she said.

"Yes," my grandfather continued, "even worse, during the Great War, in 1915, there was the biggest fire—from one end of Brest to the other, caused by the retreating Russian tsarist army. Cossack soldiers attacked and killed many Jews. One morning German planes appeared. I remember it like yesterday. More homes were burned. The marketplace was in flames. The Germans destroyed whatever the Russians didn't."

Mrs. Midler tisked and tutted.

My throat was getting dry and I could swear I smelled something burning. I suddenly thought of Perl and realized that her longing for the past, the sound of her voice that I had thought distinct, was so much like her father's.

As if she had seen my thirst, Mrs. Midler excused herself and rushed into the kitchen. I had only been in Ida's house for fifteen minutes and I was exhausted from the talking between Bashke and my grandfather. But I got the feeling that Mrs. Midler usually didn't speak that much; she seemed both flustered and embarrassed.

During her time in the kitchen, I had a chance to take in my impressions of Bashke Midler. Though Ida had described her to me, I was still startled by her appearance. A short, stocky woman, she had thick arms and legs. Her umber hair was parted to the side with a curved section dipping over her forehead, an attempt at fashion probably encouraged by her daughters. She appeared like a hearty peasant woman, a no-nonsense practical worker, uncomfortable with social niceties. I could not envision her standing side-by-side with her handsome, debonair husband. And, I could not envision her disciplining her rebellious eldest daughter.

But I was wrong. This wouldn't be the first time that outward appearances deceived me. I sensed my wrongness as soon as she returned with an ornate silver tray, complete with a silver coffee server, sugar bowl, and creamer. She lowered the tray gently on the coffee table and skittered out of the room, and returned efficiently with another tray offering orange juice, a bowl of cherries, a sour cherry compote, and a cherry pie. "Sorry," she said. "You can see we have cherry trees."

My grandfather laughed, not an easy reaction to provoke. He took off his fedora, revealing his *yarmulke.*

Then Mrs. Midler said, "Reb Cohen, You should know I only use kosher ingredients."

"That is good," he said.

"And, Esfir, have some juice and pie."

I dutifully ate a chunk, which was delicious.

"I was thinking, Reb Cohen," Mrs. Midler said, "about what you said when you lived in Brest. If I am not being too bold, what happened to you and your family? "

"After the big fire of 1915," my grandfather explained, "they didn't allow people to return until the end of 1918. Before then, the Briskers wandered in exile. When some Jews came back, non-local Poles tore off beards from the orthodox and treated them like dirt. Most Jews returned eventually but life was very hard. It was during that time of exile that we moved to Kobrin."

"Kobrin, I hear is a beautiful city."

"True, but I had to abandon my fabric shop in Brest, a great loss to me. Esfir's Aunt Perl and her husband Natan returned to Brest but the rest of our family remained in Kobrin. That's where Esfir's parents met."

Like Perl, my grandfather got wound up in the past. But I was surprised that he was so personal with Mrs. Midler. He must have realized this and ended the discussion. "And you know the rest, Mrs. Midler. Soon we became a Soviet republic and everyone became Russian again until 1921 when we were all officially part of Poland. "

"Events have a way of taking over," she said. "Please Reb Cohen, drink your coffee. My husband should be home any minute."

Before long, they were in a discussion about Agudath Israel, the political movement my grandfather belonged to, which strived to preserve rabbinical authority and believed that the Jews should have a strong voice in their own communities. I remembered Ida's chart with this group as being anti-Zionist.

Mrs. Midler showed no disrespect. Addressing him with the honorific "Reb" had been a good beginning. She knew a lot about the orthodox political movement, and she did not offer judgmental remarks. Either she had come from an orthodox background or she educated herself.

The family came trickling in. First it was Ester, the youngest at ten, but a year and a half older than me. She was going into the fifth grade at the public school, she boasted almost immediately. With thick bangs, supported by a white bow, Ester had the dark, brooding looks of Ida and the compactness of her mother.

Sala walked in the living room, stopped in her tracks by the unexpected company. She was with another girl, her best friend, Hanna Kremer.

"This is Esfir, Ida's roommate in Brisk," Ester announced, enjoying her status as the relater of information.

"And her grandfather, Reb Cohen," Mrs. Midler added.

If Ida was the exotic daughter and Ester the mischievous one, Sala was surely the beauty. Maybe this was God's way of making her, the middle child, have something special. My sister, Rivke, as a middle child could have used some of Sala's looks. At twelve, Sala was well-proportioned and lean; her hair was in the same Buster Brown style as Ester's, though it was a finer texture and lighter color like her mother's. She had a little wedge of a nose and cherubic lips. She seemed delicate like my doll Miriam, but, again, looks were deceiving regarding all the Midlers as I was gathering.

Before I could find out why their hair was dry since they were supposed to have been swimming, Sala grabbed my hand and said, "Come, Esfir, I want to show you our new gramophone. We can listen to recordings."

I heard Mrs. Midler apologize to my grandfather, who said, "They should live and be well," just what Hymie had said to us. This embarrassed me in its ordinariness.

Before long, we were sitting on the carpet listening to Chopin. Sala and Hanna waltzed around the room, giggling and stepping on each other's feet. Ester sneered as if the last thing she wanted to do was dance with me. When the recording was finished, Sala put on klezmer music and we all joined hands and skipped in a circle, then broke away and clapped ecstatically.

This scene is what Ida walked into. Though she grinned when she saw me, she held up her copy of *King Lear* and lapsed into Goneril, "Sister, it is not little I have to say of what most nearly appertains to us both. I think our father will hence tonight."

We clapped again and in walked Mr. Midler, as if he had been waiting in the wings on stage. Ida flipped pages and turned to face her father. "Sir, I love you more than words can wield the matter: / Dearer than eyesight, space, and liberty; / Beyond what can be valued, rich or rare; / No less than life, with grace, health, beauty, honor; / As much as child e'er loved, or father found . . ."

Mrs. Midler said to my grandfather, "You must think our entire family is, how should I put it, psychologically unsound."

Not missing a beat, my grandfather said, as if reciting a poem, "*Ales in eynem is nishto ba keynem.*"

Mr. Midler bowed to my grandfather for his compassionate remark, and the clapping increased in intensity.

Never would I have thought my conservative grandfather, who may have been studying in the *bes-medresh* in Kobrin at this time, would have joined in such spontaneous fun as this. I was immensely proud.

My grandfather announced that we couldn't stay more than an hour so Ida had to pack everything in. She was revved up as if she *were* in *King Lear* and was required to replace another actress without knowing her lines. This is what I loved most about Ida. Her mind worked faster than a bee, buzzing through all interference, zeroing in on the nectar. If she experienced doubt or prolonged analysis, she didn't show it. I was the one with a hesitant nature.

"Oh, Esfir, I'm so happy you came," Ida said over and over, leaping around the room. "There is so much to do in so little time. First, I must show you my house."

The Midler home was centered around two main rooms—a bedroom and a living/dining room. There was an extension on the right, which had another apartment with a room and kitchen. If they were lucky, the Midlers rented out this space. Mainly, the girls slept in the large bedroom, which was separated with a curtain. On one side, there was a regular bed for Mr. and Mrs. Midler; and on the other, there were two small feather beds. Sometimes, they slept in the attic.

The kitchen was divided in two. Half was a shop for Mr. Midler, where he sold Singer Sewing machines, being the regional salesman, and sold and repaired bicycles. The other part of the kitchen had a door that led to the garden bursting with vegetables and flowers. This was the result of Mrs. Midler's efforts; she was very particular about anyone tampering there. Ida was careful about leading me around the flowers.

The backyard also had a toolshed and a chicken coop. The chickens had been innocently intermingling with geese and pigs. The property was framed by fruit trees, including cherry, apple, pear, and peach. Beyond them in the back, there was an orchard owned by a Polish policeman. Wildflowers sprouted wherever there was room. It was my picture of heaven.

Ida took me on a quick walking tour with Ester tagging along. We passed the Jewish school that had classes conducted primarily in Yiddish. American relatives of the Volchiners helped support the school.

Then there was a large brick building, the village synagogue. We didn't go inside, but Ida said that it was beautiful with paintings and biblical verses on the walls. She described the houses we passed, reciting the names of its residents and something special about each occupant like the trade of the father or the wedding plans of a daughter. In one such house, there lived a father and his two sons. The boys were members of the Betar; the eldest was Volchin's Betar commander. This is where the Betar members congregated.

"Remember the chart I made you of the social and political groups?" Ida asked. I guess I looked dumfounded because she said, "You know Betar is the youth organization of the Revisionist Zionists." I nodded. "Of course," she added, "almost everybody in Volchin is a Bundist. The Bund is non-Zionist. It all gets very confusing. I try to stay out of these discussions. You know me, I am of two minds." I nodded again in total bewilderment.

Yet I loved when Ida spoke to me like I was her age. It was only then that I realized that Ester was not with us. She must have met someone or gone back home. Ida pointed out the large building where she had just come from, studying for her role. I wished I could have seen her perform. She took me as far as the market square, where stores were arranged in a half circle. Behind the stores, there was a passage that eventually led to the river. I longed to follow that path, but we didn't have time. The town well was in the center of the market. Villagers were drawing water from a wooden pail attached to the end.

Too bad, Ida said, that we came on a Tuesday because Monday was Market Day, when shoppers and peddlers from all over came with their carts bulging with merchandise. Mrs. Midler usually set up a small table and sold fruit and vegetables, and sometimes flowers if she could part with them. This was also the area where the villagers held weddings. I felt like I was missing out on everything special.

I couldn't dwell on my losses too long. Our time was running out and we headed back to Ida's house. I was anxious that my grandfather would be angry with me for being away for so long. Secretly, I hoped that our lingering caused us to be too late to catch the train in Visoke and we'd have to sleep at the Midlers.

I needn't have worried. When we walked in the living room, my grandfather and Mr. and Mrs. Midler were wrapped up in their talking. I was happy that they seemed to be getting along so well. They were discussing the clashes between the Arabs and Jews in Palestine, England's reduction of the Jewish immigration quota to Palestine, and whether there should be a partition between the Arabs and Jews.

While I listened, all I could think about was Velvel stuck amidst all this turmoil. We hadn't heard from him yet and I knew my mother was very worried.

What surprised me was that my grandfather presented his interpretation of events as objectively as he could, holding back his religious convictions and anti-Zionist ideas. He didn't talk about the Messiah or the afterlife, or as he called it, "The world to come." My father used to call my grandfather, "an uneasy tenant of heaven," meaning that his actions were more centered on his ordinary life here on earth.

More refreshments and then we were off. Mr. Midler kindly offered to take us to Visoke in his wagon. There was no room for more people, but Ida hopped into the wagon well, insisting that she wanted to come along. Ester and Sala asked to join her, but Mr. Midler said it wasn't a good idea to put too much stress on the wooden slats, knowing they would have been dancing around. I could see the disappointment in the girls' eyes, considering that Mr. Midler often carried bicycles and other equipment that weighed more than his daughters.

I said good-bye to Sala and Ester. Mrs. Midler embraced me and I made a vow to myself, again. Recollecting my first impressions of Ida's mother, I promised I would wait until I knew more about people— hearing them speak, watching them act—before I passed judgment.

There's not much to report about our trip to Visoke or our leave-taking. I tried not to be emotional, especially when Ida said, flippantly, "So, Esfir, see you soon in Brest." I thanked Mr. Midler for driving us; my grandfather shook his hand. Mr. Midler invited him to visit anytime, and to bring my grandmother. Maybe it was a reflex, but my grandfather said, "She would like that, God willing."

I watched the wagon and could see Ida jump from the well onto the ground and step up to the passenger seat, snuggling close to her father. Let's face it. Ida was happy that I came, but nothing compared to her joy in sharing the seat with her father.

# Twenty-One

MY MOTHER DECIDED that I should stay in Kobrin until after the High Holy Days. Now that she was more of her old self, she was becoming increasingly involved in her children's lives. She planned to take me back to Brest and have a long talk with the headmaster of my school. If she was happy with his responses, I would return but she didn't mind if I missed the beginning classes. This meant I wouldn't go back to Brest until September 16 at the earliest. It would be a month and a half until I saw Ida.

Speaking of Ida, since I couldn't attend Market Day in Volchin, I was determined to attend the August fair in Kobrin, which was held in the enormous, mazelike marketplace on the tenth day of each month and was *the* place to go. I enlisted my friend Gittel in a scheme to fool our mothers into thinking we were going to the orphanage to help the children, which we planned to do but after we snuck in the fair.

Peasants from all over Poland jammed their carts and wagons every which way. They displayed merchandise in their wagons, on crates, on the ground, in their arms, draped over their shoulders. They had cloth, seeds, wheat, wooden and tin objects, animals of all sizes, from chickens to horses, food—anything that was grown from the soil or made by the hand. There were Hasidim selling materials, peasants untying kerchiefs bursting with coins, lottery ticket sellers, organ grinders, local shopkeepers, harmonica players. With less finesse, peddlers shouted, "What do you have to sell?" I smelled onions, pickles, and horse manure. It seemed like the whole world was wheeling and dealing.

Between maneuvering around a vast area of horses, freed of their harnesses and pressed in packs, and the shoving crowds, we were suffocating. Gittel began hyperventilating and trembling as if she were hot and cold at the same time. I was frightened, too, and felt like a midget, unable to move in a stampede of giants. Gripping Gittel's hand, we shoved ahead and found a break, winding our way to a grassy area with a large oak tree. I ordered Gittel to sit and wait for me—not to move an inch.

What got into me, I cannot say. I was no less petrified by screeching animals and the hawking of shouting competitors. I could no longer distinguish a seller from a buyer, a Kobriner from an outsider. I retraced my steps and lost myself in bodies, propelled by the sway of hair, the sweep of an arm, the knock of a knee. I was a body ruled by other bodies. Finally, the give and take equaled out and I was still. It seemed like all life before me froze into a painting, and I was the artist with life or death on my palette. I closed my eyes, trying to black out the scene.

A minute, not more, passed and I was again shoved, this time in the stomach. Now I was ready to return to Gittel. On my way to her, I raised my head and smiled, saying hello to anyone who could see my face and waving to others who may have wondered why a small arm was flailing.

I reached Gittel, still cowering where I had left her. I sat next to her and put my arm around her convulsing shoulders. "It's okay, Gittel," I said as if I were pacifying a baby. "We can leave now."

Gittel stood, clutching my hand, and we moved through the periphery of the fair, avoiding much of the activity. That I had put Gittel through such an agonizing experience, for what I couldn't say. But I had this vague sense that my going back to the fair alone, greeting people even if I didn't know them, would be something Ida would have done.

Every Jew in Kobrin baked at least one extra *challah* for the poor. I had carried one in a small basket and Gittel had one too, but it was snatched from her in the melee at the fair. Gittel worried about what she would say to her mother about the missing basket. I offered her my basket since our baskets were identical. I was counting on my mother not noticing that mine was missing since we had stacks of them. With this on our minds, we hurried to the orphanage so that our day wouldn't be a total lie.

My grandmother Ruth, my father's mother, was very charitable and encouraged compassion and activism in her children and grandchildren. During the Great War, Grandma, a married woman in her forties, had gone to the train station to help the wounded and the refugees who arrived. Ruth and other women formed a committee to help the poor. Going from house to house, they brought two notebooks, one with the names of people willing to help and the other for those needing help. It was fitting that their motto was, "Give or Take."

Next on the list for Ruth and the women was to help establish a Jewish orphanage, the first in the area. Jewish doctors ministered to the children for free, and Kobriners donated food and pitched in. Soon the orphanage grew to accommodate a hundred and twenty children. The women's committee also raised money for the children to receive an education.

Life was very hard after the war. People needed interest-free loans. For that purpose, a committee of women evolved called, The Reward of Good Deeds Society. Ruth was a member of this committee, too.

Grandpa Morris was not always happy that his wife devoted so much time outside her familial responsibilities. Having only sons, Ruth tried to enlist her daughters-in-law in her causes. They would join her on occasion, but they were preoccupied with other concerns.

"It's not the same," my mother had explained to me once, "for us as it was for your grandmother. Not to criticize her work, but when you begin something that is difficult, you have an enthusiasm that comes from an inner place. Later on, when others take on the cause, they hadn't been involved in the 'fight' so they do the good works but more as a duty than a mission."

I wanted to be more like Grandma Ruth. I wanted to be the one from *my* generation dedicated to the orphans. So I went to the orphanage almost every day that I was home and Gittel often accompanied me.

On this fair day, we slipped around the building to the backyard where children were singing and dancing. Two of my latest favorites, three-year-old brother and sister twins, ran up to me and wrapped their arms around my feet. I couldn't move and then we all fell in a heap, laughing and hugging. If I'd been an adult, I would have adopted them.

It turned out that Gittel and I didn't get in trouble. Nobody ever discovered that we went to the fair and no one noticed the missing basket. When I walked into the door of my house and looked at my mother, it was apparent that something major happened in my absence. My mother's cheeks had regained some color, her steps seemed to bounce.

"It came!" she screamed, waving a paper in her hand. "It came."

"What?" I asked, unsure if I should be happy or not.

"It's a postcard from your brother." Then she said, "From Velvel," as if I didn't know my own brother's name.

"Let me see," I said. My mother was reluctant to give me the card, but I promised to give it back as soon as I read it.

He didn't write much. It was one long sentence. I copied every word in my journal: "Dear family—after a very long and complicated journey, I arrived in Palestine, which is dry and hot but I am happy in my work and live for the day that you will join me—with love always, your Velvel."

For days, my mother kept the card tucked into her brassiere. She didn't think anything wrong about reaching into her cleavage to pull it out if anyone showed the slightest interest after she hinted about her son. At first we were embarrassed. But, truthfully, each one of us would have gladly taken that card and pressed it close to our breasts. Although I didn't have anything to hold it up, I would have found a way.

Velvel had been the glue that kept our family together, more, I'm sad to say, than my father. Velvel was the one home when my father was working or at a meeting. Velvel was the one who helped me with schoolwork. He was the one to lift me when I did something he liked. And Velvel was the one with jokes and good humor, which my family seemed to need more than anything else.

I missed him so much it hurt my heart, but I was happy he was safe, and happy for my mother who was a different person.


WHEN MY MOTHER and I got off the train in Brest, we headed for my school. My mother had a satisfactory conversation with the headmaster and then dropped me off at Perl's. She had to go back to Kobrin on the next train as there was a government inspector coming to my father's shop the next day.

At Perl's, there was a war going on in the house. Predictably, the instigator was Rachel, the victim was Fanny, the weaker twin, and the defender was Ida. I never found out the reason, but it didn't matter because positions were established and loyalties declared. Not that anyone was on Rachel's side, and maybe that's why she prolonged her attacks relentlessly. The air was charged with tension and it hit me hard after the quiet contemplation of Yom Kippur, just passed. I never forgot that Rachel had something going on with the rock-throwing boys in the park. She could do anything. Was this how it would be for the new year? Arguments and hurt feelings?

My biggest disappointment by far was the reception from Ida. After visiting her in Volchin, I thought I would have risen in her affections. On my first night back, she barely said "hello." Liba came into our room and whispered into Ida's ear. I gathered they were talking about Rachel because I heard her name, but leaving me out of the conversation hurt me more than if they had been discussing me. It was like I didn't exist.

Why had I come back here? I made a big mistake. I should have insisted on returning to the school in Kobrin. At least I'd have Gittel there, my own friend, my own age. We could have continued our visits to the orphanage. I didn't belong here.

Once in Kobrin when I wanted to listen to the grown-ups and not go to bed, Grandpa Yankel had said, *"Shtup zikh nit vu men darf nit."* He was right, of course. I shouldn't push myself where I didn't belong. I missed the old goat. Ever since our trip to Volchin, we had a new fondness. It wasn't obvious to anyone else in the family, but Grandpa took extra pains to sit near me or to give a little pinch on my cheek.

And here, I had nobody special. Perl was busy. She really didn't need me. I had no place to go and no one to talk to, except, of course, Miriam. This further convinced me that I was totally unlovable. My sadness was so deep and sure I couldn't say what it was. I only knew that I wanted to crawl under the bed with Miriam and never come out.

After a bad night of tossing and sleeping only a few hours, I awoke to a wet towel slapped in my face. "What?" I screamed.

"Wake up, you old rag." Ida was jumping around the room.

"What's wrong?" I asked.

"Nothing is wrong, except for me. I was not nice to you yesterday. I don't want you to think I wasn't happy to see you. I was just so angry at Rachel, it consumed all my thoughts. I'm very glad to see you, my little friend, and I'm so sorry if I hurt your feelings."

At first I couldn't respond. I didn't want to admit that I was upset. Besides, Ida apologized. It was amazing how the world could change for me so suddenly. I needed so little to feel so much.

I MET ANIA on the way to school, and we kissed and hugged as if we hadn't seen each other for years, which is the way I felt anyhow. We had exchanged a postcard each. They both had similar messages like, "How are you? Are you having a good summer? I miss you." It was the kind of writing that is polite but means nothing. I signed it "love always," and Ania signed hers with, "your friend."

I had taken Ania's lack of affection as a sign that she was tired of me, that she had found other playmates—Polish girls who went to her church. I imagined that her family prohibited our contact because of my religion and that she was happy to drop me. I never confessed this to Ania, but I have to admit that I exaggerated my adventure at the fair with Gittel to make Ania a little jealous—my first sin to atone for this new year.

To make up for closing me out, Ida spent a half hour the next night updating me about her relationship with Mendel Feigen. I couldn't believe she would tell *me*. She said I was the only one she confided in. She said, "Mendel and I wrote letters to each other over the summer."

"You did?"

"We did. And Esfir, now that I'm fifteen, I'm almost the age that my mother had been when she met my father."

"Have you seen Mendel alone?" I asked, not admitting I had seen them kissing and more. Where I found my courage, I couldn't say.

"Esfir, I shouldn't be admitting this to you. Promise you won't say anything to anyone."

I crossed my finger across my lips.

"I saw Mendel a few times after school hours, but only so we could discuss my homework assignment, an important paper." I raised my eyebrows and she continued, "You guessed it, we talked about everything but the paper. Don't ask me where, but we walked and walked every time until it got cold and dark."

I didn't remind her that Mendel was still her teacher. I began to realize why Ida confided in me. I was the only one in the house who wouldn't criticize her. She must have known that I would have danced on ice to garner her secret desires and that I would never risk her anger by revealing them. This was real trust.

Ida was beyond judgment in my mind. If the other girls didn't approve, they were either jealous or didn't understand.

MY EIGHTH BIRTHDAY came and for the first time I celebrated without my Kobrin family. Perl stuck a candle in a honey cake and led the song at the dinner table. The girls looked embarrassed because they didn't know it was my birthday. I was glad. I didn't want them to make a fuss and be reminded of how young I was. When it was time to go to sleep, though, there was a small package wrapped in tissue paper on my bed.

Ida was reading, but looked at me innocently and said, "What is it, Esfir?"

"I don't know." I turned the box back and forth and shook it but nothing rattled. Carefully, I opened the paper and there was a small white box. Inside on top of a cotton bed lay a ring made of tiny colored beads.

"I know it's not much," Ida said.

"I love it."

And wonder of wonders, it fit perfectly on my ring finger. I couldn't stop looking at it. It seemed to change colors when I held it closer to the light. This was my first ring and it had come from Ida. I couldn't have asked for anything more.

Before long, December was over. We were all back in Brest after the holidays. The year turned again for the rest of the world—1938. I was feeling less apologetic and more talkative to those older. I didn't know why, but being around Ida made me feel that this was going to be a wonderful year.

# Twenty-Two

I WAS WRONG about 1938. Things were going on in the world that I couldn't grasp.

Mendel ran a discussion group after school and got the girls worked up about current events. One blustery day in March, he walked Ida home and I heard him talking in the parlor.

"Yes, this is already a big catalyst," he said in his uppity voice, "for troubling times." He identified the event with the word, *Anschluss*, meaning "union" in German. With Hitler standing victoriously in an open car, German troops crossed the border and occupied Austria.

"The situation changes by the day," Mendel said. "Other countries, including Poland, are agitating for their lost lands. Know this, though, when countries are vying for power, and when their borders are subject to change, this can only mean catastrophe."

I didn't pay much attention to Mendel's words, though I made Ida write some of them down in my journal. I recalled when he had been calling for Jews to immigrate to Palestine, predicting calamity if we remained in our native lands. This time no one needed Mendel to report that the borders of our neighboring countries were as tenuous as the crust of an apple pie. Or that the chancellor of Germany's Third Reich, Adolf Hitler, represented a demon other leaders couldn't ignore.

When I heard him say that Jews were being targeted for their privilege and influence, I thought Mendel must be joking. The Jews in my world were in the trades or shopkeepers—tailors, bakers, butchers, painters, seamstresses, metal workers, shoemakers, photographers, carpenters, watchmakers. Most barely made a living and that lately was becoming harder. Even if we knew a Jew in the professions or government, that person was severely restricted or couldn't work at all. Who were these Jews in power?

I was the type of person who blamed myself first if something went wrong. In the case of Germany and Poland, in particular, they were the opposite. They blamed everyone else for their troubles, never themselves.

Before going to sleep, I expressed something like this to Ida, and she said I was going to be a philosopher. I liked the sound of that and asked what it was. She said it is someone who tries to make sense of senseless things.

"Now, this Hitler," Ida said, angrily, "doesn't care about making sense or how anyone is feeling. He wants to show the world that Germany is the best."

Ida was sounding familiar to me. It was her tone rather than her words. If I closed my eyes, and with a little imagination, it could have been Mendel himself speaking to me.

She continued, "The masses listen to Hitler who stirs them into a frenzy to the point of despising anyone who isn't a German. Hitler wants more land to add to his Third Reich. For people like him, there is never enough."

As Ida was talking, she had a newspaper in her hands. Unconsciously, she tore it into strips of varying lengths and twisted them into thin shredded cylinders, lining them in columns on her night table. When she finished with about eight, she started another column and so on. Before long, she had a good-sized selection of slender ammunition. Finally, Ida realized what she was doing and quickly slid the paper pieces together, gathered them in her hand, and headed for the trash basket. She let out a loud sigh.

"I appreciate what you explained," I said. "But maybe I am just too young to understand." Now *I* was the one to say this.

Then Ida got onto her bed and stood straight, holding out her arms. "There are more things in heaven and earth, Esfir, than are dreamt of in your philosophy."

I applauded and she said that was from *Hamlet* by Shakespeare, the author who wrote *King Lear*. There was no end to Ida's talents. If I was going to be a philosopher, Ida could surely be a lawyer the way she argued and spoke out, or she could be a writer or historian because she kept a journal like the one she made for me, or she could be a great actress like Sarah Bernhardt.

IT BECAME PERSONAL. More and more Jews that we knew were being excluded from civil service and manufacturing jobs. The Jews of Brest, who by the latest count, numbered twenty-five thousand had to rely on their small trade and commerce, including supplying goods and services to the outlying peasants and city-stationed armed forces. Some Jews had small backyard factories, producing soap, cosmetics, sweets, and such. Many, like Ida, depended on dollars sent by relatives from America.

For Jews, education was also becoming more problematic. Take Yossel, Freyde's brother. He wanted to be a doctor. He had a year and a half to finish the Tarbut, but he was afraid that if he continued there, he wouldn't be able to get into a university. Few Tarbuts were properly accredited, though the Brest one was an exception, but Yossel didn't think it would last. His best chance would be to transfer to a public high school despite Jewish quotas. The government school in the area only accepted two Jews in a class of forty. After three attempts, Yossel gave up. No amount of bribing would help.

Around the dining table one night he described that he had visited a cousin at a nearby university and was shocked. "The Jewish students had to sit in the left-hand section of the lecture room," he explained. "And who knows how much longer these 'ghetto benches' would last. Soon Jews will have no place to sit."

Freyde and the other girls had two and a half years left of school, so they followed Yossel's struggles carefully. Despite great sacrifice from their families, the girls had chosen the Tarbut because they had ambitions and their parents had encouraged them. Being female, they had even fewer chances of being accepted into a university. These doubts didn't stop them from discussing what they wanted to be if they graduated from the university. Fanny said, "teacher," Liba said, "something to do with fashion, maybe running a hat shop." Liba conjectured that Ida would probably become a lawyer or even a judge, predictions Ida didn't dispute. Rachel sat silently.

"So Rachel, what about you?" Liba asked.

"I don't know yet," she said, which seemed too honest for her. Immediately, she added, "Of course, my father wants me to run his business, and my aunt wants me to go into the theater like she did."

"I didn't know your aunt was an actress," Ida said.

"Well, she did some Yiddish theater. She played Lady Macbeth."

Ida gave me one of her looks as if to say, "Esfir, do *not* tell Rachel that I was in a Shakespearean play." And we all knew that Rachel's father drove a droshky and didn't communicate with his daughter.

Not one of the girls mentioned getting married or having children. Probably they were afraid to say that in front of Ida, who would have surely made them feel like common conformists. I never felt that about Ida. The way she looked after me was strong enough proof that any child would be the luckiest in the world to have Ida as her mother.


IDA'S JOURNAL, BOUND in red leather (mine was black) had been a present from her aunt Masha in America. Being her roommate, I had seen her write and draw pictures in it like I did, especially at night before she went to sleep. Once in a while she'd show me something—a sketch of a tree or a quotation that she was copying into my journal.

One day, Ida's journal was open on her bed and curiosity got the best of me. I couldn't resist. Just my luck, Ida walked in the room and I backed away, mumbling that I was sorry. I was expecting the worst. If someone read my journal behind my back, I would never forgive them.

But Ida was, well, Ida. She said that it was okay; I could look all I wanted. There was nothing there that was so secretive that I couldn't see. Her aunt had sent her two journals. She had finished the first one and lent it to me.

Me read Ida's journal? It seemed wrong somehow—scary and wonderful. Scary that I might discover something I didn't want to know about Ida and wonderful that she would share such a treasure with me.

I shouldn't have been so flattered. She admitted that she had never asked me before because she didn't think her writings or drawings were special and couldn't imagine anyone being interested. I should have known that Ida's reasons would have nothing to do with overcoming shyness but more to do with modesty.

I turned the pages and skimmed each, looking for my name and anyone I recognized. I was amazed at how much disjointed material she could fit on each page: indecipherable pencil scribblings and smudges; fine-lined, cross-hatched ink sketches; phrases in Yiddish and Hebrew; snatches of Russian and Polish poetry; increasingly worrisome world events; amusing anecdotes attributed to Ida's family members.

On a page written that winter during a weekend visit to Volchin, Ida had described one day's activities: "Stop by butcher and baker, pick up items ordered by Bashke . . . sit on tree stump while Sala happily ice-skates with her friends." In a few bold strokes, she captured Sala's graceful form as she pirouetted solo like a ballerina and glided with friends in a hora-like circle dance. "Sala so popular," she wrote. "Less guilt for leaving her."

The adjoining page showed Sala's arms entwined with another girl, taller and heftier. The girls seemed to be gossiping, with their faces almost touching. Ida wrote on the bottom, "My sister and her best friend, Hanna. Will I ever be that close to another girl?"

When I read that sentence, I put my palm over the page as if to push the journal away, also to quiet the raging thump in my heart as its beat tripled with jealousy. How could I ever expect Ida to feel that way about me—me being even younger than her youngest sister? Now that I was nine, and had been living with Ida for more than two years, I was still not up to snuff.

Toward the end of her journal, there were only a few pen marks and random words, and a blank half page, ending with "Goodbye Journal Number I," as if she had been losing interest in writing her thoughts. That's how it was when you got something new. You'd feel so dedicated to the object and think this would always be the case.

There was a torn page folded in the back. It had horizontal blue lines; this was not a page from Ida's journal. When Ida looked over at me and saw the note, she snatched the journal away.

"Sorry, Esfir, I just remembered I have something there that is personal."

"Oh, that's okay," I said, not revealing that I had read part of it: "I can't wait to tell you this in person, to hold your beautiful slender hand in mine." And I saw enough to read the last line, "Tenderly, Mendel."

I think I turned redder than her journal cover, as if I walked into the outhouse and discovered my aunt Perl squatting down over the hole.

Ida slammed the journal shut, put it in her suitcase, and slid it under her bed. She had an identical red journal in her hand, the second one. She opened it near the beginning. She looked me up and down and I saw she was writing something.

"What are you writing about, can I ask?"

"You, Esfir, I'm writing about you. And I'm sketching your face."

I wiped the spit between my lips and smoothed my hair.

"Don't be self-conscious. I want you to look natural. This way I can remember you just the way you are."

Okay I would probably never be Ida's longed-for best friend like her sister Sala had. But her wanting a picture and description of me, in the beginning of her new journal, was enough.

# Twenty-Three

AS THE MONTHS came, my mind was like a stopwatch, frozen on certain events reported in the newspapers. I began to keep a timeline in my own journal. There was so much that occurred; Ida helped me choose what she thought had the most significance for Jews.

In April, anti-Jewish riots broke out in Dabrowa, Cracow, Budapest, and Vilna. In July, the Third Reich ordered special identity cards for Jewish Germans. In September, Mussolini canceled the civil rights of Italian Jews; Jewish lawyers were forbidden to practice in Germany. In October, the Germans demanded that Jewish passports be stamped with the letter *J.*

That same month, about seventeen thousand Polish Jews from towns across Germany, many of whom had resided in Germany for decades, were taken—in various ways—for deportation to be handed over to Poland, where they were already citizens. Some were allowed to enter Poland; most were interned at various border points and sent to military barracks, where they lived in appalling conditions.

I particularly remember Mendel's reaction to this news. One night, he was in the living room with Ida. Perl told Ida several times to get ready for dinner. Mendel remained on the couch, not seeming to get the hint. Perl gave up and invited him to join us. Ida grasped her neck as if stricken with a lethal pain. Then she grinned and I thought she was going to embrace Perl in front of everyone.

Perl didn't like to discuss world events when Mr. Kozak was around. She never knew if someone would say a bad word about the Poles. Of course, Mendel didn't know the house rules and even if he did, I don't think he could have controlled himself. He was like Ida in that way.

"Now, there is no getting away from it," Mendel said.

There was silence. All eyes were on Perl. All ears were expecting her to ask Mendel not to talk about politics. Instead, she said, "Getting away from what, Mendel?"

"Those assimilated German Jews who had thought they'd be immune to persecution, and distanced themselves from Eastern European Jewry, now have to face reality."

"How true," Ida said, her eyes twinkling.

Here was another rare time, I was disappointed in Ida. The way she fawned over Mendel was beginning to make me sick. Okay he was a serious person, and I could admit he was a good talker, with good ideas. But he didn't have to sound so "Mendel-like" with a bunch of girls at the dinner table.

Mr. Kozak said, "Yes, I see your point, Mr. Feigen. We all have to be on our toes."

This deportation was the prelude to the worst event of 1938, beginning on the night of November 9 and continuing the next day—a Thursday when I was in my fourth grade class, a week after my ninth birthday. It was called *Kristallnacht* or Crystal Night.

We read in the Yiddish newspaper that in retaliation for the assassination of a German embassy official in Paris by a young Jewish refugee, the Nazis instigated crazed rioters and gangs to smash shop windows of Jewish businesses in cities, towns, and villages throughout Germany and German-controlled lands. Stores were looted, thousands of synagogues were damaged or leveled, Jewish homes were burned, Jews were assaulted, ninety-one Jews were killed, and some thirty thousand prominent Jews were arrested and deported. It was the pogrom of pogroms.

TWO DAYS BEFORE I left for the holiday in Kobrin, I found a parcel on my bed. It was wrapped in brown paper and tied with a string. I reached in my glass that held colored pencils and pens and found a scissor. Quickly, I cut the string and opened the paper to discover a brand-new black leather journal, like the one I already had. There was a note on top: "Dear Esfir. I know you're at the end of your journal, and you have been writing in tiny letters on the margins. It's time for a new one. Happy Chanukah, Love, Ida."

Like the first one, it was entitled, *Journal of Important Words* on the first page, only she added, "*II*" after it. And like the first one, it began with a quotation. I expected it to be by Peretz, and it was: "But memory can refine everything and improve it."

There were no limits to Ida's thoughtfulness, not that I want to paint her as a saint, but it's natural to remember good about a person, or the very bad. All I had for Ida was a white scarf with long fringes that my mother had knitted. It didn't compare to a journal but I never claimed to be as thoughtful as Ida. My mother had made identical scarves for the other girls, but I requested a different color stripe on each. I gave the one with a red stripe to Ida. Red was her favorite color.

The next day, I was packing my suitcase in my room when I heard a commotion downstairs and I went to investigate. In the parlor, I saw the Midlers hanging their coats on the coatrack. They had come for a short visit and to take Ida home. Perl greeted them as if they were relatives.

Mr. Midler said, "Hello, Esfir, you're looking so grown-up. I haven't seen you in how long?"

Ester said, "It was a year and a half ago, last summer, July 1937, that is."

"Why, Ester, you have a good memory," Perl said.

"Only for certain things," Sala said, sarcastically.

"What do you mean by that?" Ester asked.

"Girls do you have to argue the first thing when we get into the house?" Mrs. Midler said.

"Yes, at least wait until we sit down to tea." Mr. Midler winked.

I loved his sense of humor.

The Midler girls came up to our room for a little private time away from the adults and vice versa for the adults.

"Esfir, why don't you show Miriam to Ester?" Ida asked.

A wash of heat zoomed up my neck. It was okay for me and Ania to dress up Miriam, and we were quiet about it because we didn't want anyone to think we were still babies. But there was no doubt that Ester, who was nearly eleven, was far too old to play with dolls. At that moment, I could have killed Ida.

"Who is Miriam?" Ester asked.

"Nobody," I said.

"Esfir is shy about showing off," Ida said.

I was not accustomed to being angry at Ida. Now, she was not only embarrassing me, but insulting. Couldn't she tell that I didn't want to pursue the subject by my reddening skin? Couldn't she sense that by saying "nobody," I wanted to avoid the subject?

Ida in her own way was trying to find something for Ester and me to have in common other than a similar first name. Further prodding from Ester and Sala gave me no choice. It was bad enough I had to unveil Miriam, but I had to reveal that I hid her under my bed, two secrets Ida gave away in one request.

"Here she is," I said, standing Miriam up on my bed. "Now you've seen her, I'll put her back."

"No, don't put her back," Sala said. "I think she is beautiful. Like a movie star. And that dress, it's shiny." Sala rubbed the material between her finger and thumb as if she were a fabric buyer evaluating the quality.

"She's okay," Ester said, walking to the window, peering toward the scene outside with fake interest.

Being from a family with three girls, I was certainly familiar with what we said and didn't say, what we felt and what we pretended to feel, how we competed and how we acted as a unit.

As if it wasn't uncomfortable enough with all these girls, Ania suddenly appeared by my opened door. She stopped in place and said to me, "Sorry, Esfir, I didn't know you had company. Your aunt Perl told me I could come up."

I introduced everyone. The Midler girls sat on Ida's bed and Ania and I on mine, with Miriam in between. Ania had mentioned that she just came from church where she was helping her uncle, Father Janusz, take food packages to a convent that cared for poor families. Ania wore a small gold cross around her neck that she had just received from the Mother Superior and she was sliding it back and forth on its chain.

Suddenly, Ania sat up straight. She must have noticed that Ester also wore a necklace, only hers featured a silver Star of David. It was as if she just realized that she was the only non-Jew in the room. Usually, at Perl's Ania met a mix of people: Poles like Mr. Kozack and Sonia, the woman who helped clean the house; Belorussians like Maria, who played with Freyde in the young people's orchestra, and a girl who was Fanny's coworker at her after-school job setting up stalls at the market. And then the Jewish boarders.

The younger Midler girls had Christian classmates and regularly associated with non-Jewish villagers. Lately, though, their father expressed wariness. Ida had told me that Iser warned them to stay away from the

churches on Sunday because the Russian orthodox and Catholics from
the outskirts came to the village to worship. The Catholics often got
drunk and started fights. When they would meet Jews, they'd give them
a hard time, often provoking fights. Mrs. Midler, on the other hand, had
stuck up for her Christian neighbors and countryside peasants. She had
only the best relations with them.

Ida was uncharacteristically quiet. She normally tried to make everyone
feel at ease. Later, when we were alone in our room, she confessed to me
that she had been preoccupied by something her parents had said at
lunch, how there were more and more restrictions on when her father
could conduct his business and with whom. Volchiners were losing their
incomes and couldn't afford to fix a broken bicycle even if they needed it
to travel for a job. It was similar for sewing machines, another necessary
luxury or, more correct, another luxurious necessity. Mr. Midler was
generous and often fixed broken parts for nothing, but he couldn't afford
to donate a new one.

When Ida had asked him about going to America, her father said
he was having trouble getting visas for the whole family, but he would
think of something. Ida's mother had said that he was always worrying
about the future, that she was sure things would get better. Then the real
reason for Mrs. Midler's reluctance came out: She could never leave her
parents who lived in a village called Bocki. They had a small farm that
they loved; they had worked hard for their land and wouldn't give it up
without a fight. And they were getting old and frail and couldn't make
the long, hard trip to America.

Ida couldn't contain herself and had blurted, "If we have to stay here,
I can give up school. Now that Sala is fourteen, she should be going to
the Tarbut, too. It's not fair."

Mr. Midler said, "Idaleh, you're right. It *isn't* fair. But it took a lot
of trouble and money from our relatives in America to get you into the
Tarbut. You will be finished in a year and a half. We have to help one
child at a time and you Ida are the oldest."

Ida had pleaded with unrealistic scenarios: that she could drop out
of school for a year while Sala went to a secondary school, maybe the
Yiddish school in Visoke, like Sala's friend Hanna did. She had never
said anything to them about her worst fear: that maybe they wouldn't
be going to America.

"This is what we have decided as a family, Ida." Mr. Midler's tone had been firm; Ida had known this was the end of the subject.

"What are you thinking, Ida?" Sala asked. Apparently I wasn't the only one who had noticed Ida's silence.

"Oh, nothing much. You know me, my mind is always somewhere else. But listen, while we are lucky to have all of you girls here, let's do something special."

"Like what?" I said excitedly, grateful to Ida for breaking the spell of silence.

"We'll play Geography," she said, making it up as she went along. "I will take out my map of the world, unfold it, and lay it on the floor. The selected person will stand in the center of the map, blindfolded with a scarf, and turn round and round until one person says, 'Stop.' Wherever she lands will be her unknown place. The others will yell out the name. Then the blindfolded girl has to spell the name, say where it is, and what she knows about it. Everyone will have a turn."

"That sounds like fun," I said.

"But it isn't fair," Sala said. "You and I will know more than the younger ones." It's strange that in a short time, both older Midler girls had been declaring that something "wasn't fair."

I couldn't decide if Sala was truly thinking of us or if she wanted to spoil her sister's plan. By virtue of her age, Ida always got to be the leader.

"Okay, Sala, you're right. The younger girls will get an extra two points, for free."

"Well, I still don't think it's fair," Sala said, without much conviction. She had little ammunition to fight her big sister, especially when she saw the younger girls eager to begin.

We played Geography for an hour. When it was my turn, I got Chile and Japan. I was able to spell both countries and knew that Chile was in South America and that the Japanese were Oriental and some of the women wore long and colorful dresses. I got five points and two free ones. Ester also got seven. Ania got eight. Sala and Ida tied at ten. It was so much fun that Ania and I vowed to play it often.

After the Midlers left, I felt better about the girls as if spanning the globe together brought us closer. In the end, we were all girls worrying about our families and our places in a new and frightening world.

# PART II
## German and Russian Occupations
## 1939–1941

# Merciful God

Merciful God,
Choose another people,
Elect another.
We are tired of death and dying,
We have no more prayers.
Choose another people,
Elect another.
We have no more blood
To be a sacrifice.
Our house has become a desert.
The earth is insufficient for our graves,
No more laments for us,
No more dirges
In the old, holy books.

Merciful God,
Sanctify another country,
Another mountain.
We have strewn all the fields and every stone
With ash, with holy ash.
With the aged,
With the youthful,
And with babies, we have paid
For every letter of your Ten Commandments.

Merciful God,
Rise your fiery brow,
And see the peoples of the world—
Give them the prophecies and the Days of Awe.
Your word is babbled in every language—
Teach them the deeds,
The ways of temptation.

Merciful God,
Give us simple garments
Of shepherds with their sheep,
Blacksmiths at their hammers,
Laundry-washers, skin-flayers,
And even the more base.
And do us one more favor:
Merciful God,
Deprive us of the Divine Presence of genius.

—Kadya Molodowsky

# Twenty-Four

ON THE LAST night in August, on a Thursday, I went to bed but couldn't sleep. I was always sad when the summer was ending. Lately, though, I was almost looking forward to it because it meant returning to Brest and seeing Ida, Aunt Perl, Ania, and the boarding girls. I loved my sisters, and my mother could do no wrong—most of the time—and I so enjoyed my adventures with Gittel (except for the fair). As the summer faded, Gittel and my sisters would be off to their schools, and my mother would be canning fruit for the winter and trying to rejuvenate my father's business. There was no role for me in Kobrin then. My place was in Brest; my bed was near Ida's in Aunt Perl's house.

I must have fallen asleep because I awoke very early the next morning to the most horrendous, ear-splitting noise. I thought I was having a nightmare. When it got louder and my eyes opened, I assumed there was a lightning storm. September, I said to myself, was coming in strong.

If I had been having a nightmare, then that dream was also happening to my mother and sisters. Everyone was screaming at once, bumping into each other near the bottom of the staircase.

"What was that?" Rivke asked, already crying. It didn't take much to open the faucet on her waterworks. She may have been almost twelve, two years older than me, but in many ways she was the baby.

"Oh my God," I said, realizing this was something outside my head.

Curiously, my mother didn't say a word. We raced toward the parlor, intending to look out the windows facing the street. The noises were increasing in intensity, if that were possible; we could feel the house shaking.

Finally, my mother spoke. "Get away. Get away from the windows. Quick. Drora, bring me the black material in the pile near the sewing machine and some pins. We need to block out the light. Then I want all of you to get dressed immediately. Take anything you have that is valuable and pack it in your schoolbag. And hurry. There is no time to waste."

"Why, Mama, what is it?" I asked.

"Hurry, I said. Don't ask questions, just get moving."

I was too scared to disobey and rushed upstairs to follow her orders. We were all downstairs within fifteen minutes, as punctual and efficient as a troop of petrified recruits.

The noises were deafening and felt like they were piercing my eardrums. The upstairs flashed light from uncovered windows. It was as if the house was ablaze but there was no fire.

None of us could resist, no matter my mother's warnings; we lined up by the sides of the blacked-out windows and peeked outside. Then we looked upward. Airplanes were flying so low we could almost see the pilot. We were being bombed.

There were new noises—whizzing, swooshing, roaring—getting louder, coming straight toward us. Away from the window, we crouched with our arms grasping each other's shoulders. This was it. I couldn't imagine the force of the bomb. It was unbelievable. Who would be doing this? We were all going to die. Let it come quickly, quickly, quickly.

The blast was enormous. It thrust us apart; shards of glass rained from the chandelier. The framed photograph of my grandparents that had been hanging on the wall fell and missed my head by an inch. From a cabinet, books tumbled to the wood floor like flapping miniature planes. Shutters banged open and windows rattled. I waited for our house to explode, our bodies to whirl in the air as if in a tornado.

There was a lull. We were still alive. My mother inched to the window, insisting that we remain close to the floor.

"Oh my God," she said, not even screaming, more in disbelief.

"What?" we gasped in unison.

"The Blooms."

"What about them?" Drora asked of our next-door neighbors.

"Their house. Their house and the house next to them, they're in ruins, leveled."

We heard people screaming and crying. My mother, still ordering us to stay put, opened the front door to take a better look at the damage and to see if she could help someone. There, in rags, his hair grayed with ash, little five-year-old Baruch Bloom was wandering in a daze, circling and crying for his mother. My mother zipped outside and took him by the hand. I followed close behind. We searched the rubble and, when my mother unearthed an arm with missing fingers poking out of a collapsed mess of wood and furniture parts, she yanked Baruch away and brought him into our house. Rivke and I took him to the kitchen and tried to clean him up and give him water. Then I went to the attic and found a shirt and pair of shorts from Velvel's bureau drawers and we gently dressed Baruch. All he did was shake and yell, "Mama, Mama."

I didn't know what to do, what to say. Clearly he would die without his mother so I said over and over that she would be here soon. But I couldn't stop the terror mounting up my throat.

By now the boy was sobbing and couldn't catch his breath. Rivke, to my surprise, put her arms around him and crooned, "Baruch, Baruch. Everything is going to be fine." Why people always said that when it wasn't true, I didn't know. But I adored Rivke for her compassion.

It was truly a miracle because maybe a half hour later my mother, who had gone out again, walked in the door with Mrs. Bloom, barely recognizable, caked in mud and dust, her clothes stuck to her in jagged slivers. Baruch ran to her, crying, "Mama, Mama."

We watched them with profound relief. Then my mother pointed toward their house and shook her head. I knew then that Mr. Bloom, their eight-year-old son, Leib, and their newborn girl, still unnamed, were dead.

Mrs. Bloom and her son left to find Mrs. Bloom's parents. My mother again instructed us to stay in the house, no matter what. She would return as fast as possible. Community adults would be gathering around the marketplace.

As soon as she left, Rivke began to sob, shaking uncontrollably. I wanted to cry too, but Rivke was so agitated that I put my arms around her ample torso and drew her close. She was stiff and unyielding. Drora was also in a daze. Realizing that at fourteen and a half and now the oldest, she had to act, she commanded Rivke to make tea and cut up the *challah* in the bread bin. When Rivke didn't move, Drora raised her voice, but gently, "Now, Rivela, Esfir also needs to eat something. You're older and it's your job to take care of her."

Mechanically, Rivke rose, took my hand, and led me to the kitchen where we sliced the *challah* and heated water for tea. After our tea and bread, which tasted like shredded hay, we brought a slice to Drora who munched absentmindedly. Drora hadn't moved from the window, unpinning the black material partly so she could position her body sideways and still have a view.

There was a creaking noise as if someone was opening our gate, and a rustling of leaves as if that person had brushed past the branches of our linden tree on the way to the front door. My heart stopped and Drora put her finger to her lips to indicate quiet, which she didn't need to do. Rivke and I were too terrified to utter a word. The front door opened and it took us a moment to recognize my mother, and we pounced on her like she was the Messiah. She kissed each of us on the forehead. She had muddy streaks on her cheeks in the shape of lightning.

"Girls, everything is alright," she said unconvincingly. "The marketplace was crowded and the town leaders said that we were hit by our planes by mistake."

We then relied on word, which came from someone who knew someone who knew someone—and we were glued to the radio, which had a lot of static and some music, I think Polish polkas. At some point, we took naps.

Late in the afternoon, we returned to sit by the radio. Drora pushed back the metal bridge of her eyeglasses. She had been wearing them more often. I wondered if she was having problems with her eyes. It wasn't the time to ask.

"It's because of that pact," she said.

"What pact?" Rivke asked.

"The Molotov-Ribbentrop Pact, between Germany and the Union of Soviet Socialist Republics. It is a nonaggression treaty."

"Well, pardon me," Rivke said, "you sound like you've memorized the names for an exam."

"Just because I know something you don't doesn't make me a snob."

"Girls, please!" my mother begged.

"So what is it anyway?" Rivke asked, holding back the sarcasm.

"It's an agreement named after the foreign ministers of each country that says both countries won't go to war with each other. They also pledged they would take no sides if another country attacked one of them."

"So what's wrong with that?" I asked, always the peacemaker like Fanny was in her family.

"Well, there are rumors of something more."

"Like what, Miss Brilliant Brain?" Rivke asked with annoyance.

"Rivke!" my mother said.

"I just heard from some people I know that Germany and the Soviets also secretly agreed to divide certain countries, particularly Poland. Eastern Poland, including us, would go to the Soviets."

"I haven't read about this in the newspapers," my mother said.

"That's because it's a secret."

"Then how do *you* know?" My mother had worried about Drora's constant night meetings and this new circle of friends whom she never invited home.

"I told you it's just a suspicion," Drora said. "I don't think anyone here really knows what went on behind the scenes."

"And how would Hitler accomplish this?"

"By having these issues agreed to in advance, Hitler could now have what he wanted without interference—to invade Poland."

Bombing. Mistakes, Secret deals. Invasions. Drora was mysterious *and* forthcoming. Did she really know something or was she just repeating what the big shot leftists were saying? Suddenly I wished Mendel was here to explain it to me.

"I can't believe that Poland would be divided again like a pie," my mother said.

"Well, it's unbelievable that the Soviets would make such a deal with the Nazis. I mean, how could they?" Drora said.

"Yes, your precious Soviets," Rivke said. She often made fun of her sister's love of anything Russian, including communism.

Perl had once explained to me, in one of her lessons, that in March 1917, there were demonstrations in St. Petersburg causing the end of the tsar's rule. There was a lot of confusion and a rise in the Bolshevik Party, led by a man named Lenin. He believed in rule by the working class, and state ownership of property. These beliefs also spread to our people, which is why so many Jews were Socialists. Now I suspected my own sister had become the kind of person who almost got me kicked out of school, a Communist.

"You don't know anything, Rivke," Drora said. "If you must know, Hitler has been making all kinds of deals to get more territory. This is just another attempt. And the Russians have been trying to negotiate a treaty for peace."

"Sure, sure."

"My friends and I aren't the only ones looking toward Russia. The Belorussians also identify with them."

"Maybe that's why the Poles are angry," Rivke said.

"They could benefit from Russia also."

"Stalin is as bad as Hitler," my mother said.

"We don't know that yet," Drora said, defending the Soviet leader.

"I still don't get it," I said. "Mama said the bombing was a mistake, so your rumors were wrong."

IT WAS *SHABBES* morning. On the radio, the patriotic music suddenly stopped. President Moscicki addressed the nation, announcing that Germany had attacked Poland. "We will fight for every Polish threshold and for every roadside crossing," he said.

The bombing wasn't a mistake after all. Germany had declared war on Poland.

This made no sense, especially since Drora said we were supposed to go to the Soviets. But Drora said that this just confirmed the suspicions. Hitler would agree to anything to get our land. She also suspected that the Russians were duped; they were innocent pawns in Hitler's devious dealings.

Rivke made a squeaky noise and mumbled to no one in particular, "Some people will believe whatever they want."

For those who had been hurt or lost homes, there was no time for such discussions. Medical and relief agencies took immediate action. For those like us, who saw destruction but remained safe, we had the luxury of worrying about the future.

Again, my mother left the house and this time spoke directly to Drora. "I know you are itching to see your friends, or should I say comrades, and find out what is going on. But as my daughter, I'm asking you to squelch your desires to get into the action for a little while. Please, stay here with your sisters. I have to see what is going on for myself. I can't afford to rely on rumors."

I had never seen my mother so focused, so tough. And Drora saw it, too. She nodded and gave my mother a tight hug, whispering, "Don't worry about us."

My mother returned in the early afternoon. She reported that at noon, flyers began to appear around the streets, plastered on kiosks, walls, doors . . . slipped under doors, asking for men to enlist in the army. She saw groups of refugees from the west, as far as Warsaw, passing through town. There were Jews, gentiles, civil servants, all escaping the Germans. They clutched bundles or sacks—whatever they could carry at the last moment. Many had been killed on the road.

The night was quiet. No one slept. On the radio, the announcer said that the Polish army was pushing the Germans back. He said, "Yes, we will win this war."

# Twenty-Five

WE LIVED IN a state of fear. It has a taste and feel of its own—metallic and parched mouth, stinging eyes, erect hair on your arms, fist in your throat. The startled response, the adrenaline flooding through the veins in your breasts, when every ounce of your body is on tiptoe and every instinct is to flatten yourself to invisibility.

From the first day of invasion, September 1, the Germans had struck Polish airfields. They bombed bridges, disrupted railroads and other lines of communication, and confiscated private vehicles.

Cut off from the rest of the world, we were like rats in a cage, totally dependent on someone else to dictate our fate. I think it was this helplessness, this not knowing that was driving me crazy. Drora was pacing continuously, no longer careful about looking out the window, even rushing to neighbors when my mother wasn't home. Rivke, when she wasn't crying, said little and resorted to her childhood habit of sucking her thumb.

Two days later, Britain and France declared war on Germany, thereby supporting Poland. They were joined by other countries, including New Zealand, Australia, and Canada. The Polish army concentrated its efforts on the frontiers, and devised delaying tactics waiting for their allies to mobilize.

Our spirits rose. Surely with all these allegiances, the Polish troops would have the backing necessary to defeat Germany. When this looked unlikely, official Polish Jewish leadership fled for the Soviet Union or abroad. There was no government. Jewish men volunteered to patrol the town square, but anything could happen with the Germans.

Drora said friends in her youth movement had seen this coming. "The Nazis planned their attack to be overwhelming and quick so that our allies wouldn't have time to mobilize."

She explained that earlier in the year, Hitler had ranted again about international financial Jewry being responsible for instigating another war. This was his pattern: spread hate and inflame the people, providing the rationale for his upcoming moves. So we were not only helpless, but condemned.

In the meantime, we had to do something. Otherwise, we were sitting ducks. Everyone had a directive. We should fill our trunks with our best clothes, linens, silverware, and jewelry; take a horse and wagon and find somewhere to bury our valuables. We should build bomb shelters. We should guard against theft.

It was difficult to have any kind of life. During those early days of German occupation, my best memory is a visit from Gittel. Although the Blooms's house was destroyed, Gittel, who lived on our other side, was lucky like us. It's strange how the bombs struck; it didn't seem like a planned attack. It was the definition of hit-or-miss. On my street, out of six houses, three were totally destroyed and one was badly damaged. I once read about a tornado in America that took an inexplicable path, demolishing trees and leveling homes. Something as insignificant as a toolshed was saved while a beautiful mansion was destroyed. You couldn't explain it.

Gittel and I didn't do much. Mostly, we spoke quietly, almost in whispers, about the people we knew who had suffered tragedies, some of them rumors and some of them confirmed. We also worried about whether we would go back to school. Maybe it was easier to focus on who was going to sit next to you in class than which student had lost his family.

I had enough experience with Gittel to expect her to be frightened to the point of total immobility, but she surprised me with a plan of action that was more detailed than Drora's. "If something worse happens, Esfir," she said, "and if God forbid I can't go home for whatever reason, I am going to my aunt's house in Gorodets. I know the way. I can walk the thirteen miles there. I already have my bag packed, with the essentials." You never know how someone will react in an emergency.

As the days went by, we grew more desperate with worry. We were hungry too, as we couldn't go out to buy food and had to rely on our garden and whatever my mother had stored in the cellar. She meted out portions, not knowing how long they'd have to last.

No longer accessible to "real" news from the radio or newspaper, we had to depend on word spread from those who had access to underground radios, the Polish military, and the secretive Yiddish press. The Zionist organizations had their own sources of information, relayed to us regularly by Drora. We could no longer deny that she held an important position in the Left Poale Zion's youth offshoot, *Freiheit*, German for freedom, sympathetic to communism and Yiddish as the national language of the Jews. This group fit into Drora's beliefs and she fit into theirs.

The "war" news was not good. My mother was frantic about Perl. We heard that on September 8, there was heavy bombing in the heart of Brest. Half the city was in flames; hundreds were killed, thousands injured. Many fled eastward. I couldn't allow myself to wonder about my beloved aunt, about the boardinghouse and all who lived there. No, not there. Not them.

One of the biggest threats to Germany came when the Polish army attempted to break through to Warsaw. For several days after September 9, German armies swung their divisions to meet the Polish attack. The Poles fought bravely but did not succeed. Their weapons and aircraft were outdated.


IN KOBRIN, THOUGH, there was a temporary lull. We didn't fool ourselves into thinking we were safe. But as human nature goes, we latched onto any hope. We were becoming a little bolder.

One morning, we heard a timid knock on the door. Any knock was cause for alarm, and Drora and I stood to the side of the door, trying to peek out the window. We could only see black material of what appeared to be a man's jacket. The soft knocking reassured us; we had heard the Germans when they came to someone's house and you couldn't even call it knocking. But we were so paranoid by then that any sound could be a prelude to something sinister.

Drora and I were pointing to each other to do something when we heard a familiar voice saying, "For God's sake, open the door."

"That's Grandpa," Drora said.

I could feel my insides ease and I opened the door a crack just to be sure. My grandfather pushed it open and Drora and I fell into his arms.

Normally not one to be sentimental or affectionate, my grandfather stroked both our heads and murmured, "*Oy, mayne sheyne kinderlekh.*"

Drora and I each put an arm through my grandfather's and led him into the kitchen where my mother and Rivke were scrubbing the floor.

"Papa!" my mother cried. "How I longed to see you. Is Mama okay? And how are Khane and the children?"

"Everyone is well, don't worry," he said. "We are too smart to let the German fascists get us." He winked at me and my fear melted like ice in boiling water. Now with my father dead and Velvel in Palestine, my grandfather was the closest male in our family. Not to say we didn't have our other grandfather, Morris, and our uncles, but we lived closer to Grandpa Yankel and saw him often. He was my favorite, I admit. And not just mine. Grandpa Yankel held the highest esteem in our house. It wasn't because he was pious or educated. It was the way he spoke and carried himself, like he was proud but not haughty.

After a few minutes, my grandfather told us a joke and we were laughing as if the Germans had never come. Drora and Rivke went upstairs to gather the dirty clothes for laundering that afternoon, and Grandpa took my mother aside. He shooed me away with his hand; and, though I tried unsuccessfully to make out what they were saying, it didn't seem too bad by their facial expressions.

"Esfir," my mother said, beckoning me, "your grandfather and I think you can have a special privilege."

My heart fluttered as if I had swallowed a beehive, and I almost swooned at the fantasy that all was well and my grandfather was again taking me to visit Ida in Volchin. Of course that wasn't the case, but they agreed that the streets were quiet, at least the three blocks from Khane's house to ours.

"Are we all going?" I asked, springing like a marionette.

"No, just you," my mother said. "We don't want to cause any attention, so we'll go one at a time. Tomorrow, it will be Drora, then Rivke, and then me. Next week, maybe we'll all go together."

I sensed that my mother wasn't a hundred percent okay with this plan. She was usually very cautious and stubborn. This time she had yielded to her father for what I imagined were two important reasons: She realized that I was again withdrawing into myself, afraid of even going to the outhouse; and she trusted her father, who was, to her, the epitome of good sense.

"Come, my little *shiksa*," he said, opening the door. Because of my blond looks, and his wry humor, it was one of his terms of affection.

I was scared but my grandfather's presence soothed me. So even with sweaty hands, I held my grandfather's, and we walked down the street as if it was just an ordinary day in September. There were only a few people on our street and the next. When we turned to Khane's block, there was a small group of neighbors surrounded by German soldiers. We crossed the street to the other side, to avoid them. One of the soldiers motioned for us to come to them; he was immediately joined by two others in helmets, rifles strapped to their shoulders.

"It's okay, Esfir, they won't hurt us," my grandfather said, undoubtedly feeling my trembling.

We recognized the local grocer, Chaim Lifshitz, being plucked from the Jews. A soldier handed him a large pair of scissors. Mr. Lifshitz was a short, balding, and beardless man. It was a hot day and my grandfather was wearing a tight-fitting black cap instead of his usual fedora. I can't remember all the words, most were in German, but it was clear that the Nazis ordered Mr. Lifshitz to cut off my grandfather's beautiful long white beard.

Mrs. Lifshitz, whom I hadn't noticed before, immediately appeared by my side and gently eased me away. No, no, go away. I must explain to the Nazis that there's a mistake, that here is my kind and brilliant grandfather. Surely they'd see that they have the wrong man. I don't remember; it's possible, I did say something because Mrs. Lifshitz squashed my mouth with her hand and pulled me even further from my grandfather—though it was only a matter of a foot or two—and I do remember squirming like a crazy person from her clutches, without success.

The Nazis continued shouting at Mr. Lifshitz, who shook his head and refused. I guess, I was lucky if you can call it that. The Nazis didn't pay attention to me. They had other things on their minds.

Then a Nazi grabbed the scissors and held it to Mr. Lifshiz's neck, plunging in the blade enough to produce blood droplets. His wife screamed.

Mr. Lifshitz took the scissors and gingerly gathered the tips of my grandfather's straggly beard in one hand, and, with the other, tried to cut off the bottom as a unit. He succeeded but the Germans weren't happy. Several shouted and shoved Mr. Lifshitz. This was not what they had ordered. With tentative motions, Mr. Lifshitz hacked the remaining beard and scraped at my grandfather's face until all that was left were uneven patches of pinkish white, the color from blood. The severed beard clumps lay on the ground like a run-over squirrel.

A loud noise came from afar and the Germans must have decided that they were bored and would investigate this new commotion. Mr. Lifshitz dropped the scissors and ran down the street, his wife scampering after him. My grandfather took my quaking hand and led me back toward my house, even though we were closer to Khane's. I don't know if he was disoriented or felt safer retracing our steps.

When my grandfather and I walked in the door, my mother tried not to show her distress but her face blanched and I heard a sucked-in gasp. She disappeared into the kitchen and returned with a wet rag and a bar of soap. She ushered Rivke to bring the "medicine," something reddish brown mixed with alcohol. She doused the rag with it and dabbed at my grandfather's chin. He winced and let out a thin but shrill cry.

I stood on the side watching, still gripping my grandfather's hand. I had a vague sense of someone speaking to me; it was sound, but no meaning penetrated through my ears. I felt pressure and my fingers were disentangled from my grandfather's.

Slowly, without asking, my mother removed his shirt. He no longer believed in the orthodox view that men and women shouldn't touch (except for close relatives, which we were anyway), but he was still a very modest man about most personal matters. Drora rubbed the blood from his shirt, rinsed and ironed it.

My mother held a glass of *shnaps* to his lips, forcing in the liquid, despite my grandfather's protestations that his insides were already on fire. By midday, he was ready to go home. My mother begged him to stay, that it wasn't safe for him to go outside again. He said he had to because my grandmother would be sick with worry. There were so many things to worry about, you needed a stepladder to put them in the proper order.

Now that I think about it, I can't remember spending so much time with my grandfather when he didn't utter one of his Yiddish sayings. In all my years since, and after everything I witnessed, that sight of my grandfather trying to smile as my mother worked on him will always stand out as my first unbearable heartbreak.

Khane related later that indeed her mother was almost a crazy woman by the time my grandfather arrived at her house. When my grandmother saw his face, she inhaled deeply and wailed an inhuman noise in a steady stream of broken air. She pulled him toward her and then quickly ran into the other room as if she were afraid that her touch would cause him more pain. She returned with Khane's dead husband's razor that she took from the cabinet, rusty from nine years of disuse, lathered my grandfather's face, and shaved the remaining patches of hair. Her breathing became more even and she gently kissed his forehead. Then she said, "I always had a soft spot for a clean-shaven man."

# Twenty-Six

THE UNDERGROUND NETWORK related war news—persecution, destruction, and death in so many cities, towns, and villages. In short doses, we heard about Brest. On September 13, the day before Rosh Hashanah, bombs fell in Brest's Jewish quarters. About two hundred died in this bombardment and thousands were left homeless. On September 17, after a fierce three-day battle with Polish forces, the Germans captured the Brest Fortress.

My sisters and I had never been religious. But every night during the German occupation, we had prayed to God for help.

Help came in the form of Russians. In Brest, meeting little resistance, Soviet forces overtook the Fortress from the German army and reached the city on the 18th when the two invading armies met. On September 19, the Polish army surrendered. The war was practically over.

The Russians were nearing Kobrin. Drora was unable to contain her euphoria. She practiced her Russian every available minute and helped formulate a myriad of secret plans with her "comrades," some, I learned by listening to Drora and a girlfriend's pressed-head talks, involved moving to Russia. I only prayed that these were merely pipe dreams because if my mother ever suspected that her oldest daughter would be immigrating to Russia, while her son was living in Palestine, I couldn't imagine what she would do.

On the morning of September 20, the Red Army entered and took control of Kobrin. No longer terrified of going outside, we all rushed to the main street and saw streams of Russian tanks and soldiers chugging along. The crowd was ecstatic. People kissed soldiers' dusty boots. Many were skinny and wearing torn or frayed uniforms. To me, they looked more like tired and dejected men than jubilant conquerors.

Within minutes, Kobrin was flying red flags that the local Communists made by tearing the white stripe from red-and-white Polish flags. Gangs scattered leaflets denouncing the fascist Polish regime. Jews greeted each other with, "*Mazel tov*."

Drora had been right all along about the "secret" partition pact
between the Soviets and Germans. I didn't always get my facts right,
but this I wrote down in my journal: Out of the deal, the Soviets
received some 77,000 square miles of new territory, with the Bug River
as part of the demarcation line; and they inherited more than thirteen
million people, including an estimated 3,500,000 Poles and 1,300,000
Jews. All-in-all, with at least half of Poland's area and one-third of its
population, the Russians got a very large piece of the pie. We were no
longer part of Poland.

THERE WERE SO many changes in our lives then, that it's difficult
to keep them straight in time. Although the war was not officially over,
we felt that it was.

To mark it in my own way, I took out Miriam from her "safe" place
under my bed. Whether I was in Brest or Kobrin, Miriam was never far
from where I slept. I stroked her hair and whispered, "Miriam, I think
all is good now. You'll see. Soon we'll go in the yard and sit in the sun.
How nice that will be." I was careful to cheer her up, but not to talk
down to her.

I stood with my back against the wall and, with a ruler flattening
my hair, I marked my height with a pencil line. My sisters and I did this
regularly. And to make Miriam feel good, I always marked her height,
too. I know this sounds crazy, but I can swear that Miriam measured an
inch taller. Still, there was no escaping the fact that the distance between
us was longer than ever. But I assured Miriam that even if I got all the
way to Drora's marks, I would never abandon her. To make her feel extra
good, I promised that we would soon be back in Brest. I know how
much she loved Ania.

Not everyone was so optimistic. When my grandfather heard that
the Soviets agreed to give Germany three hundred thousand tons of
crude oil a year, the output of Polish fields, he predicted the downfall of
our economy. He went for longer and longer periods without a joke, one
of his Yiddish sayings, or even a recitation of a religious text to make up
for our "heathen" ways.

I took on the job of cheering him up, though my mother said
that I shouldn't be disappointed if my efforts failed; some things you
couldn't fix.

Occasionally, I read my grandfather a quotation from my journal. He seemed amused at my dedication. He thought Ida was the most wonderful girl, even if she encouraged my outspokenness. Her love of literature and philosophy, especially the Yiddish and Hebrew masters, was "unusual for a girl." I made a note to tell Ida about my grandfather's praise, though I'd never include his comments about "unusual for a girl," which he had said with more jocularity than conviction.

On one afternoon at my aunt Khane's house, I found my grandfather at the desk, bent as close to the page in his book as he could be without touching.

"What are you reading?" I asked, hoping he wasn't sleeping as he continued to stare down without turning a page.

"Nothing important."

"Would you like to see more of the writings I have copied in my journal?"

"My eyes are tired, Esfele. Read me a little."

I read him some quotations, including the last by Mendele Mocher Seforim, as explained by Ida, "the grandfather of modern Yiddish and the father of modern Hebrew literature."

"So, Esfir, you think you are the only one who appreciates Jewish literature?"

"No. Ida does too."

"Oh, the famous Ida. Would you be surprised to learn that your *zeyde* has read writers like Seforim?"

"Really?"

"Really. And this *zeyde* doesn't need to put it down in a book."

Then he closed his eyes, sat back in the chair, and recited, "If two Jews were to be shipwrecked on one of those desert islands, where there was not one other human being, there is no doubt that one of them would open a shop, and the other would start some little business of his own, and they would give each other credit."

"That's funny I guess."

"You guess? That, my little girl, was directly from Mendele Seforim's novel, *The Book of Beggars*, 1869."

And *I* had wanted to impress my grandfather!

My mother had been listening to our conversation and, when my grandfather resumed his reading posture and finally turned a page, I sat next to her on the couch. She put her arm around me and kissed my cheek. "Esfir you are a compassionate girl," she said. I wasn't certain what she meant except that my grandfather acted out two lengthy jokes during dinner that night.

# Twenty-Seven

WARSAW SURRENDERED TO Germany on September 27, and the last organized resistance ceased in early October when seventeen thousand Polish troops surrendered in Eastern Poland. Now that the Germans were gone to the last one, we all relaxed. We were free from the fascists. Students returned to schools, shops and businesses reopened, the markets flourished again. It was time for me to return to Brest.

I don't remember how we communicated with Perl to announce my arrival. She met me at the train station and I ran into her arms. We stood still for awhile until someone pushed us as a unit, and then we walked for a long time. We longed to talk to each other, to catch up on family news, and to compare events in our cities. Mostly, we needed to hold onto each other's hands and swing them without fear of anyone breaking them apart.

Almost immediately, Perl reported about Sonia, the Polish woman who came from the countryside to help clean Perl's house. "I had to let her go," Perl said.

"Why?" I asked, images coming to me of a portly and cheerful woman with a gold front tooth and a nest of kinky red hair. Sometimes I'd come home from school and know she was there from the instant assault of lemon and bleach.

Perl explained, "You know I love Sonia. She has been a great help to me, but times are difficult. I can no longer afford to pay her."

"Oh," I said.

"This has been going on for a while. Little by little, I was paying Sonia less money. She loved me, I know, and said she could manage with the money I gave her. Then, last spring, I couldn't give her any money. At first, she took apples, peaches, preserves, a chicken—anything that made me feel as if I were paying her. She remained a few more weeks. In July, we both agreed that it was not going to work as it was and I promised the minute things got better, I'd summon her back. She kissed my hand and said she'd never forget me."

I had no idea Perl underwent such a drama with Sonia but I understood that Perl was purposely avoiding more personal questions.

" 'Forget, Shmorget,' I said to her," Perl went on, 'just because we don't have a working relationship anymore doesn't mean we can't be friends.' "

I tried to concentrate on Perl's story, but as we walked, each step revealed new destruction—buildings in shambles, roofs caved in, windows shattered, blackened and burned-out shops, buses and cars smashed like accordions, burlap-covered heaps revealing bodily outlines. Surely, we had gotten off the wrong train stop. This was not the Brest I left last June. Perl and I found a bench in front of the park, now strewn with piles of debris. Ragged and soot-faced children were sifting through the rubble. We cleared off a space and sat.

I closed my eyes and urged Perl to continue her story. By now, it was I who needed a diversion from the horror around us.

"Sonia immediately stood and put her hands in her pockets, aware that kissing my hand should not be the custom for friends of the same social class. So she left, swearing she would stop by for a glass of tea the next time she was working in the neighborhood."

"So has she come by?" I asked, becoming fascinated by this new relationship.

"Not yet," Perl said. "It's not easy to get around. You can see how things are." She had a faraway look; it shook me to see my beloved, jovial aunt so sad. I realized again how much she resembled her father.

Naturally, I asked Perl about all the girls. She said that before the last Germans left, Ania had practically "risked her life" to visit me, hoping I had somehow returned to Brest. Her father dropped her off as he was going to the church nearby and planned to pick her up in an hour. Ania's parents, especially her mother, had been sick with worry about their relatives in Warsaw, afraid that they were wounded or killed. That was why her father had gone to church, to pray that his relatives survived and, if they had to flee, they would make it to Brest.

Every few minutes, Ania's mother had looked out her window, hoping to see her aunt, uncle, sister, brother, her in-laws, all those close to her living in Warsaw or the surrounding areas. No matter who and where we were, we had been doing the same thing: pacing and looking out the window.

WHEN WE ARRIVED at Perl's, Ida, Freyde, and her brother, Yossel, were leaning against the side of the house. Freyde's hair was longer, side-parted and finger-waved, pulled back with a barrette. I couldn't believe she would take the time to style her hair, not *my* Freyde who rarely looked in a mirror. She wore white shoes and socks, a brown skirt and jacket, and a beige checkered blouse. And she was smoking a cigarette! She looked both studious and sophisticated, not like the awkward, mismatched girl of last June.

I was also surprised at Yossel's appearance. He had always been impeccably dressed in a clean white shirt and slacks. His normally shiny brown hair, a lock falling over his right eye, was now long and greasy. He showed the early growth of a beard and mustache. His khaki shirt was rumpled. Though, he had a flirtation—and shared a kiss—with Liba, it was clear that he was not the pursuer. If you ask me, Yossel had been smitten with Ida and wound up in an awkward situation. It was also apparent from the way he slouched toward Ida, he still had a crush on her. I can bet that Ida was oblivious.

Ida was, as she always was, unique. She wore a simple green tweed bobble-knit sweater with a rounded neck. There was a thin long black scarf draped over her large breasts and hanging to her hips. She stood with her hand at her sides as if she were modeling for a fashion magazine. She knew no more about fashion than my brother in Palestine, but she had a way of drawing attention to herself that was instinctual.

I compared her to my modest sister Drora, who was so devoted to her activities at *Freiheit*. Freyde was also involved in Hashomer Hatzair like Velvel. And, not to forget Mendel and his Revisionist Zionism. I wondered where Ida stood in all these movements. She was sympathetic to Mendel when he spoke; she commiserated with Freyde; she nodded when I related my sister's activities, what little I knew of them. But I never saw Ida attend a meeting for her own reasons.

She was, I realize now, unable to fit in with any one party, any one point of view. There was no label she wore, no banner she waved. By choosing none, she chose them all. Everyone had a valid point of view, she would be the first to say. Not that Ida didn't have strong opinions. But she never wanted to be judged for another's ideals or be a member of a "constituency." She was her own mouthpiece.

Ida was a flower, like no other. I am not exactly unbiased about her. In this, though, I am not exaggerating.

When Ida noticed me, she ran down the street and lifted me at the waist, swinging me side to side. Then she pushed me back, nodding and scrunching her lips as if she were appraising a lovely new dress, and said, "I think you must have grown at least two inches." Since I was nearly ten and self-conscious about appearing even younger, I grinned. I didn't volunteer that I had recently measured myself on the wall and *had* grown two inches!

Freyde stubbed out her cigarette and rushed to kiss me on the cheek. I could smell tobacco engulf her entire being.

Yossel gave me a nod and said, "How are you, kid?"

I said I was fine and glad to see him.

As we were standing around, Rachel and Liba walked down the street toward us, arm in arm. Naturally a bit taller than Liba, Rachel wore stylish shoes—black suede peep toes with high heels—that made her look like a giant, her exact intention. But it wasn't Rachel who was flustered when she saw Yossel lounging with the girls. Liba straightened her posture, chest forward, as if she needed to elongate herself next to Rachel. She began to fluff her Claudette Colbert short, straight bangs, which she did when she was nervous. So here was my proof: while Yossel wanted Ida, it was Liba who wanted Yossel.

During these days, it was foolish of Rachel to flaunt any extravagant dress. Where she got those shoes and why she hadn't hidden them remained another unsolved mystery. And as far as I could learn, Rachel's father had not shown up to take her to school. She had appeared one night and, with her house key, opened the front door, quietly slipped inside, for once making no notice of herself.

I was surprised to see Rachel and Liba so chummy; we were all aware how much Rachel annoyed Liba. This was one of the bonds Liba and Ida had shared: their impatience with Rachel. Ida didn't seem to mind Liba's lapse in allegiance, as she said later to me, since Liba always came to our room at night to complain about Rachel, causing both girls to howl with scheming laughter.

"Where have you girls been?" Freyde asked, innocently.

"Wouldn't *you* like to know?" Rachel said.

"Just for a walk," Liba said, apologetically.

"You girls should be more careful where you go," Yossel said, not looking at them.

"You're right Yossel," Liba said. She slipped her arm back into Rachel's and they strutted into the house.

After he left, Freyde excused her brother's appearance, explaining that he was very anxious. In his last year at the Tarbut, he had been applying to the Hebrew University in Jerusalem and for an immigration certificate to Palestine. It could take months to hear; nobody could predict when. The waiting was torture. With current political events so volatile, this could be his only chance to realize his dream of becoming a doctor.

That night, Ida seemed restless. She listened by our door and paced around the room, which was difficult to do being such a small space. It was obvious that she was waiting for Liba to deliver her report on the haughty Rachel. After Ida turned out the light and got into bed, she didn't go to sleep for a long time. I was awake thinking about things and didn't hear Ida's regular snoring snorts.

The Tarbut girls went back to school but not for long.

I HAD AN emotional reunion with Ania on the way to school in October. She was bloated and had grown a pudgy stomach. She had eaten so many potatoes—which is saying a lot because her family had them mashed every night—that her brother Piotr called her *Ziemniaczana Twarz*, "Potato Face" in Polish. Probably he wanted to get back at her for once calling him Pig Face. We hugged and skipped along, both of us looking back over our shoulders, for what I can't say.

We were early so we waited in front of school. Ania told me about the joint military parade in Brest on September 22. It was both a farewell salute to the Germans and a welcome to the Soviets. Ania had a good viewing position in the crowd.

"I saw Soviet tanks and armored cars pass while the Nazis saluted their new friends—the Communists. And there were Nazis talking to a Soviet tank crew as if Brest were their hometown."

At four p.m., she had seen an official ceremony. The Soviet Commander Krivoshein saluted the German General Guderian in the street while many—mostly the soldiers—applauded. Then in front of the German Headquarters, the red Russian flag, with hammer and sickle, flew alongside the German flag, its swastika billowing in the breeze.

The commanders had stood on a wooden platform to review the paraded vehicles. The German band played the German anthem, "*Das Lied der Deutschen.*" Ania, who studied German, noted the first line, "Germany, Germany above all." "I was so close to the trombone and clarinet section, I could hear every note," she said. Though most of the locals stared as if stunned, eventually they raised their hands and cheered. "Esfir, you wouldn't believe it. Russian soldiers were shouting and screaming."

I couldn't get into Ania's excitement. All I could think of was the hypocrisy—that the Russians felt victorious over the Germans as if the entire invasion hadn't been orchestrated.

Ania, whose family had long-held bad feelings for the Germans, couldn't help be caught up in the revelry. She had come home singing "*L'Internationale,*" the international anthem of revolutionary socialism. She repeated a line from the chorus, "This will be the final and decisive battle," raising her arm in a clenched fist. Her mother and brothers applauded, but her father suddenly slapped her cheek. Everyone froze. This had not been the first time her father hit her, but there was usually a logical reason.

Her father had said, "Ania, I'm sorry, but you should be more sympathetic to your own people. This is not a time for celebration."

Yes, Ania felt for the many thousands of Poles who had been imprisoned and persecuted by the Germans. Her father's brother and cousin, soldiers in the Polish army, had been missing for weeks.

"But, Father," Ania had pleaded, "the Russians will surely help us. Everyone says so."

"Everyone. You know everyone! But do you know that the Bolsheviks are also taking our boys as prisoners? The uniforms may change, but the bullies stay the same. As long as the Poles can't speak their own language in their own country, they're not free."

Ania had been humiliated by her father's slap. She still felt her father's coarse worker's hand grating her face like sandpaper. The word *bully* remained with her. "I decided," she confided to me, "not to voice any opinions or repeat those I heard from others." It was too dangerous, even in her own house. She spent more time doing chores or reading, retreating into her own world, a world I knew too well.

I felt so sorry for Ania and hated to see her natural good cheer dampened. Like with Perl, I held Ania's hand tightly and swallowed my tears.

Political and national allegiances became crucial in our social dealings. Most of the Poles understandably supported Polish sovereignty, while ethnic minorities, meaning mostly Jews and Belorussians, supported Soviet rule. This naturally aligned us against the Poles.

I would not allow this hostility to poison my relationship with Ania. Her family was enlightened. They had influence. Her uncle was an important religious leader, dedicated to the social welfare of the community.

As weeks went by, I realized something more was affecting her. She no longer invited me to her house. I was hoping it wasn't because she was being pressured by her family.

Then, one morning, on the way to school, I got up my nerve to ask. "Ania, is there something wrong, I mean between you and me?" I tried to swallow but my tongue curled back toward my throat.

"Esfir, why do you ask?"

"You seem different; I mean, quiet. That's all."

"Oh, Esfir, it's not you, please don't think so. Nothing will ever change between us."

This was all I needed to hear. It was sickening what she told me. Ania's uncle, Father Janusz, had been taken in the middle of the night and imprisoned. Later he was shot. Ania's oldest brother, Erek, the one I admired at the soccer stadium, had joined the Polish army and was imprisoned. Her next oldest brother, also a soldier, was missing in action. Nobody was safe.

After this admission, Ania and I didn't talk about our families, though a *P* could have been branded on her forehead as a *J* could have been seared onto mine. We still held hands when we walked to school, unconsciously dressing as alike as possible.

Yet, most of us thought that the Soviets were more interested in occupying our land than changing our lives. Businesses were allowed to run and people continued to practice their religions as before.

TROUBLE INTENSIFIED WHEN our area, already overflowing with refugees from western Poland, became inundated with immigrants from the East—Soviet officers, civil servants, commissioners, the police, along with their families. Some were placed in positions that had been involuntarily vacated by Poles. Others found little or no work.

All these newcomers needed a place to live.

We were surprised by the Russian émigrés. They, like the Soviet soldiers, looked poor and downtrodden. Some women wore rags wrapped around their feet; they carried makeshift suitcases and bundles of dirty clothes. Often they pushed themselves into one mass, walking with dazed expressions. Later, we heard from neighbors who had to vacate their homes for the Russians, that these interlopers often didn't comprehend the notion of privacy or luxury.

Suddenly, the Soviets became our evictors: seizing homes, moving people to already crowded places, imposing rules, such as each room should accommodate at least two people. There seemed to be no order to these restrictions. We never knew who would be kicked out and to where.

At Perl's we were safe, for the moment. Already, we had two girls to a room and Mr. Kozak officially moved into Perl's bedroom. She invited Yossel and his friend to share Mr. Kozak's former main floor room.

Though Mr. Kozak had to keep a low profile, he was dealing behind the scenes. He had saved a lot of money and still maintained connections. I suspected that he had paid a hefty sum to keep Perl's house from becoming a Soviet enclave and for the privilege of living with her.

New rules emerged not only regarding our living conditions but our belongings. We were allowed nothing in excess. If we had more than one change of clothing and underwear, we hid them underneath the linen in the attic chest. Occasionally, gangs burst into homes to search for anything they found that exceeded the required limit. We heard they took these goods and exported them to Russia.

Perl said we had to call Mr. Kozak by another name, Mr. Epstein, pretending he was her husband because of the anti-Polish measures. The Soviets, like the Germans before them, had been arresting Poles in great number and deporting them to the "new" Poland. We prayed no one would ask him for papers, or discover that Perl's real husband was dead.

This was the only time I could think of that a Pole pretended to be a Jew for safety reasons. And now, we Jews, instead of standing with the Belorussians against the Poles, felt a new protective kinship toward our Polish neighbors.

My mother phoned Perl at the post office and expressed her concern about Drora who still could not admit to anything wrong with the Soviets. When my sister wasn't at a meeting, she was handing out Communist leaflets on the street. She flirted outwardly with Russian soldiers. I couldn't believe this was my shy, bookish sister. Like Freyde, politics was transforming her into a bolder, more feminine person.

The love of everything Soviet began to quickly wane, even for diehards like Drora.

# Twenty-Eight

PERL, WHO HAD accepted most changes (except for the loss of Sonia) with good humor, even enjoying the new tenants, was beginning to shout unexpectedly about her valuables, often mumbling to herself. Mr. Kozak, I mean, Mr. Epstein, kept warning her to keep quiet or express her thoughts to him privately. She was able to relinquish almost anything in her house, but when it came to her Dresden china, she put her foot down. She wrapped each plate, each cup, each saucer, gently with newspapers and lay them in a small crate. Then she placed a layer of cotton bunting, followed by a thin board to protect the china. On top, she lined apples, neatly in rows, and stashed the box in a corner of the attic. Her logic was that if anyone discovered the crate and opened it, they wouldn't be interested because apples were plentiful all over our territories. That was the trick, she said, "Find something that nobody wants and camouflage your valuables in an obvious place."

Easy for Perl, maybe, but I couldn't figure out where to hide my journals and Miriam, *my* most precious valuables. I reasoned that nobody would want my journals, with every space taken by writing and drawings, but Miriam was a different story. Though Ida assured me that Soviet children were probably not allowed to have something as frivolous as a doll, I knew Miriam would be an exception, especially on the black market. So my new preoccupation was finding a place for my doll, not so distant a location that I couldn't get to her if I needed. This spot changed frequently, from between blankets in the linen closet, to under a plank in the outhouse, to being wrapped in sweaters and placed in a deeply dug hole in Perl's garden. Each hiding place lasted for a few days until I was convinced that place was ripe for discovery.

Whatever plans we had to go home for the New Year's celebrations (formerly our Chanukah or Christmas vacation) were cancelled. Staying put was the order of the day.

By the beginning of the new year, 1940, *replace* was the word we heard the most. The Russian ruble replaced the Polish zloty, and Russian and Belorussian became our official languages.

IN LATE JANUARY, we had an unexpected visitor. After midnight, I heard pinging. At first, I thought Ida was whistling in her sleep. Then she awoke and asked if I had heard something. There was another and another ping. We traced the noise outdoors, and Ida pulled the curtain back and saw a dark figure waving frantically. She opened the window and stuck out her head.

"Ida, Ida," the man called.

"Mendel, is that you?"

"Yes, Ida, shush, let me in, please."

Without closing the window, Ida grabbed a shawl and ran out the room. I heard her rushing down the stairs and the opening and closing of the front door and loud talk and then softer. They must have moved to the kitchen because the voices disappeared, and I could see the light shine on the snow outside the door from my window.

I didn't know what to think or if I had been thinking at all. I felt nauseous and dizzy, freezing and sweaty, heart palpitations and shortness of breath. Anything physical there was, I had at once. Mendel had never come here at night, alone. There must be something terrible happening.

I had to find out. The rest is very embarrassing to admit. Hugging the banister, I snuck down the stairs. I crept close to the kitchen's swinging door, which naturally opened slightly. It was enough for me to see a flash of action every now and then and enough to hear what they said.

The first thing I saw was Mendel and Ida pressed together, kissing. Mendel was moving his arms up and down Ida's back, cupping her behind. "Oh Ida," he moaned. "I want you so." As quickly as they disappeared from sight, they returned. There was a furiosity to their movements; I caught Mendel's hands pulling up Ida's nightgown and I waited for Ida to protest, but all I heard were shuffling and muffled groans. Finally, Ida, said, "No, Mendel, not here."

I backed away then, afraid they were going to come through the door at any second. I stopped by the staircase when Mendel's voice changed from caressing to imploring, going from low incomprehensible sounds to louder strings of words. He said, "You have to come, you have to."

"But, Mendel."

"Don't worry, I've taken care of everything."

"What do you mean?" Ida asked in a strange voice.

"I made secret arrangements to get to Vilnius."

"Vilna?"

"Yes, in Lithuania, where everyone goes to get to Palestine. It's the only way, believe me."

"But it's so dangerous. I've heard of those who've been caught by the secret police and sent to Siberia."

"Don't worry," Mendel said again, though, with less conviction. "I have connections—and a plan."

The couple's voices increased and seemed nearer to the door. Quickly, I took the stairs, two at a time, snuck into my room, and leaned on my door, still trying to listen. Their voices rose and disappeared. I crawled into bed, panting. I didn't know if I was more disgusted with myself for spying or anxious about Ida. Should I wake Perl and tell her that Ida was on her way to Lithuania? Since I still heard sounds, I decided to wait it out.

It seemed like hours before Ida returned. She closed our door and turned on the light. Her hair was dislodged from her braids, her eyes red and moist. She was shivering uncontrollably; her teeth were chattering. The window was still open; I closed it, scanning for any sign of Mendel. All I saw was the barren oak tree, icicles extending from branches like translucent mutations.

"What's going on?" I asked.

"Oh, Esfir, I just don't know what to do."

"What do you mean?"

"Mendel wants me to go with him, leave the country. I couldn't give him an answer, either 'yes' or 'no.' I just couldn't make such an important on-the-spot decision."

"Go alone with Mendel?" I asked.

"Yes, but how can I leave my family? If the police ever caught me, they'd kill them. How could I take such a risk?" Ida became hysterical, shaking and sobbing.

Then, she seemed to lose her speech. "He . . . he . . ."

"He, who, you mean Mendel?"

Trying to coax out her words, I spoke to her as to a child. "Ida, what is it that you want to say? Please, try."

Ida gave me a long look as if she were weighing the benefits of unburdening to me. The tautness around her mouth relaxed as if she suddenly realized that at ten, I was no longer that little, naïve seven year old, feverish with idolatry.

"What have I done?" she choked out through spasms. "By not saying 'yes,' I may as well have said, 'no.' "

"You did the wisest thing you could," I said.

"No, Esfir. You don't understand. I may never see Mendel again."

"You will, Ida. You will."

"No I won't. I just know it. I'm a coward. I said that I wouldn't risk my family, but I'm also too scared. I don't want to get sent to prison, to Siberia, to die of hunger or worse."

"Nobody wants that, Ida. This is normal."

"But, Esfir," she cried, "you don't know this, but Mendel and I are in love. It's a secret, but I know you won't tell anyone. He said as soon as we could, we'd get married. Oh, Esfir, I think I just lost my one chance for true happiness."

I reminded Ida that she had been a Shakespearean actress, that she had a tendency to be dramatic, to see life in extremes. "There is no reason to think you won't see Mendel again," I said in a timid voice. "The Russians can't continue to punish and punish. Eventually, we'll gather our strength and fight back. And, Mendel will be at the forefront, waving his own flag."

Where I got the words to answer, I don't know. I tried to sound like I knew what I was saying, but I had no idea who the "we" were who would be fighting back; and if the "we" was "us," I had no idea on the "how" and the "where." I knew Mendel had ties to the resistance movement, as well as the Zionists, the two often overlapping. He had a burning and yearning personality.

Maybe I had said the wrong thing to Ida. She was progressive, too. But, she didn't believe that the prince was going to save her. She would make her own fate. That is why America attracted her; there, she could be herself. But this time, this night, she didn't seem like a woman almost turning eighteen, but like a little girl who needed to believe in fairy tales.

For years, I had been hearing that we Jews should stay here in Poland, trek further east into Russia, emigrate to Palestine, even flee to Madagascar. Now it was Lithuania. All I wanted to do was go to a safe and quiet place with Miriam; it could even be the next street.

Something was changing in me. I realized that Ida was also much more than this saintly wonder of my construction. She was a young woman, with real feelings of love and hope. I didn't understand it all yet, how could I? Now I realize the meaning of something my mother once said: "The older we become, the more the gap between ages shrinks."


RUSSIFICATION WAS IN full swing. Private property was prohibited. Trade between city residents and peasants was halted. Food became more and more scarce. We waited in long lines for up to ten hours for a piece of bread.

The Soviets had committees and others in "cells" whose jobs were to spy on people, to make them afraid to say or do anything that could be interpreted as anti-Soviet. We were searched at random. With the arresting, killing, and deporting of huge numbers of people, the Soviet Union was trying to shift the population, to clear out all the intellectuals, the educated, civil servants, the military, and others useful or capable of independent thought. They had the perfect role model: Nazi Germany.

Special evening classes were held for training in Communist doctrine. Stores and markets were transformed into military facilities. Local hospitals shut down and government ones expanded. Private medical practice was prohibited and most lawyers were disbarred. Cinemas and theaters were nationalized. Posters of Lenin and Stalin were plastered everywhere. Loudspeakers placed around town played only Russian songs and propaganda.

The Soviets were training us into a nation of puppets.

We wore Russian-made clothes. Everyone spoke or was learning Russian. The Soviets, our saviors, turned into enemies. Perl said she wasn't surprised. She had a long memory and it went way back to the Russian pogroms of her childhood. She said, "There is no coincidence that the word *pogrom* is Russian for "to wreak havoc.""


I had been complaining less about my school life. I had been getting used to it. And I had a special soft spot for my first teacher here, Miss

Petra. All that was short-lived. Overnight, it seemed, sometime between the old year and the new, Miss Petra had disappeared and Comrade Maximov, who seemed to know nothing about teaching children, took her place. Religion, Polish history and literature, and Latin and Greek were no longer our subjects. Doctrines of Marx and Stalin were interspersed into unrelated subjects. All my favorite books were removed from libraries and bookshops. At night, we had to attend Communist lectures and "debates," receiving leaflets about barbaric nations and the need to suspect anyone who didn't adhere to superior Soviet principles.

I shouldn't have been surprised that the Soviets frowned on Zionist groups. The Tarbut girls and their friends began to hide Zionist literature and to meet in secret. No one should dream of going to Palestine, not when they were supposed to be good Russian subjects!

By then, the Tarbut school system was effectively over. The study of the Hebrew language and literature had been prohibited; Yiddish was declared the language of instruction for all subjects in Hebrew-speaking schools. Then the curricula was revamped. Russian teachers were imported. Soon the study of the Bible was prohibited, even when translated into Yiddish. Textbooks were replaced with those from Russia. Religious holidays were cancelled; national ones were established. And the final blow: a Russian school had replaced the Tarbut; Christian students replaced the Jews.

Despite all this, our Tarbut girls remained in Brest. Travel was difficult. They still held out hope that some governmental bureaucrat would provide a solution for former Tarbut students. Coming from smaller towns or villages, the girls also reasoned that they would be able to earn more money in Brest.

Free classes in arithmetic and Russian were available to the public; however, they were normally too crowded or inconveniently located. Being proficient in Russian, Ida tutored several students, especially among the Polish refugees. Most could pay little; some gave her food.

As for the other Tarbut girls, Rachel also tutored Russian, although her grasp was very limited. She hoped she could fake it enough to get by. Freyde obtained a position in a food collective; the twins got jobs as clerks in the local government service.

Unlike Mendel who "disappeared," some Zionist youth leaders voluntarily returned after months in Russia and Lithuania. Instead of focusing on those training for *aliyah*, they established kibbutz groups, underground schools, and clandestine presses. These activities gave the girls some hope, especially Ida.

In early February, Ida had a visit from a Volchin girl, Anna Gagarina, a classmate of Sala, Ida's middle sister. Since Anna was a Belorussian, it may have been easier for her to travel than for a Pole or a Jew. Anna was in Brest for some health reason. I do recall that she had to meet her father somewhere nearby. He had a horse and wagon. In those days, you didn't ask too many questions of people even if you knew them.

There wasn't too much to offer Anna except tea. Ida was embarrassed and put a cookie on Anna's saucer. Ida had been saving that cookie for a "rainy day," and as far as I could see, the sun was shining.

The girls went up to our room for privacy. After ten minutes, I couldn't stand it anymore and decided to invent an excuse to go to the room. I was becoming an expert in sneaking around Ida's private life.

A brainstorm: I needed my books for homework. Who would suspect such a simple thing? The door was ajar and I snuck in and said, "Oh sorry to interrupt, I'll only be a minute. I have to get my schoolbooks."

I fussed around the stack of books, taking one book off at a time and making another stack. Ida didn't notice what I was doing.

"Sala is good. You know her, she is friendly with the entire village," Anna said. "I don't know how she does it. I get so angry because if you walk down the street with her, she stops to talk to everyone. It can take an hour to go a quarter of a mile."

"She should be careful who she talks to nowadays," Ida said, seemingly forgetting that she had behaved similarly when she took me around Volchin, only we didn't have time to stop and socialize.

"Try convincing Sala of this."

"And, do you see the rest of my family?"

"Of course, I'm at your house at least once a week. Your family is fine, Ida. Don't worry so much." Anna patted Ida's hand as if she were the older of the two.

"How can I help but worry?"

"It's not so bad in Volchin. Who wants to bother with such a tiny village?"

"There are less places to hide there."

"You always have to think of the worst." Anna said this with good humor, though I thought it wasn't a nice thing to say. I admit I was looking for something to dislike about Anna. She was a brunette with a creamy complexion. She was beautiful, I suppose, though not as beautiful as her friend Sala.

"I'm not a complete pessimist," Ida said, "I know my aunt Masha from New York City, America, will send us money soon. My father is looking for ways . . ."

She left out the rest of the sentence, maybe realizing she had told Anna too much already. Perl warned her over and over that no matter how good a friend is, you should only divulge what is absolutely essential. It's not that the friend will squeal on you, but she could reveal something innocently. You can't be too careful. Again that word *careful*. Ida usually argued with Perl but lately her arguments were tentative and came out like a bad habit.

"Did you get what you needed, Esfir?" Ida asked.

I was so flustered that I said "yes" and ran out the room. When I got downstairs, I realized I had forgotten to take any books.

# Twenty-Nine

THE WINTER OF 1940 was one of the coldest. It was becoming more difficult to find wood for the stove than food, which was saying a lot.

It was time for all of us to leave Brest, to go back to our families. We managed to scrounge enough treats, though, for a farewell party, if you could call something we dreaded a "party."

Everyone contributed. I waited on a bread queue for hours. Perl donated a jar of plum preserves and two boiled potatoes; Ida found two mushy apples she had hidden under sweaters; Franny had traded her gold necklace for four eggs and a small wedge of Swiss cheese; Liba procured a bag of oatmeal and a cup of goat's milk; and Rachel pilfered an orange from a student's kitchen table. Mr. Kozak (Mr. Epstein) brought chocolate and *shnaps*. Perl yelled at him, unconvincingly, for corrupting minors.

Freyde brought the biggest surprise. On the dining room table where everyone displayed their treasures, Freyde plopped down eight blue school booklets and eight unused pencils. She and Yossel had stolen them from school last year when Yossel came into her class to help transport a large project back to Perl's. Near the coatrack, the supply cabinet had been open and Yossel pointed and nodded. Freyde shook her head; Yossel nodded more vigorously. Freyde must have relented and, she explained, acted as the lookout while her brother stuck the books spread around his waist and tucked into his belt. He had slipped the pencils in his coat pocket.

They had rushed out of school, and Freyde heard the insistent and increasingly loud blare of police sirens. She almost held her arms up in surrender until the cars zipped past and turned the corner. She had to hold onto the wall for support. Yossel put his arm under hers and pulled her along despite her wavering like a drunk.

"I was terrified," Freyde said. "You can imagine. But after the police were out of sight, I felt a sudden rush of exhilaration, that we got away with our crime. Since then, I hid them in my suitcase."

There were enough booklets to give one to Mr. Kozak since Yossel had also mysteriously "disappeared."

It was a Friday night and Perl lit the *Shabbes* candles. I was shocked about Freyde's stolen property, but it was followed by a bigger shock. Mr. Kozak wore a *yarmulke*—probably from the real Mr. Epstein's belongings—and holding a cup of *shnaps* substituting for wine, he recited the *Kiddush*, the *Shabbes* blessing given before the meal, in Hebrew, which Perl had written out phonetically. No one said a word. Automatically, we rose and stood until he finished. Then he raised his head and his eyes rested a second on each of us, not missing one. Clearing his throat, he said, "Now that I am Mr. Epstein, this is my duty."

Mr. Kozak-Epstein's simple declaration caught in *my* throat and I tried to breathe in my tears, but they were too heavy and I finally gave up and let them pour down wetting the linen napkin on my lap. When I looked up and around, all the girls—including Rachel—were crying.

Perl dabbed her eyes with her sleeve and said, "Let's eat this feast. Who knows when we'll be together again."

Maybe she thought that would make us feel better, but now I was sobbing and pushed back my chair and rushed into the kitchen. I didn't want everyone to see that I was so immature that I was unable to stop. I composed myself and returned. Without missing a beat for my sudden departure, they continued passing the plates—each item had been placed on a plate by itself to make it seem like we had many courses. I sat down, and Ida said, "Here, Esfir, take the apple. I saved the biggest slice for you."

There was no big ceremony for our leave-taking. In January, Jews had been forbidden to travel by train without special permission. Arrangements were therefore painstaking and unpredictable at best. Ever resilient, we all departed within twenty-four hours. The twins left first, responding to relatives who came in a wagon unexpectedly in the evening. Rachel vanished in the middle of the night. There was no note, no good-bye. If it was her father who came for her, we didn't know. I suspected that she left on her own.

The next morning, Ida had planned to get a ride with a Soviet army truck. Since Mendel left, Ida was morose and seemed to care less about matters of her safety. Perl had been horrified and tried to talk her out of it. Ida had spoken to the soldiers on several occasions and testified to their trustworthiness. We didn't believe her.

Perl scurried about packing and unpacking. One minute she decided an item was a "must," and another minute, she ruthlessly threw that same object on the floor. Her china was a necessity as were her grandmother's silver candelabra, her Chinese teapot, her embroidered tablecloth, and a selection of quality clothes that as far as I recalled, she never wore. She had arranged with Mr. Kozak to have these boxed and delivered to an undisclosed location, assured by Mr. Kozak to be invader-proof.

Last week, Perl had made, what she called, a difficult decision to come with me to Kobrin. This meant leaving Mr. Kozak, who as I mentioned before, was Catholic and, as such, was tied to his wife. Not that he planned to go back to Mrs. Kozak, but he knew he could never marry Perl and didn't want to compromise her reputation. As if anyone cared about such traditions in those days.

Perl once mentioned that Mr. Kozak had grown children, but I never heard him speak about them. So, I suppose, he had family in Brest more closely related than we were. But I don't think he stayed because of them. As a formerly influential businessman, he maintained secret contacts and had access to hideaways that hopefully would help him ride out the war. No one had to say it, but we all knew that his role as Mr. Epstein wouldn't last long because being a Jew would eventually destroy him one way or another.

I excused myself when Perl said her good-byes to Mr. Kozak. It was swift and unemotional. Perl continued packing and unpacking, and I left her to her tasks, but I noticed that her body was shaking the way it does when someone is crying.

When it came down to it, Perl didn't really have a choice. There was no place for her in Mr. Kozak's world, wherever that would take him. And, when it came down to it, in times of trouble, your blood family was your anchor.

So on a below-freezing morning in late February, Perl, Freyde, Ida, and I trudged in the falling snow to the train station. In another of Mr. Kozak's magician's tricks, he had produced train permits for Perl and me. We left Freyde near the station where she expected Yossel to "reappear." They hoped to hitch a wagon to their family in Bereza.

Ida was supposed to meet the Russians near the ticket area. As Perl and I walked away from her, I turned around and we shyly waved to each other. I can't explain it, but that wave said so many things to me. It said, "See you soon, I hope." It said, "Thanks for all the times you supported me." It said, "I pray for your well-being." And it said, "I love you."

I didn't do what I wanted, which was to rush into Ida's arms and hug and kiss her, to follow her to Volchin and hide in her attic. I couldn't afford to indulge in emotions. I was already a wreck and we had a lot to undergo until we arrived safely in Kobrin.

Perl and I found the train and shoved ourselves aboard. Almost all of the seats were occupied. There were many refugees and soldiers. We sat on a long bench along the wall of the coach. Some people sat on their suitcases or bundles. We sat and we sat. The train didn't move. It was too crowded to get out of the car. If we left for a minute, we would probably lose our seats.

We were afraid. Our papers were in order, but we were Jews and papers meant little. We shared a hunk of *challah* and dried apricots. The train was cold but heat was generated by the pressed bodies, most of us wearing layers of clothes. My bladder was bulging. Perl said if I had to let go, I should. She said, there was so much rubbish on the floor, including various liquid splotches, no one would notice. But I held it in by squeezing my legs together and daydreaming of being mashed in bed between my sisters.

By the evening, even Perl couldn't take it. Since we were close to an opened door, the easiest route was to climb over sleeping bodies and bundles camped in the doorway. We decided to go one at a time to save our places and belongings, though I was petrified to be separated from Perl for even a moment. We had rehearsed a story, loaded with fake hysterics, in case we were stopped. I dashed to the station bathroom, relieved myself in a clogged and overflowing toilet, and battled my way back inside the train to our seats. Perl stood ready to sprint.

We slept in snatches, nodding onto each other or the stranger on our other side.

The train stayed at the station all night and most of the next day. Finally it moved. Then it stopped for hours at another station, where we were able to relieve ourselves again and buy a cup of tea and bread from a vendor. While we waited, I daydreamed. I remembered that Ida had told me about the bathrooms at the Tarbut. They had immaculate English-style flushing toilets with long pull chains. I wished I could have seen one.

We made it to Kobrin. It took thirty-five hours to go about thirty miles.


WHEN WE FINALLY got to my house, after the long time it took to *shlep* through the snow at night, we were so cold and exhausted that we barely greeted my family and flopped down on the nearest bed, which was my parents'. We didn't take off our coats and slept until the next morning. I awoke and went straight to the outhouse. Then I was ready to say hello.

There were strangers in my house! I didn't know why this surprised me. People coming and going was so ordinary, you were lucky to still have your bed when you went to sleep at night. The new tenants, or I should say "occupants" because they rarely paid us anything, were a poor Russian couple and their colicky, constantly crying, rather shrieking, baby. They stayed in the living room, which was now off-limits to us. When they needed to use the kitchen or outhouse, they wandered in, never knocking. They weren't rude; it was almost like they didn't know they should ask permission for something so basic.

I tried to keep out of their way, though my mother said I should offer to help with the baby to show my friendliness. I didn't want to, not because I didn't like babies, which I did, but because I was uncomfortable around them. I knew enough Russian to communicate, but the woman looked sickly and pasty. The husband was short, almost the same height as his wife, and also appeared sickly and pasty. He had a brown beard with rust streaks, and she wore a ripped kerchief around her brown hair. The baby had a flat head with sweat-stuck blond strands and her nose was caked with dried snot. The husband and wife kept tossing the baby to each other. I wondered if this was the reason the baby, a girl named Duscha, was always crying.

So to make my mother happy, I offered to take the baby for a walk. The man and woman, I forget their names, shook their heads. I offered to give the baby milk from my glass, a big sacrifice for me, and this time the mother shook her head so much I thought she was having a seizure.

My family now spoke to each other in Yiddish, not to block the Russians from understanding as much as to maintain our privacy and safety. Their refusal of my help made my mother sad. She hoped it was more about shyness and awkwardness than anti-Semitism.

"Who knows?" my mother whispered to me, as if they secretly understood Yiddish. "Could be they think that since we are Jews, we will contaminate the baby."

"Well, the baby couldn't be any worse off."

This wasn't the only change in my house. Drora was also listless and depressed. You could have mistaken her for a relative of our new tenants. Her hair was lackluster and spotted with dandruff as if she hadn't washed it in a long time. She insisted on speaking Russian only, even to us. My mother said Drora was still defending the "poor Bolsheviks." We realized Drora had to keep up some pretense for her peace of mind so we let her go on.

Rivke was another story. Her rounded body sunk in like a concave vase; she bounced about like a grasshopper, as if she was afraid to stay in one place long enough. I had never seen her display so much energy. My mother encouraged her to go to school every day in case she could find something to eat there, maybe from another student or from the wastebasket. Was this my mother speaking? Was this the woman who wouldn't take a zloty from a customer after my father died unless she gave more than was required? I was besieged by disorientation. Where was I? Who were these people around me? Had I come to the wrong house?

FORGET ABOUT MY father's shop. Every Russian wanted a watch. The inventory disappeared overnight. The shop was collectivized and new workers took over. What they did there, my mother didn't know. She said, by that time, there were almost no watch parts left. Anything valuable, like an antique clock face or pocket watch chain, she had either sold on the black market or hidden; she didn't want to tell me where in case someone tried to beat it out of me. In a strange way, I think she was relieved to lose the business. The constant worry about buying and selling, much less keeping up with the standards set by my father, was a big burden for her, though she would never admit it.

Instead, my mother worked in a nationalized warehouse that distributed provisions, mostly food, clothing, and household supplies. Drora worked there, too. Though tempted to steal, they were under strict supervision; and if any merchandise was missing from their sector, there were severe penalties. Perl's application was just accepted for a job at the same warehouse, which seemed to have a shortage of workers.

Drora, like Ida, also tutored Russian to Polish refugees and on occasion was paid with leftover food. My grandfather went from being a bookkeeper in a yeshiva to being a bookkeeper in a shoemakers' *artel*, a cooperative association.

One day, Perl had an evening shift and came home in the morning. Drora and my mother had the following shift and returned in the late afternoon with anger on their faces. Each retired to her respective room and slammed the door. Drora wouldn't let Rivke or me inside. And Perl, who had been sharing the bedroom with my mother, didn't dare go near their door. Dinnertime came and Perl set whatever we had reserved on the dining room table. She knocked on both doors of the armed camps. My mother came out first, her lips pursed. Drora thumped down the stairs and sat down, scowling like a rejected lover.

Perl broke the ice. "Listen, you two. Whatever it is you are fighting about isn't worth upsetting the entire family. We need each other now, more than ever, so swallow your bitterness."

My mother said, "You're right, Perl. Drora and I had been discussing the Bolsheviks for a change. I don't know how she can go on finding excuses for their abhorrent behavior. Anyway, I've said this to her already."

"More than once," Drora said, sarcastically.

"I told you two to stop." Perl banged her hand on the table. "Shh, we don't need to alarm the tenants."

I think it was that remark that loosened the frown lines on both faces.

"I don't mean to talk you out of all your beliefs, Drora. But there is a reality here."

"I know, Mother," she said in Yiddish.

My mother responded with a loving voice. "Darling," she said, "I just heard from one of the workers who had seen an article in the underground Jewish press."

"And?" Drora said.

My mother's voice turned to a whisper, though she continued in Yiddish. "There was a Polish report on the September campaign, including losses inflicted by the Germans and the Soviets. I'm not sure if it's true, but even if it's close, it's frightening."

Then she lifted a tiny note stuck in her brassiere and read: "About 660,000 soldiers from the Polish Army were imprisoned, one-third captured by your precious Soviets! And about sixty thousand of the total prisoners were Jews, most of whom were murdered."

She tore the note into bits, admitting how she had written down the statistics at work, how she had disguised the numbers and names in code.

"This doesn't include the thousands upon thousands of civilians and soldiers murdered outright. And who knows how many Poles and Jews have been, and continue to be, deported," she said, no notes needed. "By anyone's calculation, these are tremendous figures and there is *nothing* in the world that excuses it."

Drora's silence prompted my mother to continue. "Don't tell me that there were losses on all sides. I know that. Nothing like we suffered, and this includes all of us former Polish citizens—Poles, Belorussians, and Jews, alike."

Finally, Drora spoke. "I know, Mother, it's beyond human comprehension." With all her pent-up emotions and her pretended indifference breaking apart, Drora began to cry, and through her sobs, she said, "I'm sorry. I know I'm a stubborn fool."

My mother could have agreed with her eldest daughter. She could have reiterated her moral "rightness," but she realized how much Drora's admission cost her. She didn't want Drora to feel utterly defeated and disillusioned. I have to say this about my mother, she had pride too, but never let it blind her from the welfare of her children.

She took Drora in her arms and intoned, "It's okay, my child. You have a tremendous gift for loyalty and integrity. I am very proud of you."

I thought at least I would find my old friend Gittel as I had left her. What had I been thinking—that she would be unscathed? That's what I had hoped to find about Ania in October, and how wrong I had been then.

Gittel was also like a different person. I never thought I'd say this, but she had no interest in any game I suggested. She went to school and was the perfect, obedient student and daughter. She did confide in me that her parents were making bundles stuffed with necessities and valuables. They had vague plans to escape eastward at the first opportunity. I thought back to the days of the German occupation, not that long ago, when Gittel proudly revealed her personal escape strategy—memorizing the thirteen-mile route to her relatives.

It was easy to fit back in school. No bullies to worry about. There were more Jewish students, and besides, there were supposed to be no differences. We were all comrades. I might as well have been in Brest. We had the same curriculum, the same books, and the teachers held a similar demeanor.

DURING THAT TIME, there was a bright spot. It had to do with Velvel.

We had often wondered what was worse—not hearing from him, or hearing about him. My mother had sent him letters and postcards but didn't know if any had been delivered. Rumors stirred about mail being censored or destroyed. Before she had worried about the Arabs, and now it was the British. Drora also had heard stories of Zionist terrorists in Palestine.

One early evening, I heard my mother shouting outside the house, definitely not desirable behavior in those days. We rushed to the door and she scuttled inside. She was beaming wider than her teeth. Without stopping to take off her coat, she waved a postcard in the air like a windshield wiper during a rainstorm. When my sisters and I gathered around her, she made sure the living-room door was closed and motioned us to follow her into the kitchen. Perl had been on an errand.

"Here, here," she said. "a postcard from your brother, Velvel." As if she needed to tell us his name. "I didn't even look to read it," she gushed. "I left my glasses at work." My mother, like Drora, was almost blind without her eyeglasses. "I want to read it with you, together, so we should all hear the same thing at the same time."

She could barely catch her breath. My mother came back from her haggard shell and emerged as the beautiful, ethereal mother of my memory.

Wearing her eyeglasses, Drora asked if she should read it. My mother nodded.

"Dear Family," Drora read. "I am happy to hear you are all eating well and feeling good. I am fine. I long to see you and help my country. Yours, Velvel."

Like a heavy curtain tumbling down on stage after a play's end, my mother's face changed color and shape. Her mouth, her eyes, and her cheeks all fell; a veil of whiteness overcame her rosy complexion.

"What?" I said. "Isn't this good news?"

'No," Drora said. "This means our brother knows about our troubles and he probably knows more than we do since he can get more news from around the world. He is not so well himself."

"I don't get it," I said. "He sounds okay to me."

"Well, Esfir," Drora said, "we have all taken to writing and speaking in code. He must realize from the news that we couldn't be eating well. He says this so we should think the opposite."

My mother said, "He said he is fine. This means he is *not* fine."

"We don't know that for sure," Rivke said, finally breaking her silence.

"And now he says, he wants to help his country," my mother explained. "He no longer considers Poland or Belorussia as his country. It is Palestine. He wants us to come there." My mother sighed and I saw a tiny tear inch down her right cheek. But, she got busy immediately, with Drora's help, writing Velvel a reply.

"What have you written to him?" I asked.

"Oh," Drora said, "Mother said that we are happy that he wrote to us. That we are doing well, working and going to school."

"Yeah," Rivke said. "Mama added a line on the bottom, 'And thanks to God you are not sick.' But then she crossed out 'to God' several times so no one could read it."

Right then I decided not to write to Velvel. I had no idea what was good to say and what was not.

THE DAYS AND nights seemed interchangeable. Aside from temperature changes, winter and spring had little distinction. Sometimes students were required to gather in school during the evening for certain exercises. A law passed in late June stated that Saturday was also a work day. Everyone was too busy and too tired to have a social life.

The person I most worried about was Perl. Not running her own home, not being with Mr. Kozak, being devious and secretive, these all worked against her nature. I rarely saw her laugh, much less joke. She was no longer affectionate with me. It was as if any physical contact was too much for her to accomplish.

When I spent time alone with her, usually cooking in the kitchen, she didn't talk about our current lives. It was always about the past. She was about my age when she visited her aunt and uncle in a village not far from Kobrin. Her uncle had leased a dairy farm. A windmill stood alongside the road, so you couldn't miss the place.

In the fields, she had wandered with her cousins and siblings among the flowers and trees. Big maples framed the house. The leaves were placed under loaves of bread while they baked. When she described the various wildflowers, she inhaled deeply as if she could still smell their aromas.

"On this farm," she said one evening, "there were animals everywhere, plus dogs and cats in the house. Birds filled the courtyard. There was a large barn with stalls for the cows and horses. A hay loft was above. Behind the barn, there were a vegetable garden and fruit trees."

"That's nice, Perl."

She continued, "I so loved the thick dark syrup made from sugar beets."

My mother heard Perl talk to me, shrugged, and left the room. This gave me the impression that Perl was exaggerating. But I didn't care, if it made my aunt happy. Then her eyes twinkled and she pinched my cheek, almost like "old" times in Brest.

In the late evenings or on Sundays, my mother and Perl sewed, embroidered, knitted—whatever they could do. They made uniforms, shirts, slacks, tablecloths. Before the summer began, Rivke and I assisted in the more menial sewing jobs like loading the spools, sorting the thread colors, cutting patterns, arranging the cut pieces. My mother would leave us instructions to follow when they were at work so that their assignments would be easier when they got home.

By mid-July, Rivke and I could sew almost anything the adults could, though we were not half as good. We also learned to forage in the garbage bins outside any place that served or contained food, including my mother's provision warehouse. If she knew, she'd have killed us.

Everyone in the family traded whatever we could, often bribing an official for a favor or two. As my grandfather said, "*Az men shmirt nit, fort men nit.*" We all broke laws; we were all suspect. We followed our prescribed paths and didn't look to our sides, though we often turned around to see if anyone was following us.

Rivke and I continued the sewing work all day in the summer, though we took time out to attend youth concerts and sporting events, usually with Gittel. Otherwise, I didn't see Gittel often. She had a job helping at the hospital. She said it was pretty disgusting work and didn't elaborate. We rarely played with Miriam. We were ten and feeling years older. We didn't talk about this, but I was sure she would have agreed that our childhoods were over.

# PART III
## German Occupation
## 1941-1944

*On Sunday, June 22, 1941 at 3:15 A.M., Hitler launched Operation Barbarossa—a massive military assault invading Russia across a broad area. The surprise attack included crossing the Belorussian border. On June 24, the Germans captured Kobrin. At the time, the Jewish population of western Belorussia, counting Jewish refugees from western Poland, was about 670,000. The Jewish population of Kobrin was 8,000.*

I am here, too, solitary,
Sick, wrapped in a shawl,
And I step slowly in the snow among the trees,
And no one knows
That I am still myself.
　　　　　　—Kadya Molodowsky, "Otwock"

# Thirty

THE PERMEATING CHOKING odor of burned rubber, singed hair, and overcooked meat; the thunderous booms and whizzing of bombs; and the sadistic nearing and waning staccato from automatic gunfire . . .

"The synagogue is burning," a man yelled, running down the street. Fire spread to other houses. I heard shouting and screaming.

We turned on the radio. The announcer said that the aggressive Nazi army had attacked the peaceful Soviet Union. The "peaceful" Soviets would retaliate.

Drora came home early from work and said that there was an onrush of people streaming into the provisions warehouse. Everyone was looting, even the Jews.

In the occasional silence of the following day, we heard the roar of airplanes in close formations. At first we thought they were Russians coming to our rescue. Then we heard they were Germans. Russian trucks and tanks clogged the streets. People climbed in open trucks. Panic swept our retreating occupier.

Tremendous explosions. Our house shook. I looked out the window at balls of fire. This is what had happened during the German invasion of 1939. Surely, the Russians would save us again. We blacked out the curtains as we had done almost two years ago and sat by the kerosene lamp all night. The streets were empty. I peered outside from beneath covered window panes; occasionally I saw beady eye pinpricks in my mirrored light and sharpened my incisors by gnawing at the skin around my lips. I had become exactly what the newspapers portrayed of my race, a harrowed burrowing rodent.

The next day, German planes flew again. Small Russian armored cars left the city. From our window, we saw German motorcycles. Each had a sidecar with another soldier holding a machine gun. Before long more Germans arrived in trucks and smaller vehicles, followed by heavy tanks and cannons on tractors.

Was it my house or my body that was in a constant state of vibration?

We couldn't believe that the mighty Soviet Union had gone down so easily.

Some of our neighbors reclaimed their houses from the Soviets. The shuffling and reshuffling of households occurred overnight. I had a moment of happiness daydreaming of running freely in our home.

"We have to get out of here," Drora said the following afternoon. She had been at a friend's house, someone she wouldn't identify. Another of her many mysterious contacts.

"Where should we go?" Rivke asked.

"To Khane's," my mother said. "I have to get to my parents."

We huddled together and tried to move as a group. Germans poured down the streets. On the next street, we saw Jewish men plucked out of the crowds and shot before us. There was a communal roar at the first one and then murmurs of "*Oy Gotenyu!*"

Clinging and clutching, we managed to get to my aunt Khane's; and they were gathering dishes, linens, towels, and wrapping them in sheets.

"What are you doing?" Perl shouted. "Are you going somewhere?"

"We have to bring belongings to the center of town. It was an order from the Germans. We heard it on a loudspeaker," Khane said. "Papa understood the German immediately."

"God will help us," my grandfather chanted like a prayer. "He will provide."

"No, Papa," my mother said. "*We* will provide, provide all our life's blood to the Germans. It's not enough that we sacrificed already to the Germans and then to the Russians."

"This can't last long," my grandmother said. "God willing."

My grandfather had been to the synagogue. As it was burning, a group of rabbis watched, praying. They said that the German commandant had asked to meet them, but they were afraid that they wouldn't be strong enough so they sent a delegation of important men. When the men returned, they reported that the Germans ordered every Jewish man and woman, from sixteen to sixty (females until fifty-five) to report for work, which was, they understood, to be hard labor.

"We have to be careful," my grandfather said.

This got me really scared. My grandfather was a man of the mind, not action. For action, he relied on God. He often said, *"Der mentsh trakht un Got lakht,"* meaning, "Man plans and God laughs."

"What?" I asked.

"Well . . ."

"Tell us! We children have a right to know," I said, amazed that I could speak to my grandfather this way.

"You're right, Esfir," he said, with a tone of defeat. "I heard the Germans rounded up a hundred and seventy leading people," he said. "They took them to a nearby village, made them stand silently. Some were ordered to get shovels and dig their own graves. Some tried to escape but were caught and torn apart by dogs."

*"Got in himl!"* Grandma Elke cried.

"They not only burned the synagogue, but the Jewish hospital and a rabbi's house."

*"Got in himl!"* my grandmother said again. On this day, those were the only words she could speak.

"The whole place is on fire," my grandfather said.

"Oh no," Perl said.

"And this is *definitely not* for the ears of the young, so go busy yourselves for a while."

This time I didn't protest. My sisters and I went into my grandparents' downstairs bedroom with my cousins, but we listened by the door to the living room.

"They threw Jews in the fire alive."

Drora ordered us away from the door so we couldn't hear the rest of the conversation. She was allowed to go back. Then she returned and reported to us. She said that they were considering what to do. Perl thought we should try and get back to Brest. My grandfather said he had heard it was much worse there. Brest had been the first military target of the Germans. In a *blitzkrieg*, German *Panzer* troops annihilated the Soviets. Those tanks! Five hours after the Germans encircled the Fortress, they entered the city of Brest.

How did my grandfather know this? I hadn't given him enough credit for having informed sources, as well as a respected voice in matters other than religious.

The adults listed every relative and friend they had outside Kobrin. Maybe they could go to my grandfather's sister-in-law in Visoke.

(His brother Hymie died shortly after we had visited.) Or hide in the countryside at another relative's farm. But since the Soviet invasion, no one could be certain where these people were or if their homes still existed.

Then we heard that the roads were being bombarded from the air. It was becoming clear that no matter what path we chose, it would be difficult, if not impossible. In any case, my grandfather said we should pack our valuables and set aside our most practical clothes for wearing layers under our winter coats—and be ready at any time. He didn't have to tell us this. We were already packed and ready to go.

When we got home, our Russian tenants were gone, leaving nothing behind.

For the next few days, we stayed home with our emergency "kits" close by. I took out a notebook and flipped though it until I found the folded-up letter I had recently stuck inside.

At the Brest train station, when I last saw Ida, she had been heading to meet Russian soldiers who were taking her toward Volchin. Perl and I hadn't wanted to leave Ida at their mercy, but Ida had been adamant and, as always, it was impossible to argue with her when she set her mind to something. Perl had said to me during those long hours on the train that she felt terribly guilty about allowing Ida to go off the way she had. She felt responsible for all the girls' safety. I shared Perl's concerns, and even her guilt, but realized that we had no better options to offer Ida at the time.

We never believed those soldiers would help her, but they did.

A few weeks before the German invasion, one of the Russian soldiers came to our house. My mother was sure this was the end for us. At first, she wouldn't open the door. The solider shouted, "Please, I have news from Ida, Ida Midler." At the mention of Ida's name, my mother opened the door partly even though there was a good chance that this was a ruse. I was standing behind her and peeked from the side. He had a broad and guileless smile, strawberry-blond hair, and gold-flecked brown eyes. There were streaks of dirt following the lines on his forehead.

"Are you Esfir?" he said. He was so much taller, all he had to do was lean over my mother.

I nodded.

"I have a letter here from your friend Ida."

"You know her?"

"Yes, we met in Brest. She's a wonderful girl."

"What do you know about her?" I walked away from my mother, not caring if there was any danger. News of Ida was worth any punishment.

"She traveled with my comrades and me in our truck. She stayed inside with the boxes of ammunition. It was dangerous. We got her to Visoke. She walked home from there."

I was getting suspicious. "How do you know that she reached her home?"

"Because I saw her again. There was a platoon sent to oversee the Bug River and on the way back, we stopped in Volchin."

I gathered that this had not been a scheduled stop.

"Volchin is a small town," he said. "We found her soon. She is well. I told her I was being sent to Kobrin, and she wrote a note and gave it to me with your address."

That was enough information to make me trust this handsome man. Ida would never have given my address to anyone who would harm me.

I took the paper and my mother insisted on giving the solider bread and fruit. He refused, but no one, not even a soldier, could argue with my mother when she was determined. So much like Ida.

The soldier ate and left quickly. I said my good-bye and thanked him and ran up to my room to read the letter, my breath ahead of my feet. I had left my journals with Mr. Kozak, who promised to keep them safe. Otherwise, if I had one then, I would have pasted the letter inside. It said:

> My dear, dear Esfir,
>
> I hope my friend Aleksandr finds you and your family well. I so long to see your beautiful face and share our thoughts and writings as we did so many wonderful times together. We are working hard. My parents send their best regards as I do to you and your family, especially to Aunt Perl. I miss you.
>
> Ida Midler

I realized that Ida couldn't reveal much. It was dangerous for her and for Aleksandr. Who was this soldier to her? Could she have forgotten Mendel? I rejected this thought, believing that Aleksandr may have been charmed by Ida, but he was just a trusted friend to her.

Why she had signed the letter with her last name, I still wonder. As if there would ever be another Ida for me!

Perl and I had been so relieved; and when she heard that Ida had singled her out for special regards, she was almost speechless, a state I rarely saw her in. Maybe quiet, sad, but never without a word if prompted. Having no children of her own, Ida calling her "Aunt Perl" was a warm embrace from afar.

During those dark early days of the German invasion, I read Ida's letter at least twice a day. Now I was so panicked that the Nazis would storm through our house and take my belongings that I ripped it into pieces and stuck each piece between stones in my cellar's walls, planning someday to put the pieces back like a jigsaw puzzle. But it didn't matter because I knew it by heart.

# Thirty-One

FROM ALMOST THE beginning of the German invasion, officers and soldiers with the letters *GFP* on their shoulder straps searched through residences. Bursting inside, seemingly at random, they dragged out the inhabitants, sometimes shooting them on the spot. We wondered why they picked one apartment and not the neighbor next door. Then Drora found out that these Secret Field Police pocketed the addresses of Communist Party and Soviet activists and anyone with an antifascist point of view. Secret agents posing as Polish refugees had formulated these lists in the fall of 1939.

Many of those rounded up were sentenced and executed in groups. We were saddened to hear that Katya Gasilevich had been one such victim. She had been an activist in the Communist Party who had already endured hardships at a Polish camp in Bereza Kartuska. When Drora said Katya's name, she was visibly upset, her voice cracking. I got the impression that she knew her.

Drora assumed that these lists also identified noteworthy or outspoken Jews since over two hundred were captured and executed in the fields of a country estate in July. Another large group was executed in August. My grandfather, Yankel Cohen, was among them.

Khane later told us that the Germans had smashed their front door. They read my grandfather's name and ordered him to come with them. He asked, "Why me? I am just a religious old man."

One soldier explained that they were taking him to register for the distribution of welfare benefits. My grandfather shook his head. Then they grabbed him by his arms and dragged him toward the door. My grandmother tried to pull him back by his feet, and a Nazi soldier knocked her down with his rifle butt. My cousins were crying and Khane was shouting, "You can't do this. You can't do this."

But they did. To this day, I don't know why my grandfather was selected. He was not a community leader. He was not a member of the intelligentsia, though he was certainly an intellectual. He was a private family man, a shopkeeper and then a bookkeeper. He was witty and brave and suffered greatly. Though he trusted God to have a reason for Jewish suffering, he attributed his inability to find it to his own failing.

Being the first of all the horrors befalling my family, it remains the hardest to write about. My grandfather's death had a profound effect on us. For some, like my grandmother, it signaled the beginning of the end. For others, like my mother and Drora, it sparked such uncorralled rage that their every minute was consumed with thoughts of revenge and escape.

I, as always, was in between. I was devoured by unremitting sorrow and anger. To keep myself from screaming, I would envision my grandfather spouting funny Yiddish sayings. His image became so vivid, so close. Even though I had become a nonbeliever, I believed that he appeared before me, saying, with a chuckle, *"Hak mir nisht keyn tshaynik!"* which was his affectionate way of saying, "Stop bothering me!"

Soon, I began to actually hear him curse the Germans. Once he said, *"Zol dir vaksn tsibeles fun pupik!,"* "Onions should grow from your navel!"

One night I heard my mother and Perl in the living room. My mother was crying. Perl was trying to comfort her. My mother said, "First it's Avrum dying, then it's Velvel disappearing God knows where, and now Papa has been murdered. There's a curse on the men of our family."

I wanted to yell downstairs and say, "No, we know where Velvel is. He's in Palestine." I held myself back, trying to remember our last correspondence from him. It had been more than a year and a half before, a lifetime. My mother was right. Velvel was God knows where.

I DIDN'T HAVE my journal to copy down dates and events. So many executions.

The Gestapo had a preferred spot, a slope off the highway by the bridge crossing the Dnieper-Bug Canal. They tied the victims' hands with barbed wire and forced them to kneel at the edge of the slope. Then the executioner would shoot each in the back of the head and push the body down the slope.

Drora had a friend—she seemed to have so many all of a sudden—who lived near this bloody area. She told Drora that sometimes the Nazis coerced people to run and tumble down the slope, followed by gunfire. She saw one couple that she knew who were newlyweds. They leapt toward their death, holding hands. Another time, she saw an entire family of partisans slaughtered.

On their way to work, my mother, sister, and Perl, though they were ordered to keep their heads down, often spied corpses at the bottom of the slope rotting in the sun. Targeted by partisans, the Germans moved the executions to the prison.

In the streets, we still witnessed enough. One day, Rivke and I were walking home and almost at the same spot that my grandfather's beard had been cut off two years before, we heard shouting. It could have been me having a hallucination because I could swear it was the same group of Nazis that had taunted my grandfather. This time, they lined up a group of male Jews against a fence and, from one to the other, the Nazis took turns punching and beating. Then, with the motion of a hachet, two Nazis went down the line and sheared off the Jews' sidelocks and beards.

At first, I thought that maybe I had missed something, that maybe the men were also being hanged from the downward position of their heads. But I couldn't see any rope or apparatus and realized that it was shame and embarrassment that was as strong as a hangman's noose.

When I saw one victim raise his head, his face a bloody pulpy mess, he seemed to stare directly at me. I wanted to shout and rescue him. Instead, I whispered to Rivke, "Let's go." We ran home.

Most of this time was a blur of restrictions and fears.

The Gestapo confiscated large buildings. Schools turned into soldiers' barracks, hotels became officers' quarters, the best homes were reserved for high-ranking soldiers. Groups of appointed Jews came to the house to collect underwear, kitchen utensils, and other items to be used for the Germans. We paid fines with gold, silver, jewelry, and other valuables.

We Jews over ten years of age—I was eleven by now—had to wear a yellow Star of David on our arms and the left side of our chests. We couldn't walk on the sidewalks except going to and from work. Anyone who fell on the street could be run over.

I saw this from my aunt Khane's window: A German soldier said, "Who is tired?" The Jewish man answered, obediently, "I am tired." The Nazi, with a joking face, said, "Lie down." He shot the man, who was then trampled by a wagon. I closed my eyes and left the window. My sadness was so deep, my shame at my inability to do anything was so overwhelming, I recognized nothing but fear. Afraid to act, afraid to hide.

Notices appeared stating that buying from Jews was forbidden. Selling to Jews was also forbidden. Using a Jew as an intermediary was forbidden. Jews couldn't go into Polish shops or the marketplace. By September, we were not allowed any physical or verbal contact with a non-Jew.

Fall was the appropriate season for the crumbling of our lives. Kobrin became an important administrative center, headed by Commissar Pantser. He was headquartered at my school. Plans for the destruction of the Jewish community were fully operational.

# Thirty-Two

NO JEW WAS surprised when we were ordered to move. We had two days to prepare our belongings. Our ghetto would be divided into two sections: A and B.

Our biggest fear (they were always getting bigger) was that we would be separated. Ghetto A was the largest in territory and population. It was designated for Jews who were considered useful like specialists, workers, the physically strong, and the wealthiest who could afford bribes. This would be the best place to be, we thought. We had sold everything valuable and hidden money for an emergency. This seemed to qualify.

There was a chain of command for bribing. My mother found her lowly contact who would pass on the request. Pooling my mother's, Perl's, and my grandmother's money, she also bargained for Khane's family, by now amounting to two teenage boys, Efraim and Mordechai. Khane's oldest son, Reuven, had been conscripted into the Red Army and was stationed somewhere in "God forsake's land" as my grandmother called it. Khane was sickly with tuberculosis and couldn't work, and my grandmother was sixty-eight and had severe arthritis.

The contact took the money without giving assurances, predicting it would be difficult for my grandmother and Khane. We hugged our relatives and vowed to find each other once we were assigned accommodations.

We worried about my father's brothers, their families, and my grandparents, Ruth and Morris. Morris had been a skilled laborer, Ruth was a strong, healthy woman, and my uncles were influential, so we also prayed for our reunion with them in Ghetto A.

I was also crazy with concern about Gittel, begging my mother to say she was our other sister. Her parents had lost their book-dealing business in 1939 and had exhausted their savings. They hocked everything of value. Although once a good businessman, Gittel's father had few practical skills that he could demonstrate and he was thin and stooped. Her mother was a talented pianist, but hadn't played in years. Gittel's brother was five. I didn't think her family had much of a chance for Ghetto A. My mother couldn't take on another child, and, even if she had agreed, Gittel's parents wanted their children with them.

Still, I prayed. Funny that I keep saying "I prayed." I admit to being one of those people who only pray when they need something, so let it be. During this time, I prayed constantly, I tapped surfaces, I repeated words, I flung salt over my shoulder. Desperation makes you cling to anything.

This is what we heard: Ghetto A was in the southern part of Kobrin; a two meter-high wooden fence separated the ghetto houses from the adjoining streets. Ghetto B was in the western side of Kobrin, on the right bank of the river. There was no fence. This was not good.

I rehearsed packing my essentials so many times, you would think I would have known what to take. I wore my coat. I had a small leather travel bag. I selected a sweater, underwear, skirt, blouse, socks, two of my most treasured books (and the thinnest), a notebook, a shawl. But there was one thing that nagged at me. Should I or shouldn't I take Miriam? I dared not ask anyone in my family because I knew the answer. I wrapped her in my shawl and placed her underneath my clothes. I couldn't close the bag. Something had to go. I spent at least an hour rearranging, discarding, repacking. Finally, I gave up my shawl and wrapped Miriam in my sweater. It was a tight fit.

Whatever my mother bribed didn't work. We all got Ghetto B. The Germans led us to a long street with rundown two-story buildings. Walking ahead of us was a bent and red-bearded man with dingy *talis* fringes hanging down from his tattered black coat. He turned around and poked my arm. "Have you seen my Hinde?" he implored. I shook my head. I heard his cries for Hinde as the Germans slapped him aside and shoved us into a brick building with exposed bags of trash piled in a heap. They pried open the front door and led us up a narrow staircase stinking of diarrhea and vomit. After pushing us inside a room, they slammed the door and I heard them rumble down the stairs. It was quiet. Then I heard another "Hinde" and a gunshot. I scrunched my shoulders and put my hands over my ears, and mumbled, "Poor Hinde."

In the apartment, we had one small room. There were two other rooms occupied by Jews. I wondered who had lived here before and where they went. Were they non-Jews? Did they go to *our* house? The ghetto rule stipulated five to six people per room. With Perl, we were five and hoped no stranger would be added.

Our room had no furniture. Anything of value had already been taken. There was no water. Luckily, we each had an apple and a piece of bread, which we didn't dare eat.

My mother asked us to remove anything soft from our bags. All of us donated a sweater and a coat. My mother and Perl also gave a wool scarf and a towel. In a short time, we improvised a sleeping area that took up all the space. It was *Shabbes* evening, our first night in the ghetto.

VERY SOON, WE adapted to the rules. I shouldn't say adapted because that implies ease. It wasn't easy. We were obedient puppets. We didn't question because there were no answers that made sense. The less conspicuous you were, the better.

We lined up for rations. Each family received some potatoes and/or a little bread.

We were forbidden to leave the ghetto unless we were part of a work detail. Rivke and I stayed home while my mother, Perl, and Drora went to work. They got up at five a.m. and marched in lines under police surveillance for ten miles in the cold and dark. Usually, the work involved digging trenches. As winter set in, many workers, worn out and improperly dressed, froze on the way and died.

Even if we had been allowed to leave the ghetto on our own, we would have been seen. We had sewn a yellow circle onto our garments on the back of the shoulder (and on the chest) that could be seen from afar. The Germans called it *Schandenflek*, spot of shame. We were branded.

When the ghetto was set up, the Germans had selected several prominent Jews to serve as our liaison. The *Judenrat* or Jewish Council, headed by a rich merchant named Angelovich, was supposedly established as our governmental body. It really was our source of news and a mouthpiece for German orders. The *Judenrat* had its own police, armed with clubs. They supervised the lines of workers when they went beyond the ghetto boundaries. We went to their "office" to complain about food and work, to beg for favors, to barter with the Nazis.

We regularly checked the lists of Jews. According to the *Judenrat* records, Gittel and her family, and Khane and my grandparents, were also on the lists for Ghetto B. It took a long time to find their whereabouts. Grandma Elke had been separated from Khane's family, and she, like my grandparents, Morris and Ruth, was placed with strangers. Thank God we had located my father's brothers and their families, who lived in a building a few streets away. We weren't certain what happened to Khane's sons as they weren't on any list; we assumed that they were taken somewhere for work as they were fit and healthy. Gittel and her family were missing.

Work duties became diversified as the Germans needed skilled labor. Our stores now were owned by Christians. *Artels* were created where Jews could work under the supervision of Christians. Luckily my mother, Perl, and Drora were transferred to a large *artel* of five hundred workers. They were hoping to obtain their skilled worker's certificates, which would give them a chance to transfer to Ghetto A.

On occasion, the Germans herded Rivke and me outside the ghetto with other older children to work at one of the smaller *artels*. We were lucky because many children over twelve were plucked from their families and transported to labor camps. Rivke was thirteen but looked my age and nobody checked the ghetto name list. We were also lucky that we were placed in one of the better *artels*; some were headed by sadistic monsters. When we walked there, we had to keep our heads down, but the signs were everywhere: "Kill the Jews." "Jews are Communists." "Jews are the troublemakers of the world." Onlookers often shouted these slogans.


ON A BITTERLY cold December day, my mother noticed a pile near me, wrapped in newspapers that I had found in the garbage outside.

"What is that?" she asked.

From her tone, I was afraid to answer. Instead, I unwrapped the paper.

"You brought your doll?" My mother's voice was flat. Her face was sweaty and red even though it was frigid in the room.

I stood still, feeling like I was getting shorter by the minute.

"You brought your doll when we are starving and freezing to death? You could have packed potatoes or another sweater." She made a fist and raised it toward my face.

I started to shake. I thought my mother was going to kill me. I never saw her this angry.

Perl gripped my mother's arm and pushed it down.

"Sheyne, no," she said, "leave the child alone."

My mother dropped on the floor. She didn't move. I thought she had frozen in that position.

"Mama?" Rivke asked.

"Let her be," Perl said.

We all busied ourselves, with what I don't know since we had no space to do anything in private. We folded our clothes, pushed them aside, rearranged our belongings, small that they were. Rivke picked up a book and started to read aloud. Perl shook her head. She made it clear that no sound should be uttered.

Sometimes we all need quiet even if we couldn't have peace.

We moved to the other end of the room with our backs to my mother. I didn't have to look at her to know she was crying.

A few weeks later, Drora didn't come home the usual time. That day, she had a different work assigment than my mother and Perl. She had been sent on a road-building detail. When it was an hour after we expected her, my mother began to pace the square room. We had one window and crowded around it, leaping when we thought we noticed Drora, only to see another girl who looked like her from afar.

We needed a diversion. The Christmas holiday had just passed. Under the Russians, all religious observations had stopped. Our one change for the better since the German invasion was that we could reclaim our traditions. Rivke sang "*Stille Nacht*" with the original lyrics in German. She had a lovely, light soprano voice and had been in a choral group years before.

My mother sank to her knees. I thought she was going to pray. Instead, she folded her arms on the floor and bent her head into them. She began to rock, I thought to the rhythm of Rivke's soft emotional interpretation. As quickly as she had gone on her knees, my mother jumped and stood. Her face was drawn and ashen. Her eyes were sunken and when she looked at Rivke, her eyeballs appeared to pop out. Her once golden hair was bland and matted. If I had seen her in *my* Olden Days, I would have thought her a crazy woman living on the streets.

She came up to Rivke and said something so low that we couldn't understand her. Rivke continued singing.

Louder, my mother said, "Didn't you hear me? I said stop, stop that singing."

Rivke stared at my mother with closed lips. "What? What?" she asked with excited trepidation. "Did you see Drora coming?" Rivke had been so captivated by her own singing, with her eyes closed in an angelic pose, that she hadn't seen my mother on the floor rocking.

"No, Rivke!" My mother was screaming now. "I haven't seen your sister. I can't believe you can be so insensitive."

"What did she do?" I asked, afraid that Rivke, who ironically was the most sensitive of us all, would start crying.

"What did she *do*?" my mother repeated. "She only sang a song about Christ. As if we don't have enough problems caused by Christians. Do we have to go about singing their songs?"

I didn't recognize my mother anymore. She didn't have an ounce of joy in her. It was as if all her waning energy was absorbed in fear and anger. Not that we were going around singing and dancing. We were still children, at least chronologically; we were desperate to find something to keep our minds off Drora.

"Is a Chanukah song okay?" I asked.

My mother didn't answer.

Immediately, we sang in Hebrew, *"Ma'oz tsur Yeshu'ati / lekha na'eh leshabe'ah,"* the first lines of the Chanukah song, *"Ma'oz Tzur"* or "Rock of Ages."

"Stop," my mother yelled, her nostrils flared.

Without hesitation, we obeyed. I was again bewildered. I understood about the Christmas song, but not about the Chanukah one. Years later, it became clear. My father had sung that song; it had been one of his favorites.

The next day, my mother and Perl left for work. Drora was due back at the *artel*. They claimed that Drora was sick, but the commandant said he expected Drora the following day or else.

Late that night, Drora slipped in the door. Those of us who had been dozing were startled. Faint light came in from the window but we knew it was Drora. She lay down on our "bedding" as if she had never left.

"Where were you?" my mother whispered with relief and reproach in her voice.

"You don't need to know," she said, sounding exhausted and defeated.

"Are you okay?"

"Yes, don't worry. Just go to sleep . . . everyone."

"Go to *sleep*," my mother repeated. "Go to sleep. As if I could get any sleep waiting for you coming back from who knows where."

"I'm sorry, Mother. I didn't mean to worry you."

I waited for my mother to repeat, "didn't mean to worry you," but she was quiet.

Sleep must have overtaken me because what seemed like a minute later, my mother was rushing Drora to wake up and get ready for work. It was still fairly dark so I couldn't see much. By daylight, I saw a little package on the floor between my shoes. I opened it and there were three potatoes and a hunk of cheese.

When they returned to our room after work, I was alarmed by my sister's appearance. She had a deep cut on the side of her eye and scratches on her cheeks and arms. I didn't see her legs, but she had a slight limp. I knew better than to ask her anything.

Word got around in the ghetto. Inside, we had little else to do but to talk. Drora had been with the partisans. How she had escaped to join them and why she came back, I didn't know. I could live with that uncertainty, but what really got to me was the sense that she could disappear again at any time and not come back.

We still couldn't locate Gittel and her family. We heard that the Nazis removed certain young people from the ghetto and placed them in special barbed-wire camps to prevent rebellion. They transported others to faraway slave labor camps. Rumors also circulated that they took some Jews to the forest and shot them. I couldn't bear to dwell on the possibilities.

Finally, we saw Gittel's family, the Auerbachs, her parents and her brother, on a list of murdered victims. Gittel's name was not there. I only prayed that Gittel, my oldest friend, had been among those sent elsewhere to work or escaped, though she would have wanted to die with her family.

# Thirty-Three

IN SECRET, AND in ever-changing apartments, a handful of adults, most former teachers—so many of them had fled eastward, joined the partisans, or had been killed—and educated older Jews provided educational or religious instruction. Most parents were afraid to let their children out of their sight. In the ghetto, it was always preferable not to bring attention to yourself.

There were children dressed in rags, carrying sheet-wrapped packages containing books for exchanges. When I saw this more than once, I became ashamed to avoid the secret lessons. One morning, I followed the children into an alleyway and through a back door into the basement of an apartment building. There in the area where the furnace was— now silent and covered with grime—I heard a sound like soft singing. Still behind the children, I ducked under dripping, rusty pipes; and, in a darkened corner, there was a group of soot-faced, raggedy young children, not very different looking from the bunch I had followed.

Rats scampered between my legs. Why this revolted me after all I saw, I can't say. But I screamed and danced around them, though they were too numerous to avoid stepping on. A thin, young man—a boy really— snuck up on me and covered my mouth with his clammy hand. His nails were long and encircled by dirt. Lice crawled in his hair. I yanked my face away, about to protest when he said, "Shh, if you want to stay here, you have to be very quiet." I apologized. The chidren moved to make room for me and I sat in a smear of wetness. The odor of ammonia and something I can only explain as burning flesh and rotting meat willfully sucked into my nostrils, jerking back my head from the shock of it.

Out of some sense of respect, I sat with the children for an hour or so while the young man led them in softly intoned Hebrew poems and songs. Unconsciously, my lips moved with the words, though I couldn't discern much melody as the voices were mostly monotone. When the man began a lesson on geography, I excused myself and, by now, lightheaded and nauseous, I literally crawled out of the basement. This was one of the rare times I had gone anywhere without Rivke and would never do it again, at least voluntarily. I never told my sister about it. I don't know if it's because I was embarrassed to have gone or to have left.

Drora frequented underground meetings. The attendees had their pretend purpose if they were apprehended: they were conducting Yiddish artistic and cultural pursuits or teaching useful trades, which seemed acceptable at first by the Germans. Their real aim was to exchange information and organize resistance. There were rumors of secret radios and arms collecting. We were all afraid to ask—afraid for the person involved and afraid for ourselves if we absorbed incriminating information.

I understand now how much these "agitators" risked their lives. Many of us "nonagitators" were complicit in our noninvolvement. We ignored a lot; we kept our mouths shut too often.

In the midst of the hell around me, I clung to my two books even though my mother had ordered me to burn them. She wasn't that vigilant as she must have realized that reading was my only real sustenance. At that point, she must have also realized that we were all doomed so why deny me a happy minute or two.

One book was a compilation of Yiddish writers. The other had been a gift from Ida on my ninth birthday, over two years before. It was a novel in verse called *Eugene Onegin* by Aleksandr Pushkin, the famous Russian poet. It wasn't until I got to the ghetto that I studied the passages, which were difficult to understand. Then, I discovered a verse, written in 1831, toward the end that Ida had underlined and written in the margin: *For you, Esfir.* I memorized it and still remember it to this day. It said:

> Reader, I wish that, as we parted—
> whoever you may be, a friend,
> a foe—our mood should be warm-hearted.
> Good-bye, for now we make an end.
> whatever in this rough confection
> you sought—tumultuous recollection—
> a rest from toil and all its aches,
> or just grammatical mistakes,
> a vivid brush, a witty rattle—

God grant that from this little book
for heart's delight, or fun, you took,
for dreams, or journalistic battle,
God grant you took at least a grain.
On this we'll part; good-bye again!

DURING *PESACH*, A wall was erected around Ghetto B. Now we were trapped, though some thought that this was a good sign, that we would stay put for a while. Yet it was now even harder to get food. We were starving. Everyone had dysentery. Our pails overflowed with bloody, mucousy stools. Even when the pails were taken outside and dumped, the stench was on our hands, between our fingers, in our hair, and in the lining of our nostrils.

I often wondered what kept my mother going. She may have been holding onto some hope, not necessarily for her, but for her children. Drora and Rivke had been almost delirious with fever and weakness. Believe it or not, I, the youngest, seemed to be the strongest. So when my mother noticed that my belly was flabby and swollen, that I, too, had succumbed, something inside her cracked.

She rushed around the apartment in circles, mumbling curses, having conversations with my father, with my grandfather. She promised that we would join them soon and hoped God would ensure our swift endings.

Yet again, Perl put her arms around her sister, trying to contain her. It was no use; my mother broke free like a caged tiger, baring her teeth and making growling sounds.

Perl said, "Sheyne, get a hold on yourself. For the children."

For a moment, my mother calmed and appeared sane again. Only for a moment. Although my mother hadn't been shot or wounded, she was dead. If her insanity had protected her from more pain, then I am happy for her.

With our mother so distraught, it was up to us. We rummaged in garbage cans for anything edible. We made soup with potato peels floating in water. We stepped on dead bodies in the street.

Evil was all around. There were *Aktions*—roundups—of all types. One demanded three hundred crazy people. I feared for my mother. Thankfully, she appeared no more deranged than most others in the ghetto. Another thing I heard from a girl, who swore her brother saw this: The Nazis set a large vat of boiling water in the center of the ghetto and threw in babies and young children, accompanied by German music to cover up the screaming. At the time, I doubted the story; this particular girl often exaggerated for attention. Now I know it must have been true.

JUNE 2, 1942. I normally didn't take note of what day it was, but I remember this was a Tuesday. It was very hot. There were rumors of a big *Aktion*. Both ghettos were surrounded.

A voice on the loudspeaker ordered us to assemble—each ghetto had a different location. Many ran away and hid. People were shot and left squirming in their blood. I heard one girl scream, "I'm too young, I want to live." A moment later she was killed.

We from Ghetto B and a group from Ghetto A gathered at our appointed place, Svobody Square (Liberty Square). From a balcony, the *Judenrat* leader, Angelovich, tried to calm us down. In a business-like tone, he said, "Nothing bad will happen to you."

"Liar," Drora yelled. There was a huge hush.

My mother grasped Drora by the arm and said, "Please, Drora, quiet."

Angelovich continued, "You are just being transferred to a new place of work. Take all necessary belongings."

Could we be moving again? But where? I looked around and everyone also seemed stunned and confused. Drora slunk away from us and I could see her in a small clearing. I was about to follow her and wrench her away when she pointed to Angelovich and yelled, "Traitor!" The crowd pushed against me and I couldn't see her well. I was clutching Rivke's hand, dragging her toward Drora. That morning Rivke and I had renewed our pact. Whatever happened, we would go together, holding hands, even if it meant certain death.

This will haunt me until the day I die. Drora was yanked by her hair and thrown. She landed on top of others and they all fell. Two SS men grabbed Drora and dragged her down the sidewalk, where Jews weren't allowed to walk, and out of our view. There was a momentary silence. Drora's screams could be heard, I was sure, a mile away. She chanted, *"L'shana ha'ba'ah b'Yerushalayim."*[1] There followed a round of machine-

---

1 "Next year in Jerusalem," the traditional wish that concludes the *Pesach Seder*.

gun fire. My mother wailed, "No, no!" It's impossible to imagine how, with all the crying and screaming and shouting, we could have heard Drora, but we did.

My memory of the time period between the announcement and our leaving is very hazy. At some point, I had made the agonizing decision to leave Miriam behind, for her own sake.

The next memory I have is to be suddenly surrounded by SS men with their ugly forthing, vicious dogs and being pushed toward the railway station. Women screaming and children crying. A few squeezed between body parts, trying to escape through any gaps but were shot like targets in a moving bullseye. Hope surged when we heard that our final destination was Bronnaya Gora, also known as Brona Gora, a forest area not far from Bereza Kartuska. Surely, this would be another camp or a work area for cutting trees. But one look at the very old and the very young among us obliterated that dream.

The sadistic seesaw of hope and terror left me teetering on the brink of madness. What could be worse? Death? No, death would be a relief, an end.

# Thirty-Four

THE TRAIN HAD eighteen cattle cars. With all the tumult and panic, I don't know why I had counted them while we lined up and waited to board. It took my mind into another realm. Armed soldiers rammed us into the next-to-last cars. We piled on top of each other, close to a hundred and fifty terrified souls.

There was a small horizontal, thickly bared window high on the opposite end of the wagon. It was clogged with tangled barbed wire. Had it been fashioned for cows to breathe only enough to make it to market?

This trip couldn't take too long. By my calculations, Brona Gora was about forty miles northeast of Kobrin, but I didn't take into account that the train would stop in Pinsk, which was about seventy-five miles east of Kobrin. And Pinsk wasn't the only stop. I lost count on how many. Every time the train slowed down, I felt both terror of the unknown and relief at the promise of finality.

Inside this roaring coffin, I heard sounds like stampedes and muffled screaming, automatic shooting and single shots, swishing of steam and clanging of bells and whistles, the jingling of chains and the sliding and slamming of doors. I felt rumbling and jostling, jabbing by elbows and hard heads. We rode for what seemed like days, but it couldn't have been much more than eight-to-ten hours. Rivke and I clung together, taking turns at crying into each other's chests. My mother and Perl squeezed as one. We were bonded by sisterly blood.

At that point, I didn't care if the train went farther. I would have rather died there smothered with my own, than to endure whatever awaited me.

The smell was unbearable. People peed, defecated, vomited. There were two buckets, one for a toilet and the other with water. I never got to either one. I was desperate for air and felt faint. At one point, I was able to crouch and press my nose smack on a crack in the floorboard. I inhaled as long as I could until someone shoved me away.

Suddenly I felt a lot of scrambling. I heard that a boy was standing on the shoulders of others, trying to glimpse out the window. After a while, he apparently spotted a town sign, and yelled excitedly. It was repeated by others so that everyone heard. "Bronnaya Gora" was the last echo.

The train shuttered to a stop, seemed to be changing tracks, and chugged forward again for a short time. Near the window, people pleaded for water. There were several quick stops and I heard clanging, shouting, barking, then a crescendo of choral screaming. When our wagon finally opened, there was a prolonged swoosh. The sudden light was blinding, and I blinked several times in a kind of shocked swoon.

Shouting in Russian, collaborating soldiers burst in and ordered us to undress, muttering something about us going to showers and having to leave our clothes in a pile. I was overwhelmed by shoving bodies, arms tugging at fabric, women howling. At first, not everyone understood. When the soldiers grabbed an old man and ripped off his tattered shirt, there was no getting away from our fate. Multiple screams of "no, no" erupted, mixed with cries of *"Shema Yisrael."*

From the wagon, the soldiers hauled out the arms and legs of those who were near-death, crushed to death, or who had died because they had already been starving when we began and gave out. Somehow, I stumbled outside. It was difficult to stand. I tripped over dead bodies. I no longer cared where we were. I only wanted air.

I stood still and hadn't stripped. An SS man approached me and pointed the bayonet at my arm, its blade lifting the edge of my sweater. He shouted to hurry, *"Schnell, schnell, macht schnell."* I was so filthy, he didn't want to touch me. By then, at twelve, I was so skinny, and wore a few layers—everything I owned—so my clothes hung in shreds; each holey layer revealed another garment underneath, plus exposed skin in places. Anyhow, I stepped out of my clothes as if I were shedding a second skin, letting the rags slip to the ground. Rivke did the same.

The Germans didn't want to miss a thing. They checked our hands for rings and yanked them off, sometimes breaking hands or fingers.

The soldiers directed us nearby onto a huge platform. On the train, some had sworn they would run into the forest when we stopped; they would rather be shot trying to escape. But there was no way to get out as the platform was encircled with barbed wire. One young bearded man found an opening in the wire and tried to shove himself through. An SS man shot him several times and his body splayed across the wires, his arms outstretched like Christ on the cross. Soldiers dragged several young women through this mangled hole. I heard their screams above the din; they were being raped and killed. In the ghetto, we had learned about rapes. You could say I was lucky that I had lost my femaleness, or it remained undeveloped.

The weather was warm yet I was cold. My budding nipples hardened and I crossed my arms. I had thought I had no modesty left, but it didn't last long. I blended in with the other walking skeletons.

Then the SS arranged us into lines through an increasingly narrow corridor, also with barbed wire, and we stumbled about thirteen hundred feet from the station. There was a sudden halt and collective intake of breath. As far as I could see, there were gigantic pits.

On some level, I heard screaming, murmuring, groaning, crying, eardrum-piercing wails, strangulated breaths, screeching dogs, blaring music, pleas to God, begging to mothers. On another, I heard nothing. I saw the lines moving forward. I saw people shot. I saw naked bodies upon bodies, masses of pulsating flesh and bones, spurting blood, poking arms, severed limbs. I saw nothing. There were leaking feces, exploding brains. I smelled nothing. I know there were bayonet piercings and rifle pokes, banged heads, wet flesh. I felt nothing. In every fiber of my being, in every sensual receptor, I was absent. Where I was, I do not know.

What I do know is that an SS officer started to pull Rivke's arms. I wrapped my arms around her waist and pulled in the opposite direction. An object smacked me in the head and I fell to the ground, but I heard Rivke calling my name, her voice getting fainter. I yelled for her, but nothing came out of my mouth.

In Brona Gora prayers and sounds were listened
The birds crying said "Kaddish."

—Elizabeta Zilbershtein (Leah Berkovitz),
"By the Common Grave"

JUST AS QUICKLY as I wasn't there, I reappeared in the scene. A woman pulled me up and the crowd pushed me forward, single file. A ladder led to the bottom of a huge pit, maybe two hundred feet long and twenty-one feet wide. Ahead of me, people tumbled down the steps. I searched for Rivke in the melee of falling bodies. My mother and Perl were somewhere behind; I couldn't be sure.

Using a combination of dogs, rifles, and shouting, the SS forced the Jews to lie face down close to each other in rows like sardines packed in a can. After a row was filled, the Nazis shot people with machine guns and the victims lay on the previous row. Bloodied bodies lay on top of layers of bloodied bodies.

Ahead, I saw another pit overfilled with piled bodies. Then, the SS finished them off with rifle shots, and workers shoveled earth and poured smoldering lime over the bodies.

It was like watching a horror movie. I was in such a state of suspended disbelief and my emotional reactions were so stifled that I was only aware that there was something I needed to do.

Here is where the details stand out like a relief on a building's frieze. I moved down the steps, getting closer to the pit in front. The nearly dead were shrieking and wailing like animals trapped at a hunt.

Chants of the death prayer: "*Shema Yisrael Adonoi Elohenu Adonoi Echod.*"[2] rose like an orchestrated chorus. Others begged for their mothers. An intoxicated SS monster lifted a wasted girl of about two and threw her into the air; her skull separated precariously from her neck. I closed my eyes. This should not be my last view of life on earth.

More descended the steps, lay on the heap, and were shot. The bodies piled high—the pit was full—and we were led to another grave. This time, the Germans didn't wait for the next group to step into the pit; they positioned them around the rim and began shooting the back of their heads, causing victims to fall inside face down. Not everyone was killed immediately. Naked bodies writhed. More shooting and the mass stopped moving.

I was suddenly at the edge of the grave. A soldier aimed his machine gun toward my head and I looked down at the pit, bracing myself for the final blow, praying it would be swift, deciding I would fall no matter

2 "Hear, O Israel: the Lord our God, the Lord is One!"

what. But his aim must have been off and the bullet hit my arm, grazing my skin. I fell, more at the edge than deep inside. I wasn't sure if I had a head wound and just didn't feel it, if my arm was my only wound, or if I would be shot again. I closed my eyes, waiting, immobile, pretending to be dead. This was the worst torture, lying there. Lying there among the still and barely moving.

Could it really have happened—amidst all the screaming and shooting? I suddenly heard Rivke calling, "Esfir, Esfir." I couldn't be mute again. I tilted my head slightly, though the weight on me didn't allow me to rise. This time, I yelled for my sister. The others around me disappeared. There was Rivke, standing defiantly with her arms in the air, shot in the head. Logically, it was another girl. Logically, it didn't even happen.

Rivke had been ahead of me; she must have been shot already. Before, I had thought Drora's death was unendurable. Now I am so glad Drora went first.


SHOOTING AND SCREAMING. Bodies dropped over me. Red and yellow and brown liquids seeped into my pores. After a while, I gently removed arms and legs and crawled upward, edging slowly, slowly. I made my way out of the rim, expecting to be shot any second. I continued creeping away, wildly digging my fingers into the earth, propelling my body forward. When I got far enough that the sounds were more distant, I stood hunched, tiptoeing, and then I ran wildly. I didn't know where I was heading, only to get away.

The Germans were busy with the shooting. There were so many people jammed together, by some miracle, they hadn't noticed me. As I stopped to catch my breath, the thoughts came: Maybe I really was invisible. Maybe I was still lying in the pit. Maybe I was already dead and this was hell.

As I crouched behind a tree, I spotted a soldier watching me from the hilltop. He aimed his rifle and I ran. Shouting, whistles, dogs. The chase started. Several Germans ran after me and bullets flew. On my knees, I snaked in and out of the trees, lying flat, and then sprinting.

I was an animal. Naked, the wound in my arm throbbing, with one terrified instinct: the need to flee. I ran and ran. I got farther into the forest. I fell in a small clearing and lay in my blood and must have blacked out. A German shepherd found me, and here is my second miracle. For some reason, the dog didn't attack me. When the Nazis came and saw me lying in a bloody puddle, with the dog licking my wound, they figured I was dead. One said, "*Kaput,*" finished, destroyed, and they left.

Until the last one they were murdered, nobody was left
In the skies their last scream still float,
They clamor not to forget their suffering and pain.

Many still alive, all of them were covered
And the blood sprang from the earth like a river,
The innocent blood sprouted a long time,
Said the gentiles that looked from a distance.

My dear mother! I want to ask,
Who left first to eternal road?
Sure you have seen the suffering,
How? do they throw your children to graves?

Words are pale to describe,
The misfortune, the pain that suffered our generation.
I stayed alive, but I feel like a stone,
Because I lost everything, I am alone.

                    —Reizel Navi Tuchman,
                 excerpts from "Brona Gora"

# Thirty-Five

I LAY LIKE this for a long time. Finally, I stood and started running again, in and out of the forest. I saw peasants in the fields; they saw me—a bloodied and muddied naked girl, probably I didn't look like a girl anymore. Probably they thought I was near-death so why bother?

I don't know how long I wandered like this. I reached the road, watching all the time for cars, motorcycles, horses, or carts. There was a pregnant woman sitting on a boulder with bundles by her feet. She took pity, my miracle number three. Without asking me a thing, she untied her head scarf and wrapped it around my arm. Then she opened one bundle, removed a dress and slipped it on me; it was so big it swept the ground. She said she was waiting for a ride to Kobrin. Kobrin, *my* Kobrin! Could I be hearing correctly? She explained that she had come from her mother's house nearby, pointing toward the direction I just ran from, and was expecting a neighbor in a horse and wagon.

She must have heard the shots, the noise, the screaming. She said to me, "Come with me. You can survive the war. I will have a baby soon, and you can stay with me and help look after it."

Could I believe this woman? Why would she trust a dirty girl with her newborn? Would they drive me back to the pits? Would she take me to the commandant in Kobrin? It didn't matter anymore. Whatever would happen, would happen. I no longer cared; I just wanted to be in one place.

The man with the wagon came. The woman—her name was Berta—said I was a poor cousin and she was taking me to help with her baby. The neighbor was expecting only one woman. I was wearing an oversized dress; my face and arms were smeared with mud and blood. I can only imagine what my hair looked like. But the driver barely glanced at me and shrugged as if it was none of his business. I don't think it occurred to him that I had escaped the killings. No one would have believed this was possible.

We passed trucks and motorcycles with Nazis. They took little notice of us, shooing us out of their way. Any minute, I expected a Nazi to stop us and haul me back onto another train going to Brona Gora.

We sat like three strangers, which we were, and rode to Kobrin.

THE DRIVER BROUGHT us to Kobrin's outskirts, to an area I didn't recognize. It was dark and most of the streets were empty. The woman pushed me in the back alley somewhere, and we climbed a flight of stairs attached to the outside. She opened a rickety wood door and deposited me on her couch. I fell into a deep sleep.

Had Berta been lying to me? Had she explained the situation to her husband, who had his own suspicions? I ask these questions because the next thing I knew, there was a Gestapo man standing over me. He took me to the station house and questioned me, accusing me of being a Jew.

I said, "I'm not a Jew, I'm a Pole." God forgive me for that lie. With my blond hair, blue eyes, and pale skin, they almost believed me. I elaborated on my story, that my name was Ruta Jablonska (the last name after a teacher), that I was an orphan and had worked as a maid for a rich Jewish family in Kobrin. I even gave this family a name. After they had been taken to the ghetto, I said, I had no place to go. I slept in the streets, changing places each night. I hid in barns, sheds, outhouses. I was starving. One night, I tried to flatten myself between bales of hay inside a wagon. The driver discovered me the next morning and took me to a deserted area and raped me. Then, he stole my clothes and left me alone in the forest. That's when I happened upon Berta. This was what I made up on the spot.

What happened afterward? I'll describe the rest in a general way because the important part of my story ended at Brona Gora.

THE GESTAPO KEPT me there, in prison, unconvinced of my story. I couldn't prove anything one way or another. Many times, they took me out of the cell and shoved me in a waiting area with other prisoners who were slated for execution. For some reason, they brought me back to the holding cell and I heard shots for the others. This happened several times. It had been the commandant's idea. I was a target in a cruel game for his entertainment—and to show off in front of his underlings. I begged him to go through with it, to have me shot and I meant it. That must have soured his enthusiasm. Eventually, he got tired of the game, or felt some sense of mercy, and handed me to the nearest convent.

The nuns treated me nicely; though they gave me a tiny room—I think it had been a linen closet—in an area separate from them. It was dark and very cold. There was a little candle wall sconce and a towel folded neatly on the floor.

I wasn't the only stray child. The convent housed four young children, orphaned by the war, and the nuns occasionally took in a sick person, usually a child. I was happy to help take care of them.

I knew many of the prayers and hymns from Polish elementary school so I went to Mass several times, to play my part as a Catholic. I don't think I fooled them; I always worried that I crossed myself in the wrong direction.

I was still very weak and frail. One day, I fainted during morning prayers. I was in a delirium state, gripped by dysentery and swathed in fever. I would sleep for long stretches and then awaken, startled at where I was. I heard the Sisters mention something about Christmas. Then I realized that I had passed my thirteenth birthday in November, nearly unconscious on this very bed. Thirteen. A teenager, almost an adult, practically a woman. My grandmother Ruth had gotten married when she was sixteen. Feeling my emaciated body, I hardly felt feminine, though a long while ago I had said good-bye to my childhood.

Sister Ursula was the one who saved my life. It was almost impossible to get good medical care; the majority of Polish doctors had been imprisoned, killed, or left the country. The German doctors catered to their own and didn't bother with peasants. Thankfully, Sister Ursula was also a nurse, hovering over my bed to constantly check my pulse and temperature. She spoon-fed me hot soup and soothed my body with cool washcloths. More than anything, she got me to eat a little something and didn't blame me if I threw it up on her.

The Sisters had gotten me a wool skirt and a blouse left by a postulant. Like Berta's dress, these clothes were too big, but I could tuck in the blouse and tie the skirt with a rope around my waist. Once I could walk steadily, the Sisters let me be.

ON A FREEZING day, I think it was January, still delirious with fever, I took my ratty wool blanket, wrapped it around my shoulders and snuck out, barefoot in the snow. I had one aim in mind: to get to my old house in the city. I had to see if someone—anyone—from my family or my friends had survived. It was a crazy plan. I had no money; I had no papers; I had no shoes. I looked like a beggar. And Germans were probably living in my house. I had no reason to believe that any Jew would be anywhere near there—or alive.

About a hundred feet away from the convent door, I collapsed. Sister Ursula found me. A large, buxom woman, she lifted me in her arms and carried me back. I was grateful to her for not admonishing me; from that day on, she watched me carefully.

Eventually, I felt better, though I was still very thin and weak. When I wasn't resting or helping with the children, I cleaned the rooms and worked in the gardens. Wash the sheets, milk the goat, mend a sock. Physical labor was the best medicine for me—to have a routine and no time to think.

Since we planted our own vegetables, had fruit trees, and a goat for milk, we had what to eat. Not that much, but compared to what I had in the ghetto, more than two kinds of food seemed like a feast. During those last months in the ghetto, Rivke and I spent hours detailing the preparation, cooking, odor, and taste of every morsel we had ever eaten. We had been beyond hunger or else we wouldn't have been able to withstand the temptations. We were like schoolgirls giggling about unattainable boys. The most fun was in the dissection, not in the actuality, not that I ever had a boyfriend.

As I got stronger I let a thought creep into my head, that maybe Velvel was alive. Fighting and killing occurred in Palestine, but we hadn't had contact with my brother for so long. I was totally out of touch with news of the day. The war could be over. The nuns were so sheltered, they wouldn't know.

My mind let go. Maybe Gittel could have escaped into the forest and had been rescued by partisans. Maybe a relative or friend had been hidden by a Christian in our very own neighborhood. Maybe my aunt Perl snuck out of the line in Brona Gora and escaped to Siberia and is waiting on my doorstep; and maybe, oh God, maybe my darling sister

Rivke, like me, had crawled out of the chamber of death and is now sitting on our bed, patting my side for me to lie down next to her in my rightful place.

I told myself, if I could survive, then who knows? Surely Ida with all her cleverness would have found a way. I held onto that hope with every ounce of my being.

Soon, I decided, I would visit Ida in Volchin and we'd play records on her gramophone. Together, we'd take the train to Brest, stop off at my aunt Perl's and go upstairs, only to find Rachel, Fredye, and the twins peacefully asleep in their beds. We'd wake them and pack lunches and go to the riverbank for a picnic.

My fantasies grew wilder. Like my mother having conversations with my dead grandfather and father when she was so disturbed in the ghetto, I talked to Velvel as if we were swimming in the river; I ate a stack of potato pancakes that my mother had cooked just for me. I observed my sister Drora get married; her little girl followed me around the orchards. I kissed a handsome and learned man who had chosen me out of all the girls in my high school.

It was a mistake, I knew, to encourage such thoughts. Time passed, at least. I could fool myself in my daydreams. At night, though, I awakened with nightmares of blood and death.

There, in the convent, I stayed. The Red Army liberated Kobrin on July 20, 1944.

# Thirty-Six

I WOUND UP in a DP camp in Germany because I had no place to go. I was still searching for information, and I was trying to get into Palestine. I had already scrutinized every list from every refugee and relief organization. I combed lists of forced laborers. I checked marriage, death, and birth records. Any piece of paper with a name on it, I saw. Any person with the remotest link to my region, I spoke to.

Shortly after Liberation in August of 1944, when I was fourteen, I went back to my house in Kobrin. It was occupied by a Russian family who wouldn't let me inside. I went to my friend Gittel's house and it was the same story. Officials said it was still too soon; the war wasn't over yet. It was impossible to predict who was alive, who would return.

I repeated my quest again in May of 1946. Now from the DP camp, it was an exhausting and difficult journey. The roads were filled with throngs of people—Jews, Poles, Slovaks, Hungarians, Germans, and Ukrainians—most of whom were returning to their homes, looking for relatives, or just wandering from place to place. They walked with their bundles or picked up whatever transport they could find, often gathering at the bombed-out railway stations not only for rides but for information on lost family members, relief organization, or political-group activity.

On the road, I met a Polish man and his young daughter, and we hitchhiked with an army truck and then with a farmer on a horse-drawn cart to Berlin in the Soviet Zone. From there, we traveled as a family; it was easier for all of us and this guaranteed that the drunk Russian soldiers would leave me alone at night. There were numerous stops for long periods—one for nearly a day—and border checks. At a five-hour stop, I bought nine ice cream cones as there was nothing else sold by the vendors who hung around the station. My mouth was frozen in vanilla sweetness, but I didn't get sick.

We changed trains a few times and stopped at Poznań, Łódź, and Warsaw, where the man and his daughter departed. The little girl, who was about four, hugged me and wouldn't leave my side. Finally, her father yanked her by the collar and patted me on the head, wishing me luck. I never found out their last names.

I had little money and, like most people, had no ticket. But it didn't matter because there was often no conductor. When there was, I had to ride on the train roof or in open boxcars. For the longest stretch to Brest, however, I was lucky and found a seat by squeezing in with a white-haired Ukrainian woman who shared her hunk of bread and Swiss cheese. She didn't say, but I suspected that she was Jewish as I heard her utter a few *oys*. Most of us travelers didn't reveal our background; it was better that way.

I arrived in Kobrin almost three days after I left the DP camp. From the train station, I walked. It was a beautiful spring day. Green and tranquil. No sign of war.

As I turned a corner, crossed a street, memories flooded me. I felt Rivke's warm and plump hand as we went to the butcher's; I imagined tagging after Drora as she hurried to her very "important" job as a delivery girl for my father; I saw my mother good-naturedly bargaining with the peddler who parked his wagon of pots and pans at the corner of my street.

My heart pounded as if this were my last minute on earth. I recognized the streets before I saw the street signs. I passed the Mukhavets River. The shops, the schools, the synagogues of my youth—squashed in burned rubble.

Only ten minutes to my house. I was the only person visible. I felt like I was going to my surprise birthday party. Any second, my friends and relatives, hunched together, would spring up and shout, "Surprise!"

But there was no one.

On Ratner Street, there were only two homes standing. In one, the windows had no glass except for jagged edges around the periphery; the front door was a rectangular dark hole; and the exterior painting peeled to reveal slivered and withered wood. The other house seemed intact. On closer inspection, I noticed that the windowpanes were made of paper; the front door was crisscrossed by large metal beams; and the brown grass was strewn with broken bottles, ripped and yellowed newspapers, and rusted food tins. Russian soldiers sat on the ravaged steps of a bombed-out temple and smoked.

At a community relations office, I met partisans waiting to cross the border. They told me of a Ukrainian soldier who caught thirty young Jewish girls hiding and shot them to death. I didn't want to hear the story but I asked if they knew the girls' names. For this, they said, there was no list.

I made it to Pinsker Street. The old cemetery was now a market. Gravestones lay flat on top of others, forming an odd, step-like backdrop to the scattered sellers sitting on wood stools in front of browned vegetables and rotted fruit sprawled on dirty blankets. In a macabre game of tag, disheveled children were running in and out of the graves, hitting each other with the stones that should have remained as visitors' markers.

The door to my house was ajar. I had been expecting Russians or by now Belorussians or Poles to be living there. I also expected that the house itself could have been destroyed or uninhabitable. I didn't expect what I found: It had been converted to a Russian army facility. I stepped inside and the Russian guards eyed me suspiciously.

"I used to live here," I said. "This is my house."

"Not anymore," one of the soldiers answered warily as if I was going to stake my claim right on his desk.

"Please," I begged. "I am not here to retake my house. I just want to look around, please."

The solider relaxed and waved me away as if to say, "Do what you want but do it quietly and quickly."

I ran through the rooms, winding in and out of army supplies, and found none of our furniture, none of our belongings. I raced up the stairs to the attic, remembering that my sister Rivke and I stuffed strips of photos between cracks on the sloped wooden beams. With the soot and cobwebs, I assumed this area had not been frequented. I ran my fingers in and around every crack and crevice. Nothing. In the cellar, I searched for the pieces of my dear friend Ida's letter that I had hidden between stones. Nothing.

Surely, with all my mother's recipes, surely for a person who was an expert at making something from nothing, there would be pots, pans, a dishtowel, a scrap of paper with a note from her perfectly neat and tight handwriting. But the only thing I spotted was the swirly moving motion of a rat diving into the open wire of a trash basket jammed with paper bags.

In a frenzy, I practically galloped to Gittel's, to Khane's, to all my friends and relatives. I went to their shops, their offices. I passed the empty lot where the yeshiva had been, the place where my grandfather had worked. I could hear his voice whispering in Yiddish to passersby, *"Fardrey zikh dayn eygenem kop vestu meynen s'iz mayner!"*

Wherever I went, the place had been demolished, closed, or occupied by Russians or Ukrainians. At my uncle Sam's Russian-occupied house, I leaned against the outside wall, my hands clutching jutting stones. The trees swayed; people across the street moved in slow motion. I was going to faint. I put my head down and felt dribble on my lips. I wiped my mouth with the back of my hand. It was smeared with blood.

Where was everyone I knew and loved? Could all of them have disappeared as if they never were?

These houses had once been occupied by Jewish families. On this street, there had been a *mikve*, on that, a yeshiva, on the other, a kosher butcher. All trace of Jewish life had vanished.

I had one last stop. I went to the ghetto and found the room in the apartment, our final family living space. It was one of the few houses left standing, though it was deserted. I could see the entire space in one sweep of my head. My doll, Miriam, was not there, where I had left her.

# Thirty-Seven

IN AUGUST 1946, I repeated my trek, only this time I got a ride with a relief organization truck to the border where I took the train to Brest, though I may as well have stayed in Kobrin. There was little difference, except the devastation was on a larger scale. I had thought it was bad that *my* house was an army facility, but Aunt Perl's was not only a place for supplies and official business, it was the headquarters of the highest-ranking officers. What had happened to the Soviet ideal of shared wealth? I didn't bother going inside.

As I was rounding a corner aimlessly, my body veered in a familiar direction. Suddenly, I was in front of Ania's house. The windows were fogged with dust, the paint stripped to the original wood, the steps dislocated and cracked. What tipped me off was a square patch of grass near the front of the house. Unlike the rest of the area, this spot had been weeded and trimmed. Tiny daisies poked out.

I went to knock on the door, but it opened with just my weight leaning against it. And here was my miracle of all my miracles. Cradling a newborn was my dear, dear friend Ania. She shrieked, not because she recognized me, but because my unexpected entrance startled her. Before she could question me, I screamed, "Ania, Ania!"

We hadn't seen each other since my last days in Brest, in the winter of 1940 when we were only ten. I would have recognized Ania's silky black hair and freckled nose anywhere. Me, I didn't look like myself or even an older version. My blond hair was long and straggly, my blue eyes dulled by sorrow, my erect posture hunched.

"Ania," I repeated, "it's me, Esfir."

"No, no, no."

This was all she could say, shaking her head from side to side. Was she going to throw me out? Would she, like the Polish woman, Berta, that I had met after Brona Gora, hand me to the police? Anything could happen to a person over six years.

Ania placed the baby on the couch and dove into me, holding me and weeping. "Esfir, Esfir, my beloved sister, Esfir. It's you, it's you."

We clasped each other as tightly as any two people could, leaned backward for a quick study to make sure each was real, and closed up again.

The baby cried and we broke apart. Ania lifted the baby and rocked it. She said it was a girl named Irenka.

I pointed and nodded. "Yours?" My eyebrows lifted incredulously, although it was not an unusal condition for a girl of sixteen.

She shook her head. "No, she's my brother Piotr's daughter. I take care of her mostly. Her mother was killed."

She announced this like she was reporting the weather. I didn't question her further. I had plenty of experience with that kind of reporting.

We didn't want to be away from each other for a second, not even to go to the bathroom. She cut my hair, lovingly sponge-bathed my entire body, forced food down my throat. She wasn't satisfied until I looked more like the girl she remembered.

On the third day, she got up her nerve to ask about my experiences. I told her that I had given my testimony to the Soviet State Commission[3] after Liberation. This had been extremely taxing. They grilled me as if I were a colossal liar, and, when they began to believe me, as if I were an otherworldly freak. Others also asked to interview me. I refused. I gave the facts once and that was all I could do.

Ania could never be unrelenting or critical, I assured her. I just couldn't handle her emotional reaction. I think she understood and didn't press me.

Though I was reluctant to talk, I was desperate to hear. Ania was happy to supply whatever information she could. She told me that her father, who worked in a dismal and overcrowded factory, had died of typhus. Two of her brothers were killed. Piotr was in the army. Her mother worked all day cleaning homes. Ania took care of the house and the baby. Sometimes, she helped her mother when she could take the baby along.

3 The full name is the Extraordinary State Commission to Investigate Nazi Crimes Committed on the Territory of the Soviet Union.

Ania was even more beautiful than I remembered, but there was flatness to her voice, a sadness that shadowed her old buoyancy. She didn't have to say that she had suffered, too.

While we drank glasses of tea, she told me what she had learned about the fate of Kobrin's Jews. On the day that we from Ghetto B were rounded up, the Jews in Ghetto A were tortured and many were murdered. Then very early on Oct. 14, 1942, Ghetto A was surrounded. The gates opened. Nazis shouted, "Get out!" They shot running women with children. Ania heard that one woman was cut into pieces in front of her children. Some young adults threw themselves into wells. Out of about five hundred who fled the ghetto—several betrayed by Polish and Ukrainian peasants—more than one hundred escaped to the forest and joined the partisans. Many more were shot on the road.

October 15th was the final annihilation of the ghetto. The Germans broke down doors, combed through attics and basements, dug through bunkers. Anyone found, including children and the sick, were shot. When there was not a Jewish soul left, looters descended and took everything they could find. All in all, Ania's friend, a policeman, told her in secret that the Kobrin region lost from ten to twelve thousand Jews during the war.


WE DIDN'T SPEAK again for hours. I lay in bed and Ania went about her chores. Later that evening, she called me into the kitchen. She took a deep breath. I knew she was saving something big to tell me, something personal that would be hard to hear.

Mr. Kozak, she was very sorry to say, was also dead. He had been a real hero. He stayed around as long as he could to protect Perl's house. Then he moved in with his original family and hid two Jews in the cellar. He was caught and everyone, including his wife, was killed. His children had grown up and were on their own. Who knows? Probably, they were dead, too.

I was holding it in, holding it in. I had to ask but I knew the answer. Here it was, "Ania, please tell me. Do you know anything about the Tarbut school girls?"

"I don't know what is true. But this is what I heard. Freyde and her brother Yossel joined the partisans and were killed. Liba and Fanny and their family were sent to Treblinka where they probably perished in the gas chambers. Rachel, I don't know. It could be that she survived. I asked the droshky drivers and they said that Rachel and her father probably went into hiding. But, Esfir, my dear, when you don't hear about a person, it usually means the worst."

I nodded, speechless for a long time. Then, I continued my quest. "Do you know anything about Mendel Feigen, you know, Ida's teacher at the Tarbut?"

"Yes, I remember him. He was shot early in the war, before the ghetto. At a work detail."

No mention of Ida and the Midlers. Ania must have been trying to prepare me. But, then I had reasoned, how would she know what happened to them all the way in Volchin? It was different for the other girls; they either lived nearer to Brest or had close family ties there.


ANIA CHECKED ON the baby in the bedroom. When she returned, all color drained from her face. I didn't want to know, but I had to hear.

"Esfir, this is going to be hard. Do you remember that Ida's sister Sala had a Belorussian schoolmate named Anna Gagarina?"

"Yes," I said. "She came to Brest once to see Ida. The only reason I remember her was that Ida emphasized that Sala had so many friends, including Belorussians. And then Anna went in my room and she and Ida shut me out of their conversation."

I was relaxing a bit, thinking that Ania was going to tell me that this Anna Gagarina was also dead.

"This woman," Ania said, "went to Perl's. The Russians had directed her to me because I told them if anyone comes to Perl's house looking for anyone at all, they must contact me. So Anna came to my house. I asked her about the Midlers and this is what she told me."

I listened but focused on the words. "No one knows for certain . . . . The Midlers could be alive . . . . Yes, it is possible they are also living in a DP camp . . . . Maybe they made it to Brooklyn in America. There may be such cases."

I refused to believe anything bad since there was no proof, but that's the way it was then. There was no proof that my mother, my sister Rivke, my grandparents, Perl, Khane, and the rest of my family were annihilated at Brona Gora. I was on the train with some of them; the others, I assumed were in another car. I had survived; maybe others had. But as Ania said to me several times during my visit with her, "You would know by now."

Though Anna couldn't swear to the Midlers' fate, she did have something definite to add, something extremely disturbing. The Jews of Volchin, like all the villages, towns, and cities in western Belorussia, were not immune to the 1942 massacres. Theirs happened on September 22. On that day, the village Jews were led to an open pit in a former sand quarry at the edge of town, forced to undress—their belongings left for others—shoved to the edge of the pit, and shot. The total killed: 497. These were not all the Jews from Volchin. Many had already been killed or left the village. Of the Volchin Jews, so far none had returned except for Hanna Kremer, Sala's best friend, who had escaped to eastern Russia, having suffered greatly.

Along with the Jews shot in the Volchin massacre was a group from a nearby village, Chernavchich, Rachel's hometown. Anna Gagarina didn't think Rachel was among the executed. I then remembered the drosky drivers who thought Rachel and her father had been in hiding. How anyone knew anything, I couldn't say.

I braced myself and shut my eyes as if I would then be unable see what only words could describe.

"Esfir, Anna was very certain of one thing," Ania said, gently.

"What?"

"Anna was sure that the Midlers were not killed in Volchin."

"This is wonderful news. I am not surprised. They were in good shape and may have been able to escape somewhere. There were locals who saved Jews."

"Perhaps, Esfir. But we don't think so. Anna said that she had heard that they had been taken to a labor camp. Ester was thought to have been smuggled to a relative's in a little village near Bialystok. You must know from your own research that Jews from that area were sent to Treblinka."

"No!" I cried.

"Finally, Esfir, Anna, from hearing about others in the area, conjectured that the Midlers probably had been killed at Brona Gora. She did say that the Midler house had been destroyed, another one replacing it that was occupied by locals."

This could not be. My mentor, my protector, my inspiration, my idol—Ida—could have been lying in the pit next to me.

The next day, Ania left me alone and went out with the baby to help her mother clean a house. She thought by the time she returned, I would have had an evening and afternoon to at least absorb her information. It was nighttime when she opened the door and called my name. She turned on the light and there I was sitting in the dark, my feet planted in a puddle of urine.

I DON'T REMEMBER the rest of the evening. Early the following morning, Ania brought a glass of tea to my bed. I hadn't been sleeping, but I was resting.

"Esfir, dear. I have something that I was saving for after I told you everything. Now you are leaving later this afternoon and I think I did the wrong thing. It may have been easier for you if I gave this to you first. I didn't know what to do. I am so sorry if I could have spared you some of this agony."

How could I be angry at Ania for anything?

Ania was holding a cardboard box.

"Oh Esfir, darling, Mr. Kozak gave me this right before he was killed. He must have known that he wouldn't live out the war. He said, 'Ania, you must keep this. No matter where you go, take it with you. Here are Esfir's journals. Keep them for her. And, if she doesn't come back, try to find her brother Velvel in Palestine. If you have no luck, keep them for you, for your children.'"

All the past years of my defended and stunted emotions melted. I sobbed for hours, on and off. I couldn't sob for my losses. I sobbed for happiness, happiness that I had a record of my life. My life with Rivke, Drora, my parents, my grandparents, Perl, Ania, the Tarbut girls, and, last but not least, Ida. Here was proof.

Ania gave me back my life.

# Epilogue

AFTER I LEFT Ania's, I returned to the DP camp and resumed my quest even though I realized that it was futile. But one day, I had a name. There on a list of Jews living in Palestine was a certain V. Manevich. His country of origin was Poland. It was not the only Manevich from Poland on the list. When my brother had left us, it was before the first German invasion. Our area had still been considered Poland.

I didn't have the stamina for another wild-goose chase but I had no choice. I wrote a letter to this person and waited. Waiting became my life. I waited for the proper paperwork. I waited for the turmoil in the new state of Israel to quiet. I waited for a place on the boat. There were so many others before me.

Soon after coming to Israel in 1949, I headed for the referred kibbutz. In my purse, folded neatly in quarters, was the answer to my letter.

I got a ride in a wooden-fenced well of a truck, and the driver deposited me in the middle of an open field, surrounded by an assortment of tents, outbuildings, and rusted farm equipment. He directed me to a woman holding a clipboard, checking off columns as she inspected goats drinking water from cement troughs.

After finding out my reason for coming, she led me past settlers milking goats and half-dressed children running in a circle. Then, she stopped and pointed to a tall and muscular man who was hammering nails on an enclosure of some sort. His back was to me. In not much more than a whisper, I said, "Velvel."

The man continued to work.

Again, I said, "Velvel Manevich, is that you?" Could this be my once-skinny brother? He jerked his head around and there he was, a handsome man around thirty, with slate-colored eyes and sun-bleached hair.

*"Feygele?"* he stammered his pet name, little bird.

His big-toothed smile and streaming tears were all the answers I needed. We rushed into each other's embrace. My brother had survived.

I HAD BEEN alone in the world. Until Ania and Velvel.

After two years at the kibbutz, I met a man, a good man, David, from Grodno. He had his own horrors—concentration camp, the death march. He didn't seem to notice my dull, stringy hair, the way my clothes hung on my skinny frame, or that my left eye continually twitched and teared. How could he know that even though I was almost twenty-two, I felt like a withered, old woman?

Instead, he called me his beautiful flower. I shook my head and let slip out what I was thinking. "No, my mother was the one who was beautiful."

"I want you to marry me," he said.

"I am not a real person," I responded. "I am a living ghost."

This time, David's eyes were the ones tearing and he said, "No, you are a living, breathing woman."

"There is nothing of me to give," I said.

He just smiled and said, "You will see, Esfele. Things will change."

Sometimes I allowed myself the fantasy of getting married without my dear ones. There would be Velvel and his family, a wife and three children. Ania, also married now with a child, wrote me that there would be nothing in the world to prevent her from coming to Israel for my wedding. In this pretend wedding, she would be my maid of honor.

I couldn't afford to live in fantasy. Instead, I busied myself with work: cutting down brush, planting trees, caring for sick children, studying English and literature. I could as well have been in the convent, but here no one saw through me; they saw me as I was—a Jewish woman with only one of her own, like so many here.

With those who experienced the Holocaust, we had a secret, silent bond. At any mention of our pasts, we nodded and shook our heads as if responding to a roll call. There was no need to recount our losses.

With others, it was different. I met an American couple working on the kibbutz for a summer. The wife questioned me about my experiences and I gave her only sketchy details. She said, "Oh I know, it was so hard for us to get food during the war."

Almost as insensitive, her husband asked me my philosophy as if I had learned a big lesson. I sidestepped the question with a few rehearsed sentences. If he had expected me to get meaning out of these experiences, he had not paid attention to my evasions. There was no meaning.

But, something nagged at me. Maybe there was no rational explanation for what had happened to the murdered Jews, but their lives were meaningful. And then, when the kibbutz held a ten-year anniversary memorial for a Polish woman's massacred relatives, I felt ready to take a peek at my past. It was time; it was time for me to bring back the dead, my dead. And I could do it in the only way I knew. I bought a new leather-bound book with lined pages and began my final journal, entitled with my announcement to the world, "Esfir Is Alive."

On the inside first page, I copied this from my favorite poet:

> I am a wandering girl.
> My heart is practiced in longing.
> And when the day eats up the dew of the night,
> I tuck up the small white curtain from my window pane,
> And look upon a new street.
> There lies coiled up
> In a little corner of my heart
> Such a singular, trembling idea:
> Maybe no one here will love me.
> Maybe no one here will want to know me!
>
> —Kadya Molodowsky, "Otwock"

SCOURING MY OLD journals brought back wonderful memories of Ida and my sisters before the carnage. But, they also triggered a recurring nightmare: I had a disease spreading across my face. It began to bulge under my skin, forming a big lump in the middle. The doctor said this was very dangerous and he had to operate immediately. He removed all the skin from my face. It was completely raw. He said after a while, when the skin grew back, my face would become grotesquely scarred. In the meantime, I walked around like this with my raw face exposed.

I met Ida. She didn't know it was me. "It's me, Ida," I garbled. "Me, Esfir." I said something personal so she would believe it was me.

She had been horrified and said she couldn't be friendly with me anymore. I woke up screaming several times and sank back into this dream. I had no control. Each time, I felt that same rawness, that same need to rid myself of whatever poison was affecting me. No matter what I did, I would be scarred for life.

I spoke to a doctor about these dreams. He told me it was a normal reaction and that they would go away. But I never understood how he could know what was normal since nobody else experienced what I had.

As I wrote my story, I remembered. I remembered my darling aunt Perl who bought me a gorgeous, one-of-a-kind doll, my Miriam. I remembered when I went to Volchin to visit Ida and, bubbling from a rehearsal of *King Lear*, she gave me a tour of her beloved village. I remembered when I once got lost going to my grandparents and my learned grandfather Yankel said to me, "Even a fart in a blizzard has a sound and a smell." I didn't remember the Yiddish translation anymore.

And there were other memories. I remembered looking at the disdainful poses of our Polish and Belorussian neighbors who came into our shop; the chest of a girl wearing a red blouse like Rivke had to give away; the faces of all those shunning us like we were vermin or worse as if we were not there. Sometimes, I had begged Rivke or Drora to hold me back. I could have killed each person with my bare hands. I had that much hate inside me—even more than for the Germans who were never my kind.

I remembered my last moments with Rivke at Brona Gora. When she had called my name, when she needed me the most, I was silent. Until I die, I will see Rivke's once-round, adorable face, her rolling eyes searching for me as she was killed. There will never be a worse moment for me.

The hole inside me is still as deep as that pit that swallowed thousands of Jewish bodies. My sorrow flows through that hole, never-ending.

By happenstance, I had survived. Me, a nothing, a nobody. My grandfather would have said it in Yiddish, a *pisher*. Had it been a fluke, luck, a miracle—who knows why? Yes, why . . . why me? I kept asking this question. If I allowed myself to believe in a benevolent God who had something more for me to do, I would have an answer.

And so, I have come to the end of my journal. People have questioned me about my life. I have been invited to speak at gatherings. I have been asked to be interviewed. I have refused them all. This is the first and the last time I will reveal my entire story.

ONE MORE THING. I would like to record the names of my family and friends, the ones who didn't survive.

My mother Sheyne Cohen Manevich, a woman of grace.
My sister, Drora Manevich, who should have been a lawyer.
My sister, Rivke Manevich, my heart.
My grandmother, Ruth Manevich, a great humanitarian.
My grandfather, Morris Manevich, a gentle man.
My grandmother, Elke Cohen, a pious woman.
My grandfather, Yankel Cohen, philosopher and linguist.
My aunt, Khane Cohen Wornick, a devoted mother.
My aunt, Perl Cohen Epstein, storyteller supreme.

Rachel Novick, a lonely girl.
Freyde Finefeld, a courageous fighter.
Yossel Finefeld, a compassionate man.
Liba Levin, who dreamed of love.
Fanny Levin, a kind soul.
Gittel Auerbach, friend extraordinaire.
Jozef Kozak, a prince among men.
Mendel Feigen, activist and orator.
Iser Midler, a man of sensitivity.
Bashke Midler, a woman of surprise.
Sala Midler, who would have been a mayor and/or poet.
Ester Midler, an irrepressible spirit.
Ida Midler, who could have been anything she wanted.

Let the world know about Freyde, Rachel, and the twins. Tell them about Mendel Feigen. Share stories about Perl, my grandparents, Gittel, Rivke, Drora. Introduce them to Ida. Explain that once upon a time, in a corner of Belorussia that was sometimes Poland and sometimes Russia, there was once a people whose only crime was being Jewish.

—Esfir Manevich, Israel, 1952

# Author's Note

The historical events in *Efir Is Alive* are factual. The real Midlers were my relatives from the village of Volchin in what is today the Eastern European country of Belarus. In June of 1942, the real Esfir Manevich was shoved into a cattle car and transported from her native city of Kobrin to a forest area between Brest and Minsk called Brona Gora. There, during the summer and fall of 1942, the Nazis systematically murdered 50,000 Jews, including an estimated 36,000 from the city of Brest.

Of the Jews who filled eight mass graves, Esfir was the only known survivor to give recorded testimony (three paragraphs) to the Soviets in 1944. At the time, she was twelve years old. She then disappeared from written history, at least from my numerous efforts. As I have learned repeatedly in my search for the truth, more information about Esfir may still be out "there."

There have been a few recent uncorroborated reports. A man supposedly survived the Brona Gora massacre. He was shot and killed later in Bereza when he tried to escape. Also, two people from Bereza and one woman from Antopol purportedly escaped the killing fields.

In my version of her life, Esfir writes her remarkable story ten years after the massacre. Many of the characters' names and experiences are a combination of real and imagined. Others are true to life—to those who believe.

# Acknowledgments

In 1997, I joined a Holocaust-related group mission to Belarus, culminating in a visit to the killing fields of Brona Gora, where we paid homage to the 50,000 Jewish victims. My subsequent research focused on the events in this area, both historical and personal, captured in my memoir, *Bashert: A Granddaughter's Holocaust Quest*. But for many years, the story of one girl's survival tugged at me, germinating into ideas, sketches, stories, and, finally, a novel. Throughout these stages, there have been many who were essential sources of literary guidance and moral support.

For help in research, my thanks to Jewish "Genners" Jenni Buch, the late Dr. Sam Chani, and Henry Neugass. At the YIVO Institute for Jewish Research, thanks to Gunnar M. Berg, project archivist; Jesse Aaron Cohen, photo and film archivist; Yeshaya Metal, reference librarian; Fruma Mohrer, chief archivist; and Marek Web, senior research scholar. Recently, I received timely and efficient assistance from the Warsaw Jewish Historical Institute's Agnieszka Reszka, head of the Archives Department. Thanks also to Kateryna Duzenko, project manager, and Jervin Gonzalez, videographer, of Yahad-In Unum (YIU) for their courteous help, especially for allowing access to testimony B139. Thank you to Rachel Shapiro, researcher at Yad Vashem.

Thanks to my new friend Hannah Kadmon in Israel who helped me search for the real Esfir Manevich and who reminded me that the reward for a *mitzvah* (good deed) is a *mitzvah*.

Belorusian historian and scholar Oleg Medvedevsky is in a category unto himself. He is a font of knowledge and cooperation, providing immeasurable and responsive help in obtaining photos and research on Brest and Kobrin.

Thanks to Ania Ciepiela Ioannides for Polish translation assistance and especially for providing me with the inspiration for my "Ania." Other translation help came from Shoshana Lew for Hebrew, and Jack Berger for Yiddish. Particular thanks to Dr. Paul (Hershl) Glasser for his scholarly help in editing the Yiddish glossary.

In the writing/editing category, there are so many to thank. For reading the early iterations of this book, loving thanks to my wonderful sister/friends from the long-lasting Madeline L'Engle writing network: Patricia McMahon Barry (and for the flowers), Stephanie Cowell, Jane Gardner, Katherine Kirkpatrick, Pam Leggett, and Sanna Stanley. For their astute comments and edits, much thanks to my many writing colleagues at the City College of New York's MFA program, particularly to Michèle Menzies-Abrash for the coffee conferences. For friendly (and no less essential) advice, thanks to early readers, Joan Katz, Penny Laitin, Karen Mann, Barbara Packer, and Carol Schweid.

For endless sources of writerly encouragement, thanks to mentor extraordinaire John Browne.

Thanks to Marc Parent for suggesting the title of this book, Alex Murawski for the wonderful book trailer, and publicist Rachel Tarlow Gul for her encouraging and comprehensive advice.

Extreme gratitude goes to everyone at Bedazzled Ink Publishing: Claudia Wilde, owner and publisher; Lynn Starner, cover designer; Sui Conrad, typesetter; and particularly to C.A. Casey, head of operations and chief editor, who expertly guided me through the editorial and production processes and onward.

For essential inspiration, thanks to the late Hanna Kremer of Volchin, the late Midler family of Volchin, and, of course, the real Esfir Manevich. Scenes of Volchin were inspired by the tireless work of Dov Bar and the late Shmuel Englender.

For overall support and encouragement: thanks to dear friend Arline Fireman; my sister, Barbara Simon Hoffmann; my number-one and only daughter, Alexis Zoe Simon Neophytides; and my one and only husband, Andreas Neophytides.

# Glossary of Yiddish Words and Phrases*

*Afn ganef brent dos hitl.* On the head of a thief, burns his hat.

*Ales in eynem is nishto ba keynem.* All in one is to be found in no one.

*A make unter yenems orem iz nit shver tsu trogen.* Another person's problems are not difficult for you to endure.

*A meydl mit a kleydl.* A cute girl showing off her dress.

*A pish on a forts iz vi a khasene on a klezmer!* A pee without a fart is like a wedding without a band!

*Az di bobe volt gehat beytsim volt zigeven mayn zeyde!* If my grandmother had testicles, she'd be my grandfather!

*Az men shmirt nit, fort men nit.* If you don't bribe, you don't ride.

*balaboste.* An excellent homemaker.

*Belz, Mayn Shtetele Belz.* Belz, my little town of Belz.

*bes-medresh.* House of study and prayer for Jewish males.

*bopkes.* Nothing; worthless; trivial.

*Brisk.* Brest.

*Brisk D'Lita; Brisk Delite.* Brest of Lithuania.

*bubele.* Term of endearment; darling.

*challah; khale.* Braided bread glazed with egg, served on *Shabbes* and holidays.

*chometz; khomets.* Leaven products.

*chutzpah; khutspe.* Nerve; gall; guts.

*davn, davening.* To pray; chanting with a swaying motion.

*Der mentsh trakht un Got lakht.* Man plans and God laughs.

*dreydl.* Spinning top used during Chanukah.

*Er est vi nokh a krenk.* He eats as if he just recovered from a sickness.

*es.* Eat.

*Fardrey zikh dayn eygenem kop vestu meynen s'iz mayner!* Go drive yourself crazy, then you'll know how I feel!

*feygele.* Little bird; a dear child.

*gants gut.* Pretty good.

*gefilte fish.* Stuffed fish.

*gelt.* *Money.*

**Got in himl!** God in heaven!

**goy (goyim).** A non-Jewish person (people); a gentile.

**Hak mir nisht keyn tshaynik!** Don't bang me like a teakettle! Stop
bothering me.

**Kaddish; Kadish.** The mourners' prayer, glorifying God's name.

**kasha kreplach; kasha-kreplekh.** Cooked cereal-filled dumplings,

**Kiddush; Kidesh.** The blessing over wine, before meal, on *Shabbes* eve
or festivals.

**kreplach, kreplekh.** Small dumplings, triangular or square.

**latkes.** Potato pancakes.

**mandelbrot; mandlbroyt.** Almond bread

**matzoh; matse.** Unleavened bread.

**Mayn sheyne meydele.** My little girl.

**Mayn zun.** My son.

**Mazel tov!; Mazl tov!** Congratulations!

**mikve.** Ritual bath.

**mitzvah; mitsve.** Virtuous deed.

**Nu?** So? Well, now.

**Nisht far dir gedakht!** God forbid! It shouldn't happen.

**Oy Gotenyu!** Oh, dear God!

**Oy, mayne sheyne kinderlekh.** Oh, my beautiful little children.

**peyes.** Side earlocks.

**perene.** A featherbed.

**Pesach; Peysekh.** Pesach.

**pisher.** A nobody; an insignificant person.

**rugelach; rogelekh.** Small, crescent-shaped, rolled-up pastries with
different fillings.

**Seder; Seyder.** Ritual feast marking the beginning of *Pesach*.

**Shabbes; Shabes.** Sabbath.

**Shema Yisrael.** "Hear, O Israel," The beginning of the most common
Hebrew daily prayer; also recited on one's deathbed.

**sheyn.** Beautiful.

**shiksa; shikse.** A non-Jewish woman.

**shivah.** Seven days of mourning.

**shlep.** Drag; pull.

**shmate.** Rag.

**shnaps.** Intoxicating spirits.

*shtetl.* Little town.

***Shtup zikh nit vu men darf nit.*** Don't push yourself into places you shouldn't be.

*shul.* Synagogue.

*shvitsbod.* Sweat bath.

*Talmud.* Massive compendium of books on learned subjects.

*talis.* Prayer shawl.

***tante; mume.*** Aunt.

*tsatskele.* A little plaything; a cute female.

*vants.* Bedbug.

***Vos makhstu?*** How are you?

*yarmulke; yarmlke.* Skullcap.

***Yeder mentsh hot zayn eygene mishegas.*** Every person has his own idiosyncrasies or craziness.

*zeyde.* Grandfather.

***Zol dir vaksn tsibeles fun pupik!*** Onions should grow from your navel!


*When there are two versions listed, the first is the popularized, common one, the second the correct Yiddish one.

# Esfir Is Alive

**by Andrea Simon**          **ISBN 9781943837601**

Esfir Manevich is a young Jewish girl who lives in the
Polish town of Kobrin in 1936. Facing anti-Semitism in
public school, Esfir moves in with her charming aunt who
runs a boardinghouse in the bustling city of Brest. Being
younger than the other boarders, Esfir struggles to find
a place in her new life, all the while worrying about her
diminishing role in the family she left behind.

As the years pass, Esfir experiences the bombing of her
hometown during the German invasion of 1939. When
the Russians overtake the area, Esfir sees many of her
socialist relatives and friends become disillusioned by the
harsh restrictions. During the German occupation, Esfir and
her family are enclosed in a ghetto where they develop
heartbreaking methods of survival.

In the summer of 1942, shortly before Esfir's thirteenth
birthday, the ghetto is liquidated and the inhabitants are
forced onto cattle cars destined for the killing fields—and
Esfir must face unimaginable horror. *Esfir Is Alive* is a
gut-wrenching historical novel capturing great pain and
resilience.

## From the Author

The inspiration for this book comes from my memoir:
*Bashert: A Granddaughter's Holocaust Quest*, published
in 2002 by the University Press of Mississippi, a personal
journey investigating my ancestral Belorussian village and
the events leading to the death of my relatives. *Esfir Is
Alive* carries many of the same themes and characters,
broadening them into a novelized arena, giving depth and
breadth to a story of great pain and resilience. I was most
interested in exploring the rich intellectual and social life of
the Jews of Eastern Europe in the interwar years, as well as
the psychological impact of extraordinary events on the life
and survival of a young person.

## Discussion Questions

1. Why does the author choose to open the book with the quote by I.L. Peretz: "I'll make you listen to me! You will have to hear me!"?

2. Esfir was a young girl when she experienced anti-Semitism in her school. What effect did it have on her and how did she respond? Have you ever experienced discrimination; if so, what was your reaction?

3. Both Ida and Esfir depend on their *Journal of Important Words* to express their thoughts and feelings. Do you have a similar creative outlet?

4. Esfir and Ania have a special relationship, despite their different religions. Do you have a friend from a different religious or ethnic background? How do you deal with these differences?

5. Yiddish is sprinkled throughout the book. What is special about the language?

6. What role does Esfir's doll Miriam play in her life and in this novel? Have you ever had a childhood object that meant so much to you?

7. One of the most wrenching scenes in the novel is the beard cutting of Esfir's grandfather Yankel and his subsequent death. How do these events change the nature of the novel?

8. Drora is a very spirited and courageous character. How does she debunk one of the stereotypes of the "passive" Holocaust Jew?

9. Discussions about the Holocaust often examine the issues of guilt and responsibility. What you would do if you or your family were threatened by torture or death? Or, what would you do if you were a witness to (or suspicious of) an atrocity?

10. The scene at Brona Gora is unimaginable. Can you understand why humans do this to each other? Can you imagine how a person can survive such an ordeal?

# About the Author

Andrea Simon is the author of the memoir *Bashert: A Granddaughter's Holocaust Quest*, as well as several published stories and essays. She is the recipient of numerous literary awards, including the winner of the Ernest Hemingway First Novel Contest, two Dortort Creative Writing Awards, the Stark Short Fiction Prize, the Short Story Society Award, and the Authors in the Park Short Story Writing Contest. She holds an MFA in Creative Writing from the City College of New York where she has taught writing. Andrea is also an accomplished photographer, and her work has been featured in international publications and galleries. The mother of an adult daughter, Andrea lives in New York City with her husband.